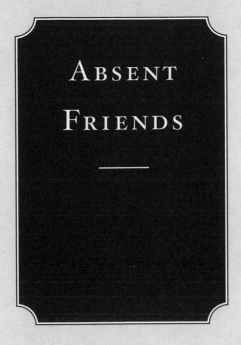

ABSENT

FRIENDS

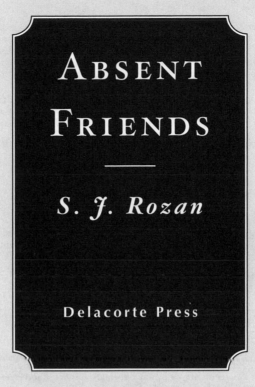

ABSENT FRIENDS

S. J. Rozan

Delacorte Press

Grateful acknowledgment is given for permission to reprint from the following:

"Musée des Beaux Arts," copyright 1940 and renewed 1968
by W. H. Auden, from COLLECTED POEMS by W. H. Auden.
Used by permission of Random House, Inc.

Excerpt from "A Martial Law Carol" from COLLECTED POEMS IN
ENGLISH by Joseph Brodsky. Copyright © 2000 by the Estate of
Joseph Brodsky. Reprinted by permission of Farrar, Straus and Giroux, LLC.

ABSENT FRIENDS
A Delacorte Press Book / October 2004

Published by Bantam Dell
A Division of Random House, Inc.
New York, New York

Book design by Virginia Norey

Library of Congress Cataloging-in-Publication Data
Rozan, S. J.
    Absent friends / S. J. Rozan.
        p. cm.
    ISBN 0-385-33803-1
        1. September 11 Terrorist Attacks, 2001—Fiction.
2. Staten Island (New York, N.Y.)—Fiction. 3. Women
journalists—Fiction. 4. Firefighters—Fiction. 5. Friendship—
Fiction. 6. Secrecy—Fiction. I. Title.

PS3568.O99A64 2004
813'.54—dc22   2004045471

Manufactured in the United States of America
Published simultaneously in Canada

BVG   10   9   8   7   6   5   4   3   2   1

for all the heroes

There are people who are as much a part of this book as the words in it. Expressing my gratitude isn't enough, but it's a start. Thank you to:

My agent, Steve Axelrod, who stayed calm, and my editor, Kate Miciak, who got excited.

Steve Fagan, Laura Lippman, D. P. Lyle MD, FDNY Lt. Simon Ressner, Betsy Harding, Royal Huber, Jamie Scott, and Lawton Tootle, for technical help and support.

Keith Snyder, Nancy Ennis, Carl Stein, Steven Blier, Hillary Brown, Monty Freeman, Max Rudin, Eve Rudin, James Russell, Amy Schatz, Nancy Richler, Vicki Trerise, Reed Coleman, Jonathan Santlofer, Paula Woods, Felix Liddell, Denise Bigo, John Douglas, Stuart Early, Jennifer Jaffee, Tina Meyerhoff, Larry Pontillo, Tom Savage, Jose Latour and his wonderful family, Jayne and Frank Krentz, Bob Hughes, and Joe Wallace, for aid and comfort.

Susanna Bergtold and Andrea Knutson, for being where they were, and being with me.

And especially, James Grady and Archer Mayor, for helping me find the floor.

As to truth, I haven't even tried to dissect its nature. All I know is that the surest way to make enemies is to always tell the truth. So, its nature probably is quite complex.

—Jose Latour

Powerless is speech.
Still, it bests a tear
In attempts to reach,
Crossing the frontier.

—Joseph Brodsky,
"A Martial Law Carol"

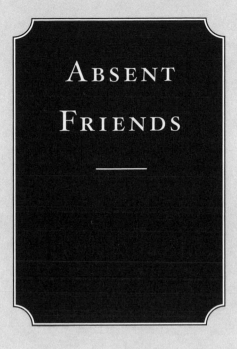

ABSENT

FRIENDS

Boys' Own Book
Chapter 1

Secrets No One Knew

July 4, 1976

Four boys, three girls, high and soaring, skin sizzling, tingling under the dizzying stars. Everything open and opening: the ragtop to the sky, the sky endlessly to the huge summer night. This night to their limitless lives.

Everything opening: In the black sky tight bright bursts eclipse the luminous moon, explode as fiery streaks, fountains of scarlet, rockets of silver, purple blooms and sprays of green. On the radio rising swells of tinny music; from the car shouts and applause.

Everything opening: the girls to the boys, not for the first time, but with a new, laughing heat. The boys to each other, grunts and shrugs and grins their fiercely sworn oaths, beer cans their glittering tokens of fealty.

Everything, everything opening: surprisingly, newly, the boys to the girls.

The boys? One is quiet, and one sure; one eager; and one flying, as always, too near the sun. The girls are royalty to these boys, have been since their memories began; and now, as the boys turn into men, the girls are knowing, wise, and real to them in ways they are not yet to themselves.

All would tell you.

And on this patriotic night, this celebration of association, when people all around them are reveling in the sheer staggering luck of being born into the community they would most want to be part of—what are they feeling, these boys and girls? Not fear, not on a night like this, when together they could conquer invading intergalactic armies, with grace and ease they could defeat rock-blind, howling swamp men burning with destruction. Not fear, but the hope of an anchor. The need for each other's weight in the whirlwind. "You Are Here" marked on a mental map. One of the boys leaving in the morning, everyone else to stay. All have been told by men and women, older and more tired, that the marked spot shrinks to nothing, that no ballast can hold, that the buoy above the anchor disappears in the bobbling waves.

Not one of the seven believes it.

It can be said that here the story begins, though it has been going on for some time. No story has a true beginning, and none has an ending, either.

From the *New York Tribune,* October 16, 2001

A HERO REMEMBERED:
CAPT. JAMES MCCAFFERY
by Harry Randall

Third in a Series of Profiles of the Lost Heroes of September 11

Note to readers: September 11 produced countless heroes. Many are still with us; others perished. Some final acts of bravery and sacrifice will never be known. The *New York Tribune* joins a grateful city in saluting all our unsung heroes.

There are others among the lost whose final deeds stand out in memory. In this series the *Tribune* profiles some of these heroes, as a testimony to their courage and to the character and pride of all New Yorkers.

"First in, last out."

With these words, spoken by a surviving member of Ladder Co. 62, Capt. James McCaffery was eulogized before a crowd of 2,500 at a memorial service at St. Patrick's Cathedral on Monday, October 15. McCaffery, 46, one of the most decorated firefighters in the history of the New York City Fire Department and the focus of a memorial fund, was remembered by speakers including the Mayor, the Fire Commissioner, the Governor's Chief of Staff, and firefighters who had served with McCaffery or under his command. Firefighters from nearly every state in the union stood shoulder to shoulder in the cathedral aisles, ceding the pews to members of the FDNY and to McCaffery's family and friends.

Because of his long and distinguished career—and, paradoxically, his lifelong distaste for publicity—James McCaffery's story has captured the imagination, and the hearts, of New Yorkers. He has been cited as a example of the courage and character of the FDNY on the day of the worst terrorist attacks in American history.

Ladder 62, housed in a landmark firehouse on West 11th

Street, was one of the first companies to respond to reports that a plane had hit the north tower of the World Trade Center, arriving at the scene minutes before the second plane struck. Multiple accounts from survivors credit McCaffery's organization of their evacuation with saving hundreds of lives. Repeatedly noted was McCaffery's "calm, in-control" demeanor and a sense he conveyed that "the situation was in hand." More than one survivor spoke of McCaffery's smile. "He didn't say anything," said Baz Woods, a law firm clerk. "But he made me feel like things weren't so bad. Like someone was in charge."

"That was definitely Jimmy," Thomas Molloy, a prominent Staten Island businessman, childhood friend of McCaffery's, and founder of the McCaffery Memorial Fund, told the *Tribune*. "You always knew Jimmy could take care of things."

James McCaffery grew up in the Pleasant Hills neighborhood of Staten Island. He left over two decades ago but is still regarded as a local hero.

"Oh, no question," said Father Dennis Connor, pastor of St. Ann's Church in Pleasant Hills. "Through all these years, we'd read in the papers about him, some brave thing he'd done, and we'd all be thinking, that's our Jimmy."

James McCaffery always wanted to be a firefighter. "He had a red plastic helmet someone gave him when he was three," said Mr. Molloy's ex-wife, Victoria. "He wore it all the time. When it got too small, he still kept squashing it on. His father had to buy him another one."

McCaffery is remembered as a quiet boy who captained the varsity baseball team at Dwight D. Eisenhower High School. "Jimmy never talked much," said Mike Pidhirny, retired head coach. "I never remember him riding anyone. It all went into his game. Jimmy expected a lot from himself, and he made the other guys want to give as much as he did. We made the play-offs every season he played. We won two division titles."

McCaffery entered the FDNY Academy in 1976 at the age of 21. His first assignment was to Engine 168, in Pleasant Hills.

"We watched him grow up," recalled Owen McCardle, a firefighter retired from Engine 168, who has been digging at Ground Zero since September 11. "Used to come around all the time when he was a kid, try to help out, wash down the truck, stuff like that. Did well at the Academy. Could have got assigned anywhere, put in for here. Once he was in, we couldn't shake him. Go out on a run, come back and this probie, not even on duty but he's frying up bacon, ready to scramble eggs."

In a move that surprised people in Pleasant Hills, McCaffery applied for a transfer in 1980 and was assigned to Ladder 10 in Manhattan. He moved to a Greenwich Village apartment near his new firehouse and never returned to live or work on Staten Island.

"He lost two friends within a year," said Marian Gallagher, the director of the More Art, New York! Foundation. Ms. Gallagher grew up with McCaffery and now heads the McCaffery Memorial Fund, whose mission is to aid the FDNY's outreach and recruitment efforts. "I think he just felt a need to start over. But he never forgot where he came from. One of the friends who died left a son. Jimmy helped raise him."

"Definitely, I joined the Department because of Uncle Jimmy," said Kevin Keegan, 24, the son of Mark Keegan, a close childhood friend of McCaffery's who died at the age of 23. Kevin Keegan is a probationary firefighter at Engine 168 who had been on the job just three months on September 11. His right leg and arm were badly burned by falling debris as he and other firefighters prepared to enter the north tower. Keegan is currently in rehabilitation at the Burke Center in Westchester. "Uncle Jimmy was there the whole time I was growing up," Keegan continued. "If I was in trouble, or had a problem or something, he'd be on the phone, he'd show up at our door. I could count on him."

Keegan, the *Tribune* has learned, is the beneficiary of Captain McCaffery's FDNY life insurance policy. "That's Jimmy. Still taking care of us," said Keegan's mother, Sally. "No matter where he was, Kevin and I could always go to Jimmy."

After Ladder 10, McCaffery served with Engine 235 in Brooklyn and then in three other Manhattan companies, including three years with Rescue Co. 1, before being given the command of Ladder Co. 62. From his probationary days at Engine 168, McCaffery's fearlessness stood out. "He wasn't reckless," said his mentor, Owen McCardle. "Jimmy never made a move until he took the situation in. But sometimes we had to pull him back all the same. One thing you learn on this job: sometimes you have to let something burn. Let something go to save something else. Jimmy never wanted to believe that. Superman, we called him. Save everyone, that's what Jimmy wanted."

In a Pulitzer Prize–winning photograph from 1984, McCaffery is in midair, leaping the gap from one rooftop to another, silhouetted against smoke and flame. Another picture, taken in 1988, shows him being lowered on a rope to rescue a baby held out the window of a burning third-floor apartment. McCaffery brought the baby up and was lowered a second time to save the mother. He tied the rope around her, signaled firefighters to pull her up, then disappeared into the building in search of another child. He found her crouching in a closet with the family cat. As the fire went to three alarms, McCaffery staggered from the building, ankle badly twisted and with bloody parallel lines of scratches on his face and hands. EMS workers rushed forward and took from him a blanket-wrapped, unhurt child clutching her terrified cat.

There are other stories: a dive into the Hudson in a rainstorm to pull a man from a sinking boat. Using his turnout coat to smother the flames on a man whose clothes were burning. Many stories. And after each act of heroism, James McCaffery—most often smiling widely—thanked well-wishers, returned to his firehouse, and refused all requests for interviews.

Three times McCaffery was admitted to NYU Medical Center, twice to the Burn Unit, with injuries that would have made him eligible for retirement. Each time he was back on the job within months. FDNY Assistant Chief Aleck Wagman acknowledges McCaffery to have been a source of "institutional knowledge." "Men were anxious to serve under him. Not just the new guys, everyone. Anyone could learn something from Jimmy. He'll be badly missed."

"At the other houses he worked, he wouldn't let them call him Superman," Owen McCardle recalls. "Like it embarrassed him. But, tell you the truth, it was always who he wanted to be."

McCaffery lived alone in a small, spare apartment on West 12th Street and never married. "The Job was his family," said Ted Fitzgerald, retired captain of Engine 235. "There's always guys like that, every generation. They're the backbone of this Department, and on 9/11 we lost way too many of them."

McCaffery's heroism on September 11 is by now legendary. Elizabeth Murray, an attorney, made the trip down 28 flights of stairs with others from her firm. Murray, her firm's fire warden, was among the last to evacuate her floor. She spoke of McCaffery's "swift and total" understanding of the tragedy. "There was fire on our floor from the elevator shaft. People were burned, and some had been hit by debris that exploded out when the doors blew open. There was a lot of smoke, and we were cut off from our stairs." The men of Ladder 62 directed the crowds away from the fire to an open stairwell, assisting the injured and, in the words of another survivor, "defusing the hysteria, everyone screaming and running around."

"He seemed to know exactly how much time we had to get out," Murray said of Captain McCaffery. "He said if we didn't panic, we'd be all right. He could have come out with us. We just barely made it. I really think he knew that the tower was going to come down. None of us remotely thought it would, at that time."

McCaffery was last seen by Murray heading another way. "He went up," she said. "He told his men, 'Get control of this, take these people out of here.' He meant the panic, the confusion. Then he looked around, like he was taking it all in. He said something like 'The job's up there.' One of the others, another firefighter, said, 'If you're going, Captain, I'm going with you.' Some of them went." Murray's eyes filled with tears. "He was smiling when he pulled open that staircase door. I'll never forget it. All the way down, I wondered what made him smile like that. I remember thinking, Well, when this is over, I'll look him up and ask him."

Deputy Chief Gino Aiello was at the north tower command station when the evacuation order was issued. "Some of the companies didn't respond," Aiello said in an interview. "A lot of the radios were out, so we don't know if they got the order. But Ladder 62 heard us. Captain McCaffery responded. He was on 44. He said he had injured up there, and he was bringing them out. He had three men with him. 'We'll be down as soon as we can, Chief. There's a lot of injured.' That's what he said. I don't know how he was planning to bring a lot of injured down 44 flights with three men, but if anyone could talk the injured into getting up and walking—the injured, maybe even the dead—it was Jimmy McCaffery."

Ladder 62 lost four men that day. Funerals and memorial services for the other three firefighters have already been held. "This is how Jimmy would have wanted it," Owen McCardle said. "He would have expected the other men to be taken care of first. He was their captain. First in, last out."

BOYS' OWN BOOK
Chapter 2

———

Abraham Lincoln and the Pig

October 30, 1968

Eleven years old: Four boys, three girls, and they weave through each
other's lives the same as through the open doors of the houses up and
down the street. These kids know one another the way they know these
blocks, the trees and sidewalks and everyone's backyard. Jimmy can't
remember—no one remembers—a time when the other ones weren't
there.

When they were little, their moms brought them to the park or to
each other's houses; on Saturday their dads took the whole bunch to the
beach, to the zoo. It's different now that they're bigger, now that they
go to school: Jimmy—with Markie, Marian, Sally, Vicky—is at PS 12;
and the Molloys, Tom and Jack, go to St. Ann's, study with the nuns. It
doesn't change who they are to each other; it's just, this way, some
things about each other are stories, legends almost: only some of the
kids see, but everyone *knows*.

Like the story (it got to be a legend) about Paulie Testa, and Eddie
Spano, and Tom's smart idea.

Paulie's at St. Ann's, too; his father has the fruit stand on Main
Street. He's little, Paulie, and right after school starts in the fall, there
go the Spano brothers knocking him down, taking his lunch money. It
happens a couple of times. It's not like Paulie says anything to any of
the kids, it's not like they say anything to Paulie; after all, he's from the
other side of the parish; after all, he's Italian. And the Spanos are
Italian, too. In Pleasant Hills people take care of their own.

But all the kids like Mr. Testa. Sometimes he gives you an apple or a peach for free; says they're bruised, he can't sell them, though no one ever finds a brown spot on one.

And weeks go by, and no one, meaning none of the Italians, stops the Spano brothers from beating on Paulie. Tom tells this to Jimmy, they both agree it's bad.

If he was bigger, Tom says, if he could look out for himself. But Paulie, he's just a shrimp, like Markie.

This makes Jimmy mad, the Spanos beating up on a scrawny kid. Paulie can't help it, or Markie, either, if they're not big; and Jimmy's had to get Markie out of trouble more than once that he got in just for being small.

Because of who their dad is, says Tom. That's why, because everyone's scared.

Jimmy knows that's right. Al Spano is a frightening man; being scared of him isn't stupid, it's smart. What should we do? Jimmy asks.

Tom says, Not you, Jim, just me.

Alone? Jimmy says.

Tom's not scared like everyone else, not afraid to go up against the Spanos. Jimmy knows why: because of who Tom's dad is.

But not being scared still doesn't mean Tom can take both Spano brothers on.

I don't think I'm gonna fight them, says Tom. I have an idea. He grins, and Jimmy does, too.

Like always, Jimmy says.

But if it doesn't work? If I need help? You got my back?

Like always, Jimmy says.

This is the way it is with Tom. Like because of who he is, he has things he has to do. All the kids have things they're supposed to do: clean your room, do your homework, do the dishes, go to church. Some kids, that's how you get your allowance: you do your chores. Tom, he has this extra job: take care of people. The kids aren't sure what he gets for doing that, but chores come from grown-ups and so does whatever you get, and Tom's father is Mike the Bear.

So one day Eddie Spano, the older brother, he's in fifth grade, Tom's grade. It's morning, the kids out on the playground before school, everyone running, yelling, the boys throwing balls, the girls jumping rope. Sister Agnes blows the whistle, the kids all run to get their book-bags and line up to go in. Eddie Spano at first can't find his bookbag. It's not where he left it, but he spots it off to the side. Goes over to get it, and it stinks. The thing's soaked in gasoline. All Eddie's books, note-books, his history report, drenched in gasoline, everything reeking and ruined. A book of matches on top, a note in the matchbook: *Lay off Paulie Testa, or next time its you.* The kids are lined up, girls on one line and boys on the other, and Tom, from his place in line, is staring at Eddie, not looking away.

That's Tom, that's his way. He could have fought the Spanos, sure, could have collected his brother Jack, and Jimmy—Jack's a year older, a lot bigger, but Tom's always in charge—and stood on the sidewalk around the corner from the schoolyard, where the Spanos had to pass, where the nuns couldn't see. Jimmy would have done it; Jack would have loved it. The Spanos would have lost.

Why didn't he?

What I wanted, I wanted them to stop beating on Paulie. That's what Tom says to the six kids sitting on the stoop, eating Heath bars and waiting to hear the story again. Marian says, Couldn't you tell a teacher? Tell someone so they'd make Eddie stop, so nobody has to get into a fight?

Vicky rolls her eyes. She's sitting next to Tom, the place Vicky usu-ally sits, on the top step. Anyway, Vicky says to Marian, they didn't get into a fight. Tom knows what he's doing. Vicky scoops up some crackly fall leaves, tries to braid their stems into a bouquet, but they crumble.

Well, I didn't want to do that, have a fight, Tom says. I mean, sup-pose we did, suppose Jimmy and Jack and me beat the crap out of them?

You would've, Tom, Markie chimes in, you would've *demolished* them. *Terminated* them. Markie's using big words, the kids ooh and ah; except Sally, she giggles and pushes Markie, and Markie grins and tries to tickle her.

Yeah, says Tom, for sure.

Yeah, says his brother Jack, for *fucking* sure, and I fucking wish we had, man. Jack says this, though he's also been heard to say, That little runt Paulie, he looks like a worm from his father's apples.

Yeah, Tom says; and the kids know there's no question in his mind who'd have won, if that's how it had gone. But, he says, but then they get some other assholes, come back and call us out. *We* get some other assholes—here he pokes Markie with his sneaker, and Markie grins again—and we call *them* out. Guineas and micks, in the middle of Main Street! World War Three!

Tom's saying words the kids aren't supposed to say. They're not dirty words, not exactly, or swearwords, like saying Jesus when you're not praying. There are other ones, too, spic and chink and kike and nigger, they're not nice. The moms don't want the kids to say them, though sometimes the dads, if they're talking to each other, they'll let one pop out, especially if they don't know you're listening. But not the kids, they're not allowed. Those other words, the kids don't know anybody to say them to anyway. But guineas, you better believe they know who the guineas are in Pleasant Hills. And the micks, that's them. It's not a nice word, but it's a good thing to be. All the kids know.

So, says Tom, so the next thing that happens, we have this big fight, and then Sister Joseph calls out my dad, and their dad. And your dad, Jimmy.

The kids all laugh, seeing Sister Joseph, a dried-up prune, standing on the sidewalk waiting to mix it up with Al Spano, with Brendan McCaffery and Mike the Bear. Jimmy laughs, though Jimmy's not really sure what odds he'd give on Mr. Molloy and Mr. Spano, or even on his own dad, if it came to that.

My way, Tom says, nobody gets hurt. Meaning, he adds, me and you assholes. Them, who gives a shit?

Tom talks dirtier than the other kids, except not dirtier than Jack. This is a privilege of rank; all the kids understand that.

Yeah, Markie pipes up. And I heard Eddie's dad beat his butt.

Tom nods. This is expected, but Markie's is the first report. That's expected, too: Markie's always hearing things, bringing the kids interesting information. Probably this is because no one—grown-ups or kids—really pays much attention to Markie. No one notices him much, who cares what he sees or hears?

Markie says, Mr. Spano, he's making Eddie buy a new math book from his fucking allowance.

Now Markie's using a word Tom saves for when he really needs it. Tom acts like he doesn't hear. Jack's eyes narrow, but he says nothing.

Markie goes on: And what else I heard, I heard Eddie told his dad he didn't know who did it, poured the gasoline. Even no matter what his dad did to him, he wouldn't tell.

Sally's green eyes get wide; Marian moves a little closer next to her and pats her hand. Everyone's quiet for a moment. The kids are all thinking about what Mr. Spano, a red-faced explosion of a man, might have done to Eddie, and about Eddie not telling.

Al Spano is just plain mean, for no reason, like his two sons. The Italians, the kids all think they're weird anyway. They wave their hands around and listen to music that you can't understand the words, and the old ladies wear black. But this kind of meanness, it's not from being Italian. All the kids keep away from Al Spano, all the kids cross to the other side of the street on the block where the Spanos live; all except Jack, who walks on that side on purpose, staring right into the windows of their house. No question Al Spano would tear out and break the arm of any man whose son was messing with his son. Even Mike the Bear: any man. But going up against Mike the Bear, that would be the end of Al Spano. Eddie Spano must know that, everyone knows that. So Eddie has to say he doesn't know who poured the gasoline.

Eddie's doing what he has to do. The kids are still scared of him, they'll never like him, and he deserves whatever he's getting; but his silence, they respect. Only Marian looks sad.

Sitting there on the stoop, everyone quiet, Jimmy's thinking, like the other kids, about Al Spano and the beating Eddie must have taken. But he's thinking about something else, too: what would happen if the Spano brothers snatched little Paulie's lunch money again tomorrow.

He sees it: Eddie Spano howling, rolling on the ground, eaten alive by flames.

He knows it won't be like that: the Spanos will never go near Paulie again. But if they did? Jimmy watches Tom, Tom's hands peeling the bark from a stick, digging with his thumbs where it doesn't want to come off.

But if they did, Jimmy thinks. Whose job would it be, then, to put that fire out?

Tom looks up at Jimmy, almost like Jimmy said what he was thinking out loud. Looks at him, but doesn't answer the question.

Tom snaps the stick, throws it away. Anyhow, he says. This way Paulie gets to keep his lunch money. The only one in trouble is Eddie, and he started it. The important thing—and now he grins, that great grin that makes them all feel good, all feel part of everything—the *important* thing, Dad don't get smacked by Sister Joseph.

The kids all laugh.

But there's something else Jimmy sees, sees and doesn't forget. What Tom wanted was to make the Spanos stop. Tom makes Jack part of it, what Jack will want is to beat the crap out of anything that moves. Kids fight, it's no big deal, not big enough for Sister Joseph to call anyone out. Except the way Jack fights. Jack gets in there, everything blows up, everyone's in trouble.

Tom looking out for little Paulie the way he did, Jimmy knows, that way instead of a different way, is also Tom looking out for Jack.

From the *New York Tribune*, October 24, 2001

A HERO'S LEGACY
by Harold Randall

Today was a happy day in Pleasant Hills.

This Staten Island hamlet of modest homes on sloping, tree-shaded streets is a town that lives up to its name. Kids ride bikes past well-tended flower beds on their way to the schools their parents went to. Main Street runs a short three blocks, lined with mom-and-pop shops. The Post Office is on the eastern end of Main Street, and the parish church of St. Ann's anchors the west. Between them, in the symbolic heart of Pleasant Hills, stands Engine 168, one of the first firehouses on Staten Island and still in use.

The purple and black bunting draped above the red doors of Engine 168 and the flags at half staff all over town suggest that Pleasant Hills hasn't had many happy days lately. Engine 168 lost two men on September 11, men who lived here, who were neighbors, fathers, and friends. The town also lost four other residents: two who worked in the World Trade Center, and two who were firefighters with other FDNY companies. And Pleasant Hills is also mourning a native son, a man who left this town 20 years ago but will always be one of their own: Capt. James McCaffery, one of the most decorated firefighters in the history of the FDNY. Capt. McCaffery died in the collapse of the north tower along with three other members of Ladder 62, the Manhattan company he commanded.

But today was a happy day in Pleasant Hills, because another native son, a little worse for wear, maybe, but alive and whole, came home.

Kevin Keegan was a probationary firefighter with three months' experience under his belt when the bell at Engine 168 rang on September 11. His shift was over; he didn't need to be there. But Keegan could often be found in the firehouse after his shift was over. Or before it began. Or on off-duty days. He liked the place: the kidding around, the stories, even the food.

"Kevin grew up here," Owen McCardle told the *Tribune*. The gray-mustached Pleasant Hills resident spent his entire career at Engine 168. Though he left the job over a decade ago, McCardle is still a part of the firehouse family; in the FDNY, that's how it works. "Jimmy McCaffery was here then," McCardle said. "He used to bring Kevin around to the firehouse after his father was gone. When Jimmy transferred out, he asked us to look after the kid."

"We made him like the prince of the firehouse," confirmed Peter Connell, recently promoted to captain and given the command of Engine 168. 168's former commander, Bill Small, is one of the men this company lost. "Kevin was two when his father died. We sort of adopted him. No kid should have to grow up without a father." Captain Connell looked back through the open firehouse door to the apparatus floor. Engine 168, damaged in the maelstrom that was September 11, has been repaired and repainted. The captain said, "I guess there are going to be a lot of kids to adopt now."

When the call came in to Engine 168 on September 11, off-duty firefighter Kevin Keegan asked Captain Small for permission to ride along. By then the extraordinary nature of the event was clear, though not yet its true and terrible extent. With the other members of the company, Keegan rode the engine into a cataclysm for which no level of experience could have prepared anyone.

"They had the bridge open for emergency vehicles, but it was slow going." In an interview last week, Keegan sat with a visitor at a picnic table on the rolling grounds of the Burke Rehabilitation Center in White Plains. "By the time we got there, the second plane had hit. The fires were burning pretty bad."

Keegan is a cheerful red-haired, freckled young man. But when he speaks of the events of that day, he turns his gaze away. He peers across the distant hills like a man hoping for the first glimpse of travelers returning home.

"Everything was chaos," Keegan said. "Girders crashing down, glass breaking. People on fire falling from the sky. It was unbelievable." Here in the green serenity of the hospital grounds, it did seem almost unbelievable that such horrors had ever been real.

"They sent us to the north tower," Keegan went on. "We were massing to go in—there was a chief there, I don't know which chief, but my captain reported to him. And there were, I think, four other companies. And we were getting set when part of the building just came twisting out of the sky. Someone shouted, and some guys ran, but some guys didn't have a chance to run."

Keegan was seriously injured by the falling debris, receiving a concussion and second-degree burns; but it's clear he knows how much luckier he is than many of the men with whom he stood.

"I lay there with something heavy on top of me. I knew I was being burned, but I couldn't move. I thought, I'm going to die. But, okay, at least I'm on the Job, I'll die as a firefighter. That was okay, you know?"

Whether or not that would have been okay is a judgment the visitor is glad he does not have to make.

"Then I heard Uncle Jimmy calling me."

Uncle Jimmy, of course, is Capt. James McCaffery, who stepped in and helped raise young Kevin Keegan after the death of his father. "There was smoke and dust everywhere, you couldn't see anything, but Uncle Jimmy told me to go left. He said it was my coat that was pinned, not me, and to take it off and stay low and head toward daylight on the left.

"So I did. I peeled out of the coat, and I could move. It was slow going, but Uncle Jimmy kept saying just a little further, he was right there waiting. I could see the daylight he meant. I got there, to a kind of hole, and saw guys up there, yelling and digging. I called to Uncle Jimmy. I figured that's where he was, that I'd made it to the right place. A couple of guys yelled back. One guy jumped down into the hole. A guy I didn't know." Keegan shook his head, clearing out memories of smoke and dust, fire and darkness. "I asked where Uncle Jimmy was, but he just kept telling me I was okay, and they got me out.

"That's the last thing I remember until I woke up in the hospital the next day. Some of the guys were there sitting in the room, the guys I rode with. They told me about Dave"—firefighter David Schwartz, the second member of Engine 168 to die that day—"and Capt. Small. I asked about Uncle Jimmy. They told me about him, too.

"The thing is"—Keegan turned his clear green eyes back to his visitor, giving up his search of the horizon for absent friends—"I reconstructed it. Over and over, in my head. Uncle Jimmy was already up in the tower when we got to the location. Thirty, forty flights up. That's where he was when it fell—on forty-four. He was nowhere near where I was. Nowhere near."

Today in Pleasant Hills a breeze ruffled the bunting above the doors of Engine 168, and the carved salamanders, legendary lizards that cannot be destroyed by fire, seemed to wink. And Probationary Firefighter Kevin Keegan walked, slowly, on crutches, but unaided, back into the firehouse where he grew up.

"Jimmy saved him." Keegan's mother, Sally, has no doubt in her mind about that. "Jimmy's been taking care of us all our lives. Since we were all kids. Kevin's dad . . ." Sally Keegan smiled. It was a day for smiling. "You had to know Markie. My husband was the sweetest man who ever lived. But he got into trouble all the time. Jimmy was always getting him out. One of the worst things for Jimmy, I think, was when he couldn't help Markie that one last time. But he's been doing things for Kevin and me ever since. And look what he did for us now."

You don't have to believe in ghostly voices to see the ways in which Captain McCaffery is still taking care of his friend's son. Kevin Keegan's FDNY health insurance paid for his stay at Burke. Jimmy McCaffery's FDNY life insurance named Keegan as beneficiary and has paid for the extras: the private room, the private nurse, the hours of physical therapy demanded by a young man eager to push himself, anxious to get back on the Job.

But even before that, years before, Jimmy McCaffery always did what he could.

Mark Keegan, Kevin Keegan's father, died in prison, according to Marian Gallagher, director of the More Art, New York! Foundation and Kevin Keegan's godmother. "Markie killed a man in self-defense. He was never charged in the killing. But his gun was unlicensed, and he went to prison for that. It was a short sentence, but he got into a fight there and was killed." Marian Gallagher's face saddened. "We were all so young. . . ."

After Mark Keegan died in prison, Jimmy McCaffery looked after Keegan's young family. "Uncle Jimmy said we should sue the State," Kevin Keegan tells the visitor. He leans on his crutches, the center of the happy chaos echoing down Main Street. "Mom and

Aunt Marian thought he was nuts. Even Uncle Phil did." Keegan grins. He pokes the ribs of a tall man standing beside him. This is Phillip Constantine, Mark Keegan's court-appointed attorney. Over many years he has remained a friend of the Keegan family. He grins also and tells the visitor, "Once in my life I was wrong, and he can't forget it."

"But Uncle Jimmy insisted," said Keegan. "So we sued. And the State settled."

All of that, of course, is family lore: Kevin Keegan was too young to remember. His mother remembers, though. "Yes, it was Jimmy's idea. No one thought it would work, but it did. That was Jimmy—just going ahead with something he believed in, no matter what anyone said. It wasn't a huge amount of money, but it came every month. I didn't have to work when Kevin was little. That made all the difference."

Sally Keegan's eyes, clear and green like her son's, broke off from her visitor's and gazed down the street, as though someone had called her name.

And Main Street suddenly seemed crowded. Not just with Kevin Keegan's friends and well-wishers, people giddy with good news in a season bleak with tragedy. Ghosts were also shimmering in the morning air. Jimmy McCaffery. Markie Keegan. Bill Small. David Schwartz. The four others that Pleasant Hills lost on a day which changed us all forever. All were there, to welcome Firefighter Kevin Keegan home.

LAURA'S STORY
Chapter 1

The Man Who Sat by the Door

October 30, 2001

Harry Randall's death broke over Laura Stone like a thunderstorm out of a clear blue sky. That was even one of her stupid thoughts, one of the notions that floated by as Georgie, who'd brought her the news, hovered, ready to catch her if she fainted or to fetch water, a sweater, whatever she wanted. Georgie who'd always loved her. I should have known, Laura thought, rubbing her arms with her newly cold hands, seeing not Georgie but the Hudson flowing splendidly through the glorious afternoon in the window behind him: It's such a perfect, beautiful day.

In New York now, beautiful days were suspect, clear blue skies tainted with an invisible acid etch. "Lovely weather," neighbors greeted one another, smiling under the generous golden sunlight of an Indian summer still unrolling into late October. Then their smiles would falter. They'd nod and walk hastily on, to avoid acknowledging the likeness, to escape seeing, in each other's eyes, how stunningly beautiful that day in mid-September had been, too.

The next equally meaningless thought that passed through Laura's mind as she stood staring down at the river: How long had Georgie known? Had he stood watching, waiting for her to leave her desk to go stand by the conference room window—a thing she could be counted on to do half a dozen times a day, to come here to watch the Hudson flowing to the sea while a sentence composed itself in her head—so he could be the only one near, the one to comfort her?

No, she told herself impatiently, as you might scold a child for making a claim he knows is false: *"I can fly,"* or *"My dog ate a car."* No, not

Georgie. I'd do that. I'd deliver bad news to Harry that way. But kind, lovesick Georgie wouldn't do that to me.

Bad news, or good news. It was Laura who'd pinned yesterday's front, the front that carried the third Jimmy McCaffery story, to Harry's corkboard. Not where everyone could see it (though of course they'd all seen it when the paper came out, all seen Harry Randall on the front again after a five-year drought, not just the front, above the fold). She'd tucked it in the corner, folded small, just the head and subhead left to shout privately to Harry how proud of him she was. It was still there, still shouting:

FUND REJECTS CONTRIBUTION
Questions Surround Hero Firefighter's
Dealings with Crime Figures
by Harry Randall

Surprising her, Harry had left it up all day yesterday. But he was sure to take it down today. No, but—twisting stomach, ice on her skin—according to Georgie, Harry wouldn't be here today, wouldn't be here again, wasn't here, was gone.

But—swept away suddenly, losing her footing to a rogue wave of hope—Georgie must be *wrong*! It wasn't Harry. Someone else took Harry's car. Who? What's the difference? It was someone else's body. She'd go, she'd go now over to the morgue, past the tent and the refrigerated trucks where all the unidentified bodies were, and this would be just another one, just someone else no one knew. She'd tell them it wasn't Harry, and later, back at home, she and Harry—

Georgie was shaking his head, reaching for her. Laura heard, horrified, her own voice, high and shrill, speaking these thoughts aloud. Shivering, she spun away from Georgie, turned to the river, willing Georgie to stay back: if he touched her, she would splinter and crack, like ice in warm water.

The river blurred, her face felt steamy: oh God, she was crying, with Georgie there. Her knees wobbled. Despising herself, she dropped onto a chair. It was the one with the coffee stain on the arm, from the morning meeting, soon after Laura had come to the *Tribune,* when Leo had complained about something—*toothlessness,* Leo's word—in a story of Harry's. Harry, to the mortal eye unperturbed, offered an insolent reply. Leo tossed the pile of copy and a disgusted snort in Harry's direction. The gods clashing on Olympus: Laura had been thrilled. The papers had upended someone's coffee, not Harry's, she remembered, but someone else's.

"Who has the story?" Confused, Laura heard an imitation of her own voice demand this of Georgie. Oh, she thought: Reporter-Laura, that's who's speaking. She who went to a hospital groundbreaking to give the donor a chance to comment on the rumor that the multimillion-dollar windfall was profit from his Mexican drug operation. She who pushed herself into the face of a mother to ask how she felt now that a fire had killed her children.

Georgie, weakly and after a moment: "What?"

"*Who?*"

"Laura, what's the difference?" Georgie had damp brown eyes and a mouth eternally open, eager to speak the right words, of comfort, of explanation, if only he could find them. He preferred to be called George or, better, to be abruptly summoned by his last name—"Holzer!" the way you'd hear "Randall!" or "Stone!" echo through the newsroom—but no one ever did that. His beat was technology, science. Half the *Tribune* staff held he was a virgin; the rest, that he visited a Korean whorehouse on 38th Street twice a week.

Laura, who never gazed long upon Georgie, looked angrily past him now, through the blue sky's reflection in the conference room glass, into the newsroom.

It was chaos there, the regular thing. The attacks had not forced the *Tribune*'s offices closed, but the rhythm, the urgent fast and steady beat of newsgathering, had been smashed and jangled. Throw a rock in water, orderly rings pulse in all directions; throw many, and the world is anarchy, confusion. It took time for the *Tribune*'s tempo to reassert, but finally it had. Keyboards clicked. Men with their polished shoes on their desks leaned dangerously back in chairs asking pointed questions into phones. Women with sharp elbows leaned forward over theirs, desks and phones, listening darkly. Someone came, someone went.

Laura turned to Georgie. "They don't know yet." It was an accusation.

"Leo's about to call us together. I asked him if I could tell you first." It was an admission of guilt.

"First? So you could—? I have to—?"

On top of her words: "Laura, you know—"

But Laura was refusing to know. A wave of fury threw her out of her chair, fury at Georgie for the news he'd brought and the way he'd brought it, at the river for flowing and the sun for shining and the leaves for falling from the trees.

Before she could scream and tear Georgie apart—he would have permitted this—a change in the tenor of the newsroom froze her. A ripple in the force field: Leo was stepping from his office. He planted himself just over his threshold, and when he stood there and roared, "People!" everything stopped.

Square-headed, white-haired, rough-faced, and bulky, Leo waited for phone calls to end and documents to be saved-as. Laura and Georgie, after a motionless moment, stumbled unthinking through the conference room door: rage, shock, and sorrow could not, even combined, begin to overcome the autoresponse triggered in a reporter by Leo's bellow from the doorway.

So Leo delivered the news, and Laura had to hear it again.

This time it was ornamented with details. If she'd been listening as a reporter, these would have been important to her. Fascinating even, as they clearly were to the colleagues around her. Unable any longer to be impressed by death, they could still be surprised by the personal nature of one like this; but not enough to keep them from scribbling notes on pads, in case Leo assigned them the story, or from stealing glances away from Leo to send them Laura's way when they thought she wasn't looking.

But she was looking, though she was determined to have nothing but scorn for their glances, and she didn't hear the news as a reporter, though she was one. She heard it as a student, as an acolyte, apologist, and lover, and the word Georgie hadn't used but Leo did, the dam-break that swept her into stunned disbelief and powerless fury, was *suicide*.

Marian's Story
Chapter 1

——

The Man Who Sat by the Door

October 30, 2001

The catastrophic force of the earthquake that would be summoned up by Harry Randall's death was not at first apparent to Marian Gallagher. All the news brought her was a disquietude such as she might have felt at faint tremblings of the ground: vibrations so weak they could be dismissed as the inventions of an anxious imagination, except by those who had passed through such times before.

The breathless last to join a cheery group of friends around a bistro table—Marian had many groups of friends—she was kissed and greeted, her wine was poured, the olives and the bread were passed her way. How are you, honey, Clark asked, and Sue, always knowing what meant the most, asked how that young firefighter was, her godson, the one who was hurt, the one the story in the paper was about? Kevin, replied Marian; he's doing very well, we're very grateful. Tomiko asked how her day had gone, how many forms she'd filled out for people (*in,* Sam said, you fill forms *in*), was it still as hard as in the beginning, working with the victims?

Marian smiled and said, Oh no, but she wasn't working with the families, those were the volunteers with the really hard jobs, she didn't know how they did it. She tasted the wine, a dry chardonnay, and nodded approvingly. Her clients were the businesses, she told them, the stores, the offices, the take-outs, and the delis. Some of them had given so much, you know that one locksmith opened his shop and told the rescue workers, Just take what you need. And now everything was gone. Everything! And the restaurants had been feeding the rescue workers, and people had donated water, breathing masks, whatever they had, people had given whatever they had. It was wonderful, now, to be able to really *do* something for *them*.

Sam reached around the table and topped off people's wineglasses. Katie asked Tomiko how the baby was. Ulrich, as usual serious about the menu, recommended that people try the mussels, they were exceptional the last time he was here, although of course that was before, but that shouldn't make a difference, should it, now that they'd reopened? Sue picked up a story she'd been telling Jeana; Marian overheard something about cell phones, being connected into some stranger's call because the lines were all still so weird downtown.

"Everything all right back at the office?" Sam asked quietly, just making sure; he'd left for meetings of his own long before Marian had gone to hers. Marian smiled and nodded. "I wish we had more phones, though." Sam shrugged agreement, brought the wine back to her. Everyone in Lower Manhattan wished they had phones. The MANY Foundation's office was luckier than most: two weeks ago, one of their six lines had been restored.

They nibbled on bread and olives; they sipped their wine. Around the table people's faces were glowing, as they leaned forward to hear one another better, as they nodded and laughed. This was not the wine, Marian thought, not the candles. This glow—she could feel it in her own smile as she watched her friends—was the light of what used to be a simple pleasure: ending a day of hard work with good food and good friends.

By the time the waiter came to take their orders—Marian had decided on the rigatoni with goat cheese and three varieties of mushrooms—no one had yet mentioned the Fund. No one had asked Marian if there were new developments, what would happen to the money if the allegations in yesterday's *Tribune* article turned out to be true.

Eventually someone would bring it up. This was the sort of juicy story that would have been irresistible when gossip was fun. No one had the heart for gossip now. But Marian was entwined in this story—much more than they knew—so someone was bound to bring it up. When they did, she would answer as honestly as she could, because these were her friends.

Marian listened to the talk around her and told herself she was glad that, for the time being, no one was asking. She told herself that their silence on this subject betokened nothing other than courtesy, an unwillingness to bring up what was sure to be a difficult subject, for her, their friend. She buttered bread with quick impatient strokes as she scolded herself for imagining that Ulrich, the most morally strident of them, had avoided her eyes since she'd sat down.

And she hoped that, when finally the topic came up, Sam would remain calm. It would only serve to make everyone uncomfortable if he exploded here the way he had in the office yesterday when the third *Tribune* article ran. Sipping her wine, Marian watched him. He and Clark were leaning toward each other, both talking at once, Clark shaking his head and laughing, Sam's hands in constant motion as he sketched out his points in the air. Sam caught Marian's eye, gave her a quick, private smile, said something in answer to Clark, and sliced at the air again.

For some time now Marian had been seeing younger men. She had been surprised to find herself drawn to the first one: Frank, a field director for Human Rights Watch. The difference in their ages was not so very great, but enough: Marian by then had roots, commitments, the quiet consolation of expected rhythms. Frank was like a dancing flame. He sought, incessantly, new things to illuminate and to feed on. When he was transferred to Prague, she had been relieved. And then two months later she found herself sitting over martinis with a Japanese video artist even younger than Frank.

The young men suited her in many ways. They had passion, they were tireless, in bed and in the world. Not yet weary, they saw the good in people, as Marian did, and also still had hopes (as Marian wished to have, but some days it was difficult) of helping it to blossom. Because they valued Marian's experience and fulsomeness, they were flattered by her attention, which flattered her in return.

And they were willing to move on. No matter their protests, their broken hearts, and their promises, Marian knew they would begin to forget her as soon as the door had closed. Their need to be lightly connected suited her. It eased the burden of guilt she would otherwise feel as her joy in and desire for each new lover bloomed, flowered, and faded. It always did; it always would. She had come to accept that. No new love was able to last through the seasons in a heart like hers; none could become established where the roots of her first love ran so deep and its branches spread so wide.

What had been between Marian and Sam had ended long ago, but the friendship that had started before and continued after seemed to Marian stronger, like a rosebush once the extraneous growth has been pruned away. She'd approached the start of their affair tentatively: Sam worked for MANY, and it had been new for Marian, poaching on her own preserve. But she'd judged Sam capable of handling the situation—its beginning, its middle, and its inevitable end—and she'd been correct. About character, Marian was rarely wrong. While others marveled at her unerring intuition, Marian understood her skill to be that of an overcompensating athlete injured when young, now running marathons even though—or because—she'd thought she'd never walk again.

Marian was grateful for Sam, for his daily, practical presence in the office, for his willingness to stay friends. Still, when the Fund came up, she hoped he would be calm. In this circle of friends, she would be embarrassed by any attempt at rescue.

A month ago, when this same group had come together for dinner, the first time some of them had seen the others since the attacks, the first time they had been together as a group, someone had asked about the Fund. Jeana, it was; she'd read about the establishment of the McCaffery Fund in the *Tribune* the day before, and she'd wondered why, with all Marian had to do, had she taken it on, this McCaffery thing? Marian answered, simply, to help, because they'd asked her. Didn't you know him, that firefighter? Katie asked. Oh, well, he was famous, Marian said.

Marian knew many famous people. She never dropped names, but when Tomiko had had trouble with her work visa last year, Marian had called someone in a senator's office; and Ulrich's pictures would not be in the permanent collection at MOMA if he had not met MOMA's photography curator over dinner at Marian's loft. The fallen firefighter in whose name this fund was established had been notoriously publicity-shy but famous for daredevil heroic deeds nonetheless; it stood to reason, then, that Marian knew him.

But though Marian did not expect to get through the evening without mention of the Fund, or of Jimmy, she was completely blindsided by the question that actually came.

She was removing an olive pit discreetly to a bread plate when Clark asked what about that guy Randall, it was on the evening news, that was that guy, wasn't it, and what the hell happened? But Marian had been in meetings all afternoon, she hadn't heard the news, and it seemed Sam had not, either: Which guy, what do you mean what happened? Everyone filled them in, slapping facts down as though in a friendly cutthroat game of hearts: midmorning, on the Verrazano—the inbound side, he must have been on Staten Island—not many other cars around; so far no note, no idea why—or else they just weren't saying; left his car keys behind, and his wallet, they say most jumpers do that, *why,* for God's sake? until someone—Sue—focused in on Marian's silence, on her wide eyes. "But, honey, you hate him," Sue said, half question, half reminder. Marian drank her chardonnay in an attempt to refloat her heart, which seemed to have suddenly run aground.

"Hate," Marian repeated, holding her wineglass by the delicate stem. "I guess. But there's just been so much death. . . ."

In the rustling forest of talk around them, in the clinking of dinnerware and the teasing and laughter, a withering drought of silence descended on their table. Marian, her stomach clenching, said, "Oh no, I'm sorry. I didn't mean to bring you guys down. Look, just give me a minute. I'll be right back." She stood, dropped her napkin on her chair, hurried from the table, but not before she stopped to smile at Sam and answer his "Are you okay?" with an unwavering "Of course." Then she headed for the ladies' room, up front by the bar; but once close, she slipped past it, out onto the street.

The night was warm; Marian was wearing a jacket of loose-woven cotton and needed nothing else. She stood at the end of the narrow street, waiting to cross the highway. The traffic seemed normal, it seemed almost like before. Two weeks ago the city had begun to allow even trucks downtown again, and the perimeter was pulled in a little every few days.

When the light changed, Marian crossed to the river. The scent of salt water overwhelmed the faint, astringent odor from Ground Zero, the odor of cars and furniture, papers, family photographs, clothing and its owners, jet fuel still smoldering underground.

The river flowed smoothly; an ocean smell this strong meant the tide was pushing the water north, and a barge moved that way, too, placidly allowing itself to be towed by a hardworking tug with yellow lights glowing in its cabin. On the day of the attacks, the squat and ugly tugboats, along with lumbering ferries and sleek commuter launches and polished yachts, had rushed to the shores of Lower Manhattan and swept dust-caked survivors across the river. The boats had worked tirelessly, into the night.

In the following days, though, river traffic had been halted. Unneeded and forlorn, the tugs had stayed bound at their moorings. Marian, her office building too close to Ground Zero to reopen right away—the cleanup, the air tests, must come first—had taken her coffee to the river each morning; standing there, she'd watched the tugs pull halfheartedly on their ropes, as the tide shifted. So much to be done, no way to do it. But now traffic on the river was moving again, and the tugs were needed. Marian imagined them joyously leaning their shoulders into their work.

She thought of Sally, and then of Kevin. Did they know about Harry Randall's death, had they heard? She was hit with a strange thought, a terrible thing to think, but she was thinking it before she could stop herself: most deaths came too soon (and this was a theme of meditation on the September 11 deaths, because so many of the lost were young professionals, young office workers, young firefighters, young cops), but this death, the death of this reporter, had come too late.

With determination Marian turned her mind from that idea. She did not want to wish anyone ill, not even this man who had so disturbed the ravaged earth just as people were attempting, warily, to find footing again.

But her thoughts, pushed away from Harry Randall and not easily managed in this uneasy time, swung back to the missing and the lost. Many were young, yes; but not all. Jimmy had been forty-six.

In Marian's most insistent, most difficult memory, they were both twenty-four. Jimmy stood with her on the rocks under the bridge. Dazzling spring sunlight streamed over them. She knew, had known for some time, that things were not right with Jimmy. Still, she was stunned, unable to speak, even to ask, as he folded his hands on hers, held her eyes with his, and told her goodbye.

She could not now, nor could she then, repeat the words he'd used. It had seemed to her she hadn't understood them, that she had abruptly lost her ability to comprehend language. Jimmy had talked about being someone different, although it had not been clear to Marian whether he was speaking of a desire, or a regret. What she did recall clearly, such a small, strange thing, was the cool dampness on her fingertips from the salt spray that had splashed on his sleeve. She remembered feeling that coolness even after, long after, he'd turned and walked away.

Over the years she had run across him, of course, and been shocked each time at the changes in him, and at the things that had not changed.

On Staten Island she'd seen him in church at Kevin's first communion, and at the ballpark when Kevin's Little League team made the play-offs; he had been a pallbearer nine years ago at Sally's father's funeral, but two years later he had not attended Big Mike Molloy's, though Marian had steeled herself for his presence. Nor had she been the only person who expected him there. Returning from the graveside ceremony to drink coffee in Peggy Molloy's hushed living room, Marian overheard a neighbor asking Tom about Jimmy.

"You were such good friends, Tom," the man said. "Your father's funeral, I'd have thought he'd be here."

"He doesn't come out here anymore" had been Tom's answer. "Only sometimes to see Kevin and Sally."

"No, not just them. Owen McCardle, that he used to work with? I saw him the other day, Jimmy, I mean, on Owen's porch. A week before that big construction fire, it was on the news? Jimmy climbing all that scaffolding. I thought he'd be here, I could congratulate him."

Tom just said, "Him and me, we lost touch."

Marian had watched the neighbor turn away, felt his disappointment that the famous Jimmy McCaffery was not going to appear. She'd tried to feel only relief.

Two years after that—five years ago—by heart-stopping accident, she'd run into Jimmy in Manhattan. Rounding a corner, she'd come upon a company of firefighters stowing their equipment after a call. The sidewalk was wet, the air smelled of smoke. The captain turned to answer someone's shouted question and was suddenly face-to-face with her, and it was Jimmy. His face had fleshed out, the hair she could see was gray. Three white scars ran down his cheek, parallel tracks that echoed the folds now etched on his forehead. But his eyes, his eyes were the same. They met hers and held them.

Only when Jimmy had swung himself up onto the truck and the company had driven away did Marian know her hand had reached for him, must have touched his coat, because her fingertips were stained with soot.

Now, as she stood gazing out over the river, another scene—Harry Randall's death—gathered itself and grew bright in her mind. She knew better than to try and stop it; she just watched. Pulling over on the bridge. (You'd have to put your flashers on, so no one drove into your car and got hurt.) Clambering over the cold steel rails. (A difficult climb, made to be so, she imagined, she hoped, to give the climber one more chance, one more reason, to turn away.) Hauling your trembling body up to stand swaying, surveying the enormous sweep of river, buildings, sun, and clouds, until that mighty moment of final choice and the dive, the long, soaring flight into blue, sparkling water. (From such a height, no difference between water and rock.)

She did a breathing exercise to rid herself of the images, and of the twin burdens of anger and guilt. The guilt was for the pall she had cast on the easy joy of her friends' evening. Joy was not an abundant crop lately; where found, it needed to be carefully tended and sheltered from the withering chill of memory.

The anger was at Harry Randall, for killing himself.

Attempting to force the truth about Jimmy McCaffery out of the dark place they'd all, without a word to one another, buried it in; exposing what he'd uncovered, now of all times, to the searing glare of front-page headlines—that had been a terrible thing. Marian had tried to make Harry Randall see that it would be that way.

Her own danger had been secondary to her. The morass opening before her now, the tangle of trouble to herself, was not important. But her work was. And especially now. In these unsteady days, when no one was able to find a firm footing, she could offer a handhold, a refuge, a place to stand. She had tried every way she could think of to make Harry Randall understand how crucial it was, right now, for everyone only to help. She had tried to make him see that truth was not, always, the highest good.

Randall, though, was a reporter. And though she had failed, she did understand his need, in these times, to cling to what he had always believed in.

But when the consequences of what he'd done began to become clear, he should have acted like a man. He owed them all that.

In times like these, no one had the right to suicide.

PHIL'S STORY
Chapter 1

———

The Man Who Sat by the Door

October 30, 2001

The thunderbolt of Harry Randall's death hit Phil Constantine at Grainger's Tavern. It was thrown from the TV over the bar by a glossy-haired anchorwoman in an insistent blue suit. The news blasted him with a powerful jolt, though no one watching would have seen that: just his eyes opening slightly, his jaw tightening as his focus narrowed and intensified.

In court Phil would sometimes cock his head, lean forward when a witness spoke—a prosecution witness, never his own—as though what he was hearing made no sense. As though he were trying to understand by moving closer to the source of his confusion. That gesture, though, was ruthlessly tactical. A lawyer who admitted to confusion was a fool. Real surprises, like being told by the evening news that that bastard reporter had jumped off the Verrazano Narrows Bridge, called for control.

Facing gravely into the camera, a trench-coated reporter spooled off as many facts of Harry Randall's life and death as he could jam into forty-five seconds. Behind him a weary-looking cop ripped down crime-scene tape. Two more linked tow chains to Randall's empty car. When the story was done, Phil asked Steve, behind the bar, to switch the channel, to try to catch it again.

"Something going on?" Steve glanced apprehensively up at the TV, tensing with someone's just-opened beer bottle in one hand.

"No, nothing new." Phil spoke reassuringly—reassurance was one of the tones in his automatic repertoire—"just someone I know," he added, to explain. Steve nodded but gave the TV another distrustful look as he reached for the remote, handed it to Phil.

Everyone was like this now. Every siren, every subway delay, every unexpected crowd as you rounded the corner, made your heart speed, your palms sweat. You walked along thinking of your day or your date or your dinner, and then you saw someone on the street run up to some- one else and whisper, and before you could stop yourself you were thinking, That's it, something else happened. What this time? Sarin in the subway? Car bombs in the tunnels, dynamite on the bridge? Smallpox, assassination, poison in the water?

Everyone was like this, Phil as much as anyone. You just had to con- trol yourself and go on anyway: it wasn't going away.

Phil flicked through channels. He found the Harry Randall story again, just ending, heard only what he'd just heard, learned nothing new. Either the other stations weren't running it, or, Harry Randall being one of their own, they'd led with it and he'd missed it already. Probably that. The death of a reporter, even a washed-up drunk like Harry Randall, was news to reporters. It would have been, even without the bullshit stories the *Tribune* had been running these past few weeks. Stories that started from the pure bright light of that fallen hero, Jimmy McCaffery, and spread in so many directions like a scorching flame. Stories with Randall's byline over them as though his name still meant something, stories meant to reignite a career long since cooled to ash.

Phil laid the remote on the bar. Steve came over and picked it up, Phil thanking him but really only half there, half aware of one televised story ending and another beginning. An anchorman offered him scenes of the war and developments in homeland defense. He paid no atten- tion to the rest of the news or the rest of the crowd, sparse still, though Grainger's, barely a dozen blocks from Ground Zero, had never closed.

On the night of the day itself, Phil, stunned, exhausted, and alone, had stood at his window looking out over the dark, silent streets of Lower Manhattan. Down the block, flickering lights caught his eye: candles in Grainger's window. That Steve had lit them that first night as a beacon was clear, though whether he was offering rescue or hoping to be rescued, Phil was never sure.

The light brought Phil down four flights from his blacked-out apart- ment to a bar nearly but not totally dark, nearly but not totally empty. That first night there were five of them, all longtime regulars who lived inside what was suddenly the perimeter, in places without power but still habitable thanks to the arbitrary nature of currents of wind and smoke.

In Phil's memory of that night, they huddled in a room that stank of smoke and sweat. Compulsively they told one another their stories: the avalanche roar, the choking black cloud, then the silence, sudden, absolute, and horrifying; and then, as in a nightmare, roar and cloud and silence again as the second tower fell.

Grainger's had no ice and no TV, but someone had brought a radio. They twirled the dial until they found a station still broadcasting. In the shuddering candlelight they sat late, drank, and talked—Phil, no, Phil not talking, just silent, just listening to others' words swirling around him, like sounds from afar brought on a whirlwind, Phil saying almost nothing but not leaving—and all of them alert to changes in the newscaster's tone as though to rumblings of the heavens from which the gods might speak. Phil remembered drinking steadily but remaining sober, scotch slipping past the numbness at his core like wind whistling around a rock.

Now, tonight, Phil sat here again, as he had almost every night before (when Grainger's was just a place, somewhere to unwind) and every night since (when anything familiar was a parachute and everyone was falling). With barroom solidarity the other regulars ignored what Harry Randall had written about Phil, as though they hadn't read the stories (unlikely); or they made it a point to tell Phil that they didn't buy one single word of that crap (to Phil's mind, people being what they were, equally unlikely). A third reaction, one nobody voiced but Phil sensed in the appraising looks he caught when he glanced in the mirror above the bar, was a surprised respect: That string-bean Jew lawyer? Mixed up with Eddie Spano, for all these years? Whaddaya know?

There was a fourth reaction now, too: Phil could see it on cops or firefighters who'd known Grainger's from before, who were working the rescue but had to get away from the tent. They'd come to the bar bringing other cops and firefighters with them, ones who'd come down from Massachusetts, up from Kentucky or Virginia. If they knew who he was—and the ones who did would point him out to the ones who didn't—they would glare at him in anger, in disgust, as though it was Phil Constantine who'd brought the great Jimmy McCaffery low. The untruth of that, the twisted irony, was so great, and secret-keeping so long a habit, that Phil could only shake his head and turn away.

Phil sipped his scotch, stared into the dimness. Harry Randall's voice, demanding, insinuating, churned in his memory. It drowned out the bar's mindless chatter and the anchorman's bland modulation. Phil watched as Randall's creased, pugnacious face formed and floated in the air before him.

In the end, Randall had won. Phil had fought him with all his court-room weapons of exaggerated rationality, sarcasm, feigned innocence, and personal attack. He'd buried his knowledge at the center of a blind-ing maze of argument, tirade, sermon, and bitter humor. But Randall, with his irritating shrug, had merely to turn and go elsewhere. Randall hadn't found his way to the truth, not all the way in. But he'd gotten his story. True? Did it matter? He'd won.

But now, it seemed, he had lost.

Phil slipped a ten onto the bar, left his drink unfinished. It was his second; he never finished the second. Before September 11 he'd never ordered a second. But early on, the crowds thin as they were, he'd tried way overtipping for the one he'd had. Steve had pointedly left the extra bills on the bar. Now Phil ordered two, left the second, tipped on both. Neither he nor Steve ever said anything about it.

Phil pushed out of Grainger's into stillness. The streets were almost empty of people, no cars at all; down here the perimeter still held. The rumble of heavy equipment faded as he moved south, away from the site. Behind him the sky glowed with an icy gleam from the enormous lights lent by filmmakers to the rescue effort. No, not rescue now; now, just recovery.

A faint breeze brought him the smell of burning. At Battery Park he walked past the wary eyes of two young men wearing military camou-flage, holding rifles, serving their country on the tip of Manhattan. Kids with guns, Phil thought. Once that would have meant either a threat or a client. Now, God help us, they were here to protect him.

He leaned on the railing near the ferry terminal. He knew this place so well, he was sometimes surprised his shoes hadn't made grooves in the pavement, his hands hadn't worn down the rail. He'd stood here so many times in the beginning years, staring across the water, letting the ferries go, telling himself he'd take the next one. And in the end turn-ing, walking home.

Telling himself it didn't matter. Telling himself it was better. Going for coffee in the morning with the blond photographer in the top-floor loft whose boyfriend had just walked out on her. Buying drinks for a girl from some southern college while she marveled at how everything was just so different here. Phil thinking, My God, they'll eat you alive, taking her home, leaving her, perplexed and a little hurt, at her apartment door.

And waiting. Until—collapsing under the weight of a need as great as his? or just simple loneliness? he was never sure—the walls Sally built to keep him out would crumble. Then for months he'd cross the harbor nearly every evening to her world, that alien place of quiet houses on shaded streets, Sunday morning church bells, and neighbors who lived in the homes they'd grown up in. He'd stay until morning, then sneak away, sailing back through the breaking mist to the sparkling towers of his own world like a prince from some idiotic fairy tale. Trying to avoid being transformed by the sun's first rays into what, exactly? What could getting caught with Sally Keegan in the hard light of day turn him into that he hadn't already become?

Phil stared across the harbor, watched the ferry, but tonight he couldn't go.

Now, when the death of Jimmy McCaffery was only one of many deaths that Sally's Staten Island neighborhood was trying to stand up under—McCaffery, gone from the place for over twenty years but still a hero there, how well Phil knew—Phil was staying away. Not because he gave a damn how the people of Pleasant Hills looked at him, the silent stares as he walked down their streets. Truth was, it wasn't so different now from the way it had always been. He'd always felt eyes on him, known things were said beyond his hearing that he wouldn't want to hear. The idea that the people of Pleasant Hills thought less of him than before Harry Randall's muckraking was almost laughable.

But Sally. She'd read the articles, too. She had never cared any more than he what her neighbors thought, and she didn't care now: but Sally wanted to know the truth. Demanded explanations he didn't have. Refused the ones he gave her.

Sally didn't believe what Randall had written about Jimmy McCaffery. Kevin didn't, either. In Pleasant Hills, no one did.

It might, though, be true.

But it appeared they were all willing to believe what he'd written about Phil.

And Phil?

Phil had to admit (but so far, only to himself) that what Randall had written about him might also be true.

He turned, to look not across the harbor but anywhere else. Up the Hudson, at buildings and ships and, above them, tiny pale stars just opening into a perfect cobalt sky. Harry Randall. That bastard Harry

Randall had killed himself. And why the hell, Phil thought, gripping the rail as though to choke the truth out of it, why the *hell,* if the old bastard was going to do this, couldn't he have done it weeks ago and spared everyone all this shit?

The river went on and the stars didn't blink. Phil's fury faded, unsustainable. The answer, of course, was that without the McCaffery story and the shitstorm that followed it, the old bastard would never have done this at all.

Staring north through the haze of the filmmakers' lights, Phil considered the crushing weight of guilt Randall must have carried these past weeks. The truth about McCaffery might have mattered once. But not now. New Yorkers didn't need truth now. Now New Yorkers needed what Sally and Kevin had always needed: for the sainted Jimmy McCaffery to have actually been the hero they thought he was.

Randall's article had come too late to do anything but harm. And Randall must have finally come—too late—to see that.

And so Phil accepted the facts of Randall's death as they had been spread before him. Oh, he had questions, when was he without questions? But not among them, not yet, was the question of whether Harry Randall's death had actually been suicide.

Boys' Own Book
Chapter 3

———

Tree, Falling

September 11, 1978: The Boys (Jimmy)

Now it's later, though not by much, and changes have come, but not so many. Not the important ones; or if they have begun, you cannot see them.

Jimmy's a fireman. Aces the Academy and has a choice of houses; and though he could have had Manhattan, where the television cameras always come, or Bed-Stuy, where the trucks go screaming out two, three times a night, Jimmy asks for and gets Engine 168, around the corner. Wants to be close, so he can trot down to the house on days off, to drink coffee, listen to the old-timers. He loves the stories, Jimmy does: lunatic bravery, elaborate pranks, offhand memories of laughing just out of Death's reach.

Four years old: Jimmy across the street, wearing the red plastic fireman's helmet he got for Christmas, so excited he can't stand still as the bell clangs and the door flies up so 168 can go tearing out. Firefighters yank their coats on, swing up on the truck as it starts to roll. One of them grins, waves to Jimmy. Jimmy's father grabs him: The kid was gonna run right up onto it, he tells Jimmy's mother later, shaking his head. He was going to the fire, weren't you, Jim? I wanted to go, Jimmy says, I wanted to go to the fire. His mother asks, You wanted to help the firemen? Jimmy nods hard. But Daddy said, Daddy said they don't let kids, kids aren't big enough. I can help when I'm bigger. When I'm bigger, I'll go to the fire and help. Jimmy's dad musses Jimmy's hair and smiles. His mother smiles, too, but then she looks at him without saying anything, just looks and looks at him.

Now, when the smoke is whipping and the flames are roaring, someone still has to hold Jimmy back, someone senior screaming, No! some soot-streaked face in his, yelling, Don't play Superman, kid, just do your job, that way you make it out and all your brothers, too. What Jimmy wants, what he *wants,* is to go howling in, come out carrying everyone in his arms.

But Brother: they're calling him that already.

So he nods through the smoke, follows his orders, shrugs when his captain shouts to him, *What the hell's so funny?* Jimmy's seen the same grin, the one he can't keep back, flash across his captain's face, and some of the other guys', too, as they're piling off the truck, eager, one more time, to cheat the dragon.

Jimmy's happy.

LAURA'S STORY
Chapter 2

———

First In, Last Out

October 30, 2001

Laura was on the street, blundering through the scattering of mid-town pedestrians. End-of-the-day rush hour, but no crowds; mostly office workers, residents, people who had to be here. Finally, on a corner, a cluster of defiant tourists, pointing cameras at the Empire State Building because it was still standing.

Laura barely noticed any of these people, or the sun, or the softness of the air. She was thinking about other afternoons, and nights, mornings, too, about the dry rough feel of Harry's hands and the taste of gin when he kissed her.

Leo had been too smart to try to send her home, to try to give Laura Stone some time off. But a dazed, hollow-eyed reporter isn't much use around a newsroom, in fact gets in the way. Too many others feeling like they have to say something, too much swampy thickness in the atmosphere. What Leo had done instead was rearrange the week's Metro sections, pulling someone's piece on the teachers' union from Friday to tomorrow, pushing Laura's SoHo merchant story to later in the week, maybe even Monday or Tuesday. Because the teachers' union piece was more timely, he'd growled as she stood in his doorway, and she should goddamn know better than to even ask.

So when Laura left soon afterward, she could have been assumed to be working: seeking out more sources, interviewing Prince Street businessmen she'd skipped in her rush to deadline, taking the extra days to dig deeper. No one really did assume this, but Laura's dry-eyed fierceness and the rigid lock of her shoulders set up enough of a barricade that the sympathetic glances and kind comments were mercifully few.

As Laura jabbed and jabbed again at the elevator button—slowest frigging elevator in New York, Harry always said, especially when thirsty reporters needed their beer—Georgie appeared and stood sadly, but Laura, her focus inward, living again an afternoon not so very long ago, did not turn his way.

Harry Randall's explosive piece on the real James McCaffery—the third story, following by two weeks the one Leo had assigned as a soft feature on the Fallen Hero, a heartstring-tugger (and assigning it to Harry, the newsroom knew, was further proof of how far Harry himself had fallen)—had been brilliant, and Laura had told him so.

But Harry had not been so easily bought.

It was the trailing edge of an afternoon in late October. Harry had discreetly absented himself as she sifted through his copy. She ran through it once, then again, was on it for a third time when he brought his worry and his gin back with him into the bedroom.

"Terrific," Laura told him, scooting over to make room. "Jesus, Harry, this'll light the fuse. It's fabulous."

Neither of them was on that day, and they had not left Harry's apartment. While Harry hunched over his desk, the clicking of keys stopping only when he was rifling through papers, flipping notebooks open and shut, or shifting folders from pile to pile, Laura kept herself mostly to the bedroom. Once or twice, pulling her robe around her, she slipped into the kitchen to make coffee. Each time she left him his without a word and carried hers back to bed, where she was working her way through a stack of yesterday's newspapers.

This was Laura's habit from journalism school days, to scan rags from all over, every week. Harry had groused when she'd first brought her habit to bed on a Sunday afternoon: "Hey, Stone, you're smearing ink all over my sheets." Laura reminded him he was supposed to be an ink-stained wretch and went on reading. She needed to know: Someone might have thought of an angle she hadn't. Someone's prose might be making readers sit up and take notice. And some young reporter—younger even than she—someone still in the sticks, might be breaking out, a star rising. She needed to know.

Though, if truth be told, the bedroom was a little chilly, the view from its windows dull, a neighbor's brick wall. Laura might have been happier out where Harry was, in the living room, wrapped in a blanket in Harry's reading chair, where she could glance up from an op-ed piece to see the river roll by and to watch Harry work. She would have preferred some conversation, maybe even a kiss and a cuddle, between the *Sacramento Bee* and the *Chicago Sun-Times*.

But the muttering Harry Randall in the other room, tossing papers, dropping folders, banging the keys nonstop as the sun slid in orange squares across the wall—this was the Harry Randall of legend. The man the newsroom, with Laura the sole exception, said was gone for good, drowned in gin and futility.

He was not gone; he was right here; and it was thrilling. Once or twice, as the afternoon lengthened, Laura slipped out of bed and stood silent in the doorway. She watched as, with a hunter's taut smile, Harry searched his notes for this quote, that date, letting out a sharp "Ha!" when he found what he'd wanted; and Laura's heart sped, and she had to wipe her eyes because they'd suddenly gone misty.

So Laura made Harry coffee, and sipped her own, and stayed out of his way. And if she did not precisely smear ink on her own shoulder patting herself on the back, still she was certain that if an exiled afternoon was the price of getting that Harry Randall back, it was a hell of a terrific deal.

And when he'd stopped, hit the keys for the printer, brought her the pages, and wandered off to find his gin, she shoved to the floor all the newspapers floating around her, read his copy through, and told him it was brilliant, because it was.

"Ummm." Standing the gin bottle on the side table, holding on to the glass, he flapped the sheet up and slipped into bed. With his empty hand he tugged the covers up again.

Laura rolled onto her hip to look at him. "You're still not sure?"

"That it's great? No, that brilliant young reporter, the up-and-coming Laura Stone, says it's great. It must be true."

Harry nestled closer to her. She giggled. "I'm not the only thing around here that's up-and-coming, am I?"

"Behave yourself, Stone. I'm an old man."

"I know." Laura traced a slow finger on the rim of Harry's ear, continued down the side of his neck. "And the one and only thing that interests you at this point—in the twilight of your life—is the pitiful and corrupted state of American journalism."

"You're right."

"You're lying."

He had been, and it was some time before they returned to story, coffee, and gin.

By then the sun had gone, striping the sky across the river with the colors of fire. Harry picked up his drink, Laura the pages he'd given her. It was too dark to read, but she did not reach for the light. She offered the pages to Harry, almost as though for the first time, almost as though they weren't his. "This is great, Harry."

He shrugged: yes, okay, maybe.

She said, "But you don't think it should run."

Harry, looking at the pages in Laura's hand but not touching them, said, "What's the point?"

"That's not really what you mean." He didn't answer, just sipped at his gin, so she went on. "You mean, 'What good will it do New York's suffering citizens?' You mean, 'Does a shell-shocked city really need more pain?' You mean, 'Does a grieving country, trying to heal, to reach closure, to find some answers in these troubled times—' " That was all there was of that; Harry was stuffing a pillow over her face.

"Finished?"

The pillow nodded. Harry removed it, and Laura charged on. "You mean, 'It's time to get back to normal'—wait, *normalcy*—'and move on. To take back our lives or the terrorists win! In this city so damaged by Recent Events—' "

"I thought you were finished," Harry complained, settling his pillow weapon behind his head.

"You mean"—the anchorman tone dropped from Laura's voice, she was Laura again—"for everyone's good, some truths are better off buried. Come on, Harry. You're not serious."

"I'm beyond serious, Stone. I'm maudlin."

"This is a great piece. This is tremendous. This is *dynamite,* Harry."

"There were firemen from forty-six states at his funeral."

"So?"

"And the Mayor, the Fire Commissioner—"

"Since when does Harry Randall give a damn?"

"You have it backwards." He inspected his gin as though for something missing. "Harry Randall used to give a damn, but he wised up."

Laura looked at Harry as he had at his gin. The skin around his eyes was loose and lined, old and dry, but the pale gray eyes were clear.

"You've been working on this for two weeks," she reminded him. "Night and day. You don't eat. You don't sleep. You don't screw."

"Wait—what was that just now?" Harry said, with mild surprise.

"You're lucky I recognized it, it's been so long." She squiggled around, settling with her cheek on his shoulder, the hand holding his copy draped across him. "If you weren't going to run it, then why write it?"

He shrugged. "I thought," he said, stopping as though surprised to hear his own voice, then going on, "I thought it might be important to find the truth."

"Of course it is." Impatience crept into her tone, and she could have kicked herself for it.

She said nothing else, just moved closer, held Harry tighter. His glass was empty; as he groped for the bottle, he said, "Maybe people need their illusions." He was talking to her, she thought, about the story; and to himself, about something else, too.

She was quiet for a moment, then said, "People need the truth."

He had hold of the bottle by the neck. "Why?"

" 'Wherever you're lost, land or sea, you can navigate by the north star. It's real; the sounds in the night around you aren't.' "

His eyebrows lifted. He poured gin, chortled, drank. "You're quoting that old charlatan Harry Randall."

"When Harry Randall said that at my graduation, it was—Jesus, Harry, it was *inspiring*."

"Stop. You're about to tell me I've been your hero since you were a child." He sighed. "On the other hand, that was only the day before yesterday."

"This story," Laura offered gently, "this is a real Harry Randall story. The kind you—the kind everyone expects from you."

"Expected." Harry nuzzled his chin into her tumbled hair.

"Expects. Harry? Tell me the truth: it was fun, wasn't it?"

"Fun?" Harry pulled back, putting on a tone of shocked disapproval. "It most certainly was not fun. Exposing the perfidy of trusted members of society, following the trail of duplicity and deception as it leads ever higher and deeper—"

"At the same time?"

"Of course! That's the thing about duplicity, it can do two things at once. Sshh. Where was I?"

"Following the trail."

"Right. Following, et cetera. This is a sacred trust, to be shouldered only with the most grave respect for its importance, to be undertaken with only the most solemn purpose and dedication. It is—"

"More fun than sex."

His eyebrows went up. She kissed him. "Go ahead, tell me it doesn't turn you on."

"That—"

"Not that! This!" She bopped him on the head with his copy.

He smiled and said nothing, and that said everything.

"And this? The way you wrote it?" she went on. "It's Harry Randall. It'll make them move, it'll smoke them out. You can't wait, can you? To see what happens next?"

Harry sighed, as though forced to acknowledge an inarguable, though unpalatable, truth.

"Harry?" Laura's heart was singing. She tried to stay calm, to not let on that she'd seen him struggle to the top of the dry, rocky mountain, and now she knew he could see the ocean, could find his way again. But she had one more thing to offer, a welcome-home gift. "This story will put you back on top, Harry. It'll show the Unbelievers." Unbelievers was their name for the powers at the paper, Leo and the inner circle.

"Hell with the Unbelievers."

"People—"

"Hell with people."

But there must have been someone Harry was not willing to dismiss, because he kissed her, slipped on his robe, and e-mailed his copy to Leo at home. Leo kept the fact-checkers working through the night, and the next morning, the story ran.

Boys' Own Book
Chapter 4

——

Complicated Work

September 11, 1978: The Boys (Markie)

He's a mechanic, Markie, same as ever, the ragtop's his, and it's still cherry. He's the first to marry, Jimmy his best man, of course. Markie's nervous: He'll drop the ring. He'll forget his words. He'll stumble walking out of St. Ann's down those stupid steps, trip, knock Sally down and fall on top of her, look like the biggest idiot ever, *ever*, man.

Jimmy grins. Markie, man, you're the only asshole I know with no troubles, so you got to make 'em up. Jimmy calms Markie down, Jimmy looks after him. Like always.

Nine years old: scrawny and small, but Markie can pitch, and he's even a lefty, in Little League that's hard to find. The game is big: not regular schedule, just midseason exhibition, but the other team's from Manhattan, the Empires. They have fancy uniforms, they have paid coaches at first and third, not dads doing it by the seats of their pants. Late innings, and the Pleasant Hills Panthers are up, but only by one run, and the Empires have two men on. Coach Roberts takes out Eddie Spano, Eddie's been throwing hard but wild, like always, ignoring the calls from Jimmy behind the plate, throwing whatever he wants. It's only the Panthers' fielding, the other kids stepping up, that's kept Eddie out of a hole. Coach watches Jack Molloy crash the right-field fence to steal one from an Empire batter, and that's enough. Coach brings in Markie, says, Shut 'em down. Eddie glares at Markie as they pass, Markie on his way in, Eddie going off.

Markie stands on the mound, looks around: when did this park get so big, how did it get to be so far to the plate? His mouth is dry. His arm hurts, he can't remember why. He fingers the ball, can't get it right, even to throw his warm-ups. The Manhattan kids grin at him, the coaches, too, and he can see they know it: no pitcher.

Jimmy straightens up from behind the plate, where he's been waiting for Markie's warm-up throws. Walks out to the mound, not fast, just like this is what he always does when they bring a relief pitcher in, goes out to talk to the guy before his first windup.

Jimmy, says Markie. He swallows, looks at Jimmy.

Throw me some bullshit, Jimmy says.

What? says Markie. Jimmy's using bad words, so Markie pays attention, but he doesn't get it.

Crap, Jimmy says. Soft, low, inside. 'Bout a dozen. They want to bunt this guy home. Jimmy's eyes move to the Empire kid on third, but he doesn't point, doesn't let the other team know what he's talking about with Markie. He says, Let them think that's all you have. Then when the batter steps up, throw the sizzler. If he connects with a bunt, it'll come right back to you. You and me and Tom, we'll run this guy down.

Markie looks over to third, where Tom seems to know what they're saying, seems ready. Then he looks at the second baseman, then at first, so looking at third won't seem like it was anything special. He looks back at Jimmy, nods. Jimmy jogs back to the plate. When he passes the batter waiting on deck, he flashes him a man-you're-in-trouble-now grin from behind his catcher's mask. Markie throws eight marshmallow warm-ups, he can hear the Empires talking, jeering. Then he nods, he's ready.

The batter steps in. Markie winds up, and he throws the fastball, what he's been working on all season, every day: getting it a little faster, a little more exact. He puts it just where he wants it, the batter shortens up and bunts before he realizes this isn't the pitch he expected, and the ball does just what Jimmy said: goes much too fast, too far, ends up right at Markie's feet. Markie scoops it up, flips it to Jimmy, Jimmy to Tom, and Jimmy and Tom close in on the runner, Markie covering the plate and the second baseman covering third, just in case, but Jimmy and Tom don't need that, they run the guy down like it was a training film.

While this is going on, the first-base runner makes second and the batter lands on first, but Markie doesn't care, doesn't care one bit, because Jimmy's behind the plate calling for the pitch he wants, and Markie knows whatever pitch Jimmy wants he's got it, and it'll work.

All he needs is one more out to end the inning. He gets it easily on a soft pop. The game goes on, Markie even singles. The Panthers beat the Empires, and the kids from Manhattan slink home on the ferry.

So at Markie's wedding, Jimmy grins and says, Markie, man, with Sally up there in that white dress, who the hell you think's gonna be looking at *you*? Markie walks up the aisle without tripping, slips the ring on Sally's beautiful hand just like he knows how, like he's practiced for this for a long, long time.

All the guys are there, at Markie's wedding, hair slicked back, shoes shined, elbows digging into each other's ribs, big grins in the church and bigger ones over beers at the reception. They dance with Sally, and they dance with their own girls and each others'. They lean on the wall and twist the tops off beer bottles, look around at the balloons and the candles, the crumbled pieces of cake. Jack says, Look at Markie, man. Guy who smiles like that, he's in shock, don't know what hit him.

Maybe that's true, maybe not. Markie keeps smiling; a year later he's smiling even bigger, handing out cigars: he has a son.

Markie's happy.

FUND REJECTS CONTRIBUTION
QUESTIONS SURROUND HERO FIREFIGHTER'S
DEALINGS WITH CRIME FIGURES
by Harry Randall

The *Tribune* has learned that, claiming concern for "our responsibility to our other contributors," Marian Gallagher, director of the McCaffery Memorial Fund, has rejected a $50,000 contribution offered by Edward Spano, a Staten Island developer with reputed underworld ties.

Capt. James McCaffery, 46, commanded Ladder Co. 62 and died on September 11 in the World Trade Center's north tower. The McCaffery Fund was established within days by Thomas Molloy, a Staten Island civic leader and childhood friend of McCaffery's. To date the Fund has topped $500,000. Contributions and pledges are flooding in daily from around the country.

Asked about the Fund's actions, Ms. Gallagher told the *Tribune*, "Some people are saying we could do a lot of good with this money and should accept it. But until the absurd rumors floating around have been put to rest, we will continue to err on the side of providing our contributors with the comfort level they have a right to expect."

Thomas Molloy said he and the Fund's board of directors "fully supported" Gallagher's decision to turn down Spano's offer.

Marian Gallagher, who, along with Molloy and Spano, grew up with McCaffery in Pleasant Hills on Staten Island, is executive director of the More Art, New York! Foundation, a Lower Manhattan–based arts-funding organization. In that capacity she is the chosen representative of Lower Manhattan's cultural community to the Downtown Redevelopment Advisory Council, a citizens' watchdog group.

Gallagher and McCaffery were well known as a couple during their days in Pleasant Hills. "That's why I asked her to take this on," Molloy told the *Tribune*. "Because she'd been close to

Jimmy." Gallagher refused to discuss the nature of her relationship with McCaffery. But in a reference to recent allegations that McCaffery was involved in dealings of an unspecified nature, financial and otherwise, with Edward Spano, Gallagher stated, "Jimmy McCaffery was completely honorable. If anything wrong was going on, he wasn't part of it."

The rumors circulating about McCaffery center on events that took place more than two decades ago.

A 1979 shooting in Pleasant Hills resulted in the death of Jonathan "Jack" Molloy, 25, half-brother of Thomas Molloy. Mark Keegan, 23, admitted shooting Molloy but claimed he did so in self-defense. According to Keegan's statement, Molloy, who had a record of arrests on minor charges, threatened him with a gun and fired two shots. Keegan returned fire, killing Molloy with a single shot. No homicide charges were filed, but Keegan pled guilty to possession of an unlicensed handgun. He was sentenced to 16 months in prison, where he died after a fight with another inmate.

According to Keegan's widow, it was McCaffery who urged her to file a wrongful death lawsuit holding New York State responsible. Sally Keegan claims the suit was filed but withdrawn when the State offered a settlement under a policy compensating the families of prisoners injured or killed in custody. Six months after Keegan's death his family began to receive monthly payments of $1,000. In 1990 this amount jumped to $2,000. Payments continued until Keegan's only child, Kevin, now a firefighter, turned 18. They were made through Phillip Constantine, the attorney who had handled Keegan's criminal trial in 1979.

However, the *Tribune* has learned that New York State has no such family compensation program, nor did it ever have one.

Reached at his Lower Manhattan office, Constantine, a prominent criminal attorney, refused to comment on the payments' source. Asked whether a lawsuit was filed against New York State, he would only say, "Lawsuits are public record." The *Tribune* failed to find any suit filed against the State on behalf of any member of the Keegan family.

Constantine refused further comment on such questions as the object of the deception or why it was taken to such lengths.

Asked whether Sally Keegan would have accepted money if she had known its source was a reputed crime figure, Victoria Molloy, former wife of Thomas Molloy, said, "Never."

Sally Keegan refused to comment. Kevin Keegan would not answer a reporter's questions except to say, "Jimmy McCaffery was my godfather and my father's best friend. There's no way he was involved in anything dirty, with Eddie Spano or anyone else."

Spano, reached at his office at Chapel Pointe, a luxury development going up on Staten Island, denied any knowledge of where or why the payments to the Keegan family originated. Asked about his relationship with McCaffery, Spano said, "I knew Jimmy when we were kids, that's all. Always admired the guy. A real hero." Pressed about his motivation for contributing to the McCaffery Fund, Spano would only say, "I just wanted to help out."

Spano called allegations of his own ties to organized crime "ridiculous."

It is a matter of public record that Spano has been indicted twice, once on charges of extortion and once for racketeering under the state RICO law. He was paroled after serving 10 months of a 30-month sentence under a plea bargain on the extortion charge. The racketeering charge was dismissed for lack of evidence after a key witness disappeared.

Spano's role, if any, in the deception remains unclear, as does the exact role McCaffery played. Based on witness accounts, Constantine, who remained close to the Keegan family, had continuing contact with McCaffery over two decades, though the men claimed to dislike each other.

The Fund director, Marian Gallagher, also stayed close to the Keegan family, although she claims to have "lost touch" with McCaffery. Asked about McCaffery's actions at the time of Molloy's and Keegan's deaths, she would say only, "They were Jimmy's friends. He was devastated when they died." On the question of McCaffery's relationships with Constantine and Spano, she refused to speculate. Asked about her own part in the deception, she vigorously denied any participation.

No criminal activity is alleged against any party at this point.

By rejecting Spano's contribution, Gallagher seems to have staved off a movement within the FDNY to shut down the McCaffery Fund, at least on a temporary basis.

"This is crap about Jimmy, that's all it is—the purest crap," said retired firefighter Owen McCardle, who served with McCaffery at Staten Island's Engine 168. "Jimmy was one of the finest members of this Department it's ever been my privilege to work with."

Nevertheless, sources say elements of the FDNY leadership, under pressure from the Mayor's office, have suggested freezing the McCaffery Fund until an investigation into McCaffery's relationship to Spano is complete.

"You've got to understand, firefighters are big heroes now, not just here but all over the country," FDNY Deputy Assistant Chief Gino Aiello told the *Tribune.* Aiello was promoted last week in the Fire Department's effort to replace high-ranking officers lost on September 11. "Schoolkids are sending us pennies. But that could turn around. You saw what happened last week." This was a reference to the October 25 melee at Ground Zero, when firefighters, protesting the Mayor's order to cut the number searching for remains, clashed with police officers. Seventeen firefighters were arrested and charged with disorderly conduct.

"Look, no one believes every man or woman in this Department is pure as the driven snow," said one Fire Department source, asking to remain anonymous. "But McCaffery was famous. Long before 9/11, people heard of him, he was a hero. Since they set up the Fund, he stands for the Department in a lot of people's minds. If it turns out he was mixed up in anything, that could hurt us. It could hurt a lot of the positive things going on."

"September 11, we lost 343 guys," Chief Aiello told the *Tribune.* "But also 92 vehicles. Equipment—radios, oxygen tanks, all sorts of things. Right now a lot of guys are putting in tremendous overtime in the search. That's all got to come out of the budget somewhere. The McCaffery Fund could be a big help, but not if it blows up in our faces."

The investigation is continuing.

PHIL'S STORY

Chapter 2

———

How to Find the Floor

October 31, 2001

It was going to be a busy day.

Halloween. In his field, they used to joke it should be a national holiday. This year made-up horrors were redundant. Not a lot of Freddie or Jason masks around this year.

And all days were busy, now as before. Phone service still spotty, even the cell phones went in and out. Some offices, courtrooms, chambers still closed, judges and ADAs needing to be hunted down and mostly on foot because of the damn phones. The building where Phil had his office had reopened, but it was inside the perimeter, making many people vastly confused about whether they were allowed to go there, and if so, how.

You might have thought, given the staggering nature, the breathtaking scale, of the crime of September 11, that criminals of lesser ambition, weaker imagination, would have paused in their pursuits, even if only from embarrassment. And for the first week or so, they had. A week when the muggers, stickup artists, con men, drug dealers, and gangbangers gave New York's stunned citizens and exhausted cops breathing room.

Then the Mayor—in the New Normal, everyone's hero, which, according to Phil, showed you how far this really was from normal—the Mayor told New Yorkers to do their patriotic duty: live their lives, get back to work.

And the city found out that crooks were as patriotic as anyone else.

For Phil, that meant new clients, new interviews, and new bullshit stories to get past: *I can't help you if you're going to jerk me around.* And the old clients still needed him to stand up with them at their arraignments, their bail hearings, their days in court.

The *Tribune* story hadn't changed this, not yet. The people Phil defended were criminals. (Aloud, Phil would have insisted on "persons charged with criminal activity.") If the odor of improper, possibly illegal, behavior swirled around their lawyer, in their minds that only made him more likely to understand. Those of his clients who even knew, who even read the papers. Most of them were hypnotized by their own troubles. Their minds were locked on the desolation of the futures they faced the way you'd stare into a bloodred sunrise, unable to take your eyes off the storm clouds massing.

So until it came to the ethics investigation, the disciplinary committee review—and it would, oh yes; already there were conversations that stopped when he walked into a room, invitations to go get a beer that he didn't have to duck because they'd stopped coming—Phil could stay busy. His clients, as before, would be desperately glad to see him, though what he was able to offer them was, compared to their hopes, a leaf in a windstorm. Until the Feds called, or the State, whichever won the fight over who got to try to take Phil Constantine down—and they would have called already, if everyone on that side wasn't scrambling, madly searching tips and phone taps they'd ignored for years to see if they should have seen this coming, if they could see anything else coming now—Phil's life could go on, no different and completely changed, like everything else.

And if he found himself now, on occasion and without warning, seized with an urge to grab a client's collar and shout, "That's it? After all this, this is still who you are and what you want?" he roped himself back under control each time, and just went on. He wasn't really sure who it was that he wanted to shout at.

Phil had been caught in the cloud on September 11, running like hell with everyone else.

His eyes burned, his lungs were crazy for air. A woman next to him staggered, so he reached for her, caught her, forced her to keep going, warm blood seeping onto his arm from a slash down her back as he pulled her along, later carried her. Somewhere, someone in a uniform took her from him, bore her off someplace while someone else pressed an oxygen mask to his face. He breathed and breathed, and when he could speak, he asked about the woman, but no one knew.

And all the time he was running, coughing and choking and seeing nothing but thick dust, no sense of direction, no up or down, all the time he was hearing screams and sirens and shouts, a clanging like a thousand railroad cars crashing off the tracks, and, in all that, explosions like gunfire that were bodies and parts of bodies hitting the ground, all that time, in Phil's mind, were his clients: skinny little José, down two strikes but he just had to try to peddle that one last goddamn bag of grass, though Phil had warned him, warned him; Mrs. Johnson, whose five children still hadn't been told she'd shot her husband's girl-friend and then her husband; that kid he called Ben, though the kid had given four different names already. Phil saw them all, locked in cells down here, in the middle of this swirling, roaring ruin and death, know-ing they were trapped, knowing they would die.

They didn't. The towers fell in, not over; the devastation, as bad as it was, was not as bad as it could have been. Acknowledging this truth, as Phil did later, did not make him share the Pollyanna optimism of the friend who had voiced it. As far as Phil knew, it was always true. Nothing was ever as bad as it could have been.

And damn little was as good, either.

So the day would be busy, and complicated in ways Phil wasn't sure about yet by the death of that bastard Harry Randall. He needed to call Sally and Kevin; probably he should've called Sally last night, when he heard. Well, not probably: should have and didn't. What reason? Choose one.

Although the biggest reason might be this, the thought he'd had last night, when, walking home from Battery Park, he'd thought about what Randall's death could mean: *This could be my chance.* Breathing space, room to maneuver.

Because some of what Randall had said in the *Tribune* stories was true.

And most of what he'd implied was a crock.

But about a lot of it, Phil didn't know.

Now that Randall was no longer clawing through their lives, drawing blood from anything that came near him, now maybe Phil could take a shot at finding the truth.

Why?

Not because it would prove his innocence, show him to be the falsely accused white knight. Far too late for that. If the truth showed that nothing Phil had done was illegal, he still wasn't innocent, no.

And not because the truth would give him ammunition. If the truth was good, he might win; if bad, he'd certainly lose. How many times, over the years, had he told that to clients who wanted to go to trial instead of taking the plea, who wanted to offer up the truth to a jury? As though truth weren't a prisoner of the ways people find to use it, just like everything else.

Markie Keegan had been the last client Phil had considered trying to talk out of pleading. Markie, Phil had been sure, could have persuaded a jury with the truth.

No, that was wrong: he had not been sure. Markie had sat on the other side of the visiting room table before he made bail and listened. He'd held his son on his lap at his own kitchen table after his family, his friends, his boss, and his church had pooled what they had to get him released, and he'd heard Phil out.

And he'd said, No, no trial. I'll take the plea.

And Phil had felt relieved.

The truth, Phil had come to understand through the years since, through the trials and the pleas, the investigations, the accusations, and the stories, rarely did anybody any good.

But in those years the walls and floors of the world were solid, not blasting air and dust and choking smoke.

Now he was thinking this: what he'd been part of all these years, what Jimmy McCaffery had led him into, Phil had always thought he'd known. What he'd thought was bad. But if Randall was right, the truth was worse.

Now, because he could grasp, hold, be sure of, nothing else, he wanted to find that truth. Just to have it? No.

To offer it to Sally. To show her, to make her know that in this new world where, suddenly, none of them were sure of anything, some truths could still prove others, and this one would prove that he loved her.

He needed to find this truth, for its use.

But that was for later. Right now, *now,* seven A.M. on another beautiful New York morning, Phil left the locker room, heart beginning to speed, and shoved through the swinging doors onto the basketball court.

The others, these people he'd been playing with twice a week for six, eight years, these teammates he rarely saw anywhere but in this gym, were already here, stretching or shooting around. They had an unwritten rule, no serious action before seven, and another, no one arriving after seven had any claim to play.

"Oh, look, it's Phil, must be ten seconds to!" This the usual needle—Phil was never late, but rarely early, for anything—from one of the three women regulars, the wiseass one. Jane, her name was, a doctor, short but quick, good D, usually played point, and she could shoot, but only from outside. That was the book on her. Phil had a book on everyone, play with him twice and he had your game in his head.

He did a couple of quick stretches, counted players. Last to come, he made ten. Shorthanded, they'd have played four on four; that was sometimes even better, if you asked Phil. The advantage: in an undermanned game, every player had to work harder.

And Phil liked hard work, especially when it accomplished something you could see.

But no one had to ask Phil how he liked to attack the game. You could see it in his grin, his glittering eagle's eyes. Those eyes were part of his teammates' book on him. Everyone else's game face was seriousness, grim determination, an intimidating glower: Phil Constantine's was shining eyes and a sharp, hungry smile. People playing with him for the first time might take this to mean that he cared less than they did about each play, about the final score.

Prosecutors sometimes made that same mistake in court.

His teammates grinned and greeted him. They had to be thinking about the *Tribune* story, they had to be wondering; Phil knew it. But here at the Y, as long as his shot was on, he was welcome; and if he was Mother Teresa but missed his layups, the trash talk would erupt.

Phil finished stretching, looked around, saw Jane squaring up for a shot. He barreled from behind and stole the ball. Cursing, she raced after him, jumped to block his fadeaway. She fouled him, but the shot was good. Brian hollered, "This a grudge match, or can anyone play?" Phil fired him the ball. Early morning sunlight filtered through the Y's high, dusty windows; they sorted themselves into teams, and leaving behind what had happened, what would happen, they started to play.

LAURA'S STORY
Chapter 3

———

Complicated Work

October 31, 2001

Laura came back early in the morning, looking for Leo.

It was Halloween, but that meant nothing to a reporter. (Christmas, Easter Sunday, their mother's birthdays meant nothing to reporters chasing news.) Some years the newsroom sprouted pumpkins and black-cat cutouts on Halloween, but this year what could be more frightening than the view out the window?

Reporters, chomping on bagels and slurping coffee, glanced up as Laura walked by. Some tried to speak to her, to say something kind. Laura nodded to each, didn't stop on her way to her desk. Seated, she fixed her eyes on the glow of her monitor as though she were waiting for something. She wrenched the lid from a coffee cup and gulped at it without tasting it at all. Her comforters retreated.

She stayed at her computer, waiting, tearing through e-mails, not understanding their messages or caring that she didn't, until finally Leo surged from the elevator and sliced through the newsroom like Sherman on his way to the sea. She watched him through the glass of his office like a sharpshooter while he dropped his briefcase, switched on his computer, pulled his fried egg sandwich and coffee from the deli bag. Then she rose and went to his door.

His eyes, colorless as tin, rested on her before he spoke. This was unlike Leo. "Stone." He pointed at a chair. Given permission, she sat. Steam from Leo's coffee cup slipped into the air as though hoping to sneak away before Leo noticed.

Laura said, "I want the Harry Randall story." She wished she knew a way to demand things from Leo, to sound imperious, not like a street beggar. Her only comfort, cold, was that all the reporters she knew felt, always, that they were on their knees before Leo.

His answer: "No."

"Leo—"

"Forget it, Stone."

"I'm the only—"

"There's no story. If there were, you'd be—"

"I knew him best."

"You screwed him."

Through gritted teeth: "No law against it. Not even *Tribune* policy, Leo."

"You checked?"

She nodded. Leo's eyebrows shot up, usually a good sign, but not this time. Another beat, and then, "Forget it." He swiveled his chair, began fingering the papers on his desk. Every reporter knew what that meant, but Laura stayed.

"Leo, there is a story."

His square iron head nodded, not turning to her. "A full and fitting obit. Carl's writing it now."

"He didn't kill himself."

Now Leo did turn, and though she never would have said as much to anyone for fear of being called insane, she swore she saw a softening in his eyes. It was not in his voice, though, each steel word spoken with equal emphasis: "He jumped off the bridge."

"No."

Laura meant to say more, but Leo's words burst open in her brain like a booby-trapped box, and out of them sprang a vision: Harry, angry first as his car was forced over, then disbelieving, kicking and wrenching against the grip, frightened, being dragged to the rail. Harry, shouting, cursing, throwing punches that missed—not much of a fighter, he'd always said, that's why he became a newsman: they let you watch. What must it have been like, the push, the fall? How much of a struggle, how tight his grip on the stinging steel? Then Harry untethered, floating, flying, Harry—she suddenly understood—exultant as he knew it was unstoppable.

She heard "Stone!" and she'd heard it before, just now, maybe two other times. The scene on the bridge receded, and Laura was looking at Leo. He held his coffee before him like an amulet, his eyebrows knit tight together. She almost laughed: Leo looked so desperate. *It's all right,* she wanted to say, *I'm a reporter, you can yell at me. I won't dissolve into a puddle of tears on your office floor.*

She swallowed the tears she was not going to dissolve into and said, "He didn't jump, Leo."

"Stone, he jumped."

"No. Leo"—leaning forward, trying to draw Leo into what she knew—"Leo, the McCaffery story was too huge. It was real. It was *Harry Randall.* He was back, he knew it, he loved it. *Loved* it, Leo." She was trembling, vibrating the way the high-tension wires did.

"Loved it?"

"Of course he did! How could he not? Harry Randall? On to something like this? It's the story he needed, Leo, all these years."

Leo threw her a sharp look, and Laura stopped herself. "He wouldn't have . . . he wouldn't have done this now, Leo. Not now." She took a breath. "Six months ago, a year ago, maybe," she offered.

In her mind she apologized to Harry for that injustice. Leo and the others had seen Harry like that. When he'd sat slumped in his chair, sleeves pushed up on a shirt he'd been in for three days, poking intermittently at his keyboard, scowling at his phone whenever it rang, they thought he was finished, suffering from inexplicable failures of nerve and direction, suffering from gin.

That wasn't the truth. The truth was this: Harry Randall had distanced himself from their work the way a man of changed appetites rises from a table of delicacies that formerly enticed him. Harry had taken his gin to a seat apart while others feasted; but he'd never begrudged them their meal, and he'd never had a wish to be invited back.

Harry had never cared what Leo or any of the Unbelievers thought of him, of his gin-fueled conversion from man-eater to vegetarian, and so Laura stoutly refused to care, either. But what Leo thought of Laura Stone—that she had not lost her judgment to grief and shock, that she had come to beg for this story because it was a juicy one, not because working on it would keep Harry's name before her all day, keep as hers whatever there was left of him—that was important now. So she agreed with Leo's idea of Harry, false as she knew it to be.

Although, a strange, unfamiliar voice inside her said, maybe right after September 11, when Harry had been more lost than she'd ever seen him, all the other reporters (Laura one of them) chasing after the stories, Harry paralyzed with sadness. Maybe then.

She silenced that voice, said to Leo, "But not since this story."

"Stone," Leo said, in a voice that could have been Leo thinking about what she'd said, or Leo thinking about how to tell her that delusional reporters had no place at his paper, "people don't fall off bridges by accident."

"No." A point of agreement. Laura forced herself to stay calm. "They don't."

Leo leaned his chair back, tapped his sapphire signet ring on the newsroom glass. Every reporter who heard looked up. At one of them, Leo pointed. Hugh Jesselson, a cop reporter. Broad, blond, and rumpled, he lumbered to Leo's doorway.

"Jesselson," Leo grunted. "You hearing anything about the Randall suicide being something else?"

Jesselson looked uncomfortably at Laura, but Leo was not giving him a pass, so he answered with a headshake.

"Nothing? No other theories?"

"No."

"You have any?"

"Me?"

"Stone here thinks he didn't jump. Is she the only one?"

Jesselson looked at his shoes, a cop reporter's oxfords, worn and dusty. "No one . . . Haven't heard it."

Contradicting his mountainous presence and abundant prose (that fullness the reason, it was said, that he'd never made the front), Jesselson pared spoken language to a nub. Talking with him was like getting telegrams.

"No police investigation?"

Jesselson looked up, but only at Leo. "Not real popular downtown these days. Randall."

Leo glared. "In our business that's a *good* thing, Jesselson. Because of McCaffery?"

"Alive, a legend, McCaffery. Dead, a saint. Untouchable."

Leo narrowed his eyes and stared at neither of them; both of them waited. "The McCaffery story, the fallout, then the reporter dies," he said to Jesselson. "No one's interested?"

"The story, the fallout? Sure. Spano, the Fund, that lawyer. Lots of money at stake. Blood in the water."

"So where are the sharks?"

"Later. When things get back to normal. Feeling seems to be this can wait."

"But Randall? No one's interested in that?"

Jesselson turned to Laura again, his eyes those of a man regretting the bad news he's brought. "No."

Leo looked at Laura.

"They're wrong," she said.

"NYPD doesn't seem to agree."

"NYPD has enough to do."

Undeniably true. Detectives in surgical masks were clambering over the landfill mountain on Staten Island, spreading out the rubble that came in in buckets, picking through it for body parts and evidence. Uniformed officers stood at concrete barricades at City Hall, at the reservoirs, at tourist sites as they reopened. Cops in every precinct answered a deluge of calls about letters and packages citizens were afraid of.

"You have anything else?" Leo rubbed his enormous jaw. "Or just that the story was too good?"

"A story like this? That he broke? Harry was never—he was never suicidal." A tough word, but she got it out. "Not since I've known him. Jesus, Leo, not even after what happened." Like all New Yorkers, Laura waved an arm toward downtown, toward Ground Zero, when she said "what happened"; and like all New Yorkers, Leo knew without question what she meant. Her voice rose, louder and higher. "Leo, he had something else, he was on to something! And we're supposed to believe he jumped off a bridge *now*? Why would he do that?"

Leo eyed her, picked up the important words. "Something else?"

Laura nodded, told Leo: "He left papers."

"Randall?"

"No, Leo! The firefighter. McCaffery. Papers no one had seen. Harry was on his way to see them. It's the last thing he told me."

Yesterday afternoon—yesterday? No, it must have been years ago, centuries, when her heart, now a barren desert, had been a boundless, teeming sea—Laura had been sitting at her desk, polishing her SoHo merchant story, checking her e-mail every fifteen minutes, as always.

It was one of the first things the legendary Harry Randall had noticed about the new kid, Laura Stone: the way she surfaced from the depths of a project to snap at e-mail like a trout at flies. Harry's desk was behind Laura's, a little off to one side. She'd never dared speak to him except, on the day she'd joined the *Tribune,* to shake his hand and tell him how thrilled she was to be working at the same paper with him. (That, in the five minutes Leo allotted a new reporter to get settled before he started asking where the hell her copy was.)

Toward the end of her second week at the paper, as she was typing a fast e-mail confirmation of a meeting finally agreed to by a reluctant source, a quiet voice in her ear made Laura jump: "You're driving me crazy."

She spun around, and Harry Randall was leaning over her, cockeyed sardonic grin, blue eyes, shirtsleeves and all.

"I—but—" In her mind Laura had been rehearsing approaches to the great man since the moment she'd started. Now, one hand on the back of her chair, the other on her desk, he was bending to talk to her as though they already knew each other well.

"It's hard," he said, "for an ancient beached whale such as myself to continue doing as little as possible, in order to avoid disturbing the balance of the universe, in the face of Leo's insistence on introducing a tiger shark such as *your*self to disrupt what small tranquillity I've been able to create in this goldfish bowl." He waved his arm to show her reporters rushing in and out, or creating private tempests at their desks. "But do I complain? No, I do not. I try to go on. At least at first. But more and more, each day, my peace is destroyed, my meditation upon the great nothingness interrupted. And finally, I must speak."

Laura, realizing her mouth was open, closed it. The only coherent thought she had was: *He has freckles.*

"Every time you check your e-mail"—he stabbed an accusing finger at Laura's monitor—"your screen flickers, a great wave crashing onto the peaceful beach of my thoughts. And you do this every five minutes."

"Fifteen," Laura sputtered.

"Aha! So you admit it, then?"

"I— Of course I do! In case something's come up. In case someone—I'm sorry. I don't mean to disturb you. What if I tilt it?"

"Don't tilt it. *Turn* it." Harry pushed Laura's monitor a quarter of an inch with his fingertip. He went back, sat at his own desk, shook his head, came back, and pushed it again. This time, back at his own desk, he nodded happily. "Thank you."

"You're welcome," said Laura. She turned back to her work, and, ignoring the heat in her cheeks, tried to remember what it was she'd been doing.

Fifteen minutes later she checked her e-mail. The only new message was from Harry Randall: HAVE LUNCH WITH ME?

* *

And so yesterday, as always, Laura had clicked on her e-mail every fifteen minutes. Routine; nothing interesting. Then, midmorning, this, from Harry: Subject Line: WOO-EEE! Text: I'M ONTO SOMETHING, MY LITTLE TIGER SHARK. MCCAFFERY LEFT PAPERS! HOT STUFF. OR SO I'M TOLD. ON MY WAY TO GET A GLIMPSE—MORE LATER. H

What had she done, when she'd read that? Smiled, probably. Seen in her mind the gleam in Harry's eye, the predatory glint he got. (They all got it, people like Harry and Laura, and though others had long said gin had dulled Harry's eyes and the glint was no more, Laura knew that was wrong.) And—oh God, this came back to her now, how was it such small things remained?—she'd hoped, before he'd gone to see his source, the person who was offering him this treasure, that Harry had remembered to shave.

A thunderclap. No; Leo's voice. "McCaffery?"

The glint in Harry's eye, his note on her computer screen, both vanished, and Leo's office swam back into view. The thunder had been a question, so Laura answered it. "Yes."

"You have these papers?"

"No."

"You saw them?"

"No."

"Randall had them?"

"I don't know."

"What's in them?"

"I don't know. Hot stuff, Harry said."

"How do you know about them?"

"He e-mailed."

"Yesterday?"

"Yes."

"Where'd they come from? Where are they now?"

"I don't know. But I can find them, Leo. So you see—"

He waved a hand, as all gods do to silence mortals.

Leo sat unmoving as a boulder. Laura prayed for Leo's phone to stay silent, for all the reporters typing and talking and buzzing around the coffee machine to be satisfied with their sources and their assignments and not need anything, right now, from Leo.

The boulder finally stirred. "Three days," a rocky voice rumbled from its depths. "Bring me something that says you're right. No extension, no maybe. Show me there's a story."

Laura, ready with her next argument, a fresh assault of convincing words, tossed away those words and grabbed some new ones. "Thank you." She stood quickly.

Leo had no more to say. Laura, afraid something would occur to him, turned and hurried away, resisting (as she was sure everyone always had to) the urge to back out of Leo's presence, bowing.

Marian's Story
Chapter 2

Complicated Work

October 31, 2001

Pedestrians were no longer required to show identification at the Canal Street barricades. Police sentries still stood two to a block, but their job now was to prevent vehicles from entering, to answer questions from the public when they could (although what answers did anyone have?), and to keep an eye out (for what, no one knew). They generally ignored anyone who neither spoke to them nor appeared suspicious according to whatever private formula for suspicion each officer used. Still, Marian offered a smile to the young policeman standing by the blue sawhorse she passed. He nodded but did not smile back, his eyes old and wary in his impassive face. The gold numbers on his collar showed him to be from a precinct far from Lower Manhattan. Marian wondered whether he was glad to have been assigned here. Was he grateful to have a useful role to play? Or did he desperately want to be home, reporting at his usual time to his usual captain, patrolling streets he knew, on the lookout for crimes he could understand?

Through the late morning sun Marian carried coffee and the morning *Times*. She had never had much faith in the *Tribune*, even before, but she used to buy it every day. Sam, back when they were together, had put forward a theory.

"Too much meditation," he declared, rising from the breakfast table to fetch the coffee press, "lowers your blood pressure. The *Tribune* raises it again."

"You can't read just one paper," Marian countered. "Even if it's the *Times*. Thank you," as he poured coffee first for her, then for himself. "You need different perspectives. You're old enough to know that."

"I thought I wasn't old enough to cross the street by myself."

"If you look both ways." Marian shook the paper out and turned the page. This was the way they dealt with the difference in their ages, making a joke of it between them. Marian believed in keeping issues in the open. Then nothing could be slowly turning bad, rotting where it couldn't be seen. "Anyway, you should try meditating. Maybe you wouldn't get so upset when you're running late to meetings."

"My boss would fire me if I didn't get upset when I ran late." On his way back to his chair Sam leaned over Marian, parted her hair, and nuzzled the back of her neck.

"Ummm," said Marian; but she leaned forward, reached across the table as though she needed the milk pitcher, though her coffee was already pale. "Oh my God, listen to this!" she wailed, and she was off again, incensed at the *Tribune* for the same quality she admired: fiery muckraking.

Tribune reporters tore into corrupt politicians, drug-dealing rock stars, millionaire athletes who beat their wives. They pounced with conviction and courage, and of those things, Marian approved. The problem was a lack of balance. Everyone had a story; every story had two sides. At least; at least that. But you never saw the other side of a story in the *Tribune*. Only the *Tribune*'s passionate indignation, its outraged cries for justice.

Or whatever powerful emotion the *Tribune* was peddling at the moment.

Two weeks ago, when they'd run Harry Randall's tribute to Jimmy, Marian had been unable to read it. She sat at her desk, her office door shut, staring at the headline, trying to make her eyes move down the page. But every time she hit a name—Tom's, Father Connor's; Owen McCardle, she remembered him—it was another bone-jarring bump on a rocky road. In the end she gave up. And what would she learn, what would this story tell her? Everything in it was no doubt true, but the truth would not be in it.

Marian recognized the irony: the McCaffery Fund had by that time already hit over $100,000 and by anyone's accounting was likely to top out at over $2 million; people were being so generous in these terrible times. And the McCaffery Fund's administrator could not bring herself even to skim a newspaper story that was sure to spark a new round of donations, a newspaper story in which she herself was quoted. Everyone else in the office was talking about it, about the sorrow and the sense of loss it brought home to them. Marian hoped no one would notice her silence, or perhaps that they would take it for deep emotion and go no further.

She had walked through that day saying little and had a paralyzing headache by noon. Still, she told herself, these articles the *Tribune* was running, these tales of the lives of true heroes—and on that day, in that tower, Jimmy had been a true hero, she did not doubt that—brought such comfort to New Yorkers that Marian was inclined to believe that the story, like any powerful, consoling myth, had been, on the whole, a valuable thing.

Then came Randall's second article. When he'd called to ask for another interview, she'd felt a heart-skip of fear, as though a solid path she walked had without warning turned marshlike underfoot.

"Just a follow-up," Randall had said. "The 'Hero' stories make people feel better."

But the *Tribune* had not run follow-ups to any of the other "Hero" stories. And precisely because Marian so desperately wanted people to feel better, she mistrusted Harry Randall's use of this as a reason. "Why this one?" she had asked. "Why Jimmy?"

"Because of the young guy" had been Randall's easy answer. "Kevin Keegan, that you pointed me to. The Fire Department torch passing from one generation of heroes to the next, that kind of thing."

She had considered refusing the interview, pleading a lack of time, pleading a concern for Jimmy's privacy, for Kevin's and Sally's, too. But in the end, knowing he'd be calling Sally in any case, calling Kevin—calling Phil Constantine and hearing, well, who knew *what* half-truths and lawyer's lies—she'd allowed Randall to come again to her office, to drink her coffee and ask his questions. The questions he selected increased her unease. Asking about Jimmy, he asked about Kevin; and when, asking about Kevin, he asked about Markie, Marian felt a flutter of desperation. She tried, as ever, to tell only the truth. But she chose truths that led in directions she wanted Randall to go, away from paths she hoped he wouldn't even see, so overgrown were they, so choked, so long untraveled.

But she was not sure she had succeeded.

When that second article ran, she forced herself to read it. Finished, she brewed a cup of ginger tea (good for a queasy stomach) and stared out the window. Close to her, the dark stone buildings and the smooth glass ones stood as they always had; but in the gaps between them the view had changed. Now she could see the twisted steel, the giant, slow-motion cranes, and the great sprays of water arcing through the haze.

Then two days ago the *Tribune* had published Randall's third story. Marian, through mounting panic, had allowed herself to be interviewed for this article, also, hoping yet to persuade Randall that the hero Jimmy had been for the last twenty years was so much more important than anything that might have come before.

And this time she knew she had failed.

Quiet, well worded, asking seemingly reasonable questions about the circumstances of Jimmy McCaffery's life, Randall's third story had had the same effect on Marian as watching a naturalist turn over rocks on a hillside with endless patience until he came on the one concealing the nest of writhing snakes.

And now Marian was privately boycotting the *Tribune*.

She knew it wouldn't matter to the paper, the seventy-five cents a day they could no longer count on from the newsstand by her office. It mattered, though, to the stand's owner, a cheerful Pakistani man trying to raise a family in New York. For three weeks after the towers fell, trucks couldn't cross the perimeter to make deliveries; the newsstands had nothing to sell. Even now, though the papers were getting through, business was down. The cheerful man's name was Muhammad; for some people, that was enough, and they were buying elsewhere. That made Marian furious, and she said as much to Muhammad, who merely shrugged. Still, in her heart she could understand. People, everywhere, wanted to do what was right, to do something that would help. They just didn't know what that was, the thing they should do.

And now that she wasn't buying the *Tribune,* now that being named Muhammad was bad for business, Marian asked for a Coke and a Kit Kat bar to go with her *Times*. Today, handing them to her, Muhammad had wished her a happy Halloween. It was Halloween? She hadn't remembered. The time in the year, she thought with bitterness, when we admit the existence of evil, in order to mock it. We hang silly skeletons and friendly ghosts and congratulate ourselves that we've vanquished demons, conquered wickedness, gone to the very gates of hell and laughed.

No, the *Tribune* wouldn't notice her boycott and would not care. But the principle was important to her. Marian did many things because of principle, not allowing the depressing truth of how little effect her gestures sometimes had to give her permission to forgo them.

As a child, sitting in the sweet-scented darkness of St. Ann's with her father and her three little sisters, holding her baby brother (the baby her mother had left behind for them to love when she went to Heaven), and listening as hard as she could to Father Connor telling them all to be good (though sometimes he said it in grown-up words), Marian had had a vision of what that would mean. What would happen if everyone tried to be good. All those small tries would be like pebbles. Everyone would bring one, a little stone, rough or smooth, and put it down. Some people would go and get another, and another, though some would not. Slowly, the pile would grow, and be a mound, and then a hill, and then a mountain, covered finally with green sheltering forests filled with birdsong.

BOYS' OWN BOOK
Chapter 5

———

The Man Who Sat by the Door

September 11, 1978: The Boys (Tom)

Tom's gone into his father's business, though it doesn't look that way. Tom's job is in construction, his uncle's company (the uncle's clean—at least, he has no sheet). Big arms, good hands, Tom can lay bricks straight and fast, but he's usually elsewhere. Tom's learning the business, the real one his father's in. Well spoken, Tom, and smart; he'll run things one day, they all see that, could even if he weren't who he is, the boss's son.

The boss, Tom's father: Big Mike Molloy. Mike the Bear.

Yes, they all can see Tom will be running things, though Tom's different from his old man, his ways are different. Tom thinks far ahead, Tom works things out before he starts. He could confuse you, the way he talks, he could sell ice to you if you were an Eskimo. And make you think it's your lucky day, he's doing you a favor, hauling that iceberg into your backyard.

Eleven years old: it's spring, and the kids want to go to the circus.

Not the small one, the Spivey Traveling Circus and Midway, that comes to Staten Island every summer with rides and a sideshow, sets up the tents and cotton candy machines in the field by Hylan Boulevard. Spivey's is great, and the kids always go. They have flashing lights and an elephant, they have sword-swallowers and the bearded lady. (The boys pretend they love her, make kissy noises; the girls roll their eyes, push the boys, say they're dumb. The girls are infinitely too grown up and worldly to care about something like this, just some freaky thing

that happened to the poor lady, puh-leese. Though they steal glances
back at her as they all walk away.)

But now the kids want to go to the big circus. Barnum and Bailey's.
In the city, in three rings, in Madison Square Garden. They want to see
a whole ring full of elephants, and tigers jumping through fiery hoops,
they want to see the spotlights slicing through the dark and hear the
ringmaster's booming voice.

For each it's different, this thing they all want.

Marian wants to see the animal parade, baby elephants holding their
mother's tails, graceful dancers twirling on the backs of proud prancing
horses. Sally wants to laugh while clowns squirt each other from bot-
tomless seltzer bottles, see dozens of them scrambling out of one little
tiny car. For Vicky, it's the strongman, the one who lifts two girls, four,
six, in his huge arms, holds them all in the air for as long as they want.

Jimmy wants to see the trapeze artists, soaring, flying, holding nothing, their faith pinned on the patient men hanging high in the air waiting to catch them. Markie's heard there are jugglers, fire-eaters,
sword-swallowers, magicians changing red silk to blue, pulling rabbits
from hats. Jack can't wait for the frantic sweeping spotlights, the clawing cats, a man exploding out of a cannon. Tom wants to see the ringmaster snapping his whip without looking behind him, because the
ringmaster always knows exactly what's happening at each spot at each
moment: clowns, acrobats, flyers, and jugglers; tigers, horses, dogs riding on elephants.

But asking the grown-ups to take them to Manhattan is like asking
for a trip to France.

The kids are in the woods by the nature preserve, sitting on logs in
their secret spot. Marian clears dead leaves away from a yellow crocus
trying to come up. Jack's squinting up into the trees, like he's trying to
find where the birds are, to spot them where they're hiding. Jimmy's
wondering what the difference is between the preserved woods and the
part where they are, why some trees are inside and some are outside and
who decides that, whether the trees are different and that's why, or
they're the same but some are lucky.

Nobody says much, because Tom's thinking.

After a little while of birds cheeping and tree branches rustling, after
a time of smelling the damp air and watching the winking gleams of
light that reach all the way down from the treetops to tickle the puddles, Tom finally says, like he's not quite sure, like he's talking to himself, *Well* . . .

The kids all look at him, and now Tom's smiling, lifting his head and showing them that slow smile that includes them all. Like he's saying, Yeah, okay, he's pretty sure he just had a smart idea, but he wouldn't have had it if everyone else weren't sitting there, too, if everyone hadn't wanted something that got him thinking. The kids feel like they always feel when Tom smiles this smile: Like Tom's been reading their minds. Like Tom can see what they want and from seeing it can find how to do it. And so Tom's smart idea is everybody's idea, really.

And they all have to be part of it, and they are, though none of them has to actually start anything or tell any lies. That's important. Marian won't ever tell any, even as much as she wants to help the kids out. And Jimmy, well, Jimmy just thinks the truth is easier. Jimmy doesn't talk much anyway, and when he does, he likes to keep it pretty plain. Lying's confusing, lying gets you all tripped over yourself sooner or later, because the truth, it'll burn through sometime, whatever you do. The kids all know that's how Jimmy thinks.

So Tom has to make a plan that doesn't need that, because if it needed that, it would never work. All they have to do, if any grown-ups ask—and probably they won't—is say, Yeah, they heard that, too. Tom says, winking at Marian, grinning at Jimmy: And that's true, you did hear it, because I'm telling it to you right now.

And the kids all be quiet, and they listen.

The next day, Sunday, after church, Tom and Jack are walking home with their dad, Big Mike. They turn the corner onto the block where the Spanos live. This is how the Molloys always go, and Tom, like it's just the house that made him think of it, tells his dad the Spano brothers, Eddie and Pete, the kids have to steer clear of them for a few days because they're really pissed off.

Why, Big Mike wants to know, what'd you do? And don't use that language in front of your mother.

Oh yeah, sorry, says Tom, even though his mom's walking ahead of them, talking with Vicky's mom, their heads leaning toward each other, Tom knows she didn't hear. Anyway, he says, they're not mad at us. Just, those guys, when they're mad, they'll pound on anything, you know? Especially, it's their dad they're pi—they're mad at, and you know Mr. Spano.

Oh, Big Mike knows Al Spano. He nods, rubs his jaw. Mrs. Molloy's gone ahead another few steps, she's listening to Vicky's mom real hard, so Big Mike grins down at Tom, winks, says, Guy's an asshole.

Tom grins back.

Serve him right, says Big Mike. Teach him a lesson if his kids took him on.

He'd cream them, says Jack.

Now, says Big Mike. Not someday.

Yeah, says Tom, but now's when they're mad. So I told everyone, watch out for Eddie and Pete, stay away.

Mike nods again. That's right, son, he says. You look out for your friends. The Spano boys, what's their beef?

The circus, says Tom.

What?

Mr. Spano, he said he'd take them to the circus. In Madison Square Garden. Now he won't.

Broke his promise?

Tom shrugs.

Bad business, breaking promises, says Big Mike.

What I hear, says Tom, Mr. Spano said Barnum and Bailey's, that's for spoiled rich kids and their snotty parents, all those folks in the city don't know what to do with their money. He said, All the way the hell into Manhattan? And seven dollars a ticket, a guy would have to be stupid to pay that so his kid could see an elephant take a crap. He said, Spivey's, that's the kind of show for people like us.

Spivey's? says Big Mike. That elephant they got at Spivey's, I thought he'd croak when they were here last summer. Wouldn't be surprised, that elephant don't come back with them this year. And that bearded lady? Ask me, she glues that thing on.

Well, I don't know about her, says Tom. But that sure is one sorry-ass elephant.

Tom and Jack and Big Mike share a laugh. But anyway, Tom says, that's what Eddie and Pete are so—Tom looks to make sure his mom is still out of range—so *p.o.'d* about. Because Mr. Spano, he says Spivey's was good enough for him when he was growing up, so it's good enough for any son of his.

Yeah? says Tom's father. That's what he says?

Two weeks later, the Saturday before Easter, the kids are bouncing up and down on Madison Square Garden's wooden seats. They're so juiced on cotton candy and the sawdust smell from the sideshow where they got to see the tigers up close in their cages, from the blaring music and the circling lights, they can hardly sit still. Mike the Bear, on one end of their row, says, Ah, settle down, you wild animals, but the kids can't. Mrs. Molloy, smiling on the other end, reaches over to stop Jack from tickling Vicky; to hand Markie a napkin so he can wipe purple cotton candy from the end of his nose; to calm them all down just enough so they're ready, really ready, when the lights go down and the music stops and the ringmaster booms, Ladies and gentlemen and children of all ages! and not looking behind him, snaps his whip.

It's true then, Tom's ways are different from the old ways. And times are changing. Not that Mike the Bear's not smart, no one would say that. But the new times, they call for another approach. A guy like Tom, he makes everyone look legit. That's what's needed now.

Tom's happy.

LAURA'S STORY
Chapter 4

―――

How to Find the Floor

October 31, 2001

The night before—the night of the day Harry died—Laura had submerged herself in a blanket on the couch in her own apartment and waited for the hours to pass. Headlights brightened the room, fell away, rose again, a seashore rhythm. Car engines purred, a motorcycle roared by. From the staircase came a sudden laugh, as pleased and tipsy people passed Laura's front door.

To all of these Laura attended, lying curled and sleepless. She would have to relearn them now. In the nearly three years that she and Harry had been together, these had become unfamiliar, the sounds, sights, and cadences of the cramped and sunless downtown studio that in any case had never been her home.

Harry had been here only twice: once, on a Sunday morning in early spring, out of a cheerful, demanding curiosity. A quick glance had shown him everything the room had to offer; he'd laughed and taken her in his arms. They'd perched with paper coffee cups on the roof and admired the view over Lower Manhattan. Harry had pointed out this building and that, one neighborhood and another. Laura had been two years in New York by then and would have bridled at a geography lesson from anyone else. But Harry, as always, took the measure perfectly of what she knew and offered detail or context, footnotes or background. And Laura, as always when she listened to Harry—and this was especially true when his subject was his first love, New York—felt a thrill that was part anticipation, part relief, part a sense of herself as privileged beyond hope. It was—and she had laughed when she'd realized this, and never told Harry—the same thrill she'd felt when, as a little girl, she had begun to learn to read.

Though even through her joy, Laura, listening to Harry's measured drawl, heard an urgency behind it, as though he saw the tide slowly rising and had much to tell her before the island where they stood was engulfed and they had to strike out for shore.

That morning they'd climbed back down the fire escape and in through Laura's window. They made laughing, teasing love on a jumble of blankets on the floor, Harry refusing to have any part of anything so tacky as Laura's fold-out couch.

Lying together afterwards, Laura asked Harry, "Can you swim?"

"I can barely float. Why do you ask?"

Laura, who had spent three summers as a lifeguard at a lakeside beach, held him more closely and answered, "I'm not sure."

The second time Harry had been to Laura's apartment was three days after the attacks. With the smoke still rising, they had climbed to the roof to stare out over Lower Manhattan again.

Leaving Leo's office now, Laura threw her bag over her shoulder, strode through the newsroom as though hurrying to an assignment. Heads turned toward her; she met no one's eyes, and they turned away again. Across the room, Georgie pivoted his chair to follow her progress but did not rise. She stood at the elevator with her back to them all.

In the normal course of things Laura had preferred to walk uptown to Harry's apartment, varying her route according to her mood. Some days she went for speed, beating traffic lights and leaping to curbs, so that she was perspiring, her heart pounding, when she arrived. Other times she meandered, ambling behind a couple or a group she'd choose for their intriguing conversation. Later she and Harry would play a game, assuming that overheard conversation to have been a critical turning point in the speakers' lives, inventing characters and circumstances of whom that could be true.

In the beginning Laura's stories were always reasonable and logical, Harry's fanciful and ridiculous. Later Laura had resolved to out-absurd Harry and had achieved, they both agreed, some significant successes. In the first weeks after September 11 they had not had the heart for the game and had stopped it. Then one day three weeks ago, as the pasta water was boiling, Harry had asked whether anyone had had anything momentous to say on Laura's walk home. From then they had begun the game again. Laura, in what seemed to her like an earlier century but was, she realized with a lurch of her heart, just the past week, had stored up two story lines for future use, to make Harry laugh.

She was grateful for the elevator's sluggishness until she realized she was, and her gratitude flashed into anger. When she finally reached the lobby, she charged straight toward the subway.

Many people feared the subway these days, since the anthrax letters and the smallpox threats and the knowledge (no truer than before, but now everyone's eyes had been opened) that any briefcase could be a bomb and any rider, a bomber. Some people had stopped taking the subway. Some wouldn't ride the bus, go to the movies, or shop at Lord & Taylor. Laura did all these things, though now on the subway or in a store her eyes roved her surroundings, she swung her head toward sudden sounds, her skin prickled the same way it did when she walked alone down a dark street at night.

No, fear of the subway was not a problem for Laura. But the subway would take her uptown quickly, and Laura understood enough about herself to know that that was the reason why, today, on her way to Harry's apartment, she was tempted to walk.

Harry's building: rough tan brick patterned with bricks of a darker brown. Sunlight flashed off the windows, cast watery squares on the building across the street as Laura approached from the west. She'd walked around the block to come up from Riverside Drive, a way she seldom used. The ploy was not effective, though. As the building came into view, even from this unfamiliar angle, her heart faltered and her feet slowed and stumbled.

The lobby: calm walls of a clear, pale blue, quiet lighting from discreet sconces, lustrous terrazzo floor. Two chairs by the elevator and a table for your mail. A painting of sailboats; a gilt-framed mirror. Music, as always, just audible from the doorman's radio. Different doormen, different music. As Laura walked in, it was opera.

The doorman himself: Hector, a Puerto Rican twenty years with the building. He hurried to the door for Laura and told her in accented English that he was very sorry. He said it again in Spanish, as though his grief wasn't complete until put that way.

The elevator: dark wood paneling, gouged and chipped with age but carefully polished. Creaky noises and slight shakes as it went about its business. Like me, Harry always said.

Harry's door: black like all the others. His name in the bronze square. Today's papers piled on the mat.

The dryness of her mouth and the chill on her skin as she turned the knob surprised Laura. Reporter-Laura pushed her forward. Reporter-Laura was not afraid of ghosts. She stumbled through the door, her heart choppy. A breeze from the open window rustled papers on Harry's desk; she jumped, then stood still and looked dumbly around. Reporter-Laura waited, her impatience growing, as the real Laura, her heart breaking, stared at the chairs, tables, rugs, and books. All these things were Harry's. He'd lived among them for so long, and now they stood patiently waiting, and they didn't know he wasn't coming back.

She could feel Reporter-Laura's amused contempt at the idea that she was feeling bad for the furniture. She didn't care. But what blurred her vision was the thought, too swift, too natural for her heart's guards to embargo and turn back, that she'd have to ask Harry if he'd ever felt this way, too.

Laura sat in the armchair and cried. A few times in the last year, she had cried with Harry there, for reasons she couldn't remember now. Except September 11, the obvious reason, which took no remembering, permitted no forgetting. She did remember Harry's silence, and the stroke of his hand on her hair. The indifferent empty blankness of the room now was so utterly unlike Harry's enveloping, companionable quiet that she could not use the same name for it.

Shakily she rose. She went into the white-tiled kitchen with the ancient fixtures Harry had refused to replace. Water hissed into the sink from bronze piping with ornate handles. She splashed it on her face, ran it up her arms, rubbed it on the back of her neck. She stared at it running away, racing to disappear.

Why had she come here, where everything was so hard?

She wasn't sure of the answer, but Reporter-Laura was.

Work.

Work was what she'd come for. Harry's desk, his computer, his file drawers—she had a lot to do. She turned off the tap. The silence that flooded the room was so thick and swampy, she had to force her way through it.

As she turned to walk back into the living room, though, she stopped, she and her heart, for a moment. On the kitchen table stood a pitcher holding roses Harry had brought her early in the week. Their buds had been tightly furled when he'd pulled them with a flourish—ta da!—from behind his back; now they'd shattered, dropping crimson petals on the tabletop, on the floor. Laura gathered the fallen petals and the sad stems, and threw them out.

She had not told Leo about the roses. She had not known how. The truth was so simple, she was afraid it would sound simpleminded, would confirm Leo's suspicion that Laura Stone was on a baseless, emotional crusade: not a reporter chasing a headline but a forlorn lover chasing a vanishing ghost.

But Harry had brought her roses.

With a clear, fathomless certainty, Laura was sure of this: Harry would not have left her without saying goodbye.

BOYS' OWN BOOK
Chapter 6

———

The Old Masters
(Sailing Calmly On)

September 11, 1978: The Boys (Jack)

And the one who once, on that long-ago night, was about to leave? That was Jack. But Jack is here.

Half-brother to Tom, he works for the clean uncle, too, in the clean side of the business, and he has his own operation, an adjunct, sort of, to his father's business. Not what he wants: Atlanta is what Jack wants, the operation down there young and new, plenty of opportunity, nothing set yet, nothing required. This is Jack, always hungry, knows the answer before the question's finished.

Jack does leave, for a time, not Atlanta but New Haven. He knows his father, Mike the Bear (Jack has always called him "Dad," his own father a loutish bully he does not remember, a man long gone), picked New Haven because it's closer to home, because they can keep an eye on him there. Other things, Jack's told, will come next, will come later. But New Haven doesn't last. There's a guy there, and a girl; there's trouble, though if you ask Jack he didn't mean anything by it, he was just spreading his wings, what's wrong with that? Everybody so *serious* all the time! Big Mike brings Jack back, smooths the trouble out (and it costs him: he has to up the take of the locals who move his goods, and he has to pretend to like it), this is how it's always been with Jack.

Jack's been here since. They tell him he's not ready; they tell him Atlanta will happen, but later. Jack hopes so, Jesus God he hopes so. He can't keep doing this, suffocating here in this tiny office—office!—next to Tom's, making calls to small-time bozos, fools who cut their prices because Jack raises his voice, or lowers it, Jack not even working up a sweat.

Jack wishes the war in 'Nam weren't over. When they were kids, there was the war. Some of the older boys in Pleasant Hills, kids' older brothers, went to fight. Jack and Tom, Jimmy and Markie, they played soldier games and couldn't wait for their turn. (Almost always it was Jimmy and Tom on one side, him and Markie on the other, and Jimmy and Tom mostly won because they were smart and patient; but it was Jack and Markie who came screaming out of trees, leaped up in muddy ambushes from drainage ditches, shot *pow-pow-pow* from the garage roof where no one else ever thought to climb.)

That would be cool, Jack thinks, going to war, that would have been so cool. Crashing through the heat, through the jungle, sneaking up on the enemy while rocket fire lights up the night sky. Leading a platoon, that would have been Jack, oh yeah. Talk about excitement, man, talk about seeing the world!

But they ended that war before the kids got their chance. The girls say that was good, they didn't want the boys to have to go. They say war is a bad thing. But girls don't know.

So Jack's here, Jack's waiting.

And this makes Jack laugh: some of the people who see how restless he is—hell, it's no secret—they think it's Tom. They think what Jack wants is to be the goddamn prince, be the one who's going to take over someday, be what Tom is. Shit. Shit, no! Best thing Tom ever did for Jack was to get born. Sitting with Big Mike for hours, Mike telling Tom: Do it this way, no, son, don't do that, call this guy, watch out for that one. If Jack had to do that, the way Tom does, the way Tom always did, Jesus, it would kill him.

No, not that bullshit.

But his own crew, Jack's okay with that. He's got some guys with balls there, guys who don't cross themselves when someone says Big Mike's name. He's got guys willing to take chances. No gain, Jack tells his guys, without risk. And no fun, either. The net don't appear, Jack tells them, unless you jump.

Eight years old: a summer morning, the kids hanging around on the rocks under the brand-new bridge, the boys and Sally fishing, Marian and Vicky sitting in the sun. The sun's hot, and the waves are crashing like this was the ocean, not just the Narrows, the water making the rocks all black and slippery. The kids can't see the far end of the bridge; it disappears into a thin, sparkly mist, and the spray from the waves makes rainbows all around them.

Vicky's counting how many fish everyone catches. You can't eat the fish from here, they'll poison you, you have to throw them back, so the only way to know who got the most is for someone to count. Mostly, the kids don't care, but Vicky likes counting. Tom usually gets the most, and Vicky always says she knew he would.

The fishing's pretty good where they are, but Jack keeps moving down the rocks, closer to the water. Tom's watching him but keeping his mouth shut. Hey, Jack calls all of a sudden, hey, cool! He puts down his pole and starts to lower himself into a place between the rocks.

What is it? shouts Markie, and he drops his pole, too, and scrambles, slippy-sliding on the slick rocks, toward Jack. Everyone else squints in their direction. Jimmy looks at Tom. Tom's mouth is a thin line, and he starts clambering over there. So does Jimmy, and then everyone else. Jack disappears down between the rocks. Marian shouts, Jack, be careful!

Markie, always fastest, gets there first. Just as he does, a big wave comes, fills up the place between the rocks with a crash of white foam. The foam backs off, and they hear Jack say, Whoa!

You okay? Markie shouts.

Jack coughs. Yeah, but shit, this shit is slippery! Markie, man, I gotta get out, help me get out of here.

The kids are all there now, looking down where Jack is, between the rocks. He's trying to climb out, but his hands and feet keep sliding on the slimy moss. Jack's face is white, he looks back over his shoulder like another wave's chasing him.

Markie flops down on his belly, sticks out his skinny arm. Jack grabs his hand. A wave comes. For a few seconds Jack disappears, comes back up sputtering, his eyes wild. Markie still has Jack's hand, but Jack's a lot bigger than Markie, Markie's just small and skinny and he can't pull Jack up, no way, but he keeps trying. Markie starts to slide across the rock, Jack pulling him down instead of him pulling Jack up, but Markie won't let go. Tom drops next to Markie, grips Jack's other arm with both hands. Jimmy plants his feet against a rock and grabs Markie's legs, keeps Markie from falling in. He pulls Markie and Tom pulls Jack, and finally Tom hauls Jack up.

Everyone ends up with skinned elbows or knees, bruises and bumps and cuts. Everyone's dripping wet. Jesus, Jack, says Tom.

Yeah, coughs Jack. Oh, shit, man, I can't breathe.

You can, says Jimmy, kneeling down so he can look right into Jack's eyes, Just in and out slowly, like always.

Jack's wild eyes skitter toward Jimmy, and he does what Jimmy says, he coughs and chokes, but he breathes in and out, in and out.

And then suddenly Jack grins. Anyway, he says, his voice raspy but tough again, almost Jack's normal voice. Anyway, look.

He sits, pulls something from the back pocket of his soaked jeans. The kids all lean around to look.

Jack coughs again, says, Some asshole lost his wallet.

He thumbs it open. Credit cards, a driver's license, pictures. From the billfold part Jack pulls out a fan of limp and soggy bills. He peels them off each other and he counts them. It's eighty-two dollars, more money than any of the kids have ever seen. They pass it around, so everyone can see how it feels.

After everyone's had a turn, Marian says, We have to give it back.

Jack yells, Are you crazy? Asshole was dumb enough to lose it, I almost got drowned going after it, Markie too. Screw him, let's go get ice cream. He waves the bills, which have come back to him.

But his license, Marian says. And his kids' pictures.

He's an asshole, Jack says.

Vicky looks at Tom. Everyone else does, too, even Jack; he scowls, but he waits for Tom to speak.

Tom says: Jack can keep the money. He says: It's not like the guy would ever get it back if Jack didn't climb down there.

Jack flashes Marian a grin and a big wink.

But we can give the wallet back, says Tom.

Hey, Jack says.

Tom says, What? You need pictures of his kids? You gonna take his Esso card and gas up the car or something?

Tom grins, and most of the other kids, and finally Jack does, too; it's a pretty funny idea, Jack pulling Mike the Bear's big Impala into the Esso station, sticking his head out the window, and hollering, Fill 'er up! Marian's the only one not smiling. She's looking at Jimmy, like this is a bad thing that happened and he's supposed to do something. But Jimmy's not so sure it's bad. What Tom says seems right to him, the whole thing seems fair. And for sure it's not bad enough to start a fight with Jack, who's pretending he doesn't care that all the kids saw how scared he was when he couldn't breathe. Right now, Jack's all lit up and promising everyone Eskimo Pies.

So Jimmy doesn't say anything. Marian, after a minute, looks away.

She doesn't say anything, either. Vicky, she's smiling at Tom, and at Jack. Not just a regular smile, Jimmy thinks. Jimmy thinks Vicky looks the way his dad looks when they're watching a Mets game on TV, the Mets not doing so well, and Jimmy says, How come they don't take the pitcher out, put in a pinch hitter? And his dad says, Don't worry, Jim, Casey Stengel, he knows what he's doing. And Jimmy's not sure, but he waits and watches, and the pitcher singles, and the Mets score. And then Jimmy sees the same smile on his dad that he sees on Vicky now, looking at Tom.

Why doesn't Jack just leave? It's a big world out there, why doesn't he go see some of it?

Because Big Mike's saying, Soon. If Jack waits, Big Mike will set him up, get him his own operation, make him part of the machine. Guys, major guys, will have a beer with him, tell him what's what, in Atlanta, in Portland, wherever this happens.

And if he doesn't wait, if he leaves on his own, he's on his own.

It may come to that. It may have to. And it might be okay if it did, thinks Jack, except this: his mom. If Jack walks out on Big Mike, he doesn't come back, that would be the deal and he knows it. And his mom, this is what she's always been afraid of, Jack knows that, too. Jack did some weird, wild things when he was a kid, does some now, and he'd probably have done even more, played with fire, stuck his head in a lion's mouth, except for the way his mom always looked at him. Not mad, the way Big Mike gets, red and furious. His mom's eyes, when Jack does something loony and gets in trouble (this is how it was when he came back from New Haven), they're happy and sad at the same time. Like she knows something bad is coming for Jack, and she's glad, so glad, it wasn't this time.

Jack would have gone long ago, if his mom's eyes didn't look like that.

So Jack stays. He goes to the office, he runs his crew and hangs out. And waits.

Is he happy? Yeah, sure. Jack's happy.

PHIL'S STORY
Chapter 3

Secrets No One Knew

Game over. Phil's team, 48–40. A fast-moving game today, a passing game, the ball getting four, five, six touches before anyone put up a shot: this on both teams. Under the shower in the echoing locker room, Phil thought about that, rifling through the game in his mind as through a card deck, picking out moments to look at again. He did this also with jury summations, with phone conversations: any situation could teach you something, lessons were everywhere if you looked for them. Most people didn't look. The reason behind that (because there was a reason behind everything)? Phil assumed it was this: most people didn't want to know they had choices. People loved the idea of *doing what they had to do*—God, his clients said that all the time. That was how they told him why they'd shot their sister's husband, why they'd snatched a woman's purse, why the whole damn crowd was cooking meth, wrapping it and dealing it from the nice frame house in Queens.

Had to.

No choice.

And by the time they came to Phil, the damn thing was, by that time, for a lot of them, it was finally true.

Toweling off, looking through the cards in his mind, Phil compared today's game to last week's, to the other games since September 11 and the games in August, in July, in days before.

Right after the attacks, in those first days, the Y was closed like so many places, and no one played games.

When the Y reopened early the next week, Phil and his teammates reassembled. They began again, as everyone tried to do.

Those first games were wild, lawless. People passed too hard or too far, fired up insane shots. No one set things up, no one was making plays. Then a strange thing: in the third game after, Terry the Ball-Hog (even Terry called himself that) made three great passes, two to Brian, who could really shoot, and the third to little Jane, who was cutting in for a layup. It was the right play, a play by the book, though Jane had no layup anyone had ever seen; and Terry, who never before in memory had given up a ball once he had his hands on it, passed for the third time that morning, and Jane took the shot. And missed it. But the next ball that came to her she sent to Brian, who swung it to Terry, and suddenly the passing game was under way, and they had never given it up.

Oh, they still ran the fast break when the chance came, they still posted up and cleared out for the big centers (on those mornings the big centers showed up), but this new thing, this was a team game. These last few weeks, Phil had seen this: the thrill of setting a teammate up in a smooth and beautiful play trumped the thrill of sinking a basket. Almost, it trumped winning.

No one spoke about it; it was possible, it occurred to Phil as he shaved, that he was the only one who thought about it.

What caused the change?

The same thing that made the players who came early to the first game after the attacks hold off starting for nearly half an hour, in case other people were coming but were late, delayed by the erratic subways or by having to show their ID to the National Guardsmen on the corner.

The same thing that made all fourteen players show up that day, something that almost never happened. (Even Arnie had come, though his brother was still missing, later declared dead with no body found; Phil went to the service.)

The fresh breeze of relief that had swept the gym every time a player pushed through the swinging doors that day had flashed Phil back to his childhood, to his Bronx neighborhood, to after-school detours to the newsstand for comic books and Cokes.

In the shadow of the El women with their wheeled wire carts stopped for gossip. Old men shuffled by, dangling loaves of bread and quarts of milk in plastic bags. Eleven-year-old Phil Constantine (Konnenstein in the old country, four generations back; Phil had cousins called Conner) was on a mission for the new Spider-Man, hoping maybe for the Fantastic Four, though that was probably not out until tomorrow. He headed up this way a couple of times a month: he'd worked out the Marvel schedule, and DC, too, he knew just when to expect his books.

He knew this, too: Sometimes when you got to the newsstand, the Irish kids from St. Margaret's would be hanging out on the corner. Sometimes if they were, all they did was look at you with stony eyes; but sometimes they wanted more. If they did, you had to fight them. Had to. Because if you didn't take it up there, in public, on the sidewalk, they'd wait for you on the ballfield at dusk, or on the corner where the construction site was: somewhere lonely, where no one would see and no adults were near to break it up.

Phil understood early that that was the point: on the sidewalk, where adults could see and stop you, no one won and no one lost. The St. Margaret's boys could throw down the challenge, could stand proud that they'd defended their territory, could claim they'd have murdered you, pulverized you, little kike bastard, if only old man Murray hadn't come out swinging his baseball bat, hadn't threatened to call the cops. They could do this safe in the knowledge that old man Murray *would* come out, or Mrs. Harper, or that old crock Lefkowitz with his bloodied butcher's apron. That someone would stop them before they had to find out how far they were really willing to go.

Phil understood that. And this: old man Murray's newsstand wasn't the only place to buy comic books. You could walk way up Broadway, twenty minutes out of the neighborhood, where the St. Margaret's boys didn't care if you went or not. You could jump on the El, ride downtown a few stops, pick up your books in the subway newsstand at 168th, and come back on the same token. You had choices. Going to Murray's, Phil was making his.

So when he had to, Phil fought those boys.

And as great as the relief was that enveloped him anytime he rounded the corner and saw the sidewalk empty, he never once considered not heading to old man Murray's newsstand the day the new Spider-Man came out.

Now, knotting his tie in the locker room mirror, he thought that same enveloping relief was where the team game came from at the Y a mile from Ground Zero, the first weeks after.

They were all relieved that this one morning ritual could continue. That among so many things so totally changed, this one hour was still what it had been. That it required no coping, no dealing-with, no brave adjustments or support groups or halting, painful phone calls.

The passing and the play-making were expressions of gratitude.

Gratitude for what?

They were grateful to one another, Phil thought, for being alive.

Two blocks east of the Y, Phil sat down at a diner counter to drink black coffee, wait for eggs and bacon, thumb through the morning papers. All five, every day: the dailies and the *Wall Street Journal*. Just to know.

The war on the other side of the world was shown in grainy photos of blossoming explosions. A story on a Pentagon briefing quoted a spokesman telling reporters that the situation was too security-sensitive for him to tell reporters anything. At home, in the twisted, smoking ruins of Ground Zero, eight firefighters were pictured saluting a flag-draped stretcher that carried the remains of one of the three bodies recovered yesterday. No one knew where the anthrax was coming from, no one knew whether the air downtown was safe to breathe, and no one knew what they would find as they pulled the rubble pile apart shovel by shovel and ton by ton. No one knew.

In the *Times* the Harry Randall story was inside, in the Nation Challenged section with all the other September 11–related news. *Reporter Dies in Suicide Plunge from Verrazano Narrows Bridge. Wrote Series of Articles About Hero Firefighter.* Phil shook his head. Son of a bitch. He hadn't liked Randall, hadn't liked him at all, but, shit, couldn't a guy even die without the glow of Jimmy McCaffery's halo throwing him into shadow?

He scanned the *Times* story. He didn't know why he was reading it, and he didn't learn anything from it. The *Post* and the *Daily News* were pretty much the same, fewer words, more pictures.

The *Tribune* was different. They carried the story, with Randall's photo, on the front page, just below the fold. The headline was different, too, a clear shot across someone's bow. Whose? Good question. Phil propped the paper against the ketchup bottle and read every word.

From the *New York Tribune*, October 31, 2001

REPORTER DIES IN FALL FROM VERRAZANO BRIDGE WROTE SERIES OF ARTICLES ABOUT HERO FIREFIGHTER

Connection Suspected Between Death of Tribune's
Harry Randall and Organized Crime

Firefighter May Be Link

by Hugh Jesselson

Sources tell the *New York Tribune* that the October 30 death of *Tribune* reporter Harry Randall, previously listed as a suicide, may be related to organized crime elements based on Staten Island.

Harold Randall, a widely respected investigative journalist and three-time recipient of the Pulitzer Prize, fell to his death from the Verrazano Narrows Bridge. Randall's death is now being investigated for possible connection to a series of articles he was working on for the *Tribune.* Revolving around the life of FDNY Captain James McCaffery, who led Ladder Co. 62 and died in the September 11 collapse of the World Trade Center's north tower, this unfinished series, according to sources, might have traced a relationship between Capt. McCaffery and reputed organized crime figure Edward Spano. If this relationship exists, police sources say, "There would be some justification for reexamining the evidence in the death of Harry Randall."

The first two articles in Randall's series focused on the heroism and legacy of Capt. McCaffery. In the third article, which appeared in the *Tribune* the day before his death, Randall began to probe the source of payments made over the past two decades to Sally Keegan, widow of Capt. McCaffery's childhood friend Mark Keegan. These payments were not, as claimed by both Capt.

McCaffery and prominent New York defense attorney Phillip Constantine from the State of New York. Their true source has yet to be disclosed.

Keegan died at the age of 24 in prison, where he had been sentenced in connection with the shooting death of Jonathan "Jack" Molloy, 25. Phillip Constantine has admitted being the conduit through which the mysterious payments were made to the Keegan family, and has also admitted being acquainted with James McCaffery. He has refused further comment on the matter. The *Tribune* has learned that the State Ethics Commission has opened an investigation into Constantine's activities. Constantine has been investigated by the Ethics Commission on three previous occasions; none of these investigations resulted in disciplinary action.

Attention is focusing on Edward Spano, a Staten Island developer and reputed organized crime figure. Spano denies any connection between himself and Constantine, the late Mark Keegan, or McCaffery. However, Keegan, McCaffery, and Spano grew up together in Pleasant Hills on Staten Island, along with two other major figures in the case: Jack Molloy, the victim, and Marian Gallagher, who heads the More Art, New York! Foundation. In addition to being McCaffery's former fiancée, Gallagher is a member of the Downtown Redevelopment Advisory Council and is also executive director of the recently formed McCaffery Memorial Fund, a nonprofit organization created in the wake of September 11.

The Fund, which has reportedly reached a half-million dollars in pledges and contributions, has as its mission support of FDNY outreach and recruiting efforts. As reported in Randall's October 29 article, Gallagher, under pressure from FDNY leadership, has temporarily suspended accepting contributions until the questions surrounding McCaffery are answered. Gallagher, who told the *Tribune* she has no doubt that the allegations about McCaffery would be quickly cleared up, is reported to have broken off her engagement to him soon after Mark Keegan's death in prison. She claims to know nothing about the payments to Sally Keegan.

Thomas Molloy, asked about a possible relationship between his brother and Edward Spano, said, "Back then, my father ran some shady businesses. Jack and I both thought that kind of life was exciting. But after Jack died, I saw things differently. I've spent my life trying to live down some of the things they did, Dad and Jack. Trying to prove a Molloy can be respectable."

Police sources who study organized crime on Staten Island tell the *Tribune* that the criminal enterprises directed by Jack Molloy "faded away" after his death, and that those of his father, Michael Molloy—known as "Big Mike" or "Mike the Bear"—were disbanded. Thomas Molloy has no criminal record. For the past twenty years he has been involved in a variety of successful Staten Island business ventures, and he is a contributor to many charitable causes. "I'm just doing what I have to do," he said. "My family and I live in this community. Like I said, it sort of makes up for Dad and Jack."

About Spano's relationship with Jack Molloy, Thomas Molloy said, "Dad and Jack didn't have anything on the Spanos. If anyone had any kind of criminal empire in those days—though I think that's overdramatic—it was Aldo Spano. He passed it on to Eddie." Asked whether his half-brother may have run afoul of Aldo or Edward Spano, Molloy admitted that was possible.

On the question of the payments made to Sally Keegan, Molloy refused to speculate. "Jimmy McCaffery was a good friend of mine when we were kids. Just because suing the state was his idea doesn't mean he knew anything about the lies that happened later. We were all taken in, it looks like."

"This is the story Harry Randall was working on when he died," *Tribune* investigative journalist Laura Stone told reporters. "Only this one, the McCaffery story. If his death wasn't suicide, it's logical to wonder what the connection is. Although he wasn't specific, Harry Randall had, in the past few days, expressed fears for his own safety." Asked about the status of the work Harry Randall left unfinished, Stone answered, "Whatever Harry Randall was working on, the *Tribune* will follow it up. If his death is related to his work, the *Tribune* will find out."

PHIL'S STORY
Chapter 4

―――

The Bodies of the Birds

October 31, 2001

Phil read the *Tribune*'s story on Harry Randall's death just as he'd read the others. Hugh Jesselson's byline was on it. Jesselson was a cop and crime reporter; Phil had run across him before, bound to in his line of work.

And Jesselson made this clear: the *Tribune*'s take on Randall's death was different from everyone else's.

Jesselson's reporting was straight and dry, but the message was clear: The *Tribune* wasn't convinced. The *Tribune* wanted to know more. The *Tribune* couldn't see a reason for a man in Randall's position to take a swan dive through the clear October air.

What position was that? Phil studied the story, digging into his eggs. He discovered, because it was not there, something else. No police sources were quoted, no investigation cited. No matter whose byline was on the story, the NYPD was apparently not inclined to dig deeper into Randall's death.

But the *Tribune* was.

Laura Stone, another *Tribune* reporter—had Phil seen her name, maybe on the Bronx chemical spill story? Something like that, something that took digging, brains, and guts, he wasn't sure what, but he remembered being impressed—Laura Stone said her colleague Harry Randall had been working on something. Something big. He'd told her a certain amount about it. He'd expressed fears for his own safety.

Phil tore a piece of toast in half, chased crumbs of bacon around his plate. Expressed fears? The Harry Randall who'd sat in Phil's office, slouching in his chair as though even dynamite wouldn't dislodge him until he'd gotten his answers—and smiling as if to say the way he knew that was that dynamite had once or twice been tried—*that* Harry Randall had expressed fears?

No.

No, not even if he'd felt them. And Phil, remembering Randall's amused, acid-sharp eyes, his relaxed, drink-worn face, the drawling slow rhythm Phil had not been able to disrupt, did not think Randall had been a frightened man.

What, then? Not hard to figure out. "Whatever Harry Randall was working on, the *Tribune* will follow it up. If his death is related to his work, the *Tribune* will find out."

Meaning: I'm here, if you want to stand up, show yourself, take another shot.

MARIAN'S STORY
Chapter 3

———

The Invisible Man
Steps Between You and the Mirror

October 31, 2001

As Marian stepped inside, the broad oak door swung shut, blockading the footsteps and fluorescent buzz of the cramped corridor, forbidding them entry into the wide quiet of the MANY Foundation's office.

Outside this well-oiled door—in the vinyl-tiled hallway, in the security-guarded lobby, on the crowded streets—frowning women and men scurried about on unconnected errands. Here within, where plant-draped partitions supported polished woodwork surfaces hovering over carpet the color of moss, all was purpose and peace. In a flight of fancy Marian had once likened herself and her staff to forest creatures, vibrant with industry, intent upon their daily tasks. "You do know," Sam had asked, "that the daily task of half those cute little creatures is eating the other half?" Marian had smiled indulgently and hadn't replied.

That smile, that flight of fancy, had been before.

Pausing now just inside the door, Marian met a hollowness that, though unwelcome, she'd known too well these past weeks. She had not spoken about it, at first hoping it would pass, later ashamed to have it mean so much to her. What was her loss, compared to others so much more profound, so much more bewildering? But she tasted its empty, metallic tang each time she walked through this door. The soothing sense she had always had here of coming home, of having found her way back once again to the place where she belonged, had vanished after September 11, along with all else she thought she had known.

In the minutes and hours of the crisis itself Marian had remained calm. (Those hours so elusive, difficult for memory to grasp: some episodes compressed, some elongated. Events recollected as following others when in reality they must have come long before. Some recalled as though only recorded by a single sense: this, an odd sweet smell. That, a shout, and someone weeping. Sticky dust clinging to skin and hair. An abrupt midday darkness that rolled away to reveal a new, ash-covered world.) She had shepherded her staff down the staircase immediately after the second plane struck. (Their building was not yet being evacuated; its security office was "assessing the situation." Marian, watching in horror as flaming bodies and massive chunks of steel twisted through the sky to crash to roofs and slice through walls of buildings around them, wondered exactly what there was to assess.)

She had directed her people to a rear exit and had stayed in the lobby after they all had dashed outside, to help others find that back way, too, visitors to the building, strangers, office workers who came here every day but in the crescendo of their panic were losing all orientation, all direction. Thus she was still inside when the roar, the sound none had ever heard before, the rumble and clamor that froze them all, began. And as the black cloud poured down the street, she watched (helplessly, through the lobby glass) the implosion's immense pressure smashing down people trying to outrun it.

When the darkness (complete, much blacker than night, than closed eyes, than your dreams) had passed, Marian was first to the lobby doors, shouldering them open against the dust and debris. She shouted to people, ordered and offered and tugged them inside, as many as understood what she was saying, or would follow her though they clearly were too stunned to comprehend.

And when the second roar and crash and dust cloud came, pounding the lobby doors shut again, Marian waited for the darkness to pass once more and resumed her work.

People said later that she was an inspiration, that her calmness kept them calm, that her bravery made them brave. During the crisis Marian never panicked, and everyone said how courageous she was; but Marian knew that was a lie. Staying in motion, being useful, was how Marian outran—how she had always outrun—the boundless hollow terror that had besieged her and of which she was much more afraid than the roar or the cloud.

After the crisis, though, came the announcement that the building would be closed indefinitely. "Indefinitely" was just three weeks, as it developed, but she didn't know that then, who knew anything then?

Marian was thrown into a state of alarm and dread. Without work, how could she go on? What would create solid ground for her to stand on, keep the void from swallowing her? She volunteered immediately for the most intense and time-consuming tasks she could find. She kept up with as much of MANY's ongoing work as she could, from home, fighting the lack of phones, the rerouted subways, the abrupt reordering of everyone's priorities.

And there was Kevin.

Kevin was in the hospital at NYU. Marian went every day, past the coroner's huge tent, past the refrigerated trucks that held remains waiting to be identified, past the crowds of relatives and friends who gathered there because others were gathering there, because someone might have glimpsed your parent or child or lover wandering dazed, lying injured, maybe they'd been taken to another hospital and someone had seen them there and you wouldn't have to come here anymore where the coroner was identifying remains.

Kevin was her godson, and she'd gone every day, and whatever time she got there, she found other firefighters sitting with him, or arriving, or leaving. Marian soon understood that Kevin, because he had lived, because he had been saved, was an emblem for these men. He represented something they could do: his brothers had saved him then, they could support him, comfort him, kid him along now. They came to visit Kevin, she understood, for the same reason that she worked and worked late into the night.

Some of the firefighters had been digging on the pile, and had conscientiously scrubbed and changed clothes before coming to the hospital. Some were on their way to dig, or going on duty, or coming off duty. They told Kevin what had happened on the site today, who was giving commands, whose body had been found; they told him what fires they had fought in the course of their normal day's work and whose funerals they had gone to. One evening Marian had arrived to hear three firefighters describing Jimmy's memorial service to Kevin: the dignitaries, the prayers, the pallbearers shouldering the bier of flowers that carried Jimmy's helmet because there was no body to bury. Kevin was in tears, and Marian, hovering outside the open door—Marian who had been there, who had sat at the back of St. Patrick's Cathedral among the largest crowd she had ever seen in a church and had found herself shivering uncontrollably—felt her own hot tears start. She'd turned and fled from the hospital before she was noticed.

The firefighters were always courteous to her and got up to go for coffee or buy Kevin ice cream so he and Marian could have time alone. Occasionally she let them go, but most often she insisted they stay. She'd smile and set to the task of keeping order among the gifts that crowded Kevin's room.

As a rule she had trouble discarding flowers; at home she let them linger until colors dulled and petals scattered. But in Kevin's room, bouquets and sprays, cut flowers and potted plants, and also balloons, fruit baskets, and candy, arrived daily, from friends and neighbors and from total strangers who sent these things to Kevin for the same reason they sent money to the Red Cross and the Salvation Army and the McCaffery Fund.

At his suggestion she distributed many of them to other patients in the Burns Unit, and to the nurses and therapists who worked so hard for these patients. Then she would sit and drink a cup of tea, telling Kevin about anything funny that had happened to her, any gossip or intriguing event that might interest him. When her tea was gone, she would rise, kiss his cheek, and leave, promising to return the following day. If Sally arrived while she was there, and Marian had the time, she'd wait in the lounge for Sally to finish her visit, and she and Sally would go for coffee, or a drink if the hour was late enough.

"Honey, he's fine," she'd reassure Sally the same way each time. "He's doing really well. I talked to the doctor."

"Thanks." Sally would squeeze Marian's hand. "I talked to him, too, but I can't understand a word he says."

Of course Sally could understand doctors, but Marian knew what she meant, and smiled encouragingly. Because the more important something was to you, the more you needed it and demanded it, the more it grew and mushroomed in your own head, and then the harder it was to hear.

There was a rhythm to Marian's visits with Kevin, and only one thing could disturb it. If Phil Constantine arrived while she was there, Marian would gather her things and leave at once. The lawyer invariably offered to be the one to come back later, but she would not allow it. And if he was there when she arrived, she would put her flowers in water and leave. She wanted to owe him nothing, not even ten minutes with Kevin. Let him owe that to her.

And after three weeks Marian's office building reopened. On that day Marian had come in alone and very early, lugging files and computer disks. Unlocking the oak door, she anticipated with a child's excitement the magic of that moment, when she would step from the wilderness—a wilderness, always; but never before as desolate as this—into the garden.

It had not happened. Disappointed, almost panicked, Marian had found no enchantment inside, only drooping plants and forlorn furniture coated with a fine white dust that had once been buildings and everything inside them.

Marian and her staff had cleaned for three days, resolutely discarding what they could not save. They had scrubbed and vacuumed floors and furniture, dusted the books in their extensive library, the photographs on their walls. They bought new file folders and computer keyboards, new potted plants to replace withered, choked foliage they had raised from cuttings, been given as gifts. They did all their purchasing downtown, using their dollars to help their struggling neighbors. In this determined, unfaltering renewal, Marian approved expenses without a second glance and did not look behind her as treasured, unsalvageable objects were carted away.

All that had been four weeks ago. Now the MANY offices were humming again. Work, that secular savior, proceeded as devoutly as before. The MANY Foundation and Marian in particular were in a position to rise to this terrible occasion.

"I'm extremely grateful; in all this disaster I've been very fortunate, very blessed," Marian had said at the press conference announcing the formation of the Downtown Redevelopment Advisory Council (a press conference she had been asked to organize, because her contacts were so good and—in those days, before the carefully worded innuendo, the well-tended nightshade, of Harry Randall's article—her credibility was so high). "I appreciate the opportunity to give something back by working for the rebuilding effort. This is a very challenging time for all of us. What happens downtown now is profoundly important. I welcome the chance to contribute. I'm eager to help in any way I can."

She had smiled and stepped away from the microphone, careful not to talk too long, making sure to share the spotlight with the other Council members gathered there.

She'd gone on, then, to add the responsibilities of serving on the Downtown Council, and a few days later those of heading the McCaffery Fund, to a workload already the amazement of her friends. Where did she get the energy, they marveled, the strength? Marian replied that she felt not burdened but privileged; did not feel put-upon but rather was anxious to do her part as so many others were doing theirs. As so many had died doing. Working late into the evening? What was that against the price so many people had paid?

Yes, Marian was relieved. She was happy to have valuable, useful work to do. She came to the office every day feeling, as she had said, lucky and blessed.

Except that when she opened the door, there was no magic.

Boys' Own Book
Chapter 7

———

The Way Home

September 11, 1978: The Girls (Marian)

Marian is Jimmy's, and Jimmy is hers, though what that means to each may not be the same. Marian knows this, and Jimmy has not asked her to marry him, not yet. But that Jimmy is what she wants Marian has always known.

Eight years old: the stray dog the kids have been feeding since Marian found him (a secret from their parents; they've named him King) is sneaking from one backyard to another. He gets stuck under a chain-link fence. The more he tries to wriggle out, the more caught he gets. He's whining; he's bleeding. Marian tries to talk to him, softly, to make him not so scared, so someone can help him, but King just growls at her. He barks, snaps at Markie when Markie tries to go up close to him, but then he looks at them so sadly. No one thought Markie could really help, not Markie, but he went right up there, like he could be the hero, maybe, this time. Tom, Tom is thinking: Stay back! he tells them. If the dog barks too loud, someone will find him. "Someone" means a grown-up, of course. A grown-up could free King—these kids are still young, grown-ups can do anything—but a grown-up, the kids are stone certain, will take him to the pound and leave him there all by himself.

But the kids know what to do: Jack runs for Jimmy. They all watch Jimmy jog up, stop, and stand still. Marian's crying, but she wipes her eyes. Jimmy looks, taking it all in. The kids are quiet, and they wait, even Jack, who never waits. Finally Jimmy walks to King, squats down;

King growls. Jimmy grins, and now he does say something, something to the dog. None of them hears.

Jimmy reaches slowly, maybe so he won't scare King. He grips the chain-link, grunts as he lifts. King yelps, howls, writhes; he barks at Jimmy, a desperate warning, but Jimmy ignores it. King barks once more, then clamps his jaws on Jimmy's bare arm. Jimmy shouts, but he doesn't stop lifting.

Then King is free, Jimmy and King rolling on the ground in dust, in growling and yelling, until Jimmy yanks his arm up and King darts away. A lot of noise now, the dog, the kids; and Mrs. Molloy, Tom and Jack's mom—the closest house—comes running out. Mrs. Molloy scoops Jimmy up, rushes him into her kitchen, wraps his arm in a towel while she calls his dad. The kids all crowd into the kitchen, watching, silent. Marian and Sally and Vicky press close together. Mrs. Molloy smiles at Jimmy while she holds the towel tight, and even though her smile is sad the way it always is, it still makes the kids less scared.

Mrs. Molloy doesn't kick them out, in fact she tells Jack, Why don't you give everybody cookies? And Jack does, grinning at the girls like it's a party. Mrs. Molloy acts like it's no big deal, Jimmy's arm is turning her towel red. The kids' hearts all slow down, stop pounding so hard, and nobody cries.

Jimmy's dad takes him to the hospital. He needs twelve stitches in that arm, Jimmy, and he does the damnedest thing. He tells his dad it was the Cooleys' funny black dog from down the street that bit him. Tells him he was throwing sticks for it, and the dog, well, it just got a little carried away. My fault, Jimmy says. Why say this? Because the Cooleys' dog has tags, the Cooleys' dog had its rabies shots. You tell someone a stray dog bit you, they hunt it, they catch it, they kill it to see if it gave you rabies: all the kids know. Jimmy tells the kids, King tore up my arm while I'm trying to help him, now they're gonna kill him, like it's for *me*? No way.

Tom smiles when Jimmy tells them this, says, Jimmy, that's a lie, you told your dad a lie.

Jimmy says, Yeah, and I sure hope he doesn't ask me anything else about it, because I'm gonna get it all screwed up.

So all the kids wait to see if Jimmy starts to foam at the mouth, but he doesn't, so everything's all right.

And from then to now, Marian's in love.
Marian will wait for Jimmy; Jimmy will ask her when he's ready.
Marian's happy.

MARIAN'S STORY
Chapter 4

The Women in the Tent

October 31, 2001

Marian stepped to the reception desk. She smiled and greeted Elena, careful to ask after her family.

"Mama was supposed to go back to San Juan yesterday, but Aunt Pilar cried and cried," Elena told her. "So she stayed." Elena's cousin had been an electrician, working in the south tower.

"Tell your aunt she's in my prayers."

"Thank you. She'll like that."

Marian took the message slips Elena handed her and said nothing else. She'd given Elena the names of three grief counselors, two of them Spanish-speaking. She wished Elena's aunt would call someone and get some help: grief was an easier burden if not carried alone. But Marian knew better than to try to push people to do what was best for them. She tried to take lessons from life—how else to keep from despairing?—and she liked to think she had many years ago learned that one.

She walked down the short corridor to her own office thinking of Elena's aunt, Mrs. Padilla, whom she'd met half a dozen years before at Elena's wedding. She thought of all the prayers, her own and others', rising as the smoke rose, climbing toward Heaven on behalf of Elena's cousin, on behalf of so many people. Marian had indeed been praying for Elena's cousin, and for the sons and sisters of the small number of people she knew personally who had lost loved ones. And for all the people she did not know, and especially all the people who might not have anyone to pray for them.

And, yes, for Jimmy.

Marian went to church in Manhattan now, at Holy Innocents, and had for many years; not every week, but often. She had not been to St. Ann's back home since she'd left, except for a few weddings, a few funerals. Until last month, when she had crossed the choppy water back to Staten Island the first Sunday after the attacks to attend mass with her father because he'd asked her to.

In the echoing dimness of St. Ann's, where she had spent each Sunday morning of her childhood (Jimmy sometimes there, more often not, his devoutness being of a different nature), Marian had sat beside her father and waited for comfort: if not the comfort of God, at least the comfort of the familiar. Through the ponderous swells of organ music, through the homily, through the prayers spoken together and those whispered alone, she waited. She did not take communion, having not been to confession. Her father's face showed his disappointment. Watching the patient, shuffling communion line, Marian wondered why she had not been to confession since the attacks. She had, through the years, permitted herself confession and therefore communion: her doubts allowed it. Because she had never been certain that keeping her dark secret was wrong (had never been sure, she reminded herself strictly, that the secret was the truth), she had released herself from the obligation to confess it. But in these times, even to prepare for this morning's mass—even to prepare for coming back here—she had found confession impossible.

Nevertheless, she prayed from the heart, as was required. Faith was a compact, like anything else, and Marian was prepared to uphold her part of the bargain. She prayed and waited.

But the music remained just sound, the smoke clouding from the bronze censers mere fragrance. Father Connor's earnest sermon was nothing but words, and Marian found herself not listening to them, hearing instead the soft weeping of people at the first of what would now be a lifetime of Sunday masses without the husbands, wives, sons and daughters, fathers and friends they were accustomed to have beside them. She saw a tear on her father's cheek. Awkward, she patted his hand. "I miss your mother," he whispered, though it was nearly four decades since Marian's mother had passed away.

So many crowded into St. Ann's that day, the faces and voices from her childhood. Marian knew why they had come, why her father had wanted her to come: just to be there, together.

* *

A memory bloomed in Marian's mind: a windy autumn Sunday when Sister Hilda, the squeaky-voiced nun they had loved because she laughed and knew what was important, had ordered the whole Sunday school class into their jackets, marched them to the park, and taught them to make Indian tepees out of sticks and tablecloths. Each leaning stick would fall, she showed them, but for the others (and the kids all tried to make one stand alone, or two; Tom had three briefly motionless, but then they clattered down). But together, Sister Hilda told them, united (as we are united in faith) and supporting each other (as we do with our prayers and our service), they created shelter.

In St. Ann's five days after the world had changed, Marian tried to feel sheltered. So many steps along her path had been marked here, so much joy and sorrow shared, so much comfort offered, taken, given. She tried to feel that comfort now.

Though even then—long before Harry Randall began his relentless excavating of their days and nightmares—even then, Marian could not rid herself of the exhausting weight of what she had never shared.

And as her clear low voice rose to join the others, filling the church with safeguarding song, she felt it, this secret, not as she always had—as a burden she could never put down—but as empty space, a tear in the fabric of protection, leaving her open to the terrifying sky.

PHIL'S STORY
Chapter 5

——

The Way Home

October 31, 2001

Tired of sitting, Phil swiveled off the diner stool, scooped up his papers, and dropped them on the pile by the door for other people to read. He exchanged ¿*Qué pasas?* with Francisco, working the register. Phil spoke passable Spanish. He'd learned it after he realized you were limiting yourself in criminal practice in New York if you didn't. He paid his bill and picked up another cup of coffee to go.

Three blocks south he stopped on the corner, took out his cell phone. The cell phones went dead and live now in a contorted checkerboard as you moved through the city. He'd searched out and found the places on his usual routes that were most likely to work: more and more of those every day, this was one of the things people meant when they said things were getting back to normal.

Back to normal.

The walk to this corner took Phil past a bus shelter, its glass walls covered, as all the bus shelters were downtown, as the blank walls of buildings were, and fences, and newsstands, and mailboxes, with wind-tattered, rain-wrinkled Xeroxes: smiling people, at birthday parties, at graduation, holding beer bottles, holding babies; height and weight, tattoos and tiny birthmarks all detailed, and long lists of phone numbers, home, work, cell, brother's cell, daughter's cell, so you could call if you saw any of these people who would never be seen again. On the sidewalk at the base of the bus shelter, a muddled rainbow of melted wax clutched candle ends. Flames shivered on two red candles in tall glass holders painted with images of the Virgin of Guadeloupe, and also on a Yahrzeit candle, plain white wax in a round squat glass. Flowers, some fresh, some withered, lay among the candles, below the pictures. And embedded flat in the wax, a small pewter cross on a ribbon. You had to look closely for that; it was hard to see.

Back to normal.

Standing on the breezy corner where transmission was good, Phil finished his coffee. He squashed the cup into the overflowing trash can and wished, not for the first time, that he still smoked. He thumbed the phone's speed-dial button and lifted it to his ear.

Sally's "Hello?" was quiet and low, the voice of a woman unsurprisable, not strong, but determined.

"It's me." So many years he had been saying this to her, just this, *It's me.* Before that, *It's Phil*; before that, briefly, *Phil Constantine,* and early on, once or twice, *Hello, Mrs. Keegan, this is Phil Constantine, your husband's lawyer.*

So many years.

But the silence that answered him now was new.

"Are you all right?" he asked. "You heard the news? That reporter?"

After the silence: "Last night. I thought you'd call then."

"I didn't know if you wanted me to."

"I didn't. But I thought you would."

"I want to see you."

"You can't come out here."

"I'll meet you on the ferry."

They had done that before: Phil took the boat to Staten Island, Sally boarded on that side, and they were together for a stolen hour in neither her world nor his. In this itinerant province, Phil and Sally angled toward each other on a worn wooden bench or stood close at the rail. No matter the weather, they never rode inside. And while Phil took pleasure from Sally's warmth when stars burned fiercely through painful winter air, he favored still more the heat that radiated from her on high-summer noons, when other pairs of lovers stood not touching, or vanished into the boat's cooled interior, when the sky was hazed over and he could hear thunder rumbling.

On these trips they would cross the water without leaving the boat, as many times as time allowed. The harbor itself was no-man's-land, but their corner of the boat was their private country, their commonwealth of two.

It was on the boat, in the early years, that their treaties were forged, that the decrees they had issued over and over against each other were broken again and again. Until finally they admitted that though the way they lived was impossible, they could not stay apart.

Sally had never accused Phil of anything but this: not wanting to live in her world. Preferring their secret country, their world of stars and fog where even Kevin was a foreigner.

Part of this was true. And an important part was wrong. As life without Sally was unbearable to Phil, life without Kevin had quietly (Phil unable to say exactly when this happened) become unthinkable.

There had been about Kevin, always, the kind of sweet, breezy innocence that adults claim for children but that Phil didn't remember from his own childhood in himself, his cousins, his friends. Kevin's eyes always lit when Phil walked through the door.

Phil knew that light, saw it every day. His clients looked at him that way the first few times he entered the visiting rooms in their jails. They smiled expectantly, waited for the magic, and nine times out of ten he disappointed them. He couldn't get them out. Couldn't send them home. Couldn't tell them it was going to be okay. The light would fade, smothered by bewilderment and the start of despair.

"But you're supposed to be a hotshot," the client would complain, always that, some variation of that.

"Right," he'd say. "That's why you got three years instead of twenty."

Phil would leave, but never before he saw the new understanding dawning in their eyes: that bars, guards, and exercise yards were their lives now. That Phil Constantine hadn't been able to save them. But what Kevin wanted—candy, a kite, someone to push his fire truck around—that was easy. Phil loved Kevin because he never had to disappoint him.

Sally said: Stay. Nothing else, nothing so difficult. The ferry would become Phil's commuter route; they would no longer need it as their Shangri-la. Sunny summer afternoons and frosted winter mornings would belong to them, to be added to their long collection of whispered nights.

Pleasant Hills would welcome him, Sally assured him, circling him in the warmth of her arms one spent evening years ago, when they were still almost new to each other.

"Sure." He'd kissed her. "As soon as they forget who I am."

They'd had this dialogue before, and most of the time her soft pressure and his refusal closed the question. But this time Sally's face took on the distant, clouded look it always had when she talked about Markie. She held Phil closer, her red hair drifting around her shoulders, and said, "It wasn't your fault."

Phil had heard Sally tell him this before. It had been the first thing she'd said to him when they'd faced each other on the steps of St. Ann's after Markie's funeral mass.

An irreverent breeze was snapping the flag on the firehouse, trying to get a game going with the treetops, tossing grit in the pallbearers' faces. The hard glances that shot Phil's way when he entered the church told him how Pleasant Hills felt about him and his being there, but he'd known that even before he'd boarded the ferry. He found a place in a rear pew. As the unfamiliar service progressed, he sat, stood, read silently and aloud, though he didn't kneel, and not knowing the hymns, he didn't sing.

Filing with the other mourners from the gloom of the church after the coffin had passed, Phil squinted in the thin, bright sun. He looked for the widow, spotted her by the line of black limousines. Beside her a little boy, his hair red like hers, dug furiously in the dirt with a stick. Phil had glimpsed the boy in church. The child had squirmed and jiggled and had had to be quieted. Not quite three, Phil thought, though Phil was no judge of children's ages. He'd met the boy just once or twice before, though Markie had talked about him all the time. His name was Kevin. Why hadn't he ever asked his age?

Phil watched as the boy sat, as a dark-haired young woman bent to speak to him. Marian Gallagher, that's who she was. Worked for some tenants' rights group, a rising star in the nonprofit world. He'd talked to her. He'd been ready to put her on the stand, a character witness, if Markie's case had gone to trial, if there hadn't been a plea. The book on her: she never lied. A useful reputation for a witness to have, if she's on your side.

Marian Gallagher lifted the child to his feet, brushed dirt from his bottom. The boy scowled, tugged; she wouldn't let him go. Forget it, pal, Phil thought. There's always someone who gets in the way of your work. But take it from me: she's doing you a favor. That hole you were digging, it'll be deeper and wider and better in your head than it ever would've been, if she'd left you alone to dig it.

He waited at the top of the steps for the press of neighbors and family to thin. When it did, he walked down to Sally Keegan, took her black-gloved hand, and told her he was sorry.

She said, "Thank you," and then she said, "It wasn't your fault." Behind her black net veil her eyes shone a deep emerald. He was surprised at their color, expecting a paler green, and then surprised at his surprise. They'd only met twice before; when had he noticed her eyes?

She squeezed his hand and held it, though having said what he came to say, he had been about to turn and walk away, leave her to those who loved her. Instead, she bent to the child, truculent in the dark-haired woman's grip, and said, "Kevin, this is Mr. Constantine. He was a friend of your daddy's."

The child stared up at Phil, eyes narrowed, looking to see if anything about him was interesting at all.

Phil was hit with a gust of childhood memory: his neck aching after Saturday morning services as, not yet allowed to go home and change into jeans and grab his comic books or his basketball, he stood around the anteroom where they made kiddush, looking up at one adult after another, wondering how so many people could find so many stupid things to say to a kid.

Crouching outside St. Ann's, Phil didn't say anything. He met Kevin's eyes; they were the same green he remembered Sally's being, the gray-green he must have been wrong about. Without smiling, he winked. From his pocket he retrieved a roll of LifeSavers. He pried the red one off the top and offered it to Kevin.

Kevin stopped squirming, and his face glowed in an instant three-year-old grin. As he popped the candy in his mouth, Phil heard and ignored a disapproving click of the tongue from Marian Gallagher. He saw and ignored the protesting look she gave Sally. He knew and ignored what it meant: *You let your child—Markie's child—take food from the hand of this man?*

She never lied, and he guessed she wasn't much on hiding her feelings, either.

Phil winked at the boy again. Kevin squeezed both eyes shut, trying to respond. They grinned at each other, and Phil straightened up. Sally reached for Phil's hand. "Thank you," she said again.

They hardly knew each other, and she owed him nothing. Yet the morning she buried her husband, standing on the steps of the church surrounded by people staring at Phil in silent accusation (he was an outsider, he was the hired professional who'd failed, he was so easy to blame), Sally Keegan cleared her throat and said again, quietly and forcefully so everyone would hear, the one thing he could not say to himself: "It wasn't your fault."

A few years later, in the soft darkness, six-year-old Kevin asleep across the hall, she was saying the same thing again.

Phil rolled onto his back. "Your neighbors disagree."

"They'd get used to you."

"Oh, I don't think so."

"Kevin would like it if you were here more often."

He turned his head to her. "Kevin gets a kick out of Uncle Phil because I bring him funny presents and take him to the ball game. If I lived here, everything would be different."

"He needs a father."

"I'm not his father. Sal, he knows that."

Sally fell silent then. An hour or so later Phil left. Riding home on the late ferry, watching as the bridge slipped by and the towers grew, Phil tried to tell himself he was wrong. Who the hell cared where he lived? How well did he know his neighbors now, how much time did he spend at home? Maybe Sally's neighbors really would get used to him. Maybe Kevin really would like it. Why not move to Pleasant Hills, if that was what Sally wanted?

Because of Sally's eyes.

Because when Sally asked him to come live in Pleasant Hills, her eyes darkened. They went from clear green jewel to troubled water. No matter how close she held him, how she promised him it would be the right thing and it would work out, he knew it never would, when he looked in her eyes.

BOYS' OWN BOOK
Chapter 8

First In, Last Out

September 11, 1978: The Girls (Sally)

Sally's married Markie already, Sally has a son. Sally's smart, and she's beautiful: all the guys say that, they've always said it. Clouds of curly red hair, pale creamy skin, deep green eyes that can really smile, like people's eyes are supposed to but almost nobody's do. None of the guys has ever been to Ireland, but ever since they were small, when they looked at Sally, they knew what Irish princesses were like, in the days when elves and leprechauns sat down to a banquet with Irish royalty at a long table in the glen.

When Sally first starts going with Markie, freshman year, some of the guys can't believe it. They ask her, laughing over a beer: Sally, they say, what is it with this guy? They want to know about the princess and the fool, though there's not one of them who'd say it that way. Why Markie? they ask. Why a guy who can trip and fall when he's standing still? A guy who can find the gremlin in your dashboard wiring in ten minutes when the dealership gave up after three days, but he can't find two socks that match?

Sally just smiles.

Eddie Spano asks Sally out a couple of times before she takes up with Markie, and a couple of times after, like Eddie doesn't know when to quit, like he figures this Markie thing, she can't be serious. Eddie's Italian, he doesn't know anything about Irish princesses, and Jack asks the other guys, What's the matter, the wops don't have any pretty girls of their own? Sally won't go out with Eddie. A few of the guys start sort of keeping an eye on her, because Eddie, he can be a problem for girls he wants to date if they don't want the same thing, and even though, since she's dating Markie, this is sort of Markie's job, well, it's not a job anyone really thinks Markie can do. The guys do it quietly, because they don't want Sally to know. Sally doesn't like help she didn't ask for. But they do it, and they don't mind. Even the ones, Tom and Jimmy, who have girls they're going steady with, even they want to put their coats across puddles for Sally, or save her from dragons, or whatever it was heroes used to do for princesses in those long-ago days.

Seven years old: it's an autumn afternoon, and Sally's crying.

She's in her own front yard. Marian's come over to play, and she's about to ring the doorbell when she hears a little sad sound from behind the tree. She tiptoes over, and it's Sally sitting there, holding her knees to her chest, shiny lines down her face where her tears are slipping from her eyes. Sally looks up at Marian, her eyes red but the green in them greener than ever, because of the tears. Marian sits right down next to her and puts her arm around her: they're best friends. What's the matter? Marian asks. Did you get hurt?

Sally shakes her head. She doesn't wipe her eyes the way Marian would if someone found her crying, so people would think she's okay and not be worried. Sally just cries more and more, and she says: Tiger ran away.

Tiger is Sally's cat. He's not a kitten, Sally's parents already had him when Sally was born, but he still plays like a kitten, jumping for a string Sally holds. His name is Tiger because he has stripes, even though his are black and gray and that's not what tigers look like.

He ran away? Marian's whispering; this is a terrible thing.

He didn't come home since the day before yesterday, says Sally.

Your mom and dad can't find him?

They looked for him. But Daddy says boy cats sometimes, just sometimes, run away.

Marian keeps her arm around Sally and looks at the leaves rolling across the grass. She thinks about Tiger pouncing on the leaves. She looks really hard, to see if maybe he'll come tearing through the hedge to catch a leaf twisting through the air and she could say to Sally, Look, there he is! But there's nothing in the bushes but the wind.

Sally? Marian says. We'll look for him. We'll all go find him. Everyone will help.

Sally looks at Marian. She doesn't say anything, but then she sniffles and stops crying. Marian gives Sally a Kleenex, and she wipes her eyes. It seems to Marian that Sally's saying, not with words, just her eyes, I'm scared but I'll try.

Marian stands up. She smiles at Sally, who stands up, too, and they go off to look for Vicky and the boys.

They find them all in the park, the little park the kids are allowed to go to by themselves because you don't have to cross any big streets to get there. They're playing on the swings, seeing who can go the highest. Jack pushes his feet way, way out and almost swings upside down. None of them has ever seen anyone do that, go all the way over the bar, and some of the kids say no one can, but Jack says sure, you just have to not be afraid and go real hard. Marian and Sally watch as Jack pushes, pushes, but he doesn't tip over, and then Marian tells everyone about what they have to do.

The other kids stop swinging and listen. Tom asks a question: Did Tiger ever do this before, run away like this? Sally bites her lip and shakes her head. Jimmy just listens until Marian's through and then he looks around, up the block, back through the park, like he's figuring what to do, what's the right thing to do.

Vicky looks at Tom. What do you think? she asks.

Jack says, Wait, wait, just one more time, and he pumps way up high. Markie, when he hears what Marian's telling them, when he sees Sally's face, he stops watching Jack and moves over next to Sally. He says, It's okay, Sally, it's okay, I'll try really hard to find him for you. Jack swings way up once more, yells, Hey! This time! and Markie jerks his head around and watches, yelling, Come on, Jack! You can do it! but Jack doesn't do it this time either, the swing just stops at the top for a minute like it's thinking and then comes swooping down.

Tom says, Okay, come on, let's go, if we go look for him now, maybe he didn't go very far away yet.

Jack's still swinging, so Tom says: Jack.

Jack says, Yeah, yeah, okay, and jumps off his swing without stopping it so he has to run a few steps, but he doesn't fall.

Yeah, yeah, okay, says Jack, glaring back at the swing, like something bad happened that's the swing's fault.

You'll do it next time, Jack, says Marian. You almost did it. No one else ever did that, and you almost did.

Jack's looking like he's mad that he had to stop, like he wanted to keep flying like that, but he doesn't say anything mean to Marian like he would if it were one of the guys talking to him.

And we really need you to help, Marian says. I know we can find Tiger if you help.

Jack's looking at his swing, still moving by itself, and he shrugs, like he's not even listening, but the kids see him sort of smile, because of what Marian said. He looks at Sally, with her weepy eyes, and he growls, Well, come on, you guys, what are you waiting for?

They spread out around the neighborhood, crunching through the brown and yellow leaves, calling Tiger, Tiger, peeking behind bushes and under people's porches. They keep on looking until it starts to get dark and the streetlights are blinking on and they have to go home to dinner, to their own houses. They haven't found Tiger.

The next day after school they try again. They do the same things, in some of the same places and in other places, but nothing works, nothing makes Tiger come home.

You know, Jack says to Jimmy and Tom, when it's almost dinnertime and the three of them are together on the corner near St. Ann's. Maybe he went across Hylan, all the way over there.

That far? says Jimmy. Why?

Wanted to go someplace, Jack says. See what things are like somewhere else.

The cat?

Yeah, says Jack, the cat.

Tom gives Jack a long look, and maybe it's the way it's starting to get dark, but Jimmy never saw before how much Tom looks like his father, Mike the Bear.

Tom doesn't say anything, but he heads down the street, toward Hylan Boulevard. Jack follows him. After a moment Jimmy heads that way, too.

They go down to the end of the street, the three of them, and stand there watching the traffic whiz by. It's an eight-lane road, Hylan, though two lanes, one on each side, have cars parked in them. But that just makes it harder to see what's coming, headlights racing toward you in the purple light, buses stopping and cars swerving out around them. Jimmy's heart starts to beat faster.

No one asks anyone anything. They all know they're going to cross this street.

Red lights mean stop; green lights mean go. They learned that back when they were small. Because Tom says to, they wait until the light changes twice, so they can see how long it is. When it turns to green again, facing them, they run.

There's a place halfway across where you can stop, like a sidewalk stuck in the middle of the street. While they're watching the lights change, Tom says, Stop when we get to that sidewalk thing, and when they get there, he stops and Jimmy stops. But Jack, who runs slowest and gets there last, only stops for a second. Come on, you guys, he says, and laughs, and takes off again. He's looking back at Tom and Jimmy. He doesn't see that the light already changed.

A horn blasts at Jack from a car that slams to a stop in front of him. Jack looks up sharply and stumbles. He goes flying headfirst across the asphalt. Tom runs there, yanks on Jack's arm to try to pull him up. Cars are charging right at them. It's dark, and they're small. Jack's on the pavement, and Tom's bending over him, and Jimmy knows without thinking that the cars can't see them.

They're in the middle of the traffic now, Jack scrambling to his feet, the bright headlights on the cars racing forward. Jack's eyes are blank; Tom's yanking at him; and for Jimmy, something happens. Later he thinks and thinks about it, it should have been scary, but it wasn't, what it was, it was right, it was perfect. It's this: Time slows way down. Jimmy's standing there, and he has all the time he needs to take it all in, and he does, and then he knows, just *knows* exactly what to do. Jimmy moves. Steps toward the cars, not away, waves his arms like he saw a traffic cop do on this same street once when he was with his mom. The headlights stop, brakes screech, and horns squawk. Tom and Jack are standing like frozen staring statues, so Jimmy pushes them. That makes them start to move. They dash to the far sidewalk. The cars start pouring down the boulevard again, horns honking. The boys duck down and hide behind a parked car in case there's a real cop around.

But there's not. Jimmy's heart starts to beat more softly. Tom stands up, then the other two: they grin at each other. Jimmy's grin seems like something he can't help, something he couldn't stop if he wanted to, something that's coming from this tingling, sizzling place under his skin.

Tom says, Jack? What are you, nuts? What's the *matter* with you?

Jack says, I could've made it.

Tom keeps staring at Jack, but maybe he doesn't think of anything else he can say to him. He looks down, and then his face breaks into a grin again, like he can't help it, just like Jimmy can't. Tom says, Jimmy, *you're* crazy.

Jimmy says, Well, you two jerks, you were just standing in the middle of the street, like you had no place to go.

Tom and Jimmy grin at each other like Jack isn't there. Then Jack says, Hey, you guys. I mean, we're over here.

Oh yeah, says Tom. The cat.

Then they all laugh, like the cat's a joke they have now, though Jimmy knows that's not what they're laughing about, not the cat.

They look. They go around the neighborhood on the other side of the boulevard, calling Tiger, Tiger, going into people's front yards and crouching to peer under bushes and parked cars.

Tiger's not there, and they don't find him. When they cross the boulevard back, they wait on the sidewalk in the middle for the light to turn red and then green again for them, even though when they first get to that middle sidewalk, the light's still green and Jack says, Come on, you guys, we can make it. But Tom just shakes his head, so they wait.

Jimmy's mom is mad at him for coming home late. When she asks where he was, he says, I'm sorry, we were out looking for Sally's cat.

Her face stops looking mad, and she says, Oh, Jimmy, that's very nice of you. But please don't worry me by being so late again.

No, he says, I won't.

He waits for her to ask where they were looking and thinks how mad she's going to be when he tells. He hopes she doesn't ask who went with him, because he doesn't want to get Tom and Jack in trouble, too.

But she just hugs him and says, Go wash up for supper.

In the park the next afternoon, Tom tells the other kids about the big street-crossing expedition, Jack waving his hands around and throwing in words from time to time, Jimmy just quiet.

When he's done, Vicky says, Tom, you saved Jack's life.

Tom says, Me and Jack would've both got squished if Jimmy wasn't so crazy, standing right there in front of the cars.

Jimmy just shakes his head. Jimmy's thinking about the way time stopped, Jimmy's thinking about the sizzling under his skin.

Marian looks at Jimmy and almost smiles, but then she looks at Sally. Sally's smiling, because Tom and Jack and Jimmy were very brave and went on a big adventure for her, just like three princes in a fairy tale. But it's a sad smile, because she still doesn't have Tiger back.

No one ever finds Tiger. Tiger's gone.

Four days after the trip across Hylan Boulevard (now legendary, and involving, in the telling, buses, convertibles, and a huge semi like the one Jimmy's dad used to drive before he married Jimmy's mom; no one mentions the cat) Markie, who hasn't crossed any big streets or gotten home late to dinner, comes to Sally's house with a box. The box has holes in the sides and on the top that Markie poked with a pencil. When he hands the box to Sally, she almost drops it because it sort of moves around by itself.

I'm sorry I couldn't find Tiger for you, Markie says. I tried and tried. I wanted to be the one who found him.

I know, says Sally. You looked very hard. It's okay.

Sally takes the top off the box, and there's a white kitten inside, all fuzzy, with big blue eyes looking up at her. It opens its mouth and makes a tiny peep, like a bird.

My aunt's cat had kittens, Markie tells Sally. She said it was okay to give you one.

Sally looks at Markie. She picks up the kitten, and it purrs and tries to crawl into the place where her elbow bends.

But, says Markie, but she didn't have any gray and black ones.

That's okay, says Sally. That's okay. She strokes the kitten and smiles at Markie and says to him, White's my favorite color.

And when Eddie Spano starts asking Sally out, Sally won't date him, but she says no in some kind of way that doesn't piss him off. The guys keep an eye on her, but they find out she doesn't need that. Everyone's impressed, but that's Sally, no one's ever pissed off at Sally, not even Eddie Spano. So Sally marries Markie, and they invite everyone to the wedding, including Eddie, and everyone comes.

Sally's happy.

Laura's Story
Chapter 5

———

Secrets No One Knew

October 31, 2001

Laura was sitting at Harry's desk.

The big soft chair with a pattern like a Persian carpet was where she'd started. But when Laura was in the big chair, Harry was at his desk; that was how it had always been, since she had begun to take space in Harry's life, since she had made space for him in hers. Sitting there, Laura couldn't shake the feeling that Harry was about to walk out of the kitchen, the bedroom, the bathroom, to ruffle her hair, go over and pull up the creaky old desk chair, and sit down to his work. She couldn't concentrate, waiting for Harry.

Her other usual spot was Harry's bed. That was out of the question.

So she sat at Harry's desk, his few files piled neatly on the left side, notebooks on the right. Two pin-sharp pencils rested eraser to eraser against the ridge on Harry's keyboard. More than once, when his syncopated clicking stopped, Laura had looked over to see Harry picking up one of those pencils, bringing it toward the blue monitor screen as though to correct a mistake, a bad thought, in the white copy glowing there. The pencil would hover, Laura never sure if it was threatening the newer technology—behave, because there's still me—or reassuring it—I've got your back. Then he would drop the pencil into the ridge again and go on typing until he hit the next bump in the road.

Laura had always meant to ask Harry how the pencil and the screen felt about each other. Always meant to.

Soon she would have to start going through Harry's files, and the notebooks, and the computer, too, though she wasn't expecting much. Harry threw things out. This was a habit from his early days, the days his Pulitzers came from, three of them lined up on the wall, all a little crooked with vibration and neglect. "That one," Harry had confided last spring, pointing an accusatory finger at the plaque in the middle, "is for a six-piece team story. Eight reporters. I wrote the fourth piece. It doesn't really count." Laura had reached out and straightened the one that didn't count and then the others. She didn't think they'd been straightened since.

Those plaques had been won and hung years ago, before Harry had developed an intimate relationship with gin. In the newsroom Laura had seen young reporters lift their eyebrows, shrug as Harry stood at the shredder, feeding it page after page of notes for stories that would be lucky to see the inside of Section Two. She never knew if Harry saw the eyebrow-lifters, or if he cared, until the day her first front-page story ran—below the fold, but it was her first—and he had grabbed her, kissed her, and murmured romantically in her ear, "Now shred your notes."

Laughing, giddy at her success, she reminded him that that sort of paranoia seemed to be out of fashion at the *Tribune*. Harry, one arm around her waist, had pointed to one of the eyebrow-lifters hard at work across the room. "That bozo," he said mildly, speaking as if he and Laura were at the zoo and he knew an interesting fact about a creature, "doesn't shred his notes. That's all right; he'll never write anything worth a subpoena. You, my little oyster, will. Keep the quotes, to protect the *Tribune*'s ass. Destroy all else." He looked at her gravely. "The great and powerful Oz has spoken."

Laura had spent the rest of that afternoon sorting and shredding her notes.

So she was not holding out much hope for Harry's files, his notebooks or computer. But there would be something. Someplace to start: a question between the lines, a name she didn't know, a call Harry had made that had never been returned. To find that starting point was why she had come.

But first, for the hundredth time, she had reread the story that had begun, and now, she thought, ended, everything.

And been stopped, frozen, by the story's final line.

The investigation is continuing.

Continuing. Laura stared at that word, unable to move her astounded eyes from such an outrageous lie. Continuing? Nothing was continuing. Everything now was new. Everything had to start over.

She shoved Harry's chair away from the desk, paced the room with her hands deep in her back pockets. Whenever she was stuck, this was Laura's way, to stride back and forth frowning at the carpet as though whatever word, phrase, fact, she needed were hiding there.

Sit down, Stone, Harry would tell her. *You're driving me crazy. Come have a drink.*

No, you drink, she used to answer, *I'm working.*

Harry would shrug and drink. Laura would go on pacing; or she would storm out the door, run down the nine flights to the lobby, and head uptown on Broadway and then, eventually (and it never took long), back again. Sometimes she stopped at Starbucks for mocha cappuccinos, extra whipped cream. Harry would accept his gravely, savor it slowly, and, when finished, go back to his bottle.

And always, somewhere on the sidewalks, like a dropped quarter, Laura would have found the word she needed. Her cappuccino would sit, cooling and untouched, as she returned to work.

Harry's advice to her: *Join a gym.*

Now Laura stood at the window. Blades of sun glinted off the river's silver. She didn't like the river to be silver, she never had; she couldn't see anything in water this color. She'd been crying again; she was through with that now, her cheeks sticky and dry, but she was stopped, frozen. These had been tears not of grief but of fury. The floodwaters of her rage had astonished her.

The anger, she now saw, had been building all the time she'd been reading, but she hadn't felt it, the way you might not feel the current changing as you drifted downstream until, too late, you heard a new roar and without warning found yourself crashing over the falls.

After she'd read the article, she'd begun to pace, striding the length of Harry's living room, toward the window, spin, away, toward again, back and forth as though she were in a jail cell. As she made a turn, the silence was splintered by a sudden shout: "Goddamn you, Harry!" She stopped, terrified. Then she realized the voice was her own, and that frightened her more.

And then another voice, mild and amused: *Me?*

Harry. She spun wildly, but of course he wasn't there. He was dead, he was gone. The hell with him, though: she wasn't letting him off that easily.

"Yes, you!" she hissed raggedly. "Why didn't you leave that story alone?"

Why didn't I—? Please, my little minnow.

Strange how she could hear him so clearly but not see him at all. But she didn't have to see him. She knew that tone, and the infuriating half-smile that went with it.

He asked, *Was it I who was spouting that bilge about the north star and the noises in the dark?*

"It was dangerous!" she shouted. "I didn't know that!"

Would it have mattered?

"Of course it would have!"

Of course it wouldn't have. Except to make it more exciting.

"Exciting?"

But she was pretending she didn't know what he meant, so he pretended he hadn't heard her.

Quietly, standing in his empty living room, she said, "Couldn't you have been careful?"

I was very careful.

"Then why are you dead?"

The savagery of her anger rolled right off Harry. *Ah,* he said indulgently. *That's the ticket to your Pulitzer, isn't it?*

"My what?"

You can't not have thought of that.

"Thought of what?"

Tsk, tsk. The truth about what happened to Harry Randall: that's a very big story.

"You can't think that's why I'm going after it?" Laura was aghast. "Harry, I'm going after it for you. To get justice for you."

Of course you are. You're going after it because, story or not, it's the truth and the truth matters.

"I don't like the way you said that."

No, why should you? You're still dew-bedecked enough to believe it. But I was old enough to know better. In fact, until you came along, I did know better. My mistake was listening to you.

"To me?"

To you, quoting me. So really, it's all my fault, you see.

Laura didn't see.

For believing such claptrap in my own misguided youth, Harry patiently explained. *And going on to fill young minds with it. Specifically, yours. So you could pour it on thick at a later date. Sucking me back under when in fact I'd escaped. Yes, my sweet octopus. My fault entirely.*

"Harry?" Laura had only one thing to say, only one thing she meant. "Harry, please. Don't leave me."

Too late. The familiar faint amusement and the unseen shrug. And silence.

And the tears of fury, then, like the cataclysmic breaking of a dam.

Now Laura stood lost, staring down at the river. She realized she was furious with it, too. Goddamn Harry, and goddamn the river!

Hating the river, she watched it flow, all that charging, hurtling water, not making a sound.

She coughed; she was thirsty, from the crying. She drank three glasses of water as she stood at Harry's ancient sink. Maybe, she thought as she gulped, maybe this water was like the river water, all water in the end the same. Maybe, once the water was part of her, its need for movement would teach her how to move.

She put her glass carefully in the dish drainer; it clinked on Harry's black mug. She squeezed her eyes against new tears. An enormous powerful need surged in her, the need to be gone, to get out of this place Harry was also gone from.

Fear rose in Laura, flowed around her, threatened to cut off her breath. She swallowed, walked tentatively back into the living room as though wading into a stream whose depth and speed she didn't know.

She could make a break for it: throw open the door, dash through the hall, circle down the stairs, and come bursting onto the sidewalk as she had done so many times.

And then what? Would she find anything, any words or ideas, lying on the sidewalk now, waiting for her to pick them up? And who would she buy cappuccino for, on her way back?

Would she come back?

Laura turned away from the door—she wasn't sure she could keep from plunging toward it, as long as she could see it—and pulled the chair up to Harry's desk. She sat at the edge of it, not her full weight, ready to leap up at any moment. Heart racing, she opened the first of Harry's files. She took from her bag a fresh new pad and two of her own new pens. She didn't touch Harry's sharpened pencils.

An hour later all she had was a list of names and numbers.

It wasn't really right to say there was nothing here. Harry's contact lists; pages torn from notebooks to preserve attributed quotes; Xeroxes of periodicals he'd researched and quoted or used for background. All these filled Harry's neatly piled files.

But what she was looking for: it wasn't here.

Harry's death hadn't been payback for anything he'd written: she was sure of that. Anyone ruined (or about to be ruined) by Harry's stories might have thought murderous thoughts, made muttered threats, nursed dark dreams. But once the cat was out of the bag, what was the point of going after the man who'd untied the string?

Poetic metaphors, Stone, the mark of an amateur, Harry would have scolded.

Laura smiled at that; then she froze as it hit her for the first time that there were people who had had nothing to do with Harry's death who were glad it had happened. People who right now, this moment, might be raising a glass to their hero, his unknown killer.

She hated them.

But those glitter-eyed vultures, feasting on Harry's death, they hadn't killed Harry. It was axiomatic in the news business: the safest time to be an investigative reporter, they told one another cynically, is the day your story runs. The story that's dangerous is the one you're working on for tomorrow.

And McCaffery's papers: that's what Harry had been working on. The new thing he'd found, just yesterday. Hot stuff, McCaffery's papers, Harry had said. That probably meant: dangerous to someone.

And Laura knew what was dangerous: the truth.

But about McCaffery's papers, there was nothing here.

She'd checked Harry's e-mail, his voicemail. She hadn't found his cell phone. Had he remembered, as he so often didn't, to take it with him? She'd studied every scrap of paper, each note she'd found. She'd gone through the pockets of the slacks and jackets left behind, in case he'd been planning to wear a thing and then changed his mind. These, of course, were his summer jackets, linen, seersucker. Harry's wool suits were in storage. Recently he'd said, as they walked home from dinner through an evening chill, that it was time to ransom them out.

When was that, that Harry had told her this? Three days ago. What had happened in between? She had no idea, except for brief, bright flashes: Georgie's face yesterday, reflected in the window above the river when she turned away from him, from what he'd told her. Herself staring at her computer screen while she waited for Leo to arrive this morning. Why hadn't she memorized every second of those days, Harry's last days, written them down, filmed and recorded them, drawn pictures, so she could have them now, so she could look at him, hear him talk, laugh with him? What had she been doing that was so damn important, what memories did she have now that she'd made in these last few days instead of the ones she ached to have?

Laura looked down at the notepad, names and numbers in a tidy list. Names on the left, numbers on the right, ruled blue lines between them like the rungs of a ladder waiting to be climbed.

Stone! she heard Harry howl. *Stop that simile! Mash that metaphor! Annihilate those allegories! Fight, team, fight!*

PHIL'S STORY
Chapter 6

————

The Invisible Man
Steps Between You and the Mirror

October 31, 2001

Almost always, when Sally spoke about Markie, Phil got the sense that where Sally was, the sun had gone behind clouds. The exception: when she was talking to Kevin. Then her eyes sparkled, and the stories she told her son about his father were funny ones, or tender. And Kevin, a child never happy unless he was in motion, would listen and be still.

"He gave me a kitten once, when we were little," she said to Kevin when he was eight. Kevin asked if it was Socks. "It was Snowflake. Socks's great-gran." It had been late on one of their excursion afternoons, the three of them returning from Manhattan, from the circus. Phil didn't like circuses, or zoos, not even aquariums: places where animals were confined to amuse people left him restless and impatient. But Kevin wanted to go to the circus.

"The first time we went, we were ten," Sally told Phil. He'd just arrived on a late-night boat. The cat had been out late, too, and had followed Phil up the walk, meowing. "Before that there was a show that used to come. Spivey's Traveling Circus. It wasn't much, but when we were little, we didn't know the difference."

"It doesn't come anymore?"

"They built a Buick dealership on the lot they used to use. Besides, the elephant was old. I think she retired."

Because Sally knew how Phil felt about circuses, she didn't ask if he'd come. Because Phil knew how Sally felt about traveling solo off Staten

Island, he'd pulled three tickets from his shirt pocket a few nights later and asked if anyone had plans for Saturday.

Kevin was wild for the circus, unable to sit still. Each time the acts changed, he tried to watch everything all at once. Finally choosing, he'd lean forward, more and more, then leap up with excitement. His seat would snap up, and every time, he'd turn, stare, and laugh and laugh, delighted that even the chairs were part of the show.

Phil loved watching Kevin, and watching Sally watch Kevin. The circus itself he'd hated, though he was unexpectedly gripped by the high-wire act. Briefly he forgot the sad elephants standing on hind legs and the great cats jumping unnaturally into fire. Jolted by adrenaline as though he were the one somersaulting into space, he waited without breathing for the flyer's arms to make contact with the catcher's. And if they hadn't? Who would have been more frightened, he wondered, who more thrilled, as the flyer fell?

At the start of the ferry trip back—because Kevin was along, it was just a boat ride, and their Brigadoon did not emerge—Kevin, wedged between Phil and Sally on a smooth wooden bench, listened to the story of Sally, Markie, the boys, and Snowflake. The second the tale was over, he pushed off the bench. He swung the circus flashlight Phil had bought him, then gave it to Sally to hold while he played a growling tiger pawing at the trainer's whip. He tried standing on his head like the clowns and asked why the ringmaster didn't do any tricks of his own.

"He's directing everybody," Sally said.

"Can I be him?"

"You could try. I'm not sure how much fun he has, though."

Kevin tried directing other passengers to get up and do tricks, but it didn't work, not even once. "It's not fun," he declared. Then, as though struck by a thought, he pushed back into his place between them on the bench and asked about Snowflake again, and Sally smiled and told the story a second time.

Phil bought them all ice cream when they got off the ferry. The flower shop in the terminal had one bunch of roses left. He bought them when Sally was busy with Kevin and swept them out from behind his back with a big "Ta da!" that made both Sally and Kevin laugh. He stayed at Sally's for another hour. When he left, Kevin jumped up from his toy fire engine, wrapped Phil in a bear hug, and said, "Thanks, Uncle Phil."

"Any time, pal."

Kevin dropped to the floor again. He started pushing the engine around the room, but stopped and looked up at Phil. "Were you friends with my daddy, Uncle Phil?"

Oh, it was so much more complicated than that: but Kevin was eight. "Yes."

"You remember Snowflake?"

"No."

Kevin's face took on a worried look, as though this were unexpected. "But you remember Socks?"

"Socks? Sure. I think he's out back."

Kevin nodded and switched his attention to the fire truck. He drove it right through the kitchen and into the yard.

Phil kissed Sally goodbye before he opened the front door. As he passed the driveway, he spotted Kevin squatting there. He would have spoken to him, said goodbye a second time, but Kevin was busy sneaking Socks an unauthorized can of sardines.

That circus afternoon, just before he left, Sally said, "Move in with us."

Phil didn't answer, but as though he had, she smiled and said, "I know. I just thought I'd try again."

It was also true that Sally had never given a moment's serious thought to the idea that she and Kevin might leave Pleasant Hills, might move across the water into Phil's world.

When he'd first suggested that, Sally's answer was that she wanted Kevin to live somewhere he belonged, not a place—Phil's downtown loft, she meant—where things had been pushed aside and room made for him.

So Phil offered neutral addresses, worlds they could create together: a co-op on the Upper West Side, and Kevin could go to private school; or a house on Long Island with a pool in the backyard. Sally smiled at these ideas, the same smile Phil had seen her give Kevin when, at six, he brought home a Valentine's Day heart, painted red and stuck with sequins and plastic pearls. And Phil came to understand that "somewhere he belonged" meant only one thing to Sally: it meant Pleasant Hills.

And so the years reeled slowly out, so many years. Sometimes Phil found himself looking around, surprised to be where he was, wondering where those years had gone, wondering sometimes if Sally wondered, too. So many years, when their lives had been locked together while their worlds, to each other, were mist-shrouded, hidden.

That was before.

And since?

Phil had seen little of Sally since September 11. Not even spoken to her as often as he'd wanted. Not since those first frantic hours when they were desperate to find Kevin, Phil calling Sally over and over as the connection broke and came back, Phil jogging thirty blocks uptown to the office of a friend whose power had not gone out so he could scan the names of missing firefighters on website lists as they were updated and grew ever longer.

Jimmy McCaffery's name was one of the first posted. Phil read it with disbelief but no other emotion; that all came later.

Kevin's name never appeared. Phil had called everyone he could think of, everyone he could reach, all of them equally despairing, no one able to help. He had been useless, come up with nothing, but another firefighter, someone Sally didn't know, called Sally in the late afternoon. He told her Kevin was at NYU Hospital, hurt but all right. Sally had called Phil, weeping a mother's tears of relief.

That day Sally couldn't cross the harbor from Staten Island to be with Kevin at the hospital: all ferries were moored, all bridges closed, all trips canceled. So she had gone to church. She wanted, she told Phil on the crackling cell phone, to give thanks for the life of her son, and to pray for the lost.

Phil, sitting at that point on a curb in a milling crowd of strangers, smoke stinging his eyes, said, Good, said, Being with people, the comfort of the church, that's a good idea. I'll go up to the hospital, he promised, I'll go see Kevin. Weeping, she said to tell Kevin she'd come as soon as she could. She asked Phil to call from the hospital. She asked him if he'd be all right. Automatically, he said he would. Maybe she believed him; maybe she just knew there was nothing she could do for him. She told him she loved him and said goodbye. He thumbed off his phone, hearing the echo of Sally's voice, the joyful catch in it. He wondered what was in the voices of the hundreds, thousands, of other mothers, wives, children, clutching for that same golden ghost, hope. What would be in their voices after the phantom flashed and vanished, leaving empty hands, empty air? Or lingered, laughing, just beyond reach, disturbing sleep, distracting days, for a long, long time? And faded, finally disappearing, after that.

Now, on this bright corner six weeks later, it was again Sally's voice that riveted Phil. This time, no joy, no warmth: just cold, windswept distance.

He said again, "I'll meet you on the ferry."

She said, "No."

"There's another reporter," he said. He felt like he was warning her. Against what? He didn't know.

"I don't want you calling me."

But she didn't hang up.

And this was his chance. To explain, persuade, to show her, tell her: it had all been for her, everything had been for her. A wizard, his opponents called him, one of the Dark Side's best, words his weapon, wielded with a wild, sweeping daring and a jeweler's precision. He could use that weapon now, surely, he could win this battle.

But she was the one to find words first, and those words were only "Goodbye, Phil," and he was left alone.

MARIAN'S STORY
Chapter 5

———

The Bodies of the Birds

October 31, 2001

One blowy, dark autumn day some years ago, Marian had lingered on the steps of Holy Innocents after mass to speak to Father Domingo about secrets.

What had been an early morning cloudburst had retrenched to a hostile dampness; a sky the color and weight of lead sagged over wet sidewalks stuck with fallen leaves. Father Domingo, the keen-eyed junior priest at Holy Innocents, lately come to this church and to his profession (and this was why Marian had selected him: she hoped for the counsel of someone to whom her questions, like most questions, was new and thus worthy of serious thought), had shown no surprise at the gravity of her inquiry or the time and place she had chosen to pursue it.

On the church steps, a cold, determined wind pushed the hem of the priest's cassock around his ankles and tangled Marian's hair. Father Domingo tilted his head to hear her question, then frowned thoughtfully, clasping his hands behind him.

The conundrum she posed was hypothetical. A man carelessly throws a match away, realizes he has started a fire, and runs inside the burning building, rescuing the inhabitants. All are grateful: the man has saved them. Their home is destroyed, their possessions lost, but the man, their rescuer, helps them rebuild. Their losses are great, but they take heart from the selfless spirit of their benefactor. They are not sure they could have gone on, they say, but for his help and his example. He never tells them, and they never learn, that it was he who started the fire.

Marian's questions were two: Do this man's bravery and good deeds outweigh his guilty action? And: Is it cowardly of him to fail to reveal the truth, or courageous of him to bear the burden of this knowledge alone so that people who need something to believe in can continue to believe in him?

"We need never bear our burdens alone," Father Domingo said, in the suede-soft accent that made him the darling of the Dominicans and Mexicans who worshiped at Holy Innocents. "God stands always ready to share the weight of our burdens."

Marian's heart sank. Still, she persevered. "Sometimes people can only come to God through good works."

"This man, then, he is coming to God?"

"I don't know. But the people who believe in him, what if they believe he was sent to them by God, to give them faith?"

"Believing in a mortal man, this is a sad delusion."

"But if he tells the truth, people might lose their faith."

"In God? Or in him?" Father Domingo's eyes fixed on Marian's. He seemed to want to bore deep within her, below the protective stones and the nurturing soil, to the roots of her heart. She wanted to look away, but she could not.

The rising wind snatched at her scarf, trying to draw her attention as though to warn her of danger, but Marian had another question, in some ways the only question. "If someone else had seen him throw the match?"

"Would you like to come into the confessional?" Father Domingo suggested.

Marian flushed and shook her head. She had been to confession earlier, had taken communion at mass. Like most people, she was not lacking in sins to confess. But how to be sure what was a sin, what required confession; it was really this that Marian was asking.

The priest met her eyes again and she shuddered: had he found her core and seen the darkness there? "Then you must ask God," he said.

Marian mumbled her thanks to Father Domingo. She walked slowly down the steps. She would ask God: tonight in her prayers, and tomorrow, and next Sunday at mass. But she had been asking God this question for many years already.

Years later, following mass at St. Ann's on the Sunday after September 11, Marian stood with Sally in the sunshine outside the great carved doors. They hugged each other, holding on, then wiped their eyes and smiled at each other.

"I went to the hospital to see Kevin yesterday," Marian said.

"He told me."

"He looks good." Marian, who would have said this to Sally in any case, was grateful that it was true.

"He's doing well, the doctor said." Sally cast her eyes down. In these times and in this place, she was ashamed, Marian thought, of the joy she felt because her son was going to live.

Marian felt a hand rest on her shoulder. "Hey, you two," said Tom. He hugged Sally, and then Marian; his strong arms were surprisingly comforting in this time when comfort was rare.

"You okay?" Tom asked Sally. "I called NYU this morning, finally got to talk to Kevin. He sounds good."

"You got through on the phone?" Marian asked.

"Took me an hour."

"He's doing well. I'm going over there this afternoon," Sally said.

"To the hospital? Want me to take you?" Tom offered. "The bridge's open."

That was sweet, Marian thought. Sally didn't like to travel into Manhattan alone; her friends all knew. And Tom was one of her friends. He always had been. He had never turned his back on her, though her husband had gone to prison for killing his brother.

Sally was hesitating. It was a lot of trouble for Tom to go to. Marian stepped in.

"I'm just having coffee with Dad, then I'm going back," she said. "Tell me what ferry you want to make, and I'll go with you."

Sally smiled. "Thanks."

"Okay," Tom said, "but the offer's still open. Marian, can we talk a minute?"

Sally gave them each a quick kiss. "I'll call you at your dad's," she said to Marian, and left them.

Marian and Tom stood in the sun, and Tom told Marian about the fund that had just been created, the McCaffery Memorial Fund. Listening, Marian felt a lurch of fear. She told herself impatiently that was foolish. Jimmy was a hero. He was famous for unselfish courage. This fund would celebrate that. This was just the kind of thing New York needed right now. What was there to be afraid of?

"They made me chairman of the board," Tom was saying. "But none of us knows anything about this. I'd like—the board would like—to ask you to be the director."

"What? Oh, no." Marian moved a small step back, as though fighting a magnetic field. "Tom, I can't."

Tom gave a shake of his head. "Please." He was handsome, as he had always been, with his dark hair and blue eyes that, when fixed on you, saw nothing else. Marian, seeking respite from Tom's eyes, glanced over the crowd. She saw Vicky on the sidewalk with her son Michael, named after Tom's father, Big Mike Molloy. When Vicky and Tom separated, Tom had been the one to move out; he'd bought a house two blocks away. Marian had asked him then if he'd considered a bigger move, a cleaner break. No, he said, sounding surprised: Pleasant Hills was where he belonged.

Marian watched Michael kiss his mother and stride away. The boy was twenty-two and looked so like Tom had looked that for a brief, disorienting moment, like a tremor or a spell, she found herself searching the crowd for Jimmy, for Markie, for herself, all of them exuberant and invincible as they had been, back then.

The moment passed, everything snapped back into focus. Marian was standing with Tom on the church steps, and Tom was speaking about the McCaffery Fund.

The idea was not Tom's, as the press later had it. Tom was inclined, as Marian was, to let Jimmy's legend rest, though his reasons were surely different. But other people—men who, as boys, had won trophies on teams Jimmy had captained; women who, when girls, had contrived innumerable accidental encounters with him in noisy school corridors, had whispered jealously to each other as Marian walked by—had elected this loss to stand for all the unbearable others. They had chosen to take action now to console themselves for their helplessness on that day, and they had come to Tom.

As he was coming to Marian.

"Please," Tom said again. "He meant a lot to a lot of people. People want to give money—hell, it's all they can do. Think of all the good you can do with this, Marian."

He'd smiled, and she'd had to smile, too. She was an Eskimo, and Tom knew, as he always had, just what to say so that she would be most likely to sign up for a delivery of ice.

She was nevertheless steeling herself and planning to refuse, when the church doors creaked open. She and Tom stepped aside to let a group of people pass. At their center walked Eddie Spano, talking on his right to someone Marian didn't know, while his left hand gripped the arm of his father, Aldo. Eddie was almost bald—had it been that long since she'd seen him? But it was the sight of Aldo Spano that stunned and scared her. When they all were young, Mr. Spano had been a legendary monster, lying in wait to eat you (or at least smack you, though you were not his) and teaching his two sons to be like him. Now he leaned on a cane, and on his son, his movements crabbed, imprisoned by that ferocious and insatiable jailer, age. The face she remembered as terrifyingly scarlet was dull, wrinkled, and soft, like something beginning to rot. While Marian watched, Aldo Spano looked to Eddie as though unsure what to do. Eddie spoke to his father calmly, then turned back to his conversation as though he had done this many times before. Marian drew a breath.

That Aldo Spano was no longer frightening was, to Marian, a fearful thing.

Tom watched her; Tom, because he was Tom, knew what she was thinking and how to turn it to his use.

"It's just us now, Marian," he'd said, as they both watched the Spanos' slow progress down the stairs, Eddie half-lifting his hesitating father to each step. "There are no grown-ups anymore. It's just us. We have to do it."

And so she'd told him she'd think about it. From the top of the steps she'd searched the crowd, found her own father in it, and hurried to him.

As Marian, still thinking of smoke and prayers, reached the door to her own office, she heard Elena call after her.

"Marian? That reporter, it was all right I gave her your cell phone? I wasn't sure, but you said, the press—"

"Yes, of course. Thank you," Marian added with a quick smile.

Since September 11 Marian had been interviewed often in print, on radio, and on TV. To discuss the rebuilding of Lower Manhattan—and the role of the MANY Foundation and the Downtown Council in it— she made herself available to any journalist at any time. It was one of her responsibilities, one of the tasks she felt called upon to perform. Because MANY's phones still didn't work, she had given her staff permission to give her cell phone number out as liberally as she had jealously guarded it before.

And since she'd taken on the administration of the McCaffery Fund, she had been repeatedly asked about that, too, and she'd always replied with her gentlest smile and most assured tone.

"Our mission is outreach and support for Fire Department recruitment," she'd told Larry King, and she'd taped that interview and later watched it carefully, to study her own face, her body language, as she said, "The New York City Fire Department was Captain McCaffery's life. His dream was to see a department that would continue to be the best in the world, because it would contain, it would welcome, *all* New York's Bravest."

As a rule Marian did not worry about her public image, what she projected or how she was perceived. She tried to tell the truth and to be kind. She did not waste her time in inordinate concern about whether those intents were understood. Time spent speculating and fretting was time wasted on vanity, and Marian did not approve of vanity, least of all in herself.

But in this interview, she'd been talking about Jimmy.

This ground was too unsteady, this path too treacherous, for her to tread without looking back: she needed to assure herself of where she'd been. She needed to prepare herself for where she was to go.

She had run the tape three times, finally deciding she was satisfied with her look of comforting, of caring and firm resolve. "Through the McCaffery Fund," she watched herself say, "we will be able to reach out to communities that have historically not had the opportunity to serve the people of New York through this extraordinary department. In this way we will help make Captain McCaffery's dream a reality."

"A rainbow department," Larry King had said. "Captain James McCaffery's dream. We'll be right back."

It was beautiful, this dream, it was comforting to imagine heroes of all races, all colors, shapes, all beliefs and loves, being given the chance to help and save, to use their courage and their caring no matter who they were, no matter what. Beautiful, and a worthy goal for this Fund in Jimmy's name. It was a condition Marian had laid down for her service to the Fund, that this be its focus.

In truth Marian did not know what had been in Jimmy's dreams since the nights when they were young. She did not know what he had hoped for, what he had feared, over the years, but she did not imagine that since those nights his sleep had been untroubled.

Marian was not sure that the dead looked down from Heaven, or that they benefited from prayers rising or actions taken on their behalf, though Father Connor had always told them this was one of the purposes of worship. She did not know if Jimmy had made it to Heaven, was not sure what kind of heroism outweighed which sins. She did not know whether good done by a person in this life could redeem the darkness of a life gone before.

Once she had been sure of these things and so many others. The unsureness that now surrounded her, the sense that the ground was shifting under her and she had no firm place to stand: was it because, after so long, after a lifetime, of working to keep a vast empty space between them, she stood so close to Jimmy now?

Accepting the leadership of the McCaffery Fund had made her a visible target for Harry Randall's sharpshooting and all that followed. But more and more Marian suspected this: her true error was not the public revelation but the private one: that the bridge between herself and Jimmy that she'd crossed, when the time came, without looking back, she had never burned.

Seated at her desk, Marian looked at the papers in her hands, not sure how they'd gotten there. There were words on her computer screen, her coffee cooling on her side table. She turned to the window, to the dust-covered buildings, the rumbling trucks, the bright fall sunlight filtering through smoke and sprayed water.

She stood, stuck her head from her door, called down the corridor to Elena. "That reporter will be coming here soon. Make sure there's milk for the coffee, would you, and cookies or something?" Not wanting to give this interview was one thing; but since she had agreed to it, upholding MANY's reputation for comfortable hospitality was quite another.

Really, though, it was not all right. Not Elena's fault, nothing Elena had done that she should not have. But giving Marian's cell phone number to Laura Stone from the *New York Tribune* so she could ask Marian questions about Harry Randall was not all right at all.

BOYS' OWN BOOK
Chapter 9

The Women in the Tent

September 11, 1978: The Girls (Vicky)

Vicky is Tom's and has always been, nothing else ever possible. Six-year-olds on the front stoop, whispering secrets only children have; twelve-year-olds giving each other their first kiss, guessing, and rightly, what the taste of one another's lips will be.

Six years old: at least, most of the kids are six, except Markie's still five for another month, and Jack, well, Jack's already seven. It's a sticky, steamy summer day, and going to rain later, to thunder and lightning and pour down in buckets, the kids can tell. They're lying on the grass in Tom and Jack's backyard, watching the clouds roll across the sky, seeing if the clouds look like anything. People in the books their moms read them are always pointing at clouds that look like dogs or flowers or ferryboats, but the kids don't see those things, they don't see any pictures in the clouds at all.

Maybe because they're thunderclouds and they're moving, Jack says, maybe clouds only look like other things when they're just sitting there, when they don't have somewhere to go.

Vicky smiles and throws a handful of grass at Jack, as though he's making a silly joke. When she does that, Jack looks surprised.

Sally says, The kids at school said there are baby turtles in the pond in the woods. I wish we could go see them.

Markie sits up. Nobody's ever seen a baby turtle, and the kids have been hanging around the backyard since after lunch. And when Sally says something like this, about something she wants, it makes the boys all want to be the one who helps her get it. But the woods are a long way off, and it's complicated, something the moms and dads know how to do, lots of rights and lefts. Some of the kids only just learned which is their right and which is their left.

Tom doesn't say anything, and Jimmy doesn't, either, but Jack says, We can go to the pond, I know how to get there.

Sally says, You do?

Sure, says Jack, it's easy. He scrambles to his feet, dusts off his pants, says, Come on.

Markie jumps up, too, and for a minute it's only him. But then Tom rubs his hand over his head. Okay, he says.

Do we have to cross any big streets? Marian wants to know, because they're not allowed to cross the big streets, not even Jack.

No, uh-uh, says Jack. It's right over there.

So the little parade of kids follows Jack up this street and around that corner, through this empty lot and over that mud at the gate of one of the places where new houses are being built. It's a long walk, and as they go along, Vicky starts to frown. Tom looks back at her, then slows down so she can catch up to him. He whispers, I know how to get there, too. I don't know this way, but I know a different way.

Vicky asks, Do you know how to go home? And when Tom nods, she smiles at him, a big beaming smile.

And Jack does know how to get there. They come to the end of a block none of the others have been on before, a dead end at some unfamiliar trees, and Jack plunges straight in. They follow him, and he goes this way and that way and they come out at the top of a ridge, and when they look down, there's the pond and the trees they know and the path that usually takes them there, when they're with their moms and dads.

Everybody says, Hey, Jack! and Markie slaps Jack on the back, and then Tom and Jimmy do, like they're grown-ups and Jack just won a bet on the Mets. Everyone slaps Jack until Jack has to say, Hey, you guys, knock it off, but he's laughing when he says it.

But, says Sally, after everyone's through telling Jack how smart he is, but how do we get down there? Because Sally still wants to see the baby turtles.

Easy, says Jack. He sits and with his heels digging in and his hands grabbing tree roots, he half-climbs, half-slides down the steep woodsy hill, splashing at the bottom into a pile of wet leaves. Vicky's eyes are shining as she watches Jack climb down. The other kids all look at each other. It's pretty far down, but there's Jack yelling, Come on, you guys, come on! Then Markie drops down and does what Jack did. He loses his grip and tumbles the last part, and Sally puts her hand on her mouth, but Markie's laughing when he stands up from the leaves. Quickly, Vicky goes, and Jack catches her at the bottom. Come on, Vicky yells to the kids still at the top, it's easy! Then Sally goes, and Marian, who isn't sure what to do, but Jimmy helps her; and after everyone else makes it all the way down, Tom goes, and soon everyone's standing and laughing in the wet, smelly leaves at the bottom of the hill.

Then Sally holds her finger to her lips and tiptoes to the pond. The other kids quiet down and follow her. Sally points, and everyone follows her finger, and they see a little sharp rock sticking out from the water, and she whispers, That's its nose. When they stare harder, they can see it's not a rock, it really is a nose, and under the water they can see the rest of the turtle, its shell and its little feet, just floating there. No one's sure it's a *baby* turtle, it looks big enough to be a grown-up one, but then Markie whispers, There's another one! and when they look where he's pointing, they see that one, too, and then Jimmy sees one, and soon everyone's found one or two, Jack sees three sitting over on a rock and they're real little. Everyone agrees probably they're baby ones.

A rumbling sound comes from far away, they almost don't hear it, or they think it's a jet plane way high up. But Tom looks around at how dark it is and says, You guys, it's going to rain.

The rumbling happens again, and of course it's thunder, and the tops of the trees are moving and a swish of wind sends leaves skittering across the dirt. Look! says Markie. A snake in the water! but no one looks except Jack.

Tom says, Come on, we better go. He heads around the pond to the path they usually come on. Jimmy and Marian and Sally follow him, Sally turning her head to keep looking at the turtles.

Jack says, I'm going back that way, where we came down. It's so cool, climbing up that!

Markie looks at Tom, and then at Jack, and says, Me too, Jack, I'm coming that way, too. Jack says, Cool! And he says, Vicky, you want to come with us?

Vicky looks at the slope, all tangled with roots. Her eyes light up again, and she takes a step that way. But she stops. She looks at Jack and then at Tom, waiting on the path. Her face turns a little bit sad, just for a second, and then she smiles at Tom. Jack, she says, as she walks toward the path, come this way. I don't think we'll get home before the storm, if we go your way.

It's true that, for a time, after Jack comes back from New Haven, his dark eyes linger on Vicky, he winks at her when someone says, Hey, sorry New Haven didn't work out, and he always answers, Hey, it's okay, I won't be here that long, and besides, they got things here they don't have in New Haven. Vicky smiles and blushes. But that passes. And had you asked her then, she'd have told you this: it was like new fashions in the magazine pages. Startling ideas, answers to questions you had never asked, so you try them on in your head. And then realize they're absurd. And discard them. Sometimes maybe you turn back to one of those pages again, take another look . . . but no, still no. Vicky will marry Tom. After the wedding she'll stay in her job at the sewing store—trimmings, notions, exotic fabrics, Vicky's good with those, all the things that make what you expected into something different, special, and sparkling—just for a while, until she leaves to have their babies.

Vicky's happy.

LAURA'S STORY
Chapter 6

———

The Women in the Tent

Laura had made phone calls (a task that had once been so simple, that since September 11 demanded patience, ingenuity, dedication). Now she had appointments.

Almost everyone had agreed to speak with her, even the people with the most reasons to hate Harry: Kevin Keegan, Edward Spano, Marian Gallagher. Well, why not? she thought as she gathered her notebooks and pens. She was offering them the opportunity to comment on Harry's death. They probably had a lot to say, each one of them.

The lawyer, Phil Constantine, the one Harry had said was a bagman for the Spano organization—*said* this to Laura; merely *insinuated* it in print—he was the only one who'd refused. Constantine had been hard to reach; his office phone was still out, and Laura had left three messages on his cell phone before she reached him. Horns honking and a general background din had told Laura he was on the street, but she didn't think that was what accounted for the way he barked his name when he answered his phone, or for the coldness of the silence with which he listened, or for the terseness of his "no comment" when he hung up. She wasn't surprised at Constantine's refusal, nor particularly thrown. Reporter-Laura knew how to handle this. You wait until one of the others says something new about him, something that's not in print yet, something even worse than what is. Then you call him back and invite him to comment on that.

It almost always worked.

And besides, Laura thought, snapping her tape recorder shut, zipping her bag, how much could you expect to learn about the truth from talking to a lawyer anyway?

She made a trip to the bathroom mirror, checking to see how red her eyes were, giving her hair a comb. While she did this she resolutely did not look at Harry's shaving things on the sink, his bathrobe hanging on the back of the door. Her pale brown hair, straight and sleek and lustrous in good times, lank and sullen now, could have used a little more work, but she stuck the comb back in the cabinet when she felt the lump start building in her throat again. You can't do interviews with a lump in your throat.

Normally, of course, Laura would never chase all over town for interviews like these. There was no time. This was work you did over the phone, in the days, so recent but in another life, when the phone was just another tool you never even thought about, you just picked it up and someone was there. You did interviews over the phone so you could write the story yourself and grab the byline, not the "reported by" that came when you phoned a story in.

Normally, you sat at your desk, scribbling as fast as you could, and you asked people, What did you think when you heard? (The river, my God, how can it be that the river just keeps running under the burning blue sky?) When was the last time you spoke to Harry Randall? (Yesterday, early morning, no time for coffee, dashing out the door, hasty kiss.) What was the substance of that conversation? (Stone [already at elevator, jabbing button]: "Aren't you working today?" Randall [rumpled, preoccupied, but offering that ever-amused smile]: "I have something to check out first. I'll be in later.") What was your relationship with Harry Randall? (Stone: The ocean with its shores? The ship with its anchor? Randall: Where do you *get* these things?) Do you have anything to add? (Long, long silence.)

But normally, when Laura asked what someone thought about a death, a disaster, that was what she wanted to know: what they thought. Today what she was going to be asking was, Did you do this? Did you kill Harry?

Not literally, of course. Reporter-Laura would be asking the questions, and she was too cool, too professional, to make a dumb mistake like that. She would be cunning and clever. She would wait and watch and listen, study them, how they sat and spoke and looked at her, when they talked about Harry. Her years in school, her years in Des Moines and St. Paul, and these years on the *New York Tribune*: Reporter-Laura had paid attention, she'd been working hard, she had learned a lot. And now she knew: it was all for this.

For this one story.

Laura walked out of Harry's apartment without looking back. She meant to continue purposefully down the hall—she was a reporter, on her way to cover a story—but she was engulfed, staggered, by a wave of panic when she heard Harry's door click shut behind her. She plunged her hand into her pocket, terrified she'd forgotten the key, and when she felt it, she dug it out to make sure that's what it was, not a whistle or a penknife or some other hard object masquerading as the way back into Harry's place. She stared at it, cold silver on her palm. Then, clutching it, she ran down the hall, chased by her echoing footsteps, and punched the elevator button, willing the elevator to come fast, fast, fast.

MARIAN'S STORY
Chapter 6

———

Secrets No One Knew

October 31, 2001

Marian had had a heavy morning of meetings: the Downtown Council, among others. There, the topics of the Fund, of Harry Randall's poisonous story, of Jimmy, of Marian's association with what had gone before, pulled at everyone's words, at their thoughts, like tree roots clutching at travelers attempting to pass through a cheerless forest.

She spoke twice, to averted eyes and yes-fine-let's-get-on-with-it nods, and after that she kept silent, one hand conscientiously taking notes on a yellow pad, the other in her lap twisting a scrap of paper into a tight hard knot. She swept from that meeting as soon as it broke, though she herself had always been the first to say the business of a meeting is truly conducted before it begins and after it ends. One or two of the others started to say something as she passed by them, but she did not stop.

The other two meetings had gone better. The downtown arts organizations involved were, in the wake of the attacks, in desperate need of money, and the MANY Foundation had money. Marian's questionable morality, her sordid past—well, that was the way Harry Randall's third story had made things appear, there was no use pretending otherwise—these things, it seemed, were important to people in absolutely inverse proportion to how much they felt she could do for them.

Marian was disappointed by this reaction, but not surprised. She'd been in the nonprofit world, cajoling money out of Peter to give away to Paul, for too long to find herself caught off guard by anyone's agenda, anyone's motives.

But she was tired. Tired from her morning, from all the other mornings this autumn, from the phones that didn't work and the diverted subways and the dust and the children's drawings from South Dakota and Virginia that were taped to schoolyard fences and announced "We Love You, New York." She was tired from the list of times and places of firefighters' funerals, half a dozen a day, that scrolled silently down her TV screen when she watched the evening news. Tired of having to fight for a place for the Downtown Council at the Lower Manhattan redevelopment table. Of acting strong so that her weary staff would take courage and be able to go on. Of declaring, over and over, that the Jimmy McCaffery she had known—the Captain McCaffery, Marian was always careful to say, to whom so many owed their lives, not just on the basis of his heroic and ultimately self-sacrificing actions in this unprecedented disaster but because of his breathtaking bravery over the years—that this man would never have been a part of any scheme of corruption or cold betrayal, as some were hinting now.

Marian wondered what would happen if she stood and walked out the door. Now, before Laura Stone arrived. She would smile at Elena. Elena would smile back, expecting Marian was going on an errand and would presently return. But she would not. She'd make her way to Grand Central Station and board a train heading north. After a day of sitting perfectly still watching the trees and the towns and the river flash by, she would get off at some nowhere stop in the Adirondacks, find a one-room cabin no one else wanted in the dense shadows of pungent pine trees that blocked the sun. She would clear a patch of earth, turning the worm-rich, fragrant soil so she could plant a garden for next spring. She'd sit wrapped in sweaters and shawls drinking herbal tea as winter shortened the days. She would give up coffee, give up wine and flesh, subsist on the bounty of the earth, which she would nurture, returning, in her labor and husbandry, more than she took away.

And who would miss her, really? Sam? He was wrapped up in the pretty actress he'd met in June—and what a relief that had been, his mooning over Marian having gone on far too long after she had ended their lovely but, from the beginning, finite affair. (She'd seen the potential, and the limits, from their first flirtatious glance; he obviously hadn't. But that was the way it had always been with Marian, since Jimmy. Jimmy was the only lover who had ever left her.)

Her friends—Jeana, Tomiko, Ulrich? Yes, of course, they'd miss her, wonder why she did it, why she'd given up so much, to go live *where* was that again? and in not very long she'd be more valuable as a topic of endless speculation, conversation, head-shaking, than she'd ever been as a dinner companion, a pal.

Sally? Kevin? Yes, they would feel a loss, an empty place in their lives, if she were gone. But Kevin was young; his life spread boundlessly before him, an infinite number of beckoning choices. She was his aging aunt, and not even that by blood: treasured, to be sure, but occupying a place in his life smaller and less vital with each passing year. And Sally had so many friends, and Sally had Phil. And perhaps—Marian was startled to find she was permitting herself this thought; it was a sign of the difficulty of the times that her self-discipline had not been powerful enough to forbid it—perhaps Sally would be in a small way relieved to have the twenty-year war between Marian and Phil finally ended, as Marian ceded the territory and went into exile.

And her work? Well, it was true some of the projects she was involved in would crumble without her. MANY might even collapse. That thought stirred her, made her sit up, straighten her shoulders. That would be bad. Clearly, bad. This was important work. Helping. Giving. Saving. She left her desk, went to get more coffee. And stood holding her mug at the coffee machine, confused as to which pot to take from, the fresh or the old, the decaf or the strong, and what to put in it, and how much she'd been intending to have.

Marian was halfway through her coffee when Elena buzzed to tell her Laura Stone had arrived. Marian put down the proposal she had been reviewing (a graphic artist who had escaped from the south tower's sixty-third floor with his life but none of his materials was asking for a grant to rent new space and to restock; Marian was inclined to approve the application provided the space he selected was below Canal Street). She shrugged on her suit jacket, gave her glasses a quick polish, and arranged the muscles of her face into a comforting, reassuring smile, but not one too broad or welcoming. Laura Stone knew that Marian had not wanted to give this interview and would not trust her if Marian pretended to be pleased that she was there.

So she put on a smile that said, We can agree that truth is important, and the search for it equally so; come, let us reason together.

Marian led Laura Stone into the small conference room. Someone else might have a meeting that required the large one, and while, as director, Marian's needs trumped everyone else's, she did not approve of such flagrant assertions of power and avoided playing that card whenever she could.

And also: the windows of the smaller room faced west. From here, in the gap between the buildings, you could see the smoke crawling skyward, see the dinosaurlike cranes, see the smoldering, twisted ruins where so many—and one was Jimmy McCaffery—had died. Marian seated Laura Stone so that Stone would have that view. Elena, warmly efficient, followed them into the room with a carafe of coffee, fresh mugs, three kinds of cookies arranged on a tray. Laura Stone turned down an offer of coffee, but the carafe and the mugs and the tray remained. Marian made the small bet with herself that she always made: how long it would take a guest who had gained an upper hand by refusing hospitality to decide her point had been made and give in to covetous tastebuds or falling blood sugar or the very human hope for reassurance through food. In the case of this thin, harried-looking young reporter, Marian predicted it wouldn't be ten minutes.

"Well." Marian nodded as Elena withdrew and she and Laura Stone arranged themselves. The reporter, not looking at Marian, rooted in her large canvas shoulder bag, retrieved a notebook, two ballpoint pens, one of which she frowned at and tossed back, and a tape recorder the size of a cigarette pack.

"Is this all right?" Laura Stone asked, lifting the recorder.

"Yes, of course," Marian said placidly; what had Marian Gallagher to hide? She went on, silkily seizing the high ground. "I was sorry to hear about Mr. Randall's death," she said. "As you might imagine, I'd been . . . dismayed . . . to read some of the things he'd written. About me and about people I know. Still . . ." She shook her head, leaving the rest unspoken, because some people were superstitious about the word *suicide*.

"Mr. Randall was a major figure at my newspaper," Laura Stone said, flipping the notebook open. "I'd like to ask for your comments about him—the stories he was working on, his approach when he interviewed you and your friends. His death. Anything you'd like to say."

A ragged edge to Stone's clear midwestern voice pricked Marian's awareness. Her sympathetic smile still lingering and her eyes still frank, Marian reinventoried the reporter's looks. Thin, she'd thought on first seeing her; but perhaps the word was *drawn*. No makeup, but that might be a statement, something political: Marian had gone makeupless herself when younger. Eyes dark-circled, restless. The way all New Yorkers' eyes were these past weeks.

Or was this something more? Were Stone's eyes ashamed, and suspicious, and hoping to hide their hurt, as the eyes of someone who had for the first time been betrayed?

As by a lover, who left without warning.

As by a lover, say, who had killed himself.

"I'm not sure how I can help you," Marian said, watching Stone as she spoke. At the sound of Marian's voice, the reporter glanced up, her eyes filled with something like hope, which faded but did not vanish when Marian's words registered. Marian softened her tones, speaking as a woman does in the presence of another who is bereaved. "Mr. Randall only came here twice, and we spoke on the telephone a few times."

Stone looked back to her notebook, where she had written nothing. Marian allowed herself a tiny, relieved smile. Not that another woman's loss and pain gave her any pleasure, of course not. But perhaps this interview would not be, as each of the interviews with Randall had increasingly been, dangerous with traps and snares. Perhaps Laura Stone was not looking for the truth, but only for the ghost of Harry Randall.

In a voice from which the shiver had all but disappeared (and Marian admired this, the reporter's dogged attempt at control) Laura Stone said, "What did you think when you heard about Mr. Randall's death?"

"What is there to think? Or to say?" Laura Stone had lifted her eyes to Marian again, and Marian met them comfortingly. Even before the attacks and the collapse of the towers, when death was a private, individual calamity, Marian had never found any words worthy of it, though she had delivered eulogies when asked and muttered sincere consoling nonsense as she pressed the hands of the grieving. Laura Stone's pen traveled over her notebook page. Marian couldn't see what she was writing, but from the rhythmic movements she suspected it was not notes, just strokes, just a way to keep control.

She almost offered the reporter the plate of cookies, but that would be unfair.

Stone, her eyes still on Marian's, said: "What if you were told Mr. Randall's death wasn't suicide?"

Marian stared at the young woman. "Not—you're saying you think someone killed him?"

"Can you tell me who might want to do that?"

"No," said Marian. "No." Then: "Are you serious?" But of course Stone was serious. And like a nightmare vine that breaks the earth and in seconds spreads, branches, and soon towers overhead, blackening the sky, a memory threw a cold black shadow over Marian, a memory she had long buried.

Herself, younger than this young reporter, in bed alone, after Jimmy had gone to Manhattan, after Jimmy had left. The siren at the firehouse going off, Marian burrowing more deeply in the blankets while Engine 168 screams down the street. And Marian thinking of Jimmy gone from that truck, and thinking how it would be, how it would be *better,* if he were missing because he'd been lost. Missing because he'd been a hero and he'd died. Instead of the way it was, when he was not a hero—although Marian said that to no one, not even, after that night, ever again to herself—and had not been lost, but had merely turned his back on what had happened and gone away.

BOYS' OWN BOOK
Chapter 10

A Hundred Circling Camps

September 1, 1979

It begins with a phone call, Tom's father to Jimmy. Soon Jimmy's in a booth at Flanagan's, waiting, sipping beer from a heavy glass mug, nursing it really. He wants to have his wits about him when Mike the Bear walks in.

Not that Jimmy's spooked, being summoned to a meet with Michael Molloy. Nothing spooks Jimmy. And he's known Mr. Molloy all his life. Barbecues in the big backyard, Mr. Molloy grilling hotdogs, Mrs. Molloy making sure all the kids have something to drink, the kids running around, squirting each other with the garden hose. Trips to Shea Stadium (without the girls, without Mrs. Molloy), Mr. Molloy springing for ice cream and Cokes for everyone. Scary carved pumpkins and the best candy take on the block at Halloween, Mrs. Molloy dressed like a witch, green hair, extra-long teeth, but you knew it was her so you were never afraid. A Fourth of July pig roast in the middle of the street, the street closed because Mr. Molloy asks the cops to close it. And then the cops who close the street disappear, every year called away on urgent business, so that they never notice the fireworks Mr. Molloy sets off as the violet sky goes to black; a convenient thing, as fireworks are illegal in New York.

But Jimmy's father, a steel-muscled Teamster, though also spooked by nothing, has always grown uneasy in Mr. Molloy's presence. His eyes will narrow, his talk become short, and he drinks at another place, not at Flanagan's.

And it is whispered that Michael Molloy became Mike the Bear when, at Jimmy's age, he crushed a man to death in his arms.

* *

Jimmy's beer is halfway gone when Mr. Molloy walks into the bar. Tribute is paid, in *How ya doin'?* and *Hey, Big Mike.* And he is big: six foot six, edging three hundred pounds, hair almost gone now but hands still hard. Jimmy feels the power in his handshake; Jimmy tries to return it with one of equal weight.

Mr. Molloy calls for a beer, and another for Jimmy. He inspects Jimmy, he asks how life is treating him.

Fair, Jimmy answers, returning his smile, nodding his head, to show Mr. Molloy he's appreciative that he's been asked.

Fair? Mr. Molloy pulls back in his seat, as though surprised. What I hear, you're hot shit, kiddo. What Tom tells me, you're the balls.

Hey, and now Jimmy's smile widens.

The waitress brings two more mugs, both full, both cloudy with frost. Jimmy's momentarily confused, not sure what's called for. He makes his choice, abandons the old beer—the one he paid for—in favor of the new one, from Mr. Molloy.

Mr. Molloy takes that first cold sip of beer. No, really, kid, it's what I hear. Last week, the Chinese restaurant, that guy in the fire, you rolled him in the tablecloth? Saved his life?

Yeah, says Jimmy, guy'll smell like moo shu pork for a year.

Mr. Molloy laughs with Jimmy.

Jimmy sips at his beer, but for a minute he doesn't see Mr. Molloy.

Last week: dark street, locked restaurant, smell of smoke even before they pile off the truck. Probably a grease fire in the kitchen, Jimmy's captain says. Calls for Door Man to bring the irons and the others to stretch a line to the front door. Door Man's Jimmy, he's right there. He pops it and they go in together, the captain and him. Place smells, smoke's banked halfway down. No one here, says Jimmy's captain. Bring it in! he yells to the men ready with the hose. He heads toward the kitchen. Jimmy stands for a second, takes it all in, thinks, that's wrong. Wait! he shouts. The kitchen door bursts open, flames push out. Jimmy's captain jumps back as the fire rolls over the ceiling into the room, looking for something to devour. And there's this guy staggering out from the kitchen, screaming, running around, covered in flames. Worst thing you can do, run: it feeds the dragon.

And then for Jimmy it happens, what he loves so much: time slows to nothing. Every sound is clear, every sight is sharp, like he can see each thing and its deepest secret, too. Jimmy feels fire under his skin, that fire that's his, inside. He knows exactly what to do, and he has time, all the time he needs, to do it.

He yanks on a tablecloth, soy sauce and teacups flying. He sees how the burning guy's running, takes a few steps, and the guy runs right into him, right where Jimmy knew he'd be. Jimmy throws the cloth over him, knocks him down, rolls him over and over and over. The guy's still screaming, but the fire's out. Jimmy's brothers open the line and the fire hisses, throws billows of steam at them. Finally it gives up, angry like always, but defeated once again.

His captain calls in the EMTs, claps Jimmy on the shoulder, says, Good work, Superman. But you better knock off that smile. Your teeth'll turn black from the smoke. Jimmy feels the grin stretching across his face, tries to control it, but it gets wider from his captain's praise. Jimmy's glad he saved the guy, glad no one else is hurt, glad the fire's out. But the fire under his skin is fading, too, and like every time, he's sorry to see that go.

Jimmy? Mr. Molloy asks. You okay?

Oh, hey, yeah. Jimmy says. Yeah, just thinking about something. He nods and Big Mike nods, and they drink beer together.

Jimmy asks after Mrs. Molloy, how's she doing, everything's good?

Tell you the truth, Jimmy, Mr. Molloy says, that's why I called you. Mr. Molloy stops to lift his beer, takes a long pull, wipes the foam from his lip with a napkin.

Jimmy says, Something wrong? Mrs. Molloy, she's okay?

Oh yeah, Peggy, she's fine, she's okay—he smiles here, Mr. Molloy does, the same smile the kids have been seeing forever when Mr. Molloy looks at his wife, mentions her name, the kids thinking he probably doesn't even know he does it—but she's worried, she's worried about something.

Sorry to hear that, Jimmy says, and he is.

Mr. Molloy says, I need a favor, kid.

Jimmy lifts his beer, too, drinks, does not answer. Sees in his mind his father's narrowed eyes, thinks: *Mike the Bear*.

Hey, Mr. Molloy, he says, trying lightness. I'm just a fireman.

Yeah, maybe so. But the guys, they look up to you. You know I've always thought the world of you, Jimmy. Mr. Molloy sounds serious now, leaning his big body forward, his eyes locked on Jimmy. The two of them are being watched by other eyes at Flanagan's, and Jimmy knows this. *What's going on?* he imagines he can hear them ask each other. *Brendan McCaffery's boy sitting with Mike the Bear. The fuck's going on?*

Mr. Molloy pulls two cigars from his shirt pocket, offers one across the table. No, thanks, says Jimmy, I don't smoke.

Yeah, says Mike the Bear, like he knows that already.

Fifteen years old: Tom, who does not smoke, sells cheap cigarettes to the other kids, from a booth at the diner, from his backpack on the playground. By the pack, sometimes by the carton, always without that stupid tax tape on them, that's why they're so cheap. The kids know this is a small piece of Tom's father's action: they could buy these same cigarettes from Junior's Corner, still a lot cheaper than at the A&P or the magazine place but for more than Tom gets. But Tom takes care of his friends.

One day on the ballfield, the kids just messing around, Tom says this to Jimmy: Anyone you know needs smokes, they don't have to come to me, you know. I could give you a couple of cartons, make it easier.

Now Tom and Jimmy, they're in different schools, and Jimmy's a jock besides, so, yeah, Jimmy knows different kids, there's some money to be made. But Jimmy sees something else, too. Jack is Tom's brother. Jack goes to St. Ann's with Tom, but he's a grade higher; different group of guys there. And Jack plays summer league softball at the Y same as Jimmy, knows some of the guys Jimmy knows. But Jack doesn't peddle cigarettes or anything else. Tom's offer, it's not about making a few bucks, not about making anything easier. It's Tom's way of asking, *Do you want in?* It's not about cigarettes.

On the ballfield, Jimmy tosses the ball high in the air, watches it streak straight up. He waits for that breathless instant at the top when it's not going in either direction. Then here it comes cutting back down through the blue sky, thumping into his glove.

He says to Tom, No, thanks, man, I'm not much good at that kind of thing, know what I mean?

Tom nods. I hear you, he says.

And that's the end of it. The kids get older, start to drink in the bars, Jimmy goes to the Bird, stays out of Flanagan's, like his dad. Tom, he's in and out of the place, happy to hang at the Bird with everyone, but

Sunday afternoons now, you're looking for Tom, you can find him at Flanagan's, watching the game.

Jack likes Flanagan's best; almost always, that's where Jack is.

And since that day on the ballfield, Mr. Molloy still grins at Jimmy when he sees him, waves his cigar, asks him, How's it hanging? Gives Jimmy a bottle of single malt when he graduates from the Academy, a whiskey so expensive Jimmy doesn't know anyone who's ever tasted it, except Mr. Molloy. Tells Jimmy how proud he is, he always knew Jimmy would do great, get to be just what he was born to be.

So here in Flanagan's, Jimmy watches Mr. Molloy slip the second cigar back in his pocket like he knew all along Jimmy wasn't going to want it. Jimmy thinks about this, thinks about Mrs. Molloy, her smile, and her sad eyes.

Well, he says, and drinks more beer. Well, he says, anything I can do. Thanks, Jimmy.

It surprises Jimmy that Mr. Molloy actually sounds relieved, as a man would who'd been worried he'd be refused.

Mr. Molloy wraps his huge hands around his beer mug, leans forward again. It's Jack, he tells Jimmy. I got a problem with Jack.

Marian's Story
Chapter 7

———

How to Find the Floor

Marian tore herself from the grip of memory, from the empty darkness of long ago, and forced herself to return to this sunlit room, her room in this office that was hers.

This morning, unlike that desolate night, she was not alone. Here, unlike in that desolate place, she had work to do. Work: always, before, the rescuer that had saved her. Work. Yes; all right; this was familiar, putting her own needs aside to do important work. Breathe in, out, slow the heart, calm the panic.

"Someone killed Mr. Randall?" Marian spoke tranquilly, gazed directly into this thin reporter's eyes. "I haven't read that. The papers all say it was . . . that he took his own life."

"The circumstances were suspicious. I'm sorry—the police would rather we didn't discuss any details. But that's why I'm here. My paper's following the story." Stone stopped, frowned at her recorder, poked a button. In her silence, Marian watched her, thinking, *The police?*

Stone glanced up again. "He was following a few new leads," she said. "They had to do with the McCaffery stories." She paused, looked at Marian expectantly.

"What are you saying?"

"Well"—almost apologetic—"a lot of people were upset about what he'd been writing."

"One of *us?*" Marian pitched her voice to sound truly aghast. "You think someone Mr. Randall was writing about could have killed him?"

Stone said, "It's the current thinking," the way she might have suggested Marian carry an umbrella because, though neither of them liked it, it was raining. "He'd caused trouble for some people by exposing secrets. Maybe he was about to expose others."

"In my experience," Marian said, restraining her voice, keeping it calm and deliberate, "it's only in books that people kill other people to keep secrets from being exposed. Generally, in life, if people are afraid they're about to be *found out*"—she put a sarcastic, Victorian weight on the words—"they either run away or kill themselves."

She watched the young woman flinch and felt bad for her. But it was necessary. This talk of secrets, of exposure. To assuage this young lover's heart? To fulfill her aching, forlorn need to believe her beloved had been taken from her, rather than that he chose to leave her?

No. Too much was at stake.

"I'm sorry," Marian said. "But I find this 'current thinking' absurd. And I haven't heard this theory on the news, or in the papers, or anywhere except from you."

Surprisingly, Stone's face lit with a satisfied smile. "The police haven't been here yet?"

"No. No, they haven't."

"They hate it when I do this."

"Do what?"

"Beat them to an interview. Let's go on before they get here and throw me out. What can you tell me about the death of Jack Molloy?"

"Before they get here?"

"Well, of course they'll want to talk to everyone Harry Randall did. I was just hoping you might be able to point me in a useful direction first. So: Jack Molloy?"

Marian had a sense of rounding a bend in the road into a landscape that had changed without warning, where withering trees stood isolated on hills grown bare and bleak.

"Jack?" Marian spoke calmly but thought quickly, weighing options, making choices. "I went over that with Mr. Randall. I don't know anything about it except what was in the news at the time."

"You were all friends back then, weren't you? James McCaffery, the Molloy brothers, Mark Keegan, you. You were dating McCaffery. Or is that wrong?"

"No, that's correct," Marian said. Except that she and Jimmy had not "dated" since they were fourteen. "Going together" was what people said then, and that covered everything from the crisp fall days when Marian wrapped herself in Jimmy's varsity jacket, with its C

for Captain, to the evening she arrived at his basement apartment—
the month he'd entered the Fire Academy—with a spare toothbrush,
a comb, and two brand-new nightgowns to fold into his bureau drawers.

"Why did Mark Keegan kill Jack Molloy?"

Marian considered the young woman. What was this?

And what could it become—be made to be? In this bleak landscape,
could Marian plant seeds?

"You think Markie shooting Jack has something to do with Mr.
Randall's death?"

"It's the story he was working on."

Marian sat back. She paused, as though reluctant to go on, and said,
"It's the money. The payments to Sally. You think there's something
wrong there. Mr. Randall thought so, too."

"Well, it's clear some people were lying about it, so something's obviously wrong somewhere. What can you tell me about it?"

"Nothing. Just that the payments came. We all thought they were
from New York State."

"Who told you that?"

"Sally. It's what her lawyer told her."

"Phillip Constantine?"

"Yes."

"Did he know where the money really came from?"

"He had to, don't you think?" Marian sipped at her coffee. It was bitter; had she forgotten sugar? "Have you talked to him?"

"I will."

She would; of course she would. "He'll lie to you."

"Why do you say that?"

Bitter or not, Marian drank. "Because he lied to me."

"What did he say?"

"That he got the money from Jimmy."

"How do you know that's not true?"

"Because it's ridiculous."

"In what way?"

"Every way! Jimmy was a firefighter, where would he get so much
money? And why on earth this absurd charade? He was Markie's closest friend. If he had money and wanted to help Sally out, why not just
give it to her?" With horror Marian heard her own voice rising. She
tried for a look of righteous indignation. "He's hiding something. Phil,"
she added, to make sure this reporter, who seemed a little dim, would

understand. "He's trying to blame something on Jimmy because Jimmy's dead. And because Jimmy's a hero, so whatever he was up to—Phil—if he can hook it to Jimmy, it won't look so bad."

Laura Stone asked, "Where do *you* think the money came from?"

Enunciating very clearly: "I have no idea."

"Captain McCaffery didn't tell you?"

"Jimmy?" A swift rush of blood filled Marian's face. Had this slow-witted reporter not heard anything she'd said? "How would he have known?"

"Did Sally Keegan know?"

Finally, a change of path. Breathe in, out. "No, I told you. Sally believed that money came from the State."

"Are you sure?"

"We all did."

"Why did Mark Keegan kill Jack Molloy?"

"You must know this! Jack shot at him."

"Were you there?"

"Of course not."

"Then how do you know what happened?"

"It's what Markie said." Marian poured herself more coffee, added milk, made sure this time to include sugar. "And if you know I wasn't there, why are you asking me about it?"

"I'm sorry if this brings up unpleasant memories."

"These aren't my favorite memories to dwell on, but that's not my question."

"I'm just trying to follow up on Mr. Randall's story." Diffident smile, and then: "Why did Jack Molloy shoot at Mark Keegan?"

"I don't know. Probably no reason. Jack was drunk."

"He'd shoot at a friend just because he was drunk?"

"You never knew Jack, Ms. Stone. What are you getting at?"

"What's your theory on where the payments to Mrs. Keegan originated?"

Anger blazed through Marian again; but then into her mind sprang a picture, a friend's black dogs she'd seen playing tag in a field. The two zigzagged, broke this way and that, barking and yapping, taking turns being the chaser and the chased. Neither caught the other until one lay down, as if exhausted. The second trotted over to sniff, and the first leaped up and threw him into the mud.

She said carefully, "I really can't imagine. Well, except for Mr. Randall's fantasy."

"His fantasy?"

Marian sighed, making sure to keep it subtle, not theatrical. "It's obvious what he was digging for. If someone paid Markie to kill Jack, and then Markie died, they might have kept paying. Mr. Randall wanted me to say that was possible."

"Was it?"

"Of course not."

"If it were, though, who would that have been?"

"Oh, please!"

"Mr. Randall seems to have thought it was Edward Spano." Stone answered her own question. "Could it have been?"

Marian gazed across the room to a large photograph of the lush growth in a neighborhood garden MANY had funded, a garden far enough uptown to have escaped the dust and ash. "I can believe Eddie would do something like that, yes. But I can't believe it would be Markie."

"But it was."

Alarm gripped Marian's heart, though her voice did not change. "How do you know that?"

"It was Mark Keegan who killed Jack Molloy, I mean."

"Well, yes." The grip slackened, her heart slowed. "But it was self-defense."

"So Keegan said." Stone scowled at her recorder again, peering through the plastic to watch the tape rolling. As Marian relaxed, Stone, still adjusting buttons, said in preoccupied tones, "That could explain the payments to Keegan's family. Especially if someone else knew."

"What do you mean? Will you stop fiddling with that thing?"

Stone looked up quickly. "I'm sorry. I'm just not very good with equipment. I'm not sure it's working. What did you say?"

"What did you mean about the payments?"

Stone frowned, then brightened, as though remembering. "If someone knew Mark Keegan had been paid to kill Molloy, the payments might have kept coming to keep her quiet."

"Her? You mean Sally? No. No possible way."

"Can you think of another explanation?"

"I don't think that's my job, Ms. Stone."

"No." Stone sighed. "No, I suppose not. What would McCaffery's role in this have been?"

"Role? Jimmy? Even if that were what happened, which is insane, Jimmy would have had nothing to do with it."

"How do you know?"

Levelly, Marian met the other woman's eyes. "I knew Jimmy."

"You broke up with him shortly after Keegan died."

"What happened between Jimmy and me has nothing to do with this!" Marian snapped. "And"—her voice chilled—"it's certainly none of your business."

"I'm sorry." Stone seemed mortified. "That's not what I mean. It's just, you'd broken up by the time the payments began. He'd moved to Manhattan. I just wondered how you can be certain what he was involved in."

"You seem to know a lot about us."

"It was in Mr. Randall's story and his background research. Do I have it wrong?"

"No. Not the facts. But the article twisted the facts. It was full of nasty innuendo. About Jimmy, about what he might have done. And by extension, about me."

"That's why I'm here," Stone said earnestly. "I'll be speaking to other people, of course, but I've come to you first because you have a stake in it."

"What stake do you mean?" *Too sharp,* Marian admonished herself. *Stay calm, keep control.*

"The McCaffery Fund." Stone sounded surprised that Marian might be thinking of anything else. "You stopped taking contributions."

"A matter of form," Marian replied. "To reassure contributors. Just until these absurd allegations about Jimmy are cleared up. Which I have no doubt will be soon."

"Meanwhile, I'd like to give you the chance to correct any misunderstandings based on what Mr. Randall wrote."

"Those were not *misunderstandings.* Those were a reporter's attempts to smear as many people as possible on the basis of extremely flimsy supposition. Especially in the face of these extraordinary times, that was unconscionable."

Laura Stone asked, "Do you know what was in his papers?"

Oh, these twists and turns, they were wearying. "Whose papers? Harry Randall's?"

"No. James McCaffery's."

Marian did not move; but her body suddenly felt ponderous, weighted down, as if the pull of gravity had doubled. "What do you mean? What papers?"

"McCaffery apparently left papers. Possibly about this. Harry was on his way to see them the day he died."

In a corner of her mind, Marian registered: *Harry*. Not Harry Randall, not Mr. Randall. All pretense dropped.

Marian summoned strength. "Who said this?" she demanded. "That Jimmy left papers?"

"Someone told Harry about them."

"Someone lied." That was not enough. "And even if he left something, who's to say it has anything to do with Jack and Markie? Jimmy could have had any number of things on his mind." Marian wondered if that sounded as hollow to Laura Stone as it did to her.

"Yes, of course," said Stone, equally falsely. "It's just, the person who told Harry about the papers said they were 'hot stuff.' "

"Hot stuff?"

Stone nodded.

Marian shook her head. "I don't believe it."

But it could be true. Jimmy, just like Marian herself, had never liked lying; but his reasons were different. He'd always said the truth would refuse to be hidden—it would "burn through," that was how he'd put it—and lies you told would trip you up. It was too hard, he always said, lying was too hard.

It could be that that was what Jimmy's papers were about. The truth, burning through.

All right. One thing Marian understood was the importance of cutting her losses, especially when the chance still existed to bear away some small victory. "I'm sorry," she told Stone. She checked her watch, as though the time elapsed meant something. "I have another appointment. We need to bring this to a close."

Stone's eyes rested on Marian, and Marian felt as though she were being probed for gaps, weaknesses where a trickle of water, introduced but barely noticed, could burst the wall, become a drowning flood.

Deep within herself, Marian felt the rumbling of a vast, awakened anger. Before it could gather and explode, however, Laura Stone was on her feet, packing her scattered notebooks and pens, the irritating tape recorder, smiling, thanking Marian for her time. "I can find my way out," she said. Nevertheless Marian accompanied her down the hallway, shook her hand; not to do so would be rude. She closed the polished oak door behind the reporter and turned back toward her own office. As she asked Elena to please clear the table in the small conference room and leave the untouched plate of cookies by the coffee machine for the staff, she realized the only coffee gone from the carafe was what she herself had had.

PHIL'S STORY
Chapter 7

———

Breathing Smoke

October 31, 2001

Phil spent the morning as he had to, with clients, with other attorneys, doing research, making calls. He moved fast. He fired orders at Elizabeth, his paralegal (she was used to it, she was young and sharp, driven and smart, going to law school at night, she wanted someday to be the lawyer he was, Phil knew that). He demanded decisions by deadlines he invented and rejected deadlines laid down by his opponents. As usual he was in the office before either Elizabeth or his secretary, Sandra, and had work laid out for both of them by the time they came. He could see from how they said "Good morning" that they knew about Randall and wanted to talk, but Phil wasn't ready yet. He had work to do first, real work in the real world that had nothing to do with arrogant reporters or sainted heroes, work from the world of Phil's life up until now. He wasn't ready to close the door on that life yet.

The trouble he was in might have made another man more cautious, but it set Phil free. He'd always flown high, pushed the limits, found the line by crossing it. Now he was accused—only in the pages of the *Tribune* and the public mind so far, but you couldn't miss the scent of the storm racing behind the wind—of going so far over the line that no reason, no explanation, would be enough.

What use was caution now?

He would rise or fall on the truth behind the truth in Harry Randall's story. Meanwhile, nothing he did could bring a risk that measured up. So Phil was free to go out on limbs, take chances, require this and refuse that. Into his cell phone he snapped and shouted; the midmorning meeting with co-counsel on a RICO case sent them, the other two, stomping from his office lock-jawed and fuming. Drafts of memos flew from his computer. He signed letters as fast as Sandra brought them. In the middle of a conference call on a totally other matter, he had an idea even he thought was harebrained for Mrs. Johnson's defense. But it might work, and God knew nothing else was going to. When he got off the phone, he sloshed coffee into his mug from the pot that was always on and outlined his inspiration to Elizabeth in a rapid-fire volley of half-sentences as he stood at her desk. Unfazed by his delivery, she jotted down key words and said she'd look into it.

When he'd hired Elizabeth two years ago, he'd been Mr. Constantine, and she'd been Ms. Grant. Phil took no liberties with intimacy. He could call her Lizzie, she said out of nowhere, working very late with him one warm April night a few weeks after she'd started. Everyone called her Lizzie, she told him, everyone always had.

Phil had three texts and half a dozen computer windows open in front of him, but a new note in Elizabeth's voice reached him in his distraction like a fresh breeze drifting into a crowded room. He looked up. The color in her cheeks was high, but her eyes were frank and stayed on his. The small smile that lifted her lips suggested an offer but no promise, held something unsaid but nothing coy. She had long hands, nails short but polished anyhow, and a gold clip in her thick dark hair.

A looming court deadline had forced Phil to break a date with Sally: he should have been on a ferry hours ago, on the windy deck watching Brooklyn slide by, and the Verrazano Narrows Bridge—he liked that side of the boat, not the other, where the Statue of Liberty was—as the secretive shadowed hills of Staten Island grew and the towers of Manhattan, always lighted, receded.

And he thought, *Why?* Or, looking at Elizabeth who wanted to be Lizzie, *Why not?* It wasn't as though he'd been faithful to Sally all these years, he didn't pretend that. In the eras when by mutual treaty they'd been banned from each other's lives—in practice, he from hers, Phil ever the one to come and go, to propose terms, Sally the one to accept or reject—Phil had always hoped to be intoxicated. Bewitched. Mesmerized and possessed. To fall under another spell that would counter Sally's. When Sally's door was barred, he'd always turned to his own world, prowling through it in search of a sorceress to free him.

Several times he'd thought he'd found her. A lawyer, a writer, a painter, once even a cop: wild nights, stolen days, two people swept away. But always the time came when the winds died down. And the salt smell from the deck of the ferry would start to come to Phil at strange times: in his office, in Grainger's, in court.

That spring night two years ago he'd met Elizabeth's eyes—plain brown eyes, exactly what they seemed to be, nothing hidden to challenge him with; Sally's were the clear green of emeralds, or pale like spring grass, or gray-green like the ocean reflecting low clouds, and why they changed he never knew—and he shook his head. "Go ahead and call me Phil," he'd said. "But I wouldn't recommend 'Lizzie.' This is the big leagues." He went back to his books and his keyboard. From that night she'd changed her name, made it formal and professional, and he'd called her by it. Though a month passed before she could be counted on to answer to it.

At midday Phil closed a file on his computer, rubbed his hands over his face, turned his chair to face the window. Six floors below, the paths of pedestrians made a sharp-angled latticework on street and sidewalk. Without the cars, the traffic lights, though switching, were meaningless and ignored. In this new downtown, people had to find their own ways and their own rhythms.

Phil swiveled his chair back and called through the open door into the outer office. "You guys come in here a minute?"

Elizabeth and Sandra, neither of them guys, showed themselves in his doorway. Sandra carried a pad and pen. Phil tried to remember if he'd ever seen Sandra's hands empty. "Should I order some lunch?" she asked.

"After. This won't take long. Sit down." He waited until they did. "You saw the news," Phil said, no lead-in. With Phil there never was. "That *Tribune* reporter."

Elizabeth nodded. Sandra said, "Died yesterday. Killed himself."

Phil rested his gaze on her, then flashed a grin. "You don't read the *Tribune*."

"Never did." Sandra wore lipstick and no other makeup, kept her graying hair cropped Army-close. She was long divorced and nobody's fool. She had started with Phil a scant few years after he'd set up his practice, not soon enough to be there for the Keegan case, the indictment, and the negotiated plea, but in time to take the phone call from Greenhaven that Markie Keegan had been stabbed by another prisoner and was dead.

Elizabeth told Sandra, but with her eyes on Phil, "The *Tribune* story implied Randall didn't jump. They think someone killed him."

Sandra raised her eyebrows, a skeptical question, a doubt.

"The *Tribune* may be blowing smoke," Phil said. "I'm not sure what they're after. But listen." He looked at Elizabeth, at Sandra. "The escrow account. The Keegan account. Neither of you ever touched it. You don't put money in, you don't write the checks. True?" He asked the question as he would in court, and as in court, because he knew the answer, he didn't wait. "If there's something wrong with it, you're clear."

"Is there something wrong with it?" Elizabeth, fearless like himself.

"I don't know." Thirty years of reading eyes and posture had given Phil a fairly good idea of when he was being lied to and an unerring sense of when—as now—he was believed. "The money came from someone who wanted Keegan's family to have it. The . . . donor . . . wanted to stay in the background. I had no reason to think the money was tainted. But I didn't ask. And I knew it didn't come from the State, and I never told the client."

"How bad is that?" Elizabeth would have asked a surgeon to explain his choices as he lifted his scalpel, even if she were the one on the table.

"I thought there was no basis for a suit against the State. This way the widow at least got something. But that wasn't my decision. The lie effectively prevented her from exercising a right to sue that she might have used. That's enough to nail me to the wall even if the money's clean."

"And if it's not?"

"Then the obvious question is what I—or whoever was paying me—wanted hidden that a lawsuit might have uncovered."

"About what happened to Keegan in prison?" Uncharacteristically, then, Elizabeth hesitated.

No, he thought, *you can't back away from this shit.* He finished for her. "Or about Keegan."

"Was there something to know about him?"

"If there was, I never knew it. But I can't prove that."

Phil watched Elizabeth mentally file, index, and cross-reference everything he'd just said. When she was done she brought out the next question. "Who was paying you?"

"No one." He saw her whirring mental machinery catch for an instant. "I've been taking the money and passing it on, but that's all. No cut, no fee. Normally that might make me look better, but not in this case."

"Why not?"

"For one thing, my relationship with the client goes way beyond the professional one." He watched the women before him to see if this was news. Elizabeth (who for the past year had been dating a doctor) nodded. (And what a courtship that must be, Phil thought: she with a full-time job and in night school, he working residents' hours, both of them young and yearning. If they were smart enough to keep their dance cards this full, missing each other's arms more than they were in them, they stood a good chance of living happily ever after.) Sandra (who claimed to have hung up her sneakers long ago) just shrugged.

"And for another thing," he said, "there's Eddie Spano. The *Tribune* implies Spano's behind it all, was from the start. If that's true, it'll be hard convincing anyone I didn't know it."

"Did you?"

"I still don't."

Elizabeth's steady brown eyes didn't change. Sandra poked her pencil impatiently into the holes at the spiral binding of her pad.

"The point is," Phil said, "if anyone's gunning for me, this could be very powerful ammunition."

Sandra smiled, the hard smile of a veteran who finds military life with all its privations preferable to the disorderly insignificance of life on the outside. Elizabeth tossed her long hair and frowned at Sandra's smile.

"You haven't been here that long," Phil told Elizabeth, indicating Sandra, that she had been. "It's been tried. But this time might be different."

Different, Phil thought. Hell, why shouldn't it be? Every goddamn thing was different now, why not this?

Sandra and Elizabeth waited, watching him. He tried to see from their eyes whether he was different, too. He gave up: he couldn't tell.

He sat back, threw the pen he'd been toying with onto the desk. "Okay," he said. "I don't know what happens next. Another reporter's following up Randall's leads. She called this morning, and I told her to get lost. She call you guys yet?"

Sandra, with the tough smile, said, "One of the good things about working off cell phones. It's hard for her to find us."

"She will, though. I'd rather you guys didn't talk to her, but it's up to you. But that's the press. If it comes to an ethics investigation, or criminal—anything official—Sandra, you know the drill, but it'll be new to you." This looking into Elizabeth's straightforward brown eyes. "When they call you in, don't stonewall, and for God's sake don't lie. You'll just get yourself in trouble, and it won't help me. And." This, too, was mostly for Elizabeth. He locked onto those eyes the way he did on a client's when he wanted to make it absolutely clear the time for screwing around was over, this was for real. "If you want out—now, during, or after—go."

Again, Elizabeth nodded: she understood. Then shook her head: she wasn't going. Sandra let out an exasperated snort: she had work to do, could Phil quit crapping around?

"Yeah," said Phil. "Okay. You want to talk about it anytime, we can talk. Now: lunchtime. Anybody know if Wally's reopened?"

Sandra said, "Not yet."

"Then get me a corned beef and a cream soda from that deli up Broadway. Get yourselves whatever you want. Elizabeth, you get a chance to go through the Johnson file?"

Elizabeth echoed, "Not yet."

Half an hour later, when his mouth was full of sandwich and his fingers were greasy, Phil's cell phone rang. He'd have said "Shit," but he couldn't manage it. He swallowed, wiped his hands, flipped the phone open, and barked his name.

A woman's voice, sounding like she was speaking from a room with a bad smell in it, told him, "It's Marian Gallagher."

Shit came to Phil again as a response, and this time he could have said it, but he kept himself in check. Short and cold: "What's up?"

A pause, a break in her rhythm before she answered. She didn't like him any better than he liked her, and the truce of years was shattered now. She'd always found him brash and rude; he knew because Sally had told him. Civility was important to Marian, Sally said, manners mattered to her. Sally had probably hoped if Phil knew this he'd tone it down, show Marian a more cultured and chivalrous face. What really happened was that in Marian's presence, Phil found himself fighting strong urges to put his feet on the table or let the long-suppressed Yiddish-Bronx rhythms of his childhood overwhelm his speech.

So he knew full well that even in the mutual distaste of their relationship, she'd be thrown off by the implied insult of his not bothering with phone etiquette. Knew it, thought less of himself, and went ahead anyway.

"There's a problem," she said, and he heard her trying to match his cold tone.

"The whole damn thing's a problem, for Christ's sake," he said. "What specifically do you have in mind?"

"Harry Randall's dead."

"Thanks for the news flash."

He could practically hear her grinding her teeth. You just can't cut her a break, can you? he asked himself.

"Another reporter was just here." On the heels of her words her breath whispered in his ear, in, out. A yoga exercise, maybe; it would be like her. He waited it out. She said, "They think someone murdered him."

"I figured that."

Silence. "What do you mean, you figured that?"

"I read the damn *Tribune* this morning, Marian. Their story just about came out and said it." It occurred to him: "You didn't, right? Read it, I mean. The *Tribune*'s too lowbrow for you, I'll bet. You ought to try it anyway. You could learn a lot. What do you want?"

He was sure what she really wanted was to hang up on him, which was pretty much what he wanted, too, but he stayed, her voice drilling into his ear, phone pressed to the side of his head, elbows parked on either side of the sandwich on his desk like he was the Brooklyn Bridge and his corned beef was a stuck barge.

BOYS' OWN BOOK
Chapter 11

——

Sutter's Mill

Jimmy leaves Flanagan's, walking slowly. The late summer day has faded to that purple hour when a mist seems to hang in the air, clouding vision, though this is an illusion: the day has been fine, and the night will continue clear.

Jimmy's heading home, to the basement apartment he rents from the Cooleys. He stops at the deli for a roast beef on rye, picks up a box of Milk Bones for the Cooleys' yellow mutt. (The funny black dog they used to have, he died years ago.) But when he leaves the deli, sipping coffee, he turns left, not right, heads for the firehouse.

When he gets there, the door's up, the floor's wet and puddled: they've just washed down the truck, and it gleams. Jimmy could swear he sees the damn thing grin: it's ready, man. He grins back at it.

Owen McCardle, one of the senior men, sits out front, tipped back in a chair. He's watching the street from half-closed eyes. Hey, Superman, he says, nods as Jimmy walks up. Like Jimmy, Owen's not a talker. Owen's seen it all, lived through it all, could tell you all the stories but he doesn't. Probably he knows it won't do you any good.

Owen, says Jimmy. He squats down beside the chair, leans on the firehouse wall. Jimmy helps Owen watch the street.

You hungry? Vinny made spaghetti, Owen says.

Yeah? That one with the sausages?

Owen grunts. Enough to feed the Polish army.

Yeah, well, says Jimmy, and he doesn't get up.

Two pretty girls, their legs long and their skirts short, walk down the sidewalk on the other side of the street. A whistle cuts their way from inside the firehouse. One girl smiles, one girl laughs, but they don't turn and they don't stop.

Guy asked me to do something for him, Jimmy says to Owen.

Owen asks, You gonna do it?

Thinking about it.

The girls round the corner, stroll out of sight.

Superman. Owen's voice is even quieter than usual. Jimmy looks up at him.

Stay out of trouble.

I don't think, Jimmy says, I don't think this is trouble.

It's not illegal, what Mike the Bear wants. Not Jimmy's part. It's not even a lie: Big Mike wants Jimmy to tell the truth. Sat Jimmy down in Flanagan's to ask for this big favor: Jimmy, do this for me, tell the truth.

But the truth, Mike the Bear says, the truth can't come from just anyone. Some guys, you want them to know what's what, you want them to do something about it, it's got to be done a certain way, he says. It's got to be *handled*.

Jimmy can see the sense in this. When you're a kid, you don't tell your mom you don't want to go to school because you want to watch the *Batman* marathon on TV. You say your throat hurts. And it does; but if today were a game day, if you had to go out on the field in front of the whole school and be a hero, slam the ball out of the park, tag the guy sliding spikes-first toward home, if that were today, would your throat matter? But it's not today, so you tell your mom about your throat, and she worries about you so she lets you stay home.

It's the same here. Mike the Bear's worried about Jack. Jack's mom, she's worried even more.

Nine years old: Jimmy sees her, Mrs. Molloy, watching out the window while Tom calms Jack down, Jack all snarly because the kids don't want to climb the tree in Mr. Conley's yard, see if they can jump to the roof of his house from there. They won't do it even on Jack's dare: For Christ's sake, you fairies, the old fart's not even home!

Jack's going to do it himself, but Marian runs up to him and whispers. Jack stops, answers her. Jimmy hears Marian laugh. Jack says a swearword, but now, it's not like he's mad, it's like a joke, and Jack laughs with Marian. Next thing, Tom's calling, Hey, Jim, you coming or what? and Jack's pounding a fist into his mitt, and they're going off to play some ball. But Jimmy catches a look between Tom and Mrs. Molloy, something he doesn't understand, but he knows it's about Jack. And Mrs. Molloy keeps watching them out the window until the kids turn the corner and Jimmy can't see her anymore.

And back in Flanagan's, this is what Mike the Bear says to Jimmy: Trouble's coming. The cops're fed up, they're ready to jump on Jack and his crew. If Jack doesn't back off, he's going down.

Jimmy frowns. You sure? he asks Mike the Bear. I mean, maybe it's not true. You know, rumors, you hear stuff.

From where I heard it, Mike says, it's a safe bet.

Jimmy doesn't ask where that is. Firemen and cops, there's no love lost. A cop would rather bust on you than help you, rather knock you down than pick you up, because he figures probably you deserve it, anything bad you didn't do you just didn't get a chance yet.

That's what the firehouse says, and Jimmy knows some cops like that. But still, mostly they're straight. Mostly they want to fight crime and stop the bad guys, and mostly they want to be Superman just like he does. He thinks what happens, after a year or two on the street, they still want the same thing, but they forget how to tell who they're for and who they're against.

Bent cops, cops on the take—that's something else. They're against everybody, even their brother cops. Everything's for themselves, and thinking about them makes Jimmy feel like he did when the kids found a dead dog once down under the bridge, its skinny legs tied together, someone threw it in the water and made it drown on purpose. Jimmy remembers how mad he was, how he didn't know who to be mad at, how he wanted to do something and the dog was already dead and there was nothing he could do. So when Mike the Bear says what he hears about Jack, where he hears it from it's a safe bet, Jimmy just drinks some beer and waits.

I can't just tell Jack, Big Mike says. Sure, yeah, I can, but it's what I've been telling him all his life. Jimmy, you know him, he's always been like this.

Jimmy nods. He knows.

I can't say, kid, this time it's real, this time you have to back off, because I can't do anything about it, this time. He won't believe me, Jimmy. He'll think I can fix it, like I always have.

Mike the Bear's talking to Jimmy, but he isn't looking at him, he's looking across the room at the pictures on the walls, racing pictures, trotters winning and losing. Jimmy wonders how many guys have ever heard Big Mike Molloy say this, that there's something he can't do anything about.

Big Mike says, Jimmy, if your father, he worries about you, he worries about your mother worrying about you, he told you to stay out of burning buildings, what would you do?

Jimmy's thinking about Mrs. Molloy's eyes; but when Mike the Bear asks him this, he has to laugh, because his father almost did say exactly this, Jimmy's first week at the Academy. He said, It's not me, son, it's your mother, she's thinking she'll be worried every day when you go to work.

He tells Big Mike, and Mike asks, And what did you do?

I took my mom to the firehouse, Jimmy says. I showed her the salamanders over the door. They always come back after a fire, I told her. Then I gave her flowers, chocolates, too, a really big box, shaped like a heart. I told her she was lucky. I told her, Not every pretty woman gets presents from a fireman.

Big Mikes smiles. Tom's right about you, he says.

Jimmy smiles, too. He's thinking about his mom, how the day after he gave her the flowers she gave him a present, too, a St. Florian medal, said, Jimmy, keep this with you, I'll feel better if you keep this with you. It's in his pocket now.

Big Mike says, And you kept going to fires.

Yes, sir, says Jimmy.

Yes. Because Jimmy, this is *you*. And what Jack was like, since he was a kid, he's still like that, too. That's why I've been digging Jack out of holes all his life. Because it's not his *fault* he gets in them. You know what I mean?

Yes, says Jimmy.

But this one, it's too deep, says Mike the Bear. Jack's gonna have to climb out himself. But he'll never do it, he won't believe it, if it's me who tells him.

Jimmy sips his beer. He's thinking two things. One is, if Jack were just some guy, maybe the cops rolling him up wouldn't be a bad thing, maybe Jimmy'd just stand back and watch.

But the other thing he's thinking is, it's Jack.

And it's Big Mike, asking him for help, saying somebody needs to tell Jack.

But even if somebody does: just Jimmy, just like that?

Uh-uh, no.

If Jimmy tries, Jack's not going to listen.

If Jimmy tries, it'll go like this: First, Jack'll laugh. Jimmy, man, you're a worrier, you always were. I got it covered. Have a brew, man.

And if Jimmy keeps on? If he says, No, Jack, it's true, I heard it?

Then Jack will mutter, Jimmy, what the fuck? This something Tom told you? I don't need this, I don't need my little brother looking out for me, you can tell Tom that, you're such good buddies. I'm cool, Jimmy, and my guys are cool, no way I'm crapping out on them. Tom and you, get off my back.

Because this is something Jimmy hasn't told Mike the Bear, but he knows: He's been getting on the wrong side of Jack lately.

Last week: Jesus, Jimmy, when'd you get to be such a straight arrow, you got that arrow stuck right up your ass. This when Jimmy orders a Coke at the Bird, because he's on duty in a couple hours. Jack says, One beer's gonna matter? Jimmy shrugs, nothing to say. Ah, Christ, Jack says, his face hard, as if Jimmy did say something and what he said pissed Jack off.

Or back in July, Jimmy on duty on the Fourth, he and the guys bring the rig to the pig roast so the kids can climb on it, play with the wheel, and make the siren scream; but they'll be leaving early, before the fireworks. Like the cops who close the street, have a quick sausage and pepper sandwich with Mike the Bear, and then have to go someplace important, the firemen will be out of here before the first fuse is lit.

What the fuck, Jimmy, says Jack, you used to like fireworks, all that shit exploding in the sky. He shoots Tom a glance. Tom shakes his head; he doesn't care, the firemen can go or they can stay, same thing to him. Used to be, when they were kids, Tom didn't care about something, Jack would say *aw, fuck it* and walk away. Now he glares. Tom glares back; this happens more and more these days, this silent war between Tom and Jack.

So Jimmy knows when Mike the Bear says it's got to be *handled,* he's right. But what Mike the Bear's thinking, that Jimmy can do it, it won't work that way.

So he tells Big Mike he gets it, he tells Big Mike he'll think. And Big

Mike, Mike the Bear, he says, Thanks, Jimmy. Mike the Bear says, That's great, I knew I could count on you.

So Jimmy thinks. He thinks how to do it: like this, like that. And now there's a way he can see.

He doesn't really like it. It's not his way, more like Tom's kind of way, something smart, almost sneaky.

But, Jimmy thinks: there's a good part of it, too, this way he sees. It solves another problem, at least it could help out.

Jimmy's spending more time at the firehouse these days, less hanging with the guys. This is one of the things that burns Jack up, though Jimmy's not sure why. But it's not Jack who's been on Jimmy's mind lately, weighing him down: it's Markie.

Mike the Bear, Tom, Jack, what they do, it's what they were born for. Like Jimmy was born for the truck, the ax, the flames. But not Markie. Those cars: engines and axles, filters and fuel gauges, grease and the smell of gasoline, Markie was born for those. You tell Markie your engine coughs, your steering pulls, maybe you even took the car three other places already but you leave it with Markie, you come back tomorrow and it's fixed. That's what Markie does, that's what's his.

That, and be a father to his son. You'd think Kevin was the first kid ever born, you saw Markie's eyes glow watching him, heard the excitement in his voice when he tells you Kevin said Mama, Kevin went backwards down the stairs, figured that out by himself! Yeah, that's the other thing Markie can do, be Kevin's dad.

But not be what Tom and Jack and Mr. Molloy are.

Jimmy and Tom, they talk about it sometimes, Jimmy worried about Markie, Jimmy knowing Tom and Big Mike won't let Markie in but Jack, he always got a kick out of Markie, always liked him hanging around. Tom knows, too, he tries to get Jack to cool it, but Jack's always saying Hey, Markie can think for himself.

Jimmy's seen the look on Markie, from the time they were kids he's seen Markie watching Jack, watching Tom.

Now, Jimmy knows it's not just Markie. In his earliest memories most of the kids want to be like Tom, want to know what to do, what to say, want to not feel stupid—or instantly, indisputably guilty—when a grown-up asks a question. It's not just that Tom can con the grown-ups when that's called for. It's more than that: it's that Tom feels entitled to try.

Another thing about Tom, he looks out for his friends and always did. Not the way Jimmy looks out for Markie. That's a different thing.

Jimmy doesn't remember how that started, just from the beginning Markie's always there, and somebody has to keep him from running into the street, has to help him climb down out of trees he's stuck in. Always, Markie's up for anything but he doesn't think ahead.

Ten years old, a Saturday at Jones Beach: some of the kids splashing on the shore, some swimming. Jack runs down the sand, dives into the waves. Jimmy's right behind. Markie laughs and runs after, though he can't swim. An extra big wave crashes over them. Jimmy's had swimming lessons at the Y; he tumbles, rolls, feels great, like when he's flying in his dreams. Bursts up through the water, shakes his head, and looks around. What he sees: Markie slipping under, Markie's arms waving, then gone.

Jimmy stares where Markie was, but it's just water, Markie doesn't come up. Jimmy dives. He doesn't have time to think any thoughts, but one comes anyway: Oh, *wow*. That's not about looking for Markie. It's about the fire Jimmy suddenly feels under his own skin.

Jimmy gropes for Markie in the gray-green murk. He can't find him. But he's not scared. Every beam of sunlight that pushes through the water, every tug of the waves, they're all there to help him, he knows how to read them and use them. Left, turn left, turn left. He does, moves his arms through the water, Markie's there.

Then the waves, they're not helping anymore, like they're teasing, like it was a joke. But it's not funny, because Jimmy can't breathe. Straining, heart slamming, he swims with the arm that's not holding Markie, kicks his legs. He breaks the surface, gulps air. He swims more, more, then here's the beach. He half hauls, half throws Markie onto the sand, stumbles and falls down next to him. Both of them panting, they can't move. The ocean curls up around their ankles. There's sand in Jimmy's mouth, he coughs and chokes.

He hears a noise, turns his head: Markie's laughing. Jimmy stares: he can't believe this. But he feels a smile spreading on his own face. Above him, a seagull and an airplane, funny how they're the same size. The sun's hot and the sand's scratchy and his mom's over there on a big striped towel with sandwiches and Cokes and *damn*. And Jimmy's laughing, too, cracking up with Markie.

Back on the towels, Markie starts telling everyone what happened, what a big hero Jimmy is. The moms and dads look at Jimmy in a funny way.

Jimmy, he's thinking about the laughing part, about the waves tickling his feet and how amazing it is that seagulls are so white when the sky's so blue. And about how cold it was under the water, but how he felt heat: the fire under his own skin. It's fading but he still feels it now. He wishes it would stay.

Markie's mom starts to say something to Jimmy, some big thank-you, and Jimmy feels weird, like he's about to get a Christmas present that belongs to somebody else.

Markie, man, he says, you gotta be nuts, you think that's what happened. Jimmy pops the top on a Coke, slurps the foam that jumps out of the can. What really happened, he says, I just sort of bumped into you. You think I'd risk my ass saving yours, you got another think coming. Jimmy's using a word the kids aren't supposed to use, and the moms and dads frown. Markie's about to say something else, but he stops. He grins, shrugs, throws Jimmy a Twinkie. Jimmy bites it hard so the cream comes squirting out the end. His mom says, Oh, Jimmy! and races a napkin to him. Suddenly everyone's eating and talking and that's the end of that.

Except Jimmy, gulping his Coke, catches Tom looking at him, just for a second. How Jimmy feels from this look of Tom's is different from how he felt when all the moms and dads were staring at him like he was the only one the sun was shining on. How he feels, it makes him think of a Mets game his dad took him to, when he caught a rookie lefthander with a scorching fastball getting a nod from a veteran reliever, a guy you could count on to close out a game but you never saw newspaper stories about. Jimmy'd seen the rookie smile a little, and nod back, and it made him wonder how the rookie felt. Now, Tom looking at him this way, Jimmy thinks maybe he knows.

About Jimmy and Markie: that's how it was then, that's how it's been. Jimmy just supposes some people are like that, born with no sense. No point in getting mad at them, it's like getting mad at people who're born deaf. It's just, if you know someone like that, you have to look out for them.

And what Jimmy's thinking now, the way he sees to do what Mike the Bear wants—the way that's like something Tom would do—maybe this is a way he can do this thing for Mike the Bear, and look out for Markie, too.

PHIL'S STORY
Chapter 8

A Hundred Circling Camps

October 31, 2001

Phil thumbed off his cell phone, slipped it back in his pocket. Marian
Gallagher's voice—a voice he'd never liked, too full of incense and intuition, earth goddesses and community trade—echoed in his mind. He
turned to the window, staring not down to the carless streets but up
into the empty sky. No, not empty. The military patrols flew so high
you couldn't hear them, but if you looked up at the right time, you
could catch the silver flashes against the blue.

Working at his desk, his back to the window, Phil had always liked
the roar of planes. It had meant someone was going somewhere, someone was getting away. Good for you, Phil thought. That sound was gone
now, lost to the no-fly zone the air over Manhattan had become. If the
no-fly was ever lifted and air travel was allowed over the island again,
the joy in that roar would still be lost to Phil, who'd heard the first plane
hit and seen the second.

It wasn't the sound of planes that was on his mind now, though, and
not the blue, blank sky. He was thinking about Marian's voice, what
she'd told him, how he'd reacted. And, equally, about how impossible
he and Marian had always found it to be decent to each other.

That Phil and Marian couldn't resist some sniping had been glar-
ingly apparent two days ago, when, drink unfinished, Marian had
stood, scowled, and strode away, leaving Phil alone in the damn foodie
bar in SoHo that had been her choice in the first place. They'd done
something they'd spent decades avoiding: they'd met alone, Phil

and Marian face-to-face. They had to talk, Marian had said when she called.

Harry Randall, then, was still alive, and who knew how many more pieces he was planning, what he might say? Randall's last story had convinced Marian (and how many others? and how many of them did he give a damn about, besides Sally?) that Phil had been cheating Sally from the beginning. The joke was this: everyone else was chasing the money—how deep was Phil Constantine in? what was it he was deep into?—but Marian had higher things on her mind.

"You lied to her," she sniffed, denouncing him over their drinks (beer for him, and though he generally preferred his beer in a glass, with Marian he made a point of drinking from the bottle; a seabreeze, whatever the hell that was, for her).

He hadn't wanted to meet her, except that he'd had some mad thought that if he could explain to Marian, she could make Sally understand. But as soon as he saw Marian's straight-backed progress through the room (God, did this woman stride everywhere, did she never just walk?), her turquoise and coral earrings (likely picked up at some tony Free Tibet fund-raiser), and her unsmiling face (this he knew was hard for her, her natural inclination being to set others at ease: but not him, never him), he wondered what spell of insanity had made him think she might ever be on his side.

"I lied, Marian," he agreed, and drank some beer.

"How could you do that? She loves you!"

"Marian, the whole thing is none of your fucking business." He watched her flush as she took a sip of her pink drink.

"After all she's been through. How could you?"

"Is the point of this meeting to tell me what a shit I am?"

"No!" She sat up even straighter and glared at him. "I'm here so you can tell me the truth." She made it sound like it was an opportunity for him, an offer he was lucky to get.

"Why?"

She blinked, and he almost laughed.

"Screw you, Marian. I don't owe you anything."

"You owe Sally."

"Sally and I—" But there was nothing about himself and Sally that he was interested in telling Marian, so he stopped.

"The truth might help you." As though pointing out something he hadn't thought of.

"Help me what? Help me how? Fix things between me and Sally? Is that what you want? To help us patch things up?"

That was a lie she couldn't tell, and to her credit she said nothing.

He signaled for another beer, put his near-empty bottle down so that the ring it made added to the chain of rings he was forging left to right across the tabletop. "I got the money from Jimmy McCaffery," he suddenly heard himself say. And this time he did laugh.

Her face darkened. "You think that's funny?"

Phil shook his head, still grinning, and lifted the beer again, finishing it in one long pull. He resisted the impulse to wipe his mouth on his sleeve. What was funny was this: even he, even now, if for half a second he glanced away, didn't keep an eye on himself, look what happened: he found he'd wandered halfway down the midway and was buying, from some quack whose booth was all tinkly music and colored lights, the patent medicine idea that the truth could set you free.

He grabbed himself by the shoulder and marched himself back through the sawdust and the horseshit. He'd already said it, so he might as well say it again. "From McCaffery," he repeated. "But I never knew anything else about it."

"How is that possible?"

"You want to know how it's possible? Or you want me to say it's not and I'm lying?" She didn't answer, so he just went on and told her the way it had been, how it was possible. "He said he felt like it was his fault."

"His fault? His fault how?" she asked, and Phil had the feeling she was speaking without breathing.

"Keegan was his friend. He should've been able to do something. I told him that was nuts, the guy was inside, but he wouldn't give it up."

"That's all he meant?"

"That's all he said."

She did breathe now, her chest rising, falling. "And the lie? Why lie about the money?"

"McCaffery thought it was the only way—the State story—that Sally would take the money."

"Where did the money come from?"

Phil grinned. "Well, Marian, that's the big question everyone's asking, isn't it?"

"Tell me!"

"Tell you." Unbelievable. Hadn't she heard what he'd said? What he'd admitted to? That he'd closed his eyes and taken money, passed it on to a client who became his lover, told himself for eighteen years that it wasn't his business where it came from? Wasn't that bad enough for her? "Marian, I *could* say that's privileged information and there's no way in hell I'd tell you. But you want the truth? I didn't know then, and I don't know now."

Whether or not she believed that, she didn't say. After a stony look: "Did you ask Jimmy?"

"I did." Phil found himself nodding, mockingly.

She waited, and he said nothing, mostly to see how long she'd give it. About twenty seconds, it turned out, and then she couldn't stand it. Tossing each word at him like she was throwing rocks: "What did he say?"

He took a moment. Then: "I asked him where a firefighter was getting that kind of money. He said he was borrowing against his life insurance policy."

"You believed that?"

"What's the difference?"

"The difference?" She spat that out so shrilly, heads turned. Seven weeks ago this bar had been a downtown hot spot for the achingly hip. Marian, Phil thought, had probably turned up her serious-minded nose at it, though just as probably she'd been the center of gravity, a magnet for the sideways glances of the insecure, every time she'd strode in. Phil, never seeing the point of an eight-dollar microbrew, had come here only twice, both times to meet with an ambitious young ADA whose pretensions made him easy to manipulate. Now the place was an echoing hangar, half full if you were flexible about defining *half* and *full*. Before, you couldn't hear yourself talk. Now you could, and so could everyone else.

Marian's voice dropped to a hiss: "You didn't ask Jimmy what he was doing?"

Not bothering to lower his own voice, Phil said, "What he was doing was supporting his dead friend's wife and child." A few people nearby exchanged glances. Enjoy yourselves, Phil thought.

"Well, the lie certainly worked for you, didn't it, Phil?" Marian sizzled on. "You got to be the brilliant lawyer, comforting the widow."

"Go to hell, Marian."

"If it was Jimmy, why didn't he just give her the money directly?"

"She wouldn't have taken it."

"From Jimmy? I think she would."

"He thought not. I agreed."

"So *you* made the decision for her?"

"McCaffery did. I just agreed."

Phil's new beer arrived. Marian sat back in her chair, sipped at the pink concoction, and imprisoned Phil with her eyes as the waitress came and went, taking with her the glass Phil waved away.

"This is all a lie," she pronounced. "You didn't get that money from Jimmy. That's just a convenient story now that Jimmy's dead."

"Believe what you want. It doesn't make a difference."

"Yes, it does!" She leaned forward, shortening the physical distance between them as though she hoped that would bring them closer in understanding. He recognized the gesture. The earnest vulnerability with which she offered it was uniquely Marian; still, it was as carefully strategic as any shrug or raised eyebrow in his own courtroom repertoire. He wondered how many times a day she used it.

He lifted his new beer and searched the room, hoping for a pretty girl, a celebrity, a ray of light from a transporter beam. But though he was not looking at her, Marian just went on. "Phil." Okay, he thought, I get it, we're really serious now, you're speaking my name. He used hers whenever they talked because he had a feeling it made her cringe; she rarely let his pass her lips. "Phil, right now, New York really needs Jimmy McCaffery."

In amazement he turned back to face her. He almost spoke. Then he took a long pull of his beer, swallowing his words with it.

"New York needs heroes now, Phil." A desperate tone clung to her voice like the smell of smoke on clothing. "Jimmy's an important one. He's become a symbol—no one's choice, but it's real. People need to believe in Jimmy. What Randall's implying in the paper, and now what you're saying—can't you see it? You're destroying something bigger than we are."

"Oh, for God's sake, Marian, put a cork in it. New York needs McCaffery? *You* need McCaffery. You need him to stay a bright and shining hero or you're fucked, aren't you? You and the Fund. Listen, Randall's jammed me up as bad as you, worse maybe, but the truth is what it is." He leaned forward, too. What the hell, a move's a move. "Marian, that money came from McCaffery. Every month for eighteen years. And—wait, listen—and you're the only person I've ever told."

She frowned. Her hands hovered just off the table, fingers curved as though she were holding something breakable. Or strangling something. Finally: "You didn't tell Randall?"

"Why the hell would I?"

"Then why is he saying it?"

"He's not."

"Between the lines! Anyone can read it!"

"He didn't get it from me."

As he had a few times over the years, on odd occasions (mostly when they were angriest at each other), Phil surprised himself by noticing she was beautiful. Not "aging well": That implied making the best of a bad situation. Marian's beauty had grown richer with time, a clear summer morning unfolding into luxuriant, abundant day.

"If you've never told anyone this, why are you telling me now?" She asked that with a triumphant smile, as if it had come to her that if he was telling *her* a secret, that in itself proved it was a lie.

He was tempted to agree with her: *You're right, I'm lying, very clever of you to figure that out, goodbye.* Let her read all about it in the paper like everyone else.

Instead he told her what was coming. "What Randall's charging is enough to trigger an investigation. It'll come out then."

"Who'll say it?"

"I will."

"After all these years?"

"No one ever asked before. I spent eighteen years looking the other way, but that's not the same as perjury. I know you think I don't know the difference. You think I'm a lying snake—"

"You're a lawyer."

That was a low blow, unworthy of her. She must be really shaken up, Phil decided. "If they ask me, Marian, I'm going to tell them."

"Not from Jimmy," she said. "Not from Jimmy. You're making him the scapegoat because he's dead. That money was from somewhere else. And I'll bet anything there was more than you passed on to Sally. Something for your trouble."

Her eyes, hard as gems, allowed him no entry. He judged silence to be his most effective weapon, so he used it.

"That's what Randall really wants to know, isn't it?" she asked. "Where that money came from."

He smiled. Over the years he'd found it multiplied the effect of silence the way caffeine did for aspirin when your head was pounding.

Marian said, "And that's what this smoke screen about Jimmy is for. To distract Randall."

Quietly, deliberately, Phil said, "Bullshit."

"I knew Jimmy! I knew them all! I was there in those days, remember?"

"And what are you hiding?"

Her face flushed again, became a mask of openmouthed disbelief the same color as her drink.

"Oh, come on, Marian!" Phil slammed his beer bottle on the table-top. People were staring at them now, but he didn't turn to look. "You came here for the truth. I'm telling you the truth, and it doesn't make you happy, it pisses you off. You're scared shitless something even worse is going to happen. What are you so afraid of?"

Her eyes blazed at his. He hadn't had to ask the question, not really. He knew. All these years, he'd known. Though even tonight, until right now, he'd hoped he was wrong, hoped someone—Marian, even Marian—could prove to him what a mistake he'd been making. Because she'd been Jimmy McCaffery's lover back then. Because she'd know, if anyone knew.

She didn't answer him.

And that was answer enough.

As if he'd said that out loud and it made her furious, Marian slapped both palms on the table and stood. She dealt a twenty-dollar bill to the tabletop in the contemptuous stroke of a gypsy turning over a card of ruin. Phil understood the insult for what it was: *Money's been so important to you all these years, you bastard, well, here's more of it.* She stalked out, and he watched her go. After the door drifted shut behind her, he motioned the waitress over, handed her his credit card. He covered the whole bill including the tip and left the twenty lying among the coasters and napkins, across the water-ring chain. In spite of himself he grinned as he left the bar, astonished, as he'd been so many times before, by the human capacity for costly, meaningless gestures.

Now, in his office two days later, staring into the sky, Phil heard the echo of Marian's voice, telling him what she had called to say: that Jimmy McCaffery had left papers behind. Harry Randall, according to the second *Tribune* reporter, had probably seen them.

And Phil wondered what was in those papers. And where they were. And what the hell McCaffery had been thinking, writing any of this down.

And, he asked himself, how do you measure the meaning of a gesture—or its cost—when someone else pays?

LAURA'S STORY
Chapter 7

A Hundred Circling Camps

October 31, 2001

Laura's head was pounding. Squinty-eyed even behind her sunglasses, she turned south from Marian Gallagher's office and stopped at the first open coffee shop she saw. Before she found it, she passed another, a place called Wally's, where a dark and ghostly interior showed through a grimy plate-glass window. Everything inside was smothered in sticky, poisonous ash. Gray coffee cups and ketchup bottles stood on a gray counter in a trickle of sunlight that was cheerfully yellow out where Laura was but gray inside. Laura tried to imagine this place, filled with the smell of toast and the splatter of frying bacon and the shouts of orders being barked back and forth, as it would have been before, as maybe in another universe it still was.

The second coffee shop, the one she came upon two blocks later, had been scrubbed, polished, restocked, and renewed. The owner, awash in smiles, greeted her like a long-lost friend, though she'd never been there before.

She ordered coffee; as an afterthought, she asked for a cherry Danish. Marian Gallagher's cookies had been some delicate gourmet brand, and Laura felt she deserved a reward for resisting them. Not to mention the coffee she had not had, which might have cured her headache. Although probably not. It was an article of faith with Laura that lack of caffeine in the bloodstream was the most common cause of headaches, and a dose of caffeine would melt them away, repeat as needed. This headache, though, had additional causes, and from experience Laura knew that caffeine, while it would be useful, would, like sunlight on an ice floe, not quite be enough.

Laura pushed her mind away from the additional causes. She was working. She swirled milk and sugar into her coffee, used both hands to lift it, and drank down half with her eyes closed, instructing the caffeine to plow straight to the headache. Sometimes that worked.

After she'd sliced a wedge off her Danish—she'd never learned to feel comfortable picking up an entire pastry and taking a bite out of it, like other New Yorkers, like Harry—she licked her fingers and reached into her bag for the tape recorder. Pressing rewind and then play, she lifted the machine to her ear, nodding to herself when she heard, as she expected to, Marian Gallagher's voice: "What do you mean? What papers?" She lifted the tape out, labeled it, and popped in another. Of course the recorder worked. It always worked. She'd done her research, consulted *Consumer Reports,* and chosen this brand for reliability. She rooted around in the bag for the other recorder, listened to it for a moment, too. The sound from this one was much murkier, having been recorded through canvas, but the whole interview was there.

As Harry had taught her, as Harry had been, Laura was a great believer in backup.

"Like a chameleon," Harry had saluted Laura, his voice soft with admiration, when he'd worked with her enough times to have watched her, when he understood. "Like a puzzle piece changing its shape to fit in."

Laura remembered that conversation; she remembered she had smiled. "Okay," she'd said. "But you want to know how I think of it?"

"Most certainly I do."

"Like a virus."

"Explain?"

"Isn't that how a virus works? It imitates something the cell was expecting and prepared for. The cell doesn't call in any defenses because it doesn't think it needs any. The next thing it knows, the virus is inside and the cell is giving up all its secrets."

"My sweet amoeba, that's disgusting."

He was right; but the fact that it was disgusting didn't stop Harry, after that, from calling her his precious little virus at the most surprising moments.

* *

Laura, heading for the Staten Island ferry, climbed a plywood slope covering the temporary cable Verizon had laid along the curbs downtown. This close to the site, a smoky scent drifted on the air. Fires were still burning under tons of dust and steel. Like everyone downtown, Laura had been smelling this odor for weeks; but still she was unsure whether it was a bitter smell, or sweet. The acridness was the scent of smoldering plastic, and steel, and jet fuel. The sweetness, she had been told, was flesh.

The smell brought with it a familiar discomfort. She'd felt it from the first, inhaling this air, and recognized it. It was the same queasy sense that washed over her whenever Reporter-Laura crossed the line, from running after a story to trampling on private grief, from digging for facts to probing an open wound. Some things were too intimate, not made for strangers to intrude on.

Laura focused on the work ahead. She walked the blocks trying to ignore the smell, ignoring the traffic lights, as everyone now did. When cars were finally allowed downtown once more, she knew, pedestrians would start minding the lights, and ten minutes after that they'd be jaywalking again. People, especially New Yorkers, Harry had observed a few weeks ago to the newsroom in general, were infinitely adaptable.

Laura swept Harry's voice from her mind. She was working; she marched on. As she neared a building on Broadway, though, she found herself stopping. Small heaps of dust lay on the building's windowsills and protruding brick, but the bronze address numbers were newly burnished and they shone. The address clicked for Laura. The lawyer, Phil Constantine. The only one who'd refused to see her. He had his office here.

Laura checked her watch. She had time. Considering, she walked away from the glass doors. It was foolish to linger outside a downtown office building: security guards, like everyone else, were on edge these days. Circling the block, Laura called up everything she knew about Phil Constantine.

By the time she turned the corner again and approached the building's entrance, her stride had been transformed, her shoulders set. Her voice, when she spoke to Constantine, would be different from the voice that had come from her in Marian Gallagher's conference room, with its gently obvious view. The distracted, bumbling girl reporter was unlikely to elicit anything but impatience from Constantine. A man like him would need an equal, a worthy opponent. All right then, Laura thought, swinging her shoulder bag down, unzipping it for the guard in the lobby, taking out whatever he asked to see, then stuffing it all back in. All right. If that's what was most likely to work on him, that's what Phil Constantine would get.

And if that's what she gave him, Laura might get her interview.

And for sure, another headache.

PHIL'S STORY
Chapter 9

———

First In, Last Out

Phil glanced up when the outer door opened. He heard Sandra's challenge and the cocksure reply. So. Saying no hadn't worked on Laura Stone any better than it ever had on Harry Randall. *Tribune* reporters, he knew them. But this was Phil's way: unless he needed the press for his own purposes, he always told them to get lost. The mediocre reporters bought it and went away. It saved time and energy and left Phil to deal only with people who had something on the ball.

He watched as Sandra sat back, dragged his book a quarter inch closer, asked the gate-crasher whether she had an appointment. Sandra didn't look at the book: she had his day memorized, his week, and his upcoming month. This was just the game it was her job to play. When the answering volley came, she'd give the icy smile, lay down the smash, and this short match would be over.

Laura Stone looked past Sandra into Phil's office, right into his eyes. "I'm on my way to Pleasant Hills to talk to some people there. I thought Mr. Constantine might want to see me first." This with her eyes still on Phil's.

"Mr. Constantine doesn't see anyone without an appointment."

"I have a deadline. If Mr. Constantine doesn't speak to me before I have to file, *Tribune* readers won't get his side of the story."

Not bad, Phil thought. Looking only at the back of Sandra's head, he still could have described the knife blade of a smile with which she said, "I'm sorry."

Laura Stone said, "First in, last out."

Sandra was thrown. Oh, she disliked that. Phil heard her irritation: "Excuse me?"

"People remember the first thing they read. Even if it's wrong. After that, it's hard to correct. A retraction never has the impact of the original story."

Below her cropped hair the back of Sandra's neck was red. She could keep this reporter at bay all day and late into the evening, Phil knew that. Especially if she got mad. But the hell with it. He was sure she had better things to do.

"It's all right, Sandra." Phil rose, though he didn't come out from behind his desk. Let her in, sure; trek to the border to greet her, no. "Come on in, Ms. Stone. Thanks, Sandra."

With Sandra's bellicose glare following her—and Elizabeth's stare also, less hair-trigger, more weights and measures—Laura Stone marched into Phil's office. She sat down and plunked her massive shoulder bag to the floor beside her. Flipping it open, she pulled out a pad, two pens, and a tape recorder. She did this so fast and so smoothly he had to figure the bag, despite its bulging, chaotic look, was the kind with dividers, holders, pockets, and tabs. Velcro and zippers and snaps. Everything in the right place, instantly accessible.

He used one like that himself.

Stone held up the recorder, lifted her eyebrows.

"No," Phil said, sitting again.

Laura Stone dropped the machine back in the bag. Phil couldn't see whether it was running, but he assumed it was. He'd have told her to turn it off, but the second one, which she was almost sure to have, would be running, too. His choices were: he could search her, including patting her down to see if she was wired, or he could watch his mouth.

"I'm here to give you a chance to comment on the death of Harry Randall," Stone began, colonizing a chair, ankle on knee, elbows out, taking up more room than he'd have thought such a thin woman could. She flipped open her pad, held her pen poised.

Phil grinned. How about that? Another woman offering him an opportunity to do something he didn't want to do. "I told you this morning I had nothing to say."

"I didn't believe you."

"Does telling people that work in your business?"

"Does blowing off reporters work in yours?"

"Ms. Stone, with all due respect, after the last couple of weeks, why the hell would I want to talk to the *Tribune*?"

"To correct any misconceptions, I'd think."

"Yeah, I bet that's what you'd think. But all right. About Harry Randall's death?" He glanced at the ceiling, frowned, nodded. "Harry Randall was a fixture in this town. A fine example of the old-fashioned muckraking reporter. They don't make them like that anymore. New York needs him now more than ever, it's a goddamn shame what happened to him, and he'll be missed." He smiled, slid his chair back from his desk to give himself room to cross his long legs. Ankle on knee. "You can quote me."

She wrote as he spoke, quick sure strokes, and he studied her as she wrote. In that wholesome midwestern way, the way that called up the bucolic farming life (early morning rising, direct and sweaty work, lit evening windows, neighbors bringing pies), Laura Stone was pretty. Straight brown hair brushing her shoulders, features small and neat, pale skin that would probably be smooth and clear once she got some sleep. Phil's forebears were rabbis and ragpickers, salesmen and stevedores. Not a farmer among them, back to the windswept horizon. Why, then, this—not just attraction, no, not only desire—this wistful nostalgia, this homesickness a woman like this had always been able to make him feel? Her bedroom: heightening heat and the crescendo of pounding hearts under quilts in the crystal winter night; but also the breeze through the window of her sunny kitchen on a spring morning. Her soft skin, her soft hair, the feel of them under his fingertips; but even more her quiet companionship by the fire on a blustery fall day. He longed for all that, at the same time—maybe for the same reason—as he knew he'd last maybe a week in that lonesome prairie farmhouse.

Someone who's homesick for somewhere they've never been, Phil thought. The definition of an American.

Laura Stone stopped writing and flipped her hair from her face. It fell back to exactly where it had been. "If I print that," she said to him, "people will know you're lying."

What the hell had they been talking about? Oh, right, his tribute to Harry Randall. "Everyone who reads your paper already thinks I'm lying," he said.

"Then set them straight. Now's your chance."

Hey, there's an idea. Just tell the truth. After all these years? Then what had been the point? Though, when you looked at this mess, what had been the goddamn point anyway? "No. Thanks."

"You were Mark Keegan's attorney in 1979?"

"That's public record."

"Keegan was accused and convicted of possessing an illegal hand-gun—the gun that killed Jack Molloy—but not of the killing itself. Why not?"

"That was the plea deal."

"Your idea?"

"The opposition's."

"The District Attorney's?" Her eyebrows went up as if she needed more light in those morning-colored eyes.

"Yes."

"What did you think?"

"I thought if we went to trial on the manslaughter charge, we were screwed. I couldn't believe I was being offered the deal, but I jumped at it."

"Why did they do it, do you think?"

"A bird in the hand."

"Nothing else?"

"It didn't matter to me."

"But you think there might have been something else?"

"There always is. An election's coming up. The accused looks like the ADA's cousin. They don't want to waste time and money on a first-timer who killed a gangster they're happy to have out of the way."

"Or someone buys off someone in the DA's office."

"It happens."

"In this case?"

"Who the hell knows? If anyone was up to anything, it wasn't me. My client got a hell of a better deal than I thought he'd get, going in. That was all I cared about."

Laura Stone turned her head, as though looking around Phil's office, taking in the books, the pictures, and the mess. What was she, Elizabeth's age? No, a little older. The age he'd been when Markie Keegan was assigned to him. The fingertips of her left hand lifted to her temple, pressed. Headache? Or maybe he was supposed to think she had one, so he'd be gentle with her.

He waited to see.

Laura Stone brought her eyes back to him. "It didn't turn out so well for Mark Keegan, that deal."

"You think that's the fault of the deal?"

She wrote and moved on. Plainly, what she thought wasn't a topic of this meeting. "What's your relationship with Mark Keegan's widow?"

"Private."

"You and Sally Keegan have been intimate since you met, isn't that true?"

No, it's not true. Markie'd been in jail five months and dead sixteen before the foggy cold night on the Staten Island ferry when I first kissed Sally. "No comment."

"What's your relationship with Edward Spano?"

Ah, Eddie. I knew we'd get to Eddie. "No comment."

"Is it true you were taking money from Spano all these years and passing it on to Mark Keegan's family?"

Not directly. Not that I knew about. "No comment."

"But you don't deny the money didn't come from New York State?"

"That's public record."

"Where did it come from?"

Wish to hell I knew. "No comment."

"You're acquainted with Marian Gallagher? Of More Art, New York? And the McCaffery Fund?"

"Yes."

"Ms. Gallagher suggested that you, as the attorney handling the payments, would have to know the source of the funds."

"Did she?"

"Would you care to comment on that?"

"No."

"Is she wrong?"

"Usually."

Laura Stone let go a sudden smile. "You don't like her?"

Shrug. "You met her."

She reined the smile in, as though it had escaped by mistake, all business again. So, he thought, now we share a secret. Now we're buds. Good move, and well done. Probably usually works.

She said, "But you received the money from somewhere."

"True."

"Close to $350,000 over the years, that's a lot of money. Harry Randall thought it came from Edward Spano through McCaffery. Do you want to deny that?"

I'd love to. "No comment."

"What was its purpose?"

"The money? To support Keegan's wife and child."

"Who would want to do that?"

Anyone who knew them. "No comment."

"Would Edward Spano have any reason to do it?"

"Not that I know about."

"If Spano had paid Mark Keegan to kill Jack Molloy, would he have had a reason to support Keegan's family once Keegan died?"

If he had, you bet he would. "No comment."

"Why did Jack Molloy threaten Mark Keegan?"

"He didn't just threaten Mark Keegan, Ms. Stone, he shot at him."

"Why did Jack Molloy shoot at Mark Keegan?"

No change of tone. Phil had to grin. He'd have done it just that way himself. "He was drunk and from what I hear, he was crazy."

"He'd been like that all his life, and he'd never shot at Keegan before."

"How do you know?"

"Had he?"

Hope in her eyes, something new to uncover? Too bad. "No. Not according to Markie, no."

"Then why?"

Not a secret. If he didn't say, she'd get it somewhere else, then come back at him again, confirm or deny. "Jack was a gangster. Markie had heard that Jack was the subject of a police operation and was about to get the ax. He told Jack about it."

"That upset Molloy? I'd think he'd be grateful."

"Jack checked it out. It wasn't true."

"Checked it out how?"

"He called the Answer Man. How the hell do you think?"

Her eyebrows rose at his sharp tone. She shifted in her chair. If she hadn't been wearing slacks, he'd bet she'd have tugged her hem down.

"If it wasn't true the police were running an operation against Jack Molloy, why would Mark Keegan say they were?"

"That's what Jack wanted to know."

"Did Keegan think it was true? That the police were cracking down on Jack Molloy?"

"He told me he did."

"Where did he hear it?"

"He never said."

"You were his lawyer, and he never told you?"

"Never."

She gave him a conspiratorial look that said, Come on, we both know you're better than that, you can get all kinds of things out of people.

Hmm, Phil thought. That's a good one. I'll have to try it.

He didn't answer her, so after a moment she went on. "Maybe Keegan was working both sides."

He'd been waiting for that. "Neither side."

"What does that mean?"

"Markie hung around the fringes, but he wasn't in Jack Molloy's crew, and he wasn't on the NYPD payroll, either."

"So he said?"

"So everyone said."

"True?"

"As far as I know."

"But it's what Molloy thought, wasn't it? That it was Keegan himself who was ratting him out to the police?"

"Might have been."

"If it were true, it could be the reason for the plea deal. To keep Keegan from revealing his source."

"Could be. As I said, I didn't think so. But I never knew."

"They dropped the manslaughter charges."

"It was a good deal."

"It could be construed as the NYPD showing gratitude for services rendered."

"It could. Or as overworked ADAs with no witnesses, a defendant with an infant son and no priors, and a victim no one would miss." If there was any such thing. Jack Molloy had a brother, a father, and mother. Phil had seen her over the years, Peggy Molloy. One of the few people in Pleasant Hills with a smile for him, one of the people he'd least expect it from.

"Even if the story wasn't true," Stone said, "couldn't it have been planted by the police?"

"What do you mean?" he asked, though he knew exactly what she meant.

"Maybe they couldn't make anything stick to Molloy, so they were trying to scare him, make him think they were out to get him. So he'd back off. Maybe even leave town, get to be someone else's problem."

Well, whatever she was, she wasn't stupid. "Markie wouldn't say where he heard it. But I looked into it at the time. I couldn't find anything either way."

"Or," Laura Stone mused, "maybe it was something else entirely. Maybe somebody else wanted to scare Jack Molloy. Could the story have been planted on Keegan by Eddie Spano, do you suppose?"

"I asked Markie that flat out. He told me if I thought he was working for Spano, I could go to hell."

"Any thoughts on it now?"

Now? Now, when they're pulling thousands of bodies in small pieces from smoking rubble around the corner? Now, when ash could mean anthrax, and loud sounds made you jump? Now, when Sally's not speaking to me and Kevin tells me Fuck off, Uncle Phil? Shit, lady. Now you could ask me if Eddie Spano was the Messiah, and I'd have to say it was possible. "I haven't thought about it."

"What would you say if I told you Harry Randall didn't kill himself?"

"I'd say your paper already made it clear they don't think it was suicide."

"There's evidence that points that way."

"Not strong evidence."

"Why do you say that?"

"If the police bought your theory, they'd be camping in my office."

"Maybe they just haven't gotten around to you yet."

"Around to me? I'd be the first."

"You consider yourself a suspect in Harry Randall's murder?"

"I consider myself a successful criminal defense attorney. To some cops that makes me guilty of a lot worse things than murder."

"Did you kill Harry Randall?"

He stared at her. "That's a hell of a technique. Does it work?"

"Sometimes."

"I'm inclined to tell you to go to hell."

"Go ahead, as long as you answer my question."

"No."

"No, you won't answer, or no, you didn't kill Harry Randall?"

"I didn't kill him. Is this what this is really about? The *Tribune*'s looking for a few bad men?"

"Harry Randall was murdered because he knew something."

"Harry Randall was a drunk who jumped off the Verrazano Narrows Bridge."

She shook her hair back from her face again. Phil was startled to see her eyes moisten. She blinked twice, and that was gone. Maybe he'd imagined it. But her voice seemed to quiver just slightly as she repeated,

"Harry Randall was killed because he knew something." The quiver vanished, though, as she went on. "One of the things he knew was that the money you've been giving to Mark Keegan's family came from, or at least through, James McCaffery."

No surprise there. But what else did Randall think he knew? And how do *you* know what he knew? Is this story a potential Pulitzer for you, or is it personal? And which is more dangerous? "No comment."

"But you knew James McCaffery?"

"Yes."

"And it's true the money-from-the-State fiction was his idea?"

"Yes."

"Did you know he'd left papers behind?"

"Yes."

The lifting of the brows again. But look: her eyes weren't the clear blue of the morning sky, as he'd thought, but the deeper, opaque blue of evening. Had he been wrong? Or did Laura Stone's eyes change, like Sally's, according to rules he would never understand?

"You know that?" Her voice took on a quick note, hope again. "Have you seen these papers?"

"No." And because he could tell where she was going: "I only just found out."

"Where from?"

Indirectly, from you, about an hour ago. "No comment."

She gave him an appraising look. Well, let her figure it out.

"Do you know what's in them? McCaffery's papers?"

"No."

"Any guesses?"

Yes. "No."

"What if it's this whole thing—Keegan, Molloy, where the money came from?"

"Then we'll get McCaffery's thoughts on the matter."

"Would that bother you?"

"Depends what he thought."

"Are you telling my readers you have nothing to hide?"

"I'm not telling your readers anything. You can tell them whatever crap you want, just like Randall did."

"What did you think of him?"

"Randall? I already told you."

She shook her head, her soft hair swaying. "McCaffery."

One missed beat, and then: "He was a hero."

As though he hadn't answered, with no change of tone, just the way he himself would have done it, she repeated, "What did you think of him?"

I thought he was a lying, grandstanding, murderous hypocrite. "He was a hero."

BOYS' OWN BOOK
Chapter 12

The Water Dreams

By the time Jimmy gets home, Marian's there already. She has her own place, shares it with two other girls, because how would that look, if she just moved right in with him? And on the new job she stays late a lot, and Jimmy's working straight tours, so it's not that often they get to spend the night together. Jimmy sees her through the window as he's coming down the stairs from the sidewalk, stops a minute just to look at her.

She's reading, bare legs crossed Indian-style on the big leather chair. Her back's to Jimmy. The light from the lamp is soft on the side of her face, makes little swells and shadows on her T-shirt. As he watches, her black hair—short, sharp, simpler than the other girls wear theirs—sweeps across her cheek. She lifts a hand to tuck it away again: she doesn't like to be distracted, she always says, when she's reading. So many different colors of black in Marian's hair: this has always amazed Jimmy, and amazes him now.

Marian looks up, sees him through the window, smiles. He realizes he's grinning like a kid, wonders how long he's been doing that.

They kiss at the door, before they speak. The night's gotten cool, but Jimmy only realizes this when his hand's touching Marian. He's aware—he's always been aware—of the solidity under the creaminess of her flesh: Marian plays volleyball with her girlfriends, she rides her bike everywhere, in high school she was on the girls' softball team, she was captain. All that just makes her skin's silky softness better for Jimmy, like it was somehow honest, somehow earned.

Jimmy's other hand can't resist touching Marian's midnight hair.

Marian's lips play with Jimmy's, but she does not embrace him: she snakes her arms around him, slips her hands into the back pockets of his jeans, moves him toward her that way.

Oh God, thinks Jimmy.

After, they lie in the darkness for a while, just together. This is not a deep, heavy darkness, like the smoke at the center of a fire, all directions the same and the blasting air itself almost solid, itself your enemy; not like your dreams, where your eyes are open, wide open, but you can't see anything and you try to shout, scream, tell someone but you make no sound. This is just the apartment in the basement of where the Cooleys live, the apartment that's Jimmy's now. It doesn't get dark that way here.

Beyond the swaying, half-closed curtains, the soft glow from the Cooleys' porch light is backed up by lights from other porches and yards, by lit windows in the neighbors' places, and by streetlights that rise over the rooftops. The place is quiet, but the silence never gets so huge you could wander around lost in it. It's bordered, hemmed in, by a dog's bark, someone's laugh, the left-to-right flare of a car radio in the street out front.

So, Superman, Marian says to Jimmy, and her voice close to his ear sounds to him the same way her skin feels, satin with metal under it, though he doesn't think it's iron under her voice like under her skin, he thinks it's silver, maybe gold. She asks him, How many people did you save today?

'Bout a hundred, says Jimmy.

Marian gives him a poke in the ribs. You weren't even on duty today.

That's how I saved them. Stayed out of their way.

Marian laughs, nibbles on his ear.

How about you, he says, you save anyone?

Nope, slow day. She rearranges the sheet they're under, smooths it. I tutored that little Jeanine, worked on her reading, but that kid, she doesn't even need me, Jimmy. She'll do great, no matter what.

Jimmy grunts. Wasn't for you, she'd end up like her old lady. Any chance that kid has, it's because you made a project out of her.

Well, she's a good kid. She can't help it if her whole family is bums.

I know, Jimmy says. It's not that. It's more like, on one side is you, on the other side is her whole family and her whole life. Jimmy's hands, palms up, balance above the sheet like scales; one rises, one falls.

Yes, I know. Marian nods. But you can't tell. One little pebble might do the trick. You can't tell unless you put it there.

The tip of Marian's finger barely touches the palm of Jimmy's up hand. She draws little delicate circles. Then she presses, pushing down.

Jimmy's hand resists. What if it doesn't? he asks. Do the trick?

Marian keeps pushing, Jimmy resisting. She smiles. Her other hand grabs at Jimmy's down hand, lifts it high in the air. Then it'll do some other trick, she says. In surprise, Jimmy laughs. Marian laughs with him. He wraps his hands around hers, wraps himself around her.

Jimmy knows Marian's right. Little Jeanine, Marian can't just give up on her. But if Jimmy told the truth, it would be this: Marian's kind of saving, he's not really sure about it, if it ever works, if it's even right.

Marian's sure. She's sure about little Jeanine: People aren't born to be one thing or another, she tells Jimmy. People decide. Jeanine can go anywhere she wants to go.

Jimmy doesn't argue. But he thinks about himself and fires. Markie and cars. Tom and quiet talks at Flanagan's with suit-coated men who come and go. He thinks about Mrs. Molloy's eyes when she looks at Jack, always the same look since they were kids, like she sees something bad standing behind him that the rest of them can't see. He's not really sure how many choices any of them has, about which way to go.

But Marian's sure. She wants to do it for her job, help people find their ways to go. A career of saving people. That's what Marian went to college for, saving people.

Business, she tells him, laughing, the first time he says this to her. Business administration, Jimmy, that never saved anyone. But Jimmy knows what she wants, he knows why she's doing it the whole time she's in college, the only one of them to go. It's so she can work at one of those places, the Red Cross or someplace, when she's finished, an important job where she can save people.

And now she is finished, graduated back in June up at City College, Jimmy late because he has to trade shifts, take that long train ride into Harlem. Graduation's outdoors, clear and warm and not a cloud in the sky. Jimmy's way in the back, way on the side, when the graduates march in. The wind is up. They have to hold their flat hats on and their black gowns flap and Jimmy has a little trouble picking Marian out, he's so far back and they're all dressed the same. But when the dean calls her name and she strides across the stage like someone really tall on her way to someplace important—though she's shorter than Jimmy, and she's only going to shake the dean's hand and sit down again—Jimmy watches her and knows that if he forgets his own name, forgets where home is, forgets why you fight fires, he'll always remember how Marian walks.

When she starts the new job two weeks later—she lined this job up before she graduated, that's Marian's way, how she does things—Jimmy takes her out to celebrate. Just the two of them at Montezuma's, in St. George, they eat paella and lobsters and drink wine, neither of them knows what paella is before they order it, but it's great. Though Jimmy thinks maybe they could be eating cardboard and on this night he'd like it.

Jimmy lifts his wineglass, offers a toast.

To saving people, he says.

Candlelight sparkles in Marian's wineglass and her eyes. To saving people, she says, smiles at him. Your way and mine.

That smile, when Jimmy sees it, he'd slay dragons if they were keeping Marian from finding her way.

Someday, he says, and though he's still smiling, his voice has gone quiet in a way that makes Marian lower her glass and really listen, someday you'll be the one. The one making decisions, how to save people, who to save.

Marian tilts her head. Someone has to, she says.

Her eyes are almost black, with tiny lights, some reflected from the candles, but some Jimmy's seen before, light that's always there in Marian's eyes. I'm glad it's going to be you, he says.

And he doesn't say: And I'm glad it doesn't have to be me.

To do the kinds of things Marian does, the things she wants to do, you have to be pretty sure you know what's good for people.

But, Marian would say if he said this to her—he knows she would, because she has—like little Jeanine: her sister's a hooker, her mother's a drunk. How can you *not* be sure it would be good for her not to be like them?

When she says things like that, Jimmy can't argue.

But still.

His kind of saving, it's different. Buildings are going to burn, he puts the fires out. People inside are going to die, he fights a tug-of-war with death, and if he wins—so far, he's usually won—they live. There's not much to figure out: not burning is better than burning, living is better than dying.

Anyone knows that.

When they leave Montezuma's, Jimmy puts his arm around Marian.

Her shoulders are warm under her soft sweater, and he has to stop and kiss her. The way she holds him when she kisses back, he almost abandons his plan so they can go straight home. Instead he takes her hand and leads her downhill.

Where are we going?

You'll see.

They wind up at the terminal. Jimmy pays two nickels, and they're on the ferry. As the boat starts to move, he unslings his backpack on the deck, pulls out a bottle of real champagne from France, and two glasses. Marian laughs, like music. Jimmy pops the cork. Champagne fizzes up, spills over his hand and tickles. She holds the glasses while he pours, and they drink champagne all the way to Manhattan, watching the towers with their sparkly lights get closer, get bigger. And then, all the way back home.

That night, Marian's graduation night, summer was starting; tonight it's close to ending.

In bed in the Cooleys' basement apartment, Marian walks her fingers along Jimmy's ribs as though she's counting them. Superman, she says, something on your mind?

Me? No, uh-uh. Jimmy smiles. Only you.

Seems like you're worried about something.

Jimmy's surprised. On his way home he was thinking about Markie, about Jack, about Mr. Molloy asking for help over a beer in Flanagan's. He was trying to figure what to do. But when Marian opened the door, kissed him in the doorway under the stairs, well, that was the end of that.

Just stuff, says Jimmy.

He could tell her: what Mr. Molloy's problem is, what he wants Jimmy to do. But there's two things about that. One is, Marian gets mad at Jack a lot these days. Grow up! she tells him. Anyone else saying the kinds of things to him that Marian does, Jack would blow up. But Marian always had special ways she could talk to Jack, ways no one else could. And Jack could always make Marian laugh. Always before; but not now. Now when Jack's wild, when he does his stupid stuff, Marian gets mad.

And even though it's kind of impossible not to like Tom, she doesn't want to be around him a lot, not for a while now. Not since they were all too old not to know what Mr. Molloy does, what Tom now does. Jimmy doesn't push it when Marian says she has to work the night Tom has Mets tickets (though Marian loves baseball) or when she drops by only long enough for one quick eggnog at Tom and Vicky's Christmas party and spends most of that time talking quietly with Peggy Molloy. Sometimes Jimmy wonders what he'd do, himself, if he and Tom weren't part of each other's first memories. But they are.

Tom goes far back in Marian's life, too, of course, as far as he goes in Jimmy's, and Jack does, too. But with girls it's different. The girls see this kind of thing, see most things, a different way.

For the girls, Jimmy thinks, it's not just who people are. Not just that they've all always known each other, been in the middle of each other's lives like all the different colors making up the same picture, all the different sounds in the same song. That's not enough. For the girls, it's the kinds of things you do, too. For them, those can change how they think about people. For him, for the other guys, what you do, that's one thing, but who you are, that's another.

Maybe the way the girls see things is right, and his is wrong. That wouldn't surprise Jimmy. But whose way is right, he thinks, that's not what matters sometimes.

And there's the other thing, too: Marian wouldn't get it, why Jimmy can't just go to Jack and tell him what's going to happen, tell him he has to cool it or he'll be screwed. But if it's the truth, Jimmy, she'd say. Why can't you just tell him, if it's the truth?

Jimmy knows having the truth is only part of the answer, but he doesn't know how to tell this to Marian.

So when Marian asks what's on his mind, Jimmy says, Just stuff.

Nothing I can help with?

Jimmy smiles and says, You are. You're helping.

Marian smiles, too. She says, Okay. She kisses him, says, It's Saturday night. Do you want to go out?

Jimmy wraps his own hand around hers, kisses each of her fingers separately. The curtains shimmy, someone's screen door creaks. Not tonight, Jimmy says. He slides closer to her under the sheet, folds his arms around her from behind. He kisses her ear, her throat. He parts her hair and kisses the back of her neck. Not unless you can think of somewhere to go, Jimmy says, somewhere we would go that would be better than here.

Marian turns to face Jimmy and her answer is her smile, and the slow way she circles her arms around him.

**

So why doesn't Jimmy marry Marian, why hasn't he asked her? He knows she'd say yes. He knows how he feels.

But sometimes when she looks at him—and he sees this most when he's coming off his shift, when they've had a big job and one of the guys, maybe, has almost fallen, almost been lost—the way she looks at him, Jimmy's not sure it's for him. It's for what he does, but not even that: it's for what Marian thinks he does, and for the man she thinks he is for doing it.

That look, that's what's been stopping Jimmy. He needs to be sure of what he is not sure of now: that Marian knows the man who is asking her, the man she'd be marrying, is Jimmy.

Not Superman. Just Jimmy.

Marian's Story
Chapter 8

The Way Home

October 31, 2001

Marian hesitated outside. She had always disliked Flanagan's. She had been the one to call; but now, standing on the sidewalk in the amethyst hour when day surrenders to night, she wondered why she had agreed to have this encounter here. She could have demurred when Tom suggested it. (Though *suggest* was wrong: "Meet you at Flanagan's, five-thirty," was what he'd said, and she'd said, "Fine, see you there," as though Flanagan's ponderous furnishings and hushed talk had not, from the first, given her the uncomfortable feeling that something was happening just beyond the borders of her experience, something she was not welcome to know.) She could have requested another location. He would have consented, perhaps even apologized for not remembering how she felt, she who had not been inside Flanagan's for twenty years. But truly, how could he be expected to remember? You should have said something, she admonished herself, you should have spoken up if it mattered to you. It was not Tom's responsibility. People do not read minds.

Though Tom did, Tom sometimes did. She wished he had, on this occasion as so many times when they all were young, read hers. They might have met at the chrome-wrapped little diner, or they might have sat together in the Hilltop Café, finally somewhere to go in Pleasant Hills for a latte and a croissant. But it was as it had always been: what Tom offered sounded right, and without even considering another possibility (and in truth this was what most unnerved her: not that she had compromised, for Marian had built her life around her belief in the value of compromise; but that she had assumed without question that what he wanted was what she wanted also), she had agreed.

Impatient with herself, she pulled the door open into a room so startlingly unfamiliar that at first she was afraid she had somehow come to the wrong place; and then, for a brief time, she wanted the old Flanagan's back.

Dark, that tavern had been. Its linoleum floor stuck to your shoes, and its ancient jukebox throbbed with music from the days before your parents were old enough to drink. What had covered the walls? Stories clipped from newspapers, photographs behind glass. Horses, now she remembered, horses in the photos, trotting with sulkies behind. (Marian had always thought sulky races eerie and graceful, a little frightening. A trotter was expected to win, was cajoled and lashed by the man in the carriage behind, but could not run. How must that feel for the horses, she worried, what must it be like trying to do your best, having your best demanded of you, while forced to hold back?) There had been mirrors on the walls then, too, "Schlitz" or "Miller" scrawled across them in chipped gold leaf. Seeing in her mind the places where the mirrors had been, Marian realized that they had been set on the walls in such a way that from every part of Flanagan's, a customer could see the door.

She wondered whether she had always known that.

The mirrors were gone. The dark furniture and the sticky linoleum and the jukebox, the trotting horses locked behind glass, all had been replaced. Bentwood chairs, light and cheaply elegant, sat on a patterned tile floor beneath glass lamps that glowed seductively. Two television sets above the bar and three more by the green vinyl booths broadcast college football (one team a local one, their helmets bearing FDNY and NYPD logos alongside their tiger mascot's image), stock car racing (each car painted with its sponsor's name and colors and a large Stars and Stripes), and a sports interview show (tiny flag pins in everyone's lapel). You could swivel your head and take your choice. (Did they ever tune in Yonkers Raceway or the Meadowlands now, Marian wondered, where the trotters ran?)

Marian strained to hear the music. Over a lifelessly exact electronic beat a sad and sexy woman warned her man that he'd hurt her too often, and one day soon he'd find her gone. The rhythm and the melody were new, the sentiment the same as in Marian's youth, and her parents', and forever before. The raucous voices of the young crowd slammed the music down. A table or two, a booth here and there, were occupied by people Marian's age or older, resolutely eating burgers or plates of linguini, drinking their beers and watching the game. They sat in the date-night crowd like stolid old trees in a tangle of wild new growth. It was the kind of landscape, it occurred to Marian, that springs up after a forest fire. Most of Flanagan's patrons were kids, kids the age she and Jimmy had been when, finally legally permitted to drink—meaning, able to drink in public, not just in the woods or in the parking lot at Eisenhower or on the rocks under the bridge—they had only rarely chosen to come in here.

Tom, of course, had come here often; and he was here now. It was like Tom to be early, to be waiting so that she would not feel uneasy, alone in what had always been foreign territory and was now a numbingly unfamiliar country.

He stood when he saw her, and eyes in the crowd lifted to him as he rose. The plaintive woman quavering from the jukebox could be heard more clearly as conversation faltered and people glanced at one another. Tom walked to where Marian stood, just inside the door. He kissed her cheek and led her through the room.

He was no longer what he had been in days of old, the crown prince; and the kingdom he was to have inherited, he had dissolved. The young people in this new Flanagan's might not even know his name, not know what it was about him that drew and held their glances. But the older ones surely knew. They nodded to him as they had nodded to his father, smiled back when he smiled at them as though they shared a secret.

Tom led her to his table. Nothing in the new Flanagan's was familiar to Marian except this table of Tom's. Set for two and holding a half-drained pilsner of beer, it breathed an inch or two easier than the crowded tables around it and stood in precisely the spot on the floor where his father's table had always been.

And he was still Tom Molloy. His blue eyes were still clear, and his thick short hair was dark as a boy's. He still walked like a warrior, and his smile still told you that seeing you was the best thing that had happened to him all day.

Over the music, Marian said, "It's changed."

Tom shrugged, and his smile turned rueful. "What hasn't?" He looked around, and she did, too, her head full of the past twenty years, the leisurely, incremental, inescapable alterations of time; and the last six weeks, the violent flashes of disaster.

"They still make a great cheeseburger, though," Tom said, bringing them back to the solid world, the facts of the moment, and Marian, surprising herself, nearly laughed with delight at the persistent memory and hope of a world in which cheeseburgers were worth discussing.

She did not laugh, though, only smiled, and Tom did, too. She examined the menu and chose a pasta primavera. She also ordered wine, excusing herself for thinking this might be a difficult conversation to get through without something to encourage her. The new Flanagan's apologized for having no sauvignon blanc (the old Flanagan's would have laughed in her face), but the chardonnay, when it came, was surprisingly good.

Marian sipped at her wine, Tom at his beer. Tom brought up the Fund, only to say the board was still a hundred percent behind Marian, every step of the way. Marian smiled and didn't tell him that long, weary experience told her what that meant: someone on the board—at least someone, though most likely an entire faction—had questioned her decision-making, and probably her overall suitability in light of the *Tribune*'s allegations, and had no doubt urged her replacement. If the board was still behind her, it was only because Tom and his faction had prevailed.

Marian thanked him and asked after his children. All were doing well. Michael, the oldest, who looked so like Tom had when they all were young, was home. He'd been in his senior year at college, in Syracuse; after the attacks, he'd rushed home and would finish school somewhere else, somewhere near. "He wants to stay in New York," said Tom. "He doesn't want to be one of those people."

Marian knew who those people were: the ones who ran from what had happened and what might happen, who deserted, escaped to other, less endangered cities. Or to cabins in the woods. "But he could come back next year," Marian said, as though next year were something that could be counted on, as though next year would for certain come and be different from now. "Don't you think he should go back now and finish?"

"I'm his father. He doesn't ask me what I think."

"You could tell him anyway. That's what my father does."

Tom smiled at her again and looked down, and she thought he must be remembering his father, Mike the Bear, gone just over seven years now. How long that seemed! And yet it was not the Mike Molloy of seven years ago, or seventeen, whom Marian suddenly longed to see come striding through Flanagan's door. That had been a diminished and weary man, the exhausted king who had not fought his son's determination to democratize the kingdom and give away its wealth. No, the Mike Molloy whom Marian wished for was the Big Mike of her childhood, the old-time boss of Flanagan's. In charge, running things, and obeyed.

But she was being foolish. Big Mike was gone. And when the world had been his, it had not been a good world, not a fair one, and that world had ended badly, and that was why she was here with Tom right now. Tom had said it on the steps of St. Ann's in September: There are no grown-ups, only us. If Marian, and Tom, and everyone else who had been placed in positions they had not asked for, did not accept their situations, take responsibility, do what they had to do, they would find that no one was in charge.

Oh, Marian knew how much was in her hands. Still, reluctant to begin, to open a conversation she had avoided for twenty years (though it could not be that Tom did not know why they were here, so why did he not help her, why did he not begin?), Marian twirled her pasta, drank more wine, and asked after Tom's mother. "I saw her in September," she told Tom. "At St. Ann's. But I didn't have a chance to talk to her."

"That's too bad," Tom said. "She'd have liked to see you."

Marian had not spoken to Peggy Molloy at the mass she had come back to Pleasant Hills to attend, five days after the attacks. But not really because she had not had the chance.

Everyone, that day, was stunned and confused and trying to manage. All around her Marian had seen people working, for their own sakes and the sake of others, to hold themselves together, and she'd seen the different small things that made each fall apart. The sight of the empty apparatus floor through the open door at Engine 168 had been too much for one friend; another broke down sobbing as she spoke of talking to her neighbor while he watered the vegetable garden that now he would never harvest.

For Marian, strong and useful for those past five days, offering support to those weaker than she, volunteering late into the night and bearing up, that small thing had been the sight of Peggy Molloy. Seeing her shoulders bent as though carrying weight, her head covered in the old style with a black lace shawl, had brought Marian to unexpected tears.

If Tom was the abdicated prince, living now by choice as a commoner, Peggy Molloy, widowed seven years, was still the sad queen she had always been. She dressed as other women did, and walked like them, sat and talked among them in the same gentle voice she had always used; her grandchildren's friends adored her as her sons' friends always had. Others in church that day had lost loved ones; Peggy Molloy had not. But seeing her clothed in mourning out of respect for other mothers' sons had swept Marian back through years, to another mass, also at St. Ann's, when the loss had been all of theirs but Peggy's more than anyone's: the funeral mass for Jack.

PHIL'S STORY
Chapter 10

————

Sutter's Mill

October 31, 2001

The phone again. Goddamn it. There might be something to be said, Phil thought, fumbling for the damn thing in his pocket, for a city where the phones don't work.

"Constantine." More of a threat than a greeting, but screw whoever it was if they couldn't take a joke.

"It's Kevin."

Shit. Good going, Phil. Courtroom technique, swift softening of voice: "Hey, Kev. How're you doing?"

"You need to come out here. I need to talk to you."

"I've been wanting to. But your mother—"

"Mom doesn't want to see you. We'll meet somewhere. You and me." Kevin was on edge, his voice tight and cold, but at least he was calling.

"Wherever you say."

"I'd come in—"

"No, no problem." Come in, Kev—on the crutches, with the pain pills every four hours. "Where's good?"

"There's a bar called the Bird."

"I know it. On Main Street?"

"That reporter's dead, Uncle Phil. I need you to tell me what's going on."

"Kev? Kev, I don't know."

"The paper says someone killed him."

"I saw that." And was just told it, by a girl not much older than you are, who's sure it's true and wonders if it was me.

"Did they?"

Do you mean, did I? "There's no evidence he didn't jump, Kevin."

"Evidence? Oh, fuck evidence! What the fuck does that mean, there's no evidence? You think you're talking to a jury, you can just throw words around and convince me?"

"I'm not trying to convince you of anything."

Kevin's anger fell back, a quick blaze that flared itself to embers. "What's going on, Uncle Phil? What does it have to do with Uncle Jimmy?"

And there you had it. The way it had always been: Uncle Phil and Uncle Jimmy. One weaving through the world the other came from, like the wind, everywhere in it, never part of it; the other a shining light so bright his glow had colored that world long after he'd left it. Now he was gone from all worlds, Jimmy McCaffery was, but his radiance was still blinding.

"Kev . . ." At a loss for words. Phil Constantine? Amazing, incredible. Thou who dost not believe how much the world has changed, check this out. Finally, with colossal effort: "I'll meet you. I'll tell you what I know. But it's not much. Kev, how's your mother?"

"Mom's . . . yeah, Mom's fine. When can you come?"

Yeah. Mom's fine. "I'll take the next boat. Half-hour, forty-five minutes at the outside."

"Okay. The Bird. See you there."

The end. Click off. Rise, tell Sandra to cancel appointments. Tell Elizabeth you'll be in touch about Mrs. Johnson.

Tell yourself, at least Kevin's calling.

Phil rode the boat in his usual spot, outside, facing the Brooklyn waterfront and the Verrazano Narrows Bridge. The day was calm, but not on the ferry. (On the ferry it never was.) Wind churned up by the boat's single-minded rush for the opposite shore slapped his jacket around him. He tugged off his tie (always wear a tie in the office, always look ready) and folded it into his pocket. Clouds slipped along the sky escaping east, out to sea, away from entangling treetops and tall buildings. Poetic but inaccurate: clouds only got snagged on trees on the peaks of high mountains, where the earth reared up to stab the sky. And among buildings, few were tall enough to touch them.

* *

The towers had been.

Phil had never been a regular at Windows on the World. The food was good, the drinks were big, but the scene at the bar was relentlessly social. Investment bankers on the make. Talkative tourists standing locals a beer. Hand-holding, starry-eyed couples glancing over each other's shoulders to the door in case something better slouched in. But once or twice, walking home at night from Battery Park after letting the ferry go, he'd looked up to find the towers' tops lost in mist. Before he thought about it, he was stepping off the huge, silent elevator and ordering a scotch. He'd turn his back on the room, on the piano trio and the strangers anxious to become his friends. He'd stand, looking out the narrow, tall panes of glass at nothing. No: at *almost* nothing. Here and there, no matter how thick the clouds, a pale light reached him through depthless gray. He never could tell, once the clouds had dropped this low, where the lights were coming from.

His visits to the bar had been rare. But often, in the middle of a workday, in the course of crisscrossing Lower Manhattan—especially if the day were clear, with a breeze clipping along, and he'd just come from seeing some client in a windowless holding cell, someone who would not be free for a long, long time—Phil had hopped the elevator in the south tower to the observation deck. He'd grip the rail and just stand in the wind and the sun. From a height that extravagant you could feel the endless miles not just left and right, front and back, but above and below, too. And every now and then, leaning on the rail 110 stories up, Phil would find himself swept back to his childhood, and he'd laugh. If he stared hard enough at the towers of Manhattan below, he could see, almost, Spider-Man swinging between them. And see himself as Spider-Man, the way he had as a kid, long-limbed and skinny and bringing justice to New Yorkers threatened with all kinds of evil. Yeah, Phil, he'd think, yeah, you need a break, guy. Take a vacation, get out of town. He'd given himself that order, but he'd never obeyed it. The deck at the top of the tower had always been enough.

* *

The boat docked. Phil went indoors, as you had to, to reach the ramp, to get back out. He took the train, quicker than a cab in the middle of the day. The car was half empty, but he didn't sit. Holding the rail, he watched out the windows. First rooftops, then the train cut, blank concrete walls racing by. This was a view of nothing, too, he thought. Different, but the same.

BOYS' OWN BOOK
Chapter 13
———

Turtles in the Pond

September 2, 1979

It's Sunday, it's Labor Day weekend, summer's turning to fall. Jimmy and Marian show up at noon at Markie and Sally's place, the apartment they rent from the O'Neills, who live upstairs. Marian's got her arms around a paper bag: franks, buns, and sauerkraut. Jimmy's hefting a couple of six-packs. Marian goes inside with Sally, to talk about potato salad and nail polish and whatever girls talk about; Jimmy roots in the garage for the basketball, bangs layups into the hoop over the driveway while Markie fires up the grill. That hoop, all the O'Neill boys played there, their little sister, too, right with them. Danny, the youngest, he's the one Mr. and Mrs. O'Neill fixed up the downstairs apartment for; but Danny went off to Vietnam, and when he came back he didn't stay long. He's in Alaska now, working on the pipeline: says he wants to be as far away from the jungle as he can get, for the rest of his life.

Smoke from the grill suddenly switches direction, trying to ambush Jimmy, but he's too smart, dribbles the ball up the driveway to get away. Markie jumps back, too, but not fast enough, coughs and wipes his eyes. Through the kitchen window, Jimmy and Markie hear the girls hooting with laughter about something.

Must be a potato escaped, Jimmy says to Markie, while the cloud of smoke swoops like a flock of pigeons and soars over the next-door fence. Potato's probably running all over your house, man, tearing up the place.

Yeah, probably, says Markie. Think we should go in and rescue the girls?

Potato rescue, says Jimmy, I'm great at that.

But they don't have to, because Marian and Sally come out the back door and down from the porch, Marian with two big bowls, Sally with Kevin. She puts Kevin in his crib on the grass, but the kid's too big for a crib and he knows it. He wails, so Jimmy goes and picks him up. Right away Kevin giggles, grabs for Jimmy's nose, looks in his baby hand to see if it's there.

Markie, man, says Jimmy, this kid's so big and good-looking, if it wasn't saying something bad about Sally, I'd just *know* he wasn't yours.

Because he's smart, too, says Markie, knows enough to take after her side of the family. He lays the franks on the grill, grins at Kevin in Jimmy's arms.

They eat franks, cole slaw, potato salad, pop open beers, watch Kevin stomp around the tiny yard in that funny kid walk. You'd think he'd tire himself out, but he can't sit still. When he falls, his eyes get wide like he can't believe it, then he just laughs. Sally and Markie take turns jumping up and grabbing him back from crawling through the bushes, running up the driveway, chewing on sticks; he's just like Markie, Jimmy thinks, the kid'll try anything, never thinks ahead. Then laughs at himself: for Pete's sake, he's a *baby*, how's he gonna think ahead? Jimmy and Marian jump up after Kevin, too, because Kevin, it's like he's everyone's first kid.

Marian doesn't say she got a promotion at work, so Jimmy does. Oh, Jimmy, it's no big deal, Marian protests, but Jimmy says, Come on, you've only been there two months, I mean, come on. Markie and Jimmy talk about cars: Sally tells them that Steve Fagan at the repair shop says Markie's got the best hands of any mechanic ever worked there. Jimmy tells funny stories about the firehouse. Sally says, The Chinese restaurant fire, Jimmy, I heard you were a big hero in that one.

Yeah, well, says Jimmy. I mean, the pressure was on. You save a Chinese restaurant from burning down, you know they send free egg rolls to the firehouse for the rest of your life?

Everyone laughs, and no one asks anything else about the Chinese restaurant fire, what it was like in the greasy black smoke, how it felt to grab that guy with flames all over him, roll him over and over in that tablecloth, save his life. No one asks about the fire under Jimmy's skin. No one knows anything about it, to ask.

Marian says to Sally, I'm glad your dad's better; Sally's dad's been sick on and off all summer. Everyone toasts Marian with beer cans because her middle sister, Eileen, just left to go to college. Not in New York like Marian; Eileen's going away, she got a scholarship to a fancy school in Boston. Oh, come on, you guys, I didn't do anything, says Marian, Eileen's just smarter than anyone.

Yeah, you only brought them up, your sisters and Davey, says Markie.

Well, Davey can take care of himself. But the girls, someone had to keep guys like you away from them. Marian says this and everyone laughs, but they all can see how proud Marian is.

They finish the franks and start to play a little ball, the girls against the boys like back in grade school, but Kevin tries to play. Jimmy bends down and hands the ball off to him. The kid takes it in both arms and lifts it toward the hoop, hops up, and lets it go with a big grunt like he really expects it to fly up there. Sally starts cracking up, and then Markie does, too, and then they're all laughing too hard and they have to stop. Jimmy, sitting in a rickety lawn chair, sips a cold beer, swears he can feel the heat from the sun leaning on him like it weighed something, thinks he could just sit here like this forever.

But he can't. The sun keeps moving, gets to where half the yard's shaded by the branches of the big oak tree old man O'Neill's father planted when he bought the place. Marian needs to drop in on her dad and her two sisters who still live at home, just to check up. And Kevin's getting cranky: he needs his nap, says Sally. She scoops him up, tells him to wave bye-bye to Uncle Jimmy. Marian goes in with her, carrying the bowls and plates they used. Jimmy hears the water running in the kitchen, thinks, Well, now's the time.

Markie, man, he says, just him and Markie in the yard now, the shadow of the oak tree's trunk dark on the grass between them, Markie, you seen Jack around lately?

Jack? Yeah, around, sure. How come? Markie looks away from Jimmy when he says this, quick and then back at the grass, like there's something he wants to see. But there's nothing there, and in that looking-away and looking-back Jimmy knows he's right.

Tom and Big Mike, they know enough to keep away from Markie. Whatever Markie thinks he wants, it wouldn't work out, and Tom and Mike know it even if he doesn't. But Jack thinks differently. Like always, Jack will try something just to see what happens. If trouble comes, well, that'll be what happened. Markie's always had that in him, too, though more than once Jimmy's seen on Jack's face that the trouble, for Jack, sometimes that can be the good part. For Markie, it's not that. It's more he never sees the trouble coming.

LAURA'S STORY
Chapter 8

———

Leaving the Cat

October 31, 2001

In the late afternoon Laura stood at the bow of the Staten Island ferry, heading back to Manhattan. She shut her eyes and breathed moisture and salt. It was a scent that from the first had smelled like home to her, though it was not. She had grown up in a state where all water was sweet. She had never known this scent until she came to New York at seventeen, a late-summer visit to serve as the border between childhood and the adult life she could not wait to live: she was on her way to college the following week.

From that weekend until she found this scent again was, in her memory, yet another lifetime. It was Harry who, hearing her confess she had never been to an ocean beach, declared himself shocked and appalled and hauled her off the next morning on the Long Island Rail Road for a Jones Beach picnic. She had protested that it was December. December 1999, he'd said, and she could not afford to enter a new millennium with such deficits of experience as she was clearly suffering from.

And from that day to this was, again, a lifetime. Gulls screeched and the ferry's engine growled. Laura opened her eyes. Manhattan grew steadily in the late autumn sunlight as though its towers were marching forward and Laura's boat were standing still. The arched sky ran from cobalt above the hulk of Brooklyn, through lighter blues, to the first hints of what would soon be strips of glowing salmon and gold behind the machinery of the New Jersey waterfront.

Travel on the Staten Island ferry had been another of the experiences Harry had determined that she required, and they had crisscrossed

Staten Island many times, Harry hailing cabs at the terminal and taking Laura on eccentric journeys: to a Tibetan museum in the island's eastern hills, riding stables in the south, a day of fishing under the bridge. These trips were all occasions of giddy laughter, of teasing and touching. (And once, on a sultry June day, of lovemaking on slippery black rocks, spreading their blanket in a hidden cove like teenagers. "What if the regulars want to use this place and we're already here?" Laura had fretted, pointing out beer cans and cigarette butts, proof of recent occupation. "It's a school day." Harry smiled, pulling her toward him. "We have until two.")

But her most profound joy had always been found on the trip back, when she and Harry, tired and at peace in each other's company, would lean on the rail to watch Manhattan swell toward them. Silent, they would sip at their drinks (for her, the ferry's strong coffee; for Harry, of course, the gin from his pocket flask) and breathe this salt scent.

Before this trip, Laura had only once been on the ferry without Harry, and that was earlier this same day, on her way to interviews in Pleasant Hills. She was not finished there, but she had enough for now, enough to file a story tonight in case Leo wanted something for tomorrow. She had not found the answer to who killed Harry. But all Leo had asked was that she show him there was a story.

She could do that.

She could have done that without going out to Staten Island at all.

Marian Gallagher was hiding something; that had been obvious from the way the color had risen in her face, from her attempts to divert the course of Laura's questions. It was possible—likely even, because she had appeared to Laura as essentially a kind woman, warmhearted and hurt—that Marian Gallagher did not know anything directly about Harry's death. But that she knew something about McCaffery and the events of years ago, Laura did not doubt.

And Phil Constantine? That interview had been more complicated. The crushing headache that had come on as she sat watching his glittering eyes and his grin had been even worse than the one Marian Gallagher had brought her. But Reporter-Laura had chosen well. She'd thrown at him trick after subtle trick; he'd seen through them all, as she'd thought he would, and it had made him cocky. He'd given her more than she'd had coming in. Whether it was more than he knew he was giving her, she wasn't sure, but she didn't care. He too was hiding something, and if she could show Leo there was something to hide, Leo would be happy.

* *

Usually on her way back to the office Laura would have her tape recorder pressed to her ear. She'd be making notes, trying out leads, referring to her spiral pad when muddied words came up on the tape. Review when fresh, one of Laura's many mottoes. (Not Harry. Harry liked to let things settle, to come back to them. Whatever surprises you when you hear it the second time, he told her, that's what's important.)

But right now she couldn't move. Outbound, she'd turned her back on Manhattan. She couldn't afford to attend to what was behind her.

She was paying for that now.

It wasn't the bright glow from the recovery lights, just coming on now as daylight started to fade. Not the cranes, or the still-rising smoke. Not quite. As the shore moved toward her at a measured pace, Laura stared at the Manhattan skyline. She'd been to the site, to Ground Zero, how many times since it happened? And how many times in the years before, for interviews, to change subways, for a drink with a source at Windows on the World? Laura's theory, which she shared with Harry, was that the grandeur of the view from the 107th floor made people feel insignificant, and so more willing to talk.

"To build themselves up so they can feel important again?" Harry wanted to know.

"No, I don't think so," she had answered. "More because, why not? You can see from up there how little really matters."

Laura knew the World Trade Center well, then, from the days when it had been a gleaming array of sharp-cornered buildings standing over a weave of train lines. And knew it well from the last seven weeks, since it had become Ground Zero, an alien, incomprehensible place with a horrifying new name. She had watched from behind the fence and sometimes, because she was a reporter, from inside it, as torches sliced through twisted steel and trucks carted it away, as masked firefighters threw wreckage aside to reveal yet more wreckage. And she'd been taking notes and climbing mounds of destruction once as all work stopped and steelworkers and firefighters stood in silent lines, saluted the flag-draped body carried past them, wiped tears away with filthy gloves, and returned to work.

And Laura had seen the countless aerial photos, in her own paper as well as the others, starting from the day itself.

But still.

Still, as she stared at the looming skyline, the long low rays of sun and the piercing searchlights, she felt disoriented, and wrong, and stupid. And guilty, for being wrong.

Everyone knew the towers had been on the tip of Manhattan. The island, New York City itself, culminated in them, grew and swelled and pushed them soaring into the air when the unstoppable energy of Manhattan had rolled south to the water and could go no farther.

But that wasn't true. Of course it wasn't. As she stared at the place now, it was clear the lights and the cranes and the smoke were uptown from the end of the island, west of it, visible only between and above the crowd of buildings that occupied Manhattan's tip and always had. Her memory of leaning on the rail with Harry, sipping coffee and sailing from Staten Island straight toward the gateway of the towers was wrong, and if she thought back more carefully, if she meticulously unbraided meaning from fact, she knew that, and had always known it.

Harry would have laughed. Laura shivered as she heard a sound like the chortle that so often preceded a hug from Harry; but it was someone else, and impatient with herself, she shook off the idea, which was really a hope, that Harry was on the boat with her as he always had been, every time, before.

So I'm confused, so what? she demanded, of herself, the water, the gulls. The gulls just wheeled, looking for another boat to follow, and the water just flowed. This close to Manhattan the salt aroma on the wind was mixed with smoke from Ground Zero. As the ferry's engines cut to ease into the pier, Laura stared at her coffee cup. Carefully peeling back the plastic top, she upended it, pouring untouched coffee into the dark harbor water.

MARIAN'S STORY
Chapter 9

———

The Old Masters
(Sailing Calmly On)

Marian sat in Flanagan's with Tom, in a swirl of unfamiliar people, sounds, sights. His mother was well, Tom told her, in answer to a question she must have asked. Peggy went to mass almost every day, he said, as she had for many years, and she did what she could to offer solace to others, those whose recent losses were greatest, most heartbreaking (though in Pleasant Hills, Marian knew, everyone's heart was broken). Peggy took great comfort in the company of her grandchildren, said Tom, his own two sons and daughter. It was like Tom, Marian thought as she drank from a second glass of wine, not to say how comforted his mother surely was by his own presence, as she always had been, even when Peggy Molloy was the reigning queen and the royal family was whole. In the odd light and strange colors that made up this new Flanagan's, the Molloys shimmered and appeared before Marian as though in a posed photograph. In the center sat Peggy, with her straight back, her smile, and her worried eyes. Big Mike stood behind her, stolid and strong. At Mike's side, looking squarely into the camera, was Tom; and next to Peggy, grinning, shoulders forward, as though he was ready to race somewhere else as soon as the photographer was finished, Jack.

The autumn night when Jack died had been sticky and hot, a night of slamming doors, screeching brakes, and lovers' quarrels. Because he had not died naturally (though there were those who muttered that death from a gunshot wound was a natural one for Jack Molloy), because an investigation was under way, criminal charges pending, the laws of the city demanded that the Medical Examiner conduct an autopsy. Thus the wake and funeral were delayed by days, and the weather turned colder. The morning the bells tolled to summon them to St. Ann's, a raw wind marauded through the streets, driving before it a thin cruel rain. Marian walked to church beside Jimmy. All of Pleasant Hills was scurrying along the sidewalks, shivering in hastily unearthed coats and dark wool suits, converging on the vortex of St. Ann's, with their umbrellas held like shields.

Marian clutched an umbrella with two hands, unreasonably angry with the wind for coveting it, for attempting to wrench it from her and leave her unprotected. Jimmy carried no umbrella, and he wore no hat. The rain darkened his hair and ran in glistening trails down his cheeks, and it occurred to Marian that rain like this was a perfect disguise for hiding tears. Jimmy's hands, for warmth on this bitter day, were thrust deep, deep into the pockets of his good coat, and Marian struggled with the umbrella, and so perhaps it was not surprising that he had not put an arm around her shoulder or taken hold of her elbow to steer and steady her. Or perhaps it was.

From the night Jack had been killed, and Markie arrested, Jimmy had spoken little. Marian sat with him in soft silence over their morning coffee, kissed him, and smiled into his eyes when he left for his shift at 168. At night she held him, and he nestled tight to her both awake and asleep, though she knew he slept very little, and not deeply. Once, in a night syncopated with bursts of lightning and rumors of thunder but without rain, he turned suddenly (did he know she was awake also, waiting for the storm?) and made love to her with a furious urgency she had not known in him before. Afterward the thought came to her that this might be what it was like for him in a fire: to act before thought prevented action, to seize the chance before the chance was gone.

So Marian held Jimmy close, and lay awake, and the weather changed. The authorities, their work complete, released Jack's body for burial. The police made their arrest, and after an unexplained delay—but the police never explained, and who could insist?—charges were filed and a lawyer assigned. Jimmy traded shifts with a fireman brother to be free for Jack's funeral.

The day was dark, and the church was dark. Watery trails crisscrossed the tile in the echoing entryway. Parishioners plunged umbrellas into brass stands as though they were swords thrust into rock to attest to an oath (of community? of justice?) that everyone had sworn.

Marian furled her umbrella and placed it with the others, though gently. She reached for Jimmy's hand as they walked toward the front pews where the Molloy family already sat. Peggy Molloy's head was bent forward; black lace hid her face. Vicky, married to Tom in this same church, as Sally had been to Markie, sat beside Peggy, whispering something, holding her gloved hand. Tom and Big Mike stared straight ahead, their unblinking eyes keeping watch over the bronze-handled coffin before the altar. The air smelled of damp wool, of cedar and camphor. Jimmy's hand in Marian's was rough and cold, as though he had been laboring for hours in the icy morning.

Marian looked around for Sally. Some days before the funeral, Sally had asked Marian what to do, what the right thing would be.

"But, my God, you grew up with Jack," Marian had answered. "It was an accident. No one blames Markie."

Accident was the word they were all using, as though they had debated, negotiated, and come to an agreement, but it was not an accident. Markie had told them what had happened. Jack had said to Markie he would kill him. He had fired a shot that may have been meant to scream as it did over Markie's head and shatter the wooden frame of the half-built house where Jack and Markie were sharing a six-pack. And a second shot, which might have been meant to burn as it did into the plywood flooring. Or both bullets may have been meant to rip bloody holes through Markie's heart. Markie thought they had been, or Markie was too scared to think. He tugged a gun from his own jacket. (They all looked at one another with wide eyes when they heard this and asked, "Did you know Markie had a gun?" and told one another, "No.") He only wanted, he told them, to startle Jack, to slow him down, to show him how ridiculous it all was, how nuts this moment was, the two of them with guns pointed at each other in the middle of an unfinished building in the middle of the night. Maybe Jack, seeing Markie—Markie!—with a gun, did suddenly see that, maybe he looked at his own gun and wondered what the hell he was doing. Or maybe he was too drunk. The accident was that Markie's gun went off.

Three days after Jack died, Sally, on the phone to Marian, asked her about attending Jack's funeral. Since high school Marian and Sally had called each other two or three times a day, always something that could not wait, something funny, amazing, or in doubt.

Marian said, "You have to come."

Sally said, "I'm not sure it would be right."

"Oh, Sally, no! You should come, of course you should. If Markie's out, I think he should come, too," Marian added. Surely Markie's bail would be set by then, and they all could pool their savings and get him out. Or the court, seeing the true nature of things, would drop all charges and Markie could come home.

Markie was not out—his bail hearing was finally set, for the day after the funeral, Marian wondering silently how hard his court-appointed lawyer, that arrogant man Constantine, had really tried—but when she went over to Sally's later that day, Tom was there, drinking coffee in Sally's kitchen while Kevin cheerfully pulverized cookies into crumbs on the table.

Marian, who always knocked at Sally's unlocked door but never waited for Sally to come open it, called out, "Hi, Sal," and had nearly reached the kitchen before she saw Tom. She stopped, unsure of what to do. Tom was a criminal, in his father's profession, and the time had long passed when she was able to pretend that that made no difference. But Tom was also a childhood friend in mourning for his brother.

Kevin beamed and giggled when he saw Marian, pounding his chubby fists in his crumbs as a gesture of welcome. Sally's smile was tired and uncertain. Her beautiful face was ashen, the only color in her skin the smudges below her eyes. Marian crossed the kitchen with fast steps and took Sally in her arms. She hugged her the way she had when Sally fell on her roller skates or spilled her milk when they were young, when no disaster of childhood ever loomed so large that Marian was not able to comfort her, and Marian wanted to wrap her arms around Sally now and keep all bad things from her, to hold her and protect her until Markie came home again.

"I saw Markie this morning," Sally told her. "He says not to worry, everything will be okay."

"What about bail? Did you talk to that lawyer?"

"Just now. He thinks bail will be around fifty thousand dollars."

The figure staggered Marian, but she concealed that. "We'll raise it," she said. "Jimmy's checking how to borrow against his insurance, and my job has the credit union, and Markie's boss . . . Sal, don't worry— we'll find it."

Sally nodded, biting her lip. "Mr. Constantine says that's low. For . . . for something like this." She glanced at Tom, as though afraid what she'd said had hurt him.

Marian, too, looked at Tom. He met her eyes; he rose, moving wearily, and Marian drew a breath: for the first time she could ever remember, Tom looked not like his father, but like his mother, with Peggy's soft, sad smile. "I'll come back, Sal," he said, his voice quiet.

Sally turned to Marian.

Marian said, "No, Tom. Stay."

Tom hesitated, then nodded and sat again.

Sally set a cup and saucer in front of Marian. "Shall I make you some tea?"

"No, don't bother. I'll be happy with coffee."

"It's no trouble."

"Sally, please, coffee's fine. Thanks," she said as Sally poured for her. Tom's nearness disquieted her. She turned to Sally. "Sal, this lawyer. Is he really . . . I mean, Legal Aid, they're so overworked—"

"He's not Legal Aid," said Sally. "When it's . . . when it's this serious . . ."

When her voice faltered, Tom took over, as though explaining this to Marian was his responsibility. "If it looks like the charge'll be homicide, they appoint lawyers who're experienced in that. They pay them more than Legal Aid. This guy Constantine, he has his own criminal practice. I checked him out. He knows what he's doing."

Marian stared. "You checked him out?"

Tom nodded.

"Why?"

Looking into his coffee, Tom said, "If he wasn't any good, there's a guy I know."

"Tom . . ." Marian wasn't sure what she wanted to ask, what she wanted to say.

"Look," said Tom, but he stopped also, and he, too, seemed unsure. And then he said the same thing Marian had. "No one blames Markie."

Marian could not take her eyes off Tom. She gazed at him the way she sometimes stared at spring shoots in her garden, the beginnings of plants she had not grown before, wondering exactly what this one or that would become. Jimmy had laughed when, one morning, he'd come upon her peering at the tiny sprouts and she'd told him what she wondered. They're whatever they were when you put them there, he'd said, wrapping an arm around her, nuzzling her neck. They don't change.

Sally sat and poured coffee for herself. "Your parents, Tom," she said. "How could they not blame Markie?"

"It was Jack. It was what he was like." Tom stirred sugar into his cup.

His face was pale, and gray crescents underlined his blue eyes as they did Sally's green ones. He seemed about to say more, but Kevin swept his hands gleefully across the table, knocking a cookie into the air. Tom grabbed for it and caught it before it hit the floor. Kevin chortled. Tom gave him a smile and put the cookie on the table again. Kevin looked at Tom and giggled, then pushed it over the edge. This time Tom was too slow. The cookie flew to pieces when it hit the floor. Kevin peered over the edge of the chair, and then up at Tom, his face uncomprehending.

"Okay, enough." Sally lifted Kevin out, hugging him tightly. He squirmed. She kissed his cheek, wiped his face, and set him down. He scuttled over to a red fire truck and made *eee-eee* noises as he rolled it around.

Tom, his eyes following Kevin, said to Sally and Marian, "If it's anyone's fault, it's mine."

"How can you say that?" Marian asked hotly, defending Tom as though an accusation had been made. "You weren't even there."

"I'm supposed to keep an eye on him. I'm supposed to know when he gets that way."

Marian reached for a cookie, and Sally poured more coffee, and everyone pretended they hadn't noticed Tom speaking as though he would one day again have the chance to do what he'd been doing all his life, what he was supposed to do.

"It wasn't your job," Marian heard herself say. "Looking out for everyone all the time. Especially someone like Jack." She said this although she knew it was not true. Words could not change the past, change who they all had always been.

Kevin pushed his truck under the table and through the legs of their chairs.

"The funeral," Marian said quietly, to Sally. "You'll come with us. Jimmy and I will pick you up."

"No," Tom said. "Let's make sure everyone understands. You'll come with Vicky and me. Come with us."

In the end Sally did go to Jack's funeral, but alone. Vicky called to repeat Tom's offer, to assure her that Sally would be welcome to go to church with them; Sally thanked her and turned her down. She would not impose herself on the Molloys, she replied: she would not intrude on the family. To Marian, over another cup of coffee on the following day, she said she thought her presence would be difficult for Peggy and Big Mike, even if it was true they did not blame Markie. She shook her head and wondered how they could not, even if it was not Markie's fault; and though Marian insisted it would be unfair if they did, Jack was drunk, Jack threatened Markie, everyone believed that, everyone who knew Jack, though she said that, in Marian's heart she knew what Sally knew: Jack was dead and Markie had killed him, and if she were Jack's mother, her own grief and guilt would be burdens so enormous that she would be desperate to find someone else to whom they rightfully belonged.

Nor did Sally go to the church with Jimmy and Marian: this was a matter of having to wait for Kevin's sitter, she said, though when Marian walked with Jimmy down the drafty aisle of St. Ann's to the front pews where Jack's friends were gathering, she found Sally already seated, a black hat covering her bound red hair.

Jimmy and Marian slipped in beside Sally, and Marian took her hand. Jimmy's hand in her right, and Sally's in her left, her lover and her best friend, and yet she trembled deep within, shivering with a chill she feared neither the incense-streaked warmth of the church nor the presence of people she loved could ever cure. The cold wind from the abyss of Jack's death whispered of darkness to come, possibilities they had all known about and none had believed would come true.

And Marian shivered, too, for fear of what could be waiting now for Markie, and for Sally and Kevin. She was stunned, bewildered by the way one terrible instant could destroy so much.

And the bleakness within her was made colder, more vast and empty, by another certainty: Jimmy was lying to her.

No, she told herself, oh no, it was not that simple. Not lying. Not in words, telling her things were true when he knew they were false. Marian did not expect Jimmy to speak to her of what was in his heart. That was not Jimmy; he didn't know how, had never known how. And Marian had always loved Jimmy, always, and she knew that what was in his heart came out not in words but in other ways, Jimmy's ways.

She was not surprised that he had secrets, questions or answers, worries or knowledge that he would not talk about. But when he said he did not have those things, when he kissed her, told her he guessed he was just shaken, just could not get over what a mess this was, what a nightmare, Marian's stomach clenched. She would study him, walking down the street, or sitting in the living room, or flowing with her in bed so close, so perfectly, each time over the years an echo of that first, wondrous time when they were both afraid it wouldn't be as good as their dreams of it together and found instead, as they moved and touched, that they had always known these things about each other, and it was better beyond imagining. She would study him, and she saw that his eyes were seeing nothing, or at least nothing that she could also see; she would look for the tiny slant at the side of his mouth and it wasn't there, and Marian knew.

He had always held things in his heart; he was doing it now. He had never told her all his secrets. But he had never said to her, before this, that he did not have one.

Laura's Story
Chapter 9

———

Turtles in the Pond

October 31, 2001

A *ratta-tat-tat,* and the newsroom looked up: Leo's sapphire signet ring on the glass.

Everyone followed the line of Leo's pointing finger, breathed, and went back to work. Except for the person the finger pointed at. That reporter, lifted by a tractor beam, rose and was carried through the newsroom to Leo's office along the most direct route.

Laura picked up her head momentarily, saw the decree was not for her (the chosen was Del Leffler, a cop reporter confederate of Hugh Jesselson's; his beat was Vice), and immediately snapped back to work. Organizing, outlining, getting ready: she wanted to show her work to Leo, as soon as the searchlight of Leo's focus found her.

Before that she would have to sit through the end-of-day meeting, of course. If a reporter was missing, morning or afternoon, Leo had better know why, and Laura had no reason good enough. No reason at all, except the pounding of her head at the thought of reporters and editors crowding the conference room. Some would watch her with curiosity they wouldn't bother to disguise: they were reporters, Harry's death was a story, and Laura was a part of it. Others would slide their eyes right past her. They would find fascination in their yellow pads and the caps of their pens if she spoke: she was a young woman, she'd lost her lover, and polite people don't pry. Which would be worse? Laura wasn't certain.

At five-thirty precisely, Leo lumbered toward the conference room looking neither left nor right. He did exactly this every morning and every afternoon; the first time Laura had seen him do it had been her first morning at the *Tribune*. Personnel had instructed her to be in by eight-thirty sharp, but she had arrived before eight, with the cardboard box she'd packed up in St. Paul. She was putting her drawers in order, transferring computer files and phone records, unpacking her Rolodex and her coffee cup, everything she'd brought, everything she had. At eight-thirty she looked up to see Leo pushing past her desk in his march through the newsroom. Every other reporter stood and followed, like a school of fish. Laura watched, uncertain (what is this? does it include me, should I go, too, should I wait to see?), until Harry Randall, the last to file through the conference room door, stuck his head back out and tapped his watch. Laura jumped up and headed in, grabbing a notebook and pen in case she needed to take something down, or to look as though she did.

That meeting, like all but the most extraordinary since—the morning meeting on September 12 for example—lasted exactly twenty minutes. Everyone briefed Leo (Leo had a strict definition of *brief*) on the stories they were working and their plans for the day. Everyone took quick suggestions from one another and growled orders from Leo. Everyone rose at ten to nine and went back to work.

The afternoon was the same, with twenty minutes truncated to fifteen. Now, when they assembled, fast reporters as usual filled the chairs and slower ones leaned on walls. Leo pointed, people began to talk, and Laura didn't listen.

In the past she always had. She'd concentrated hard. She'd wanted to know. What were the stories, what were the angles? Could she contribute? Become part of it? Think of a different way, a new way, a way so unexplored and promising as to bring Laura Stone's abilities to the attention of senior colleagues who might, next time, think to include her when the story was big? Today, though, she was busy. Busy not noticing people not noticing her, busy returning the stares of the starers. She felt Georgie's mournful, helpful gaze, but she didn't look at Georgie. She was busy not seeing the chair Harry was not sitting in, the wall against which he was not slouching.

But not so busy that she didn't respond when Leo called her name. "Stone."

"The Harry Randall homicide." Instantly she answered. She'd practiced this in her head, over and over through the day, through the night as she lay awake on the pull-out couch in her unrecognized apartment. (What had she been thinking, buying this carpet? Didn't those curtains ever shut out the light? Did the refrigerator always hum and stop like that? It must be the noise, that must be why she couldn't sleep.) *The Harry Randall homicide.* She worked on this phrase with the precision and persistence she brought to all her writing. Words, she had always believed, made thoughts visible. Nothing was so gossamer or so incarnate, so transitory or so steadfast, that words could not reveal its secrets. Even the incomprehensible, even the unfathomable. Even this, Harry's death, could be made comprehensible by the right words.

"I was on Staten Island this afternoon," she said, "to talk to a couple of people."

"You have anything new?"

Leo wanted a piece. Laura's heart skipped. "I will by deadline, Leo."

Raised eyebrows and traded looks told her how intensely the group was following this exchange. Within minutes of her leaving Leo's office yesterday, the substance of their meeting and its outcome had flash-flooded through the newsroom: Stone has a crackpot theory that Randall didn't jump. But Leo signed on; what the hell does that mean? He's probably just humoring her. Because, you know, of her and Harry. Leo? You must be crazy. Then Jesselson's piece ran this morning, and agnosticism replaced atheism: might be something there, I mean, Leo's got Jesselson on it, too, let's see what comes next.

Leo grunted, a sign he'd heard Laura and that was all for her. But before he could draw down on his next target, words from the other side of the room: "Laura? Write this down." Hugh Jesselson, rumpled in gray slacks and wrinkled white shirt, propped up the far wall. "Angelo Zannoni. Sergeant, retired, 124." Glancing at a three-by-five card in his hand, he pounded out a phone number. Laura scribbled it down, then looked at him inquiringly. "Arresting officer," he said. "Mark Keegan, 1979. Expecting your call."

Laura smiled. "Thanks, Hugh."

Jesselson shrugged. "Thanks for yesterday."

A snicker wiggled around the room. Laura flushed. Jesselson's mouth turned up at the corner, which didn't help.

It had been Laura's idea to run this morning's story on the investigation of Harry's death under Hugh Jesselson's byline. "We can make it look like the cops care. Maybe scare someone out of the woodwork. Let Hugh have it," she'd argued to Leo. He sat lodged behind his desk, rendered as close to wordless as she'd ever seen him by the spectacle of a reporter offering a front-page byline to someone else.

Jesselson, summoned by sapphire, read her copy. "Doesn't sound like me," he'd objected.

"Rewrite it," ordered Leo.

So he had, and Hugh Jesselson, after eight years with the *New York Post* and six at the *Tribune,* had finally made the front.

Meeting concluded, reporters and editors went back to work. Laura dropped into her chair and dialed the number Jesselson had given her.

Four rings, then a growled "Hello."

"Angelo Zannoni?"

"Who the hell is this?"

"Mr. Zannoni, I'm Laura Stone of the *New York Tribune.* Hugh Jesselson suggested I call you—"

"He suggest you call me at suppertime?"

Laura glanced up to the newsroom clock. The hour hadn't occurred to her, and in the face of the important work she was trying to accomplish, she was surprised to find time mattering to anyone.

"I'm sorry if—"

"Yeah, sure. You want to come out here?"

"Yes. Yes, if that would be—"

"1491 Fitzgerald, Pleasant Hills. Think you can find it?"

"Yes, I—"

"I'm here."

Laura took the receiver from her ear, replaced it on its console. She might as well; Zannoni had already hung up.

Marian's Story
Chapter 10

Sutter's Mill

October 31, 2001

"It was Jimmy, wasn't it?"

For the second time since she'd entered Flanagan's, Marian felt conversations stopping and eyes turning their way. This time she was wrong, though, and she knew it immediately. The beat of the music continued, the talk and the laughter. No one had heard her words but Tom; no one's eyes burned, no one stared silently, but Tom.

"What the hell are you talking about?"

"It was Jimmy who killed Jack." She'd never said this before, though she had somehow always known it, known it since Jimmy stumbled, wordless, through the first numb days, sweated and could not lie still beside her through the first sleepless nights. She had known it and never said it and now she was terrified that dragons and fire-spitting serpents would come screaming down from the sky, that the enclosing, sheltering walls would crash down and bury her in endless, crushing darkness.

"You're shivering." Tom's hand was on hers. What would Vicky think? Marian wondered, absurdly. But Vicky and Tom weren't together anymore, hadn't been for years, so why would it matter? She'd just slip her hand out, pretend she wanted to lift her wine to her lips (and drinking wine was not a bad idea right now, her glass was almost empty, where was the waitress so she could order another?); or she could turn her cold palm to Tom's warm, strong one and hold tight to him, and that was what she did.

"Marian . . ."

He said no more. She reached for her wineglass with her free hand. As she took an emptying sip, Tom signaled the waitress and another was on the way.

"Marian, why are you saying this?"

"Because it's true. I know it is."

"Did Jimmy tell you that?"

"Jimmy's dead."

She couldn't think why she'd said that. Tom knew. Everyone knew, everyone in New York, even people who had never known Jimmy, everyone knew he was dead. They had all mourned him as they had mourned all the heroes, until Harry Randall told them Jimmy was not a hero, and broke everyone's heart, and her heart all over again.

"Marian. Back then. What did Jimmy say?"

Tom was leaning toward her. Suddenly she was irritated with him. "Jimmy never said anything. You knew him. He'd never say anything." She pulled her hand from Tom's. She found her new wine arriving, which was a good thing, because her mouth was dry and her face felt hot. The waitress took her other glass away. But she had emptied it anyhow, there was nothing there anymore, who cared? She reached for the new one and took a luxurious swallow, nothing to do with Marian Gallagher's sensible, moderate ways.

More beer had been delivered for Tom, too. He picked it up, drank, and put it down. Blue eyes steady, straight at her, the way he used to look at them, at each of them and all of them, ever since they were kids.

In Marian's experience (and her experience was vast: meetings were her medium, conversation her métier) most people, if regarding you in extended silence, were not seeing you at all. Their minds wrestled with whatever concerned them, their eyes did not focus, you were not really there to them. But not Tom. Whatever he was concentrating on, if he looked at you he saw you, he considered you and measured you and worked you into his plan. Across the table from Marian he sat now like that, as he had so many times in their childhood, Tom thinking something up, how to get out of something or get into something and the rest of them sitting quietly, waiting for it, waiting to be told their parts.

But the world had changed, and Flanagan's had changed. The noise of the crowd was setting Marian's nerves on edge, and she didn't want to sit and wait, not now. "Jimmy was there that night, wasn't he?" she asked Tom, thinking it might be easier for him to answer that, thinking maybe, maybe, he could tell her that wasn't true and then the other thing wouldn't be true, either.

"Jesus, Marian." Tom rubbed his mouth. He looked around, at the strangers, at the walls. His gaze traveled as though he were searching for the mirrors that were gone. He brought his eyes back to her. How blue they were. "Jesus, Marian. We were all there."

LAURA'S STORY
Chapter 10

———

The Old Masters
(Sailing Calmly On)

October 31, 2001

Earlier, on Staten Island, Laura had caught a cab. Now she found the cab stand deserted and dashed impatiently to the train. She jumped aboard as the bell rang, yanking her shoulder bag through doors determined to squash it.

Laura peered at the map, counted the stations to her destination, and swung onto a seat as the train lurched through a curve. Gazing around, she realized she knew these benches, this lighting, and these floors. The Staten Island train, it seemed, used the same cars as the subway, was in all respects identical (turnstiles and fare, ads and announcements).

But no: not identical. On Staten Island the tracks ran on elevated trestles or through open cuts, no tunnels. The rhythm of dark-while-moving, bright-when-stopped was replaced, first by a disorienting view of rooftops; then quickly and even more disconcertingly by the blank plane of endless concrete wall.

The same yet different. One more thing.

At the Pleasant Hills stop Laura climbed up out of the train and cut to a busy street of one- and two-story shops. Fitzgerald Drive was a hike from the train station, but she welcomed the walk. Already—and this was only her third trip—the ferry ride across the harbor was beginning to weary her. Harry's absence, the towers' absence, the smoke and dust lifting into the sky; the hush, and the pointing. Maybe when she went back tonight, Laura thought, she'd ride inside, on the lowest level, where she and Harry had never sat. She'd review her tapes or read over her notes or stare into space and not know anything until it was time to get off.

She stopped for coffee at a chrome-sided Main Street diner with cardboard black cats in the windows. Harry would have said it looked like it had been there since the Flood. (She could hear him say it, see the rueful smile adding that he recognized it from then.) She shook her head as a dog shakes off a rainstorm and concentrated on finding her way through Pleasant Hills. She was working.

Leaving the business strip, Laura made the required lefts and rights. At Fitzgerald Drive she crumpled her coffee cup into a trash can and followed the street's suburban curve to a three-story clutch of white-stuccoed condos. Third building, top floor, "Zannoni" on the bell, and apparently Zannoni on the balcony: a balding fleshy man, dressed in a white polo shirt and jeans, called down, "You Miss Stone?" and when, squinting past a streetlight, she told him she was, he disappeared inside and buzzed the door open.

He was waiting at the top of the stairs. His lined face and the slack skin of his arms told her he was over sixty, but he greeted her with a firm handshake. So many men shook a thin woman's hand gingerly, as though afraid to break her (though Laura had always detected a certain macho posturing in that, the message of "I could hurt you if I'm not careful" translating easily into "if *you're* not careful"). He led her through a white-walled, sparse living room and onto the stucco-wrapped balcony, where Laura found sling chairs on metal frames, a low plastic table, and an astonishing view.

She stared over shadowed rooftops and breeze-blown trees. Beyond, the lights of the Verrazano arched over the sparkling Narrows. On the far shore the buildings of Brooklyn crowded their waterfront, windows lit.

"Not bad, huh?" Zannoni stood beside her, looking over the vista with satisfied pride, as though he owned it. "Bought the place for the view. You want some tea?" He waved his hand in the table's direction.

Laura left with regret the sight of so much glittering dark water, such promised distances. She sat in a canvas chair and turned down the offer of tea.

"All I have," Zannoni said, still standing, as though she might change her mind if she knew no other offer was forthcoming. "All I drink. I'm the only Italian in the world doesn't like coffee. You sure?"

When Laura said she was, Zannoni sat.

"I appreciate your seeing me," she began. Based on the phone call, the sight of him on his balcony, and the handshake, she'd taken on a frank and direct demeanor with a faint undertone of gratitude that acknowledged Zannoni was in charge. The role she was playing was that of a straightforward reporter who did not play roles. "I'm sorry about interrupting your dinner—"

"No problem. Caught me by surprise, is all."

"I know what you mean. I don't like surprises, either."

"Yeah." He nodded, sipped his tea, and said, "Your boy Jesselson says you're interested in the Mark Keegan thing, from back then."

Laura gave up trying to find a position on the sling chair that made her feel professional, or at least adult. She swung herself sideways so she was facing Zannoni and fished her pad, her pens, her recorder, from her bag. "Is this all right?" she asked Zannoni, setting the recorder on the table.

He eyed it without love. "For now. Might ask you to turn it off, though."

"Of course. Do you want to start with me asking questions, or do you just—"

"What's your interest?"

"Excuse me?"

"Your interest in Keegan. Jesselson hunted me up, asked if I'd talk to you. Why?"

"I don't know if you've been following the stories in my paper—"

"Yeah." Zannoni nodded. "You're the guys saying Jimmy McCaffery was laundering Eddie Spano's money through that lawyer, paying off Keegan's widow."

Laura jumped right on it: "Is that what was happening?"

"What's your interest?" His eyes under thick brows held hers, not fiercely, not tight. An old cop, used to interrogations. A man who could sip tea on his balcony all day long asking the same question, while a stranger decided whether or not to answer him.

"The reporter on the original story," Laura said. "The one who died. He was a friend of mine."

"Good friend?"

"Yes."

Zannoni stared into the distance. Probably, Laura thought as she blinked back tears, the view from where he sat had not suddenly started to shimmer and melt.

He said, "Jesselson says you think someone killed him."

Laura answered, "That's true."

"Any idea who?"

She shook her head. Zannoni, still watching the water, answered his own question. "Well, me either."

"I didn't—"

"Just wanted to make sure, in case that's what you came for. I'm not going to guess. Speculate. Any of that bullshit. But back then."

"That's why I came," Laura said. "To hear about back then."

At that Zannoni turned to her. Laura sat still and returned his look.

"I was a detective at the 124 then," he said. "Later got transferred to the Bronx. Christ, what a schlep. Those days, right after the Knapp Commission—you heard of that?—they didn't have this community policing thing, like now. They wanted you to live outside your precinct. Keep down graft. Pile of crap. Cops running all around the goddamn city, damn waste of time. I retired eight years ago."

Zannoni took a gulp of tea. A fresh breeze blew in from the Narrows, got trapped in the cul-de-sac of the balcony. It lifted a page from Laura's notebook; it brought with it the scent of the sea.

"Officers responded to a shots-fired, found Molloy," Zannoni said. "Called in me and my partner, Jeff Miller. Jeff retired fifteen years ago. Condo in Tucson. Died there last year. The desert, Jesus." He looked toward the water and shook his head. "Keegan showed up half an hour later. Said he did it, ran because he lost his head but came back to do the right thing. You know the story—Molloy and Keegan?"

"I know what the papers reported."

Zannoni waited. Laura went on. "They were drinking in a house under construction. Jack Molloy got wild, waved a gun around, and Mark Keegan shot him by mistake."

"Helluva mistake," said Zannoni. "Right through the heart."

Laura said, "Couldn't it still be an accident?"

Zannoni shrugged. "Close your eyes and squeeze, likely to hit something as something else. That's how the defense played it, anyway."

"Phillip Constantine?"

"That was him, the lawyer. But he came later. Right then Keegan said it himself: I was scared, he shot twice, I just pointed and pulled the trigger. Never figured I'd hit him. I'm not real good with guns, he kept saying."

"But you think there's something wrong with that?"

Zannoni turned back to Laura. "What the hell was he carrying it for?"

"People carry guns. Especially young punks that age."

"Mark Keegan wasn't a punk. Grew up with Molloy, but nothing we had said he was connected. Far as I could see, he had no enemies. Everyone liked him. From what people said, even Molloy did, far as he liked anyone, crazy fuck that he was. 'Scuse my language."

"Don't worry about it."

Zannoni didn't look worried. "Auto mechanic with a wife and kid. 'Seventy-nine, guns weren't as easy to get as now. Today, okay, everyone has one, same as sneakers, gotta look good. Back then, gangbangers all over the Bronx, yeah, but a mechanic out here, family man? Why'd he have a gun?"

"Do you have an answer?"

"Yeah. He didn't."

"It wasn't Mark Keegan's gun?"

"Not his, and he wasn't carrying it."

Lights flashed on the distant flank of a tanker. Carefully, Laura said, "The gun was someone else's? Someone else was there?"

"Always thought so."

"Who?"

"Never knew." Zannoni cupped his tea with both hands. "That investigation, it wasn't what you'd call thorough. They pulled me and Jeff off it the second Keegan took the plea. Not like we minded. Plenty of open cases on our books. Guy pleads, hell with it, that one's closed."

"But you didn't like it?"

For a moment, she didn't think he'd answer. Then he said, "They came out there with a six-pack, Keegan said. We didn't find a single can. Keegan said he picked them up when he ran, in case of prints."

"Sounds reasonable."

"I went back the next day. Before they pulled us, you know? I went back in the light. I found two plastic ring tops. In the dirt near the foundation. Like someone tossed them over the edge. Molloy's prints on one, nothing we could make out on the other. I asked Keegan, how many six-packs did you say? He said, Yeah, I don't remember, maybe two. Seemed like a weird thing to me, guy can't remember how many six-packs he cracked open. Especially, he picked up the cans."

"He'd have to have been flustered. Couldn't one of those tops have been from another time?"

"Keegan said that, too. Backpedaling. Um, um, um, could be a couple of nights before, um, um, we go over there a lot. So maybe it's one, maybe it's two, maybe from last night, maybe last week. Great. Anyway, it was a pretty clean site. No other trash. Strange that a ring top would have stayed, from last week."

"And you think . . . ?"

"Someone else was there. Three guys, two six-packs. And that's why the cans were gone. That's the prints they were worried about. We tested Molloy's blood-alcohol level. Keegan's, too. Molloy tested high, but not Keegan. Not two six-packs' worth. And me and Jeff, we asked ourselves this: These were grown men. What the hell are they doing drinking on a construction site, like they're kids, they have to sneak around? Every third building in Pleasant Hills was a bar, those days."

"Did you ask Keegan?"

"He said they liked it out there, those half-built houses. Reminded them of this place they used to hang out when they were kids. Horsepucky."

"What do you think was going on?"

"It was a private meet," Zannoni said. "Keegan, Molloy, somebody else."

"A setup?"

"More like a fuckup. If it was a hit, they'd've been prepared. Everybody would've disappeared. Keegan wouldn't have had to take the fall. There wouldn't have been a fall."

"But you think that's what happened? That's what Keegan did, take a fall?"

"Sure as hell."

"But you don't know who for?"

"Like I say, I never did. Until I read that story in your paper. Hey, you cold? We could go inside."

"No, I'm fine. It's just a little windy here." *That story. The investigation is continuing.* Laura hated that story, hated it.

"When I read in your paper that Jimmy McCaffery was behind the money—you know that for a fact?"

Laura, who right at this moment knew nothing for a fact, nodded.

"All that money, all these years, in secret," said Zannoni. "It had to be him. It had to be him."

———

Tree, Falling

October 31, 2001

Laura stared out from Angelo Zannoni's balcony, following a ship whose lights were so bright she could see the colors of the containers piling its deck. Orange, yellow, blue. The ship slid under the Verrazano Narrows Bridge and steamed west to offer its cargo to the huge waterfront cranes at the Port of Newark, right across the river from Lower Manhattan. You were supposed to worry about the cargo now, about what disastrous freight, what catastrophic future, could burst from newly arrived, colorful crates.

"Back then," Laura asked Zannoni. "About someone else being with Keegan and Molloy. Did you say anything?"

Zannoni shook his head. "Only to Jeff. He thought the same as me, but except the ring tops, the backpedaling, we didn't have shit. For a while, we looked. We talked to the detective who knew this crap best, the Molloys and the Spanos, see if there was something going on. Checked the gun dealers around, to find where Keegan got the gun. Turned up nothing. Then Keegan took the plea, and that was the end of it."

"You didn't talk to anyone else about it? Your commanding officer?"

"Make a hassle when there wasn't one? Why? Look. Even if someone else was there that night, even if the gun was this other guy's, Keegan still could be our shooter. His prints on the gun, his confession."

"But you believe there was a third man. And you think it was James McCaffery."

"All I can say, anyone was drinking with Jack Molloy in a deserted spot like that, it sure as hell wasn't some goombah."

"But Keegan never admitted there was anyone else?"

"Keegan sat in jail a day or two. They charged him with possession of an unlicensed weapon." Zannoni snorted. "The weapon? Molloy gets shot through the heart, Keegan admits to shooting him, the best they can do is the weapon? Tell me the fix wasn't in on that one."

"You're saying McCaffery fixed it?"

"Fix like that," Zannoni said, "you know why they do it?"

"Why it's fixed?" Laura wasn't sure what Zannoni was getting at. "To get the accused a lighter sentence."

"Why the DA goes along. You know why?"

"Tell me."

"So the guy keeps his mouth shut."

"About what?"

Zannoni shook his head. "Never figured that out."

"But you're telling me you believe McCaffery was the one who fixed it?"

Laura was sure Zannoni's tea must be cold by now, but he sipped at it, once, twice. "He's somebody now, a big hero, even before this"— waving his tea in the direction of Lower Manhattan, invisible through the trees— "but back then he was just a fireman. Twenty-three, twenty-four years old. No way he had the juice."

"Who did?"

Somewhere on the street below, hidden by the treetops, a car horn honked. Birds tweeted, evening birds, and a seagull screamed; Laura couldn't see them. What she could see—the black water, the bridge, the ships—was silent.

"You know much about the history around here?" Zannoni made a circle with his tea.

"Of Pleasant Hills, you mean? No."

"Area was settled by Irish. Farmers, mostly. Before the train, especially before the bridge, towns out here were more separate than now. A lot of Italians on Staten Island, but in Pleasant Hills, mostly Irish.

"Not to say there weren't Italians. Grew up here myself." Zannoni shifted in his chair; Laura remained sideways on hers, facing him. "Not so easy, sometimes, being Italian in Pleasant Hills. To the Irish kids, all wops were Mafia, so they were hot shit if they beat the crap outta you. Fighting for truth, justice, and the American way. Bad blood, micks and wops out here, and a lot more of them than us."

"Sounds pretty rotten," Laura said, to let Zannoni know she was on his side.

"Old history now. But one thing was true. Not so much Pleasant Hills, but Staten Island. Lot of Mafia out here. The Italians-are-like-everyone guys will tell you that's not true, but it is.

"Around here—Pleasant Hills—the Irish had their crook, but we had ours, too. Theirs was Big Mike Molloy. Jack Molloy's father? Ours was Aldo Spano. You heard of them?"

"I've heard of Molloy, only because of this. And Aldo Spano—he's Eddie Spano's father?"

Zannoni grunted. Laura took it for agreement.

"Molloy was the big fish. Pleasant Hills was pretty much Mike Molloy's. Spano nibbled around the edges. Spano put up with Molloy because he had a big organization and he'd've been hard to dislodge."

"Why did Molloy put up with Spano?"

"The Irish, they operated independent, each organization. Molloy was big, but he was on his own. Italians, you're hooked up with someone, one of the families, or you're out of business. Al Spano's hookup was the Bonnanos. Spano wasn't a big enough deal for them to go out of their way, clear-cut a territory for him, but they would've jumped if Molloy made a direct move."

"So it was a stalemate?"

"Worked pretty well. Each side had their rackets."

Laura, feeling she was tiptoeing out onto thin ice, asked, "What did the police do?"

"About them?" Zannoni stared at her as though she'd asked what the police did about the weather. "Shit, those guys were a lot heavier hitters than we were. Now you got prosecutors, state and city, like Rudy before he was mayor, people like that, they'll take on these guys. But back then nobody did. All we could do was keep the noise down."

The ice hadn't cracked, so Laura took another step. "You're telling me that's what you did in the Molloy case?"

Zannoni put down the mug. It was, Laura saw, finally empty. "You ever ask yourself where McCaffery got the kind of money he was passing on to Keegan's family, if it was him? Salary of a fireman just starting out, those days, no way. Hell, even today, no fucking way."

"It was someone else's money?"

"Sure as God made little apples."

"Whose?"

"Like you said, you only heard of Big Mike Molloy because of this. The guy is history. His organization's history. You know he had two sons?"

"Jack and Thomas. I interviewed Thomas Molloy yesterday."

"No kidding?" Zannoni raised his eyebrows. "You put that in today's paper?"

"Yes."

"Didn't get the paper today. What'd he have to say?"

Laura spoke to what she guessed was the point. "I asked him about ties between his brother and the Spanos. He said there weren't any, as far as he knew, but Jack could have angered someone in the Spano organization."

"What'd you think of him? Tom?"

"You mean, did I think he was legitimate? I got the impression he was."

Zannoni nodded. "When I was at the 124, word was Tom was being groomed to take over Big Mike Molloy's organization. But what happened after Jack got killed, it seems like Tom got cold feet. Or maybe we were reading it wrong. Anyway, over the next couple years—long before Big Mike died—a lot of the Molloy rackets got sold off, shut down. And guess who ended up with whatever was left, added them to his own? Guess who's the only game in town now, in Pleasant Hills?"

"Spano?"

"Eddie Spano," Zannoni agreed. "In the end, it's the Italians on top."

Zannoni stared straight ahead, over the trees and roofs. An American flag snapped in the wind in the yard of a nearby house. Laura had learned in grade school that the flag was supposed to come down at night, but these days the flags weren't coming down.

"It sounds to me," she ventured, "like this was something you were thinking about even back then. With the second ring top and everything. But—"

"Case was closed. Perp took the plea. Me and Jeff had other things to do. And," he added, as though he knew she was going to keep pushing, "I didn't know about McCaffery then. Didn't have an idea who the other guy that night was. But I could see who could come out ahead. Without Jack, maybe the Molloy organization's in trouble. Maybe Al Spano ends up the big fish." Zannoni pushed himself out of his chair and walked to the balcony rail. Staring out to sea, he said, "I'm older than those Molloys. Jack and Tom. Never took a punch from either of 'em. But, Jack—guys just like him gave me black eyes, bloody noses, threw my schoolbooks down the sewer, whole time I was growing up.

"So Molloy gets shot, and word comes down the next day: pick up Keegan. I look and I see: Jack Molloy's out of the way. Mark Keegan's taking the fall, I don't know who for. But is this so bad? Is it bad enough, I want to throw a monkey wrench in the works, my third guy theory? Maybe risk my chance of making sergeant? For what?

"And Jeff points out to me: Spano's guys I know. I talk their language. We need something, maybe it's easier if it's Spano's guys than Molloy's. And even," Zannoni said with emphasis, as though he were stacking his reasons onto a pile, counting on the pile's height to justify its existence, "Big Mike Molloy, what he's seeing, a buddy of Jack's shot his kid. A fuckup. Bad, but shit happens."

People die, Laura thought. *Vanish, never come back. Shit happens.*

"If I'm right and Spano's involved and it comes out, hell, we got a war here. We can't handle it, everybody knows we can't. Like I said, back then, you didn't take those guys on. War, it's the civilians who pay." He nodded, as though answering an unspoken question. "So that was that."

Black sky, white stars, lit ships, glittering water. This far south on Staten Island, you couldn't see the tip of Manhattan, couldn't see the smoke rising.

"So why now?" Laura asked. "Why come forward now?"

Zannoni was silent. His hands lifted from the balcony rail, separated, came back together. "You see what those motherfuckers did over there?" Now his hands gestured in the direction of the invisible smoke. "Killing Americans, that's all they wanted. Didn't matter, you were Italian, you were Irish. Didn't matter you were a cop or a fireman. Those SOBs decided you were dead, you were dead. Italian, Irish, Jewish, black, so fucking what? That shit's gotta stop. Those motherfuckers are out there blasting the hell out of Americans. *Americans.* And I'm sitting here on my fucking balcony, I'm sitting on my butt, there's nothing I can do.

"Then your boy Jesselson calls.

"And I think, Maybe I can do this.

"I think, This shit's gotta stop."

BOYS' OWN BOOK
Chapter 14

———

Leaving the Cat

September 2, 1979

Jimmy's sitting in the backyard with Markie. The sun's warm on his back, and everything's so quiet he can hear the Addonisios' radio from three houses away. The Addonisios are old, and they sit on their porch and listen to the opera every Sunday in the summer. A lot of the other guys rag on it, they say those wops, they like lady singers who sound like cats with their tails in the door. Jimmy doesn't mind the opera. Vinny down at the firehouse, he puts it on sometimes when they get back from a run. Jimmy likes to hear it then, it sounds kind of the way he feels, all those voices, loud and soft, alone and together. But he doesn't know anything about opera.

Jimmy looks at Markie, wonders why Sally and Kevin and his job at the garage aren't enough for Markie. He thinks about himself, the sizzling that starts deep inside him when the bell's ringing and the guys are all yanking on turnout coats, swinging onto the truck. Is this what Markie feels when he's with Jack?

Ten years old: early Sunday morning, the kids over where the new subdivision is going up, no one knows what *subdivision* means (someone says it sounds like math, everyone groans), but they all love the outlines of the houses drawn in wood against the sky like skeletons. They like to play here. You can jump down from a porch, or maybe it's a dining room, onto a huge pile of sand; you can hide in the dark, damp space underneath the kitchen, not big enough even for Markie to stand up in, but full of dirt and puddles so when the other army comes to find you, you can ambush them with mudballs. A big yellow machine with a claw in front is standing on top of the hill like a dinosaur. Jack knows what it's called: it's a front loader, you jerks, he says. And he says something else: he says he knows how to drive it.

Tom looks at the thing a minute, then shakes his head, says, Forget it, man. He says, I want to see if I can climb that chimney over there, and he heads that way. Jack looks in that direction, too, maybe he's thinking about going with Tom, but Markie says, Really, Jack? Can you really drive it? And Jack looks back at the dinosaur, and says, Fuckin' A, because you know, Markie, man, I saw it, I saw where the asshole who left it there Friday, I saw where he left the keys.

And Jack and Markie are charging up the hill, kicking up sand, racing each other, of course Jack wins. Tom's shouting, but Jack's already sticking his hand into the doorless cab, feeling under the seat, and then he and Markie are in the cab and the yellow machine growls and roars, like it really is a dinosaur. Jack yanks back on a lever. His face is scrunched up, he's peering through the windshield just like Mr. Molloy trying to decide which bridge to take coming back from the Jersey shore. Markie's beside him laughing his head off. The machine jerks like it's trying to throw them out, then changes its mind; they want to go for a ride, all right, okay, they asked for it.

Jimmy watches as the machine pulls itself forward, lurching over the mud; he thinks hard, the way the hill is, the way the machine's leaning, and he runs in front, around, and yells for them to jump now! out THIS side, now! Markie laughs, slaps Jack on the back, the dinosaur's still roaring, but then Markie sees Jimmy's face, and Markie's face changes, maybe he feels how far over he's leaning, and suddenly he leaps. It's a high fall now, into the dirt, and Markie lies there forever before he gets up. All the kids stare at him and stare at the dinosaur as one side of it starts to sink into the mud. Slowly, still moving downhill, it tilts more and more, the side Markie jumped from is almost straight up in the air. Jimmy and Tom are both yelling for Jack, and then there Jack is, standing on the edge, then flying through the air, his legs pumping like he's running. He hits the ground at the same moment the dinosaur, mad because it lost its balance, roars, starts to fall, and smashes onto the corner of one of the houses. The kids hear wood splintering. Tom hauls Jack out of the mud—Markie's already on his feet—and everyone runs like hell. Jimmy's heart's pounding, Tom looks mad. But Markie's grinning as they run away, and Jack grins at Markie, too, and Jimmy sees that happen, remembers it.

This morning? We were down by the rocks, Tom says later, when the grown-ups ask. We were fishing. Yeah? says Jimmy's dad. Good morning for it, bet the bass were running. Catch anything? Jimmy shakes his head, but he doesn't say anything. Anything he'd say wouldn't be true, and he doesn't want the words to mess him up.

So when Markie looks down at the grass now, in his own backyard, like he needs to check it out, Jimmy *knows*.

Yeah, says Markie. Yeah, I guess I saw Jack around. How come?

Just wondering, I don't know, says Jimmy. Just, I heard something.

Something like what?

Jimmy drinks some beer. That crew Jack's got, Jimmy says. They fly kind of high.

I don't get you.

Yeah, says Jimmy, shaking his head. Like, Mr. Molloy? He stays pretty much under the radar. You know? Doesn't embarrass anyone.

Embarrass who?

Anyone. You're a mosquito, you sneak up and bite someone, fly away, you could do okay for yourself like that. You buzz around their ear, they're gonna squash you.

Jimmy drinks some beer, thinks that that's not exactly what he means. Still, it's close enough.

I'm gonna tell Big Mike, says Markie. That you said he was like a mosquito.

They both grin, but Markie's is the grin that makes Jimmy worried, the one he's been seeing since they were kids, seeing more of lately, when Markie's got a family and Jimmy thought he ought to be seeing it less. The grin Markie had just before he and Jack climbed into the dinosaur all those years ago.

And Jimmy's saying Mr. Molloy, same as since they were kids. But Markie's saying Big Mike.

But I'm talking about the buzzing, says Jimmy. That's Jack's problem, that's what I heard about.

Markie says again, I don't get you.

The cops, Jimmy says. The cops are getting ready to roll up Jack, his whole crew.

For a few seconds Markie says nothing. The water's not running in the sink anymore, but Jimmy hears Marian's voice, she's singing a song to Kevin. Jimmy loves Marian's voice: when he listens to her sing, he believes the words in the songs.

Shit, says Markie finally. Oh shit, you sure?

Jimmy shrugs. I don't know that much, he says. I mean, maybe I didn't hear it right. Somebody said somebody said, you know how it goes?

What about Big Mike? Does he know?

Maybe. But if he does, what's he gonna do? Everything he could do, he must've done already.

Markie nods. Jimmy watches him, sees that Markie knows that what Jimmy's saying is true, that Mike the Bear can't help Jack out anymore.

Jack's crew, they don't keep their heads down.

For one thing, they operate too close to home. Some of the businesses Mike the Bear runs—the shylocking, the bookmaking out of Flanagan's—are in the neighborhood, they have to be. And everybody always said Mike has some girls, in a boring-looking two-family you'd never notice, in the old section. But when Mike's crew takes off a truck or second-stories some fancy house, you can bet it's not around here. Not on Staten Island at all, usually, but someplace like Brooklyn or Queens or New Jersey, where the bridges go. (Jimmy remembers when the Verrazano Narrows Bridge opened, how he heard Mr. Molloy say that was the best thing the city ever did for him. Jimmy was a little kid then, but he already knew Mr. Molloy was Mike the Bear: didn't know yet what that meant, but was not surprised to hear the city did things for him.)

But Jack, ever since Mike the Bear gave him the go-ahead to put a crew together, to get something started on his own, Jack doesn't keep a lid on it. Even when they boost goods from somewhere else, there's usually stuff, watches or whatever, sometimes a car, that ends up in the neighborhood. Or some guy, from some other crew, from outside—maybe a Puerto Rican from Harlem, something like that—gets beat to shit, everybody's asking each other what the spics are doing in the neighborhood: but knowing he came to do business, he wouldn't take No for an answer, this is just Jack's way of saying he means No. It's trouble: it's not the way it's done. Over the years there've been lots of people Mike the Bear doesn't want to do business with: they get talked to, roughed up a little if they have to be, but not like this. And if it has to be this, you use the bridges, the guy gets found somewhere else.

Markie and Jimmy both know this, everyone does.

Tom and Jack have argued about it more than once, evenings in Flanagan's, Tom tight-jawed, low-voiced, while Jack leans back, drains his beer, says, Yeah, yeah, all right, like Tom's making a big deal out of nothing. These arguments leak from Flanagan's into the surrounding streets, get passed from neighbor to neighbor over backyard fences or in the aisles of the A&P.

And sometimes something even gets in the paper; the *Advance* runs a story, "Crime on the Rise." Sometimes things flare up, then suddenly go quiet, and you know Mike the Bear's had a word with someone, cash has changed hands somewhere, something has been promised, or delivered.

But that has its natural limit. Cops are like anyone else: you can pay them to protect your ass, but not if it costs them theirs. Sooner or later, if there's enough complaining, something has to be done, or at least it has to look that way.

And this is what Mike the Bear told Jimmy in Flanagan's yesterday, and this is what Mike wants Jack to learn. From wherever he gets things, Mike the Bear got this: the cops are coming for Jack, and Mike can't stop them. Jack's only chance is to back off, cut his crew loose, turn into Mr. Model Citizen, at least for the duration. Of what? Until the NYPD forgets about him. However long that is.

Jimmy looks up from his beer, realizes Markie's asking him a question he asked once already.

What's gonna happen? Markie wants to know.

Jack's got to go straight, Jimmy says. He's got to start going to church and helping little old ladies across the street. He has to quiet down.

He's gonna hate that. Like wearing a tie.

Jimmy smiles, because he's remembering Jack yanking off his tie at the party after his first communion, and every time since that he had to wear one, funerals and weddings and every time, saying, I'm smothering, this thing's gonna choke me, man, I got to get out of it. Jack, always afraid of smothering, always needing to get out.

Jimmy says to Markie, But that's what's got to happen.

You think he'll do it?

Only, Jimmy says, if someone tells him to.

Who? Big Mike? Tom?

Jimmy shakes his head. If they did that, he says, Jack'll just say it's because Tom wants his operation.

Tom? What does he want that for? When Big Mike retires to Florida or something, Tom's gonna have everything. What does he want what Jack has for?

I didn't say he does. I said Jack'll think he does.

Markie frowns, then looks up. You, Jimmy. You gotta tell Jack. You gotta warn him.

Yeah, I guess, I guess I better. Trouble is, all the people around here, I'm the one he's most going to think is bullshitting him. What the hell does a fireman know about this shit? You know what, I'll bet he'll think Tom told me to. Or even I thought it up by myself, because now I'm too straight, I don't want guys like him having any fun.

Markie laughs. Yeah, it's true, he thinks you got pretty uptight since you went on the Job.

Jimmy shrugs. Probably I did.

Yeah, says Markie, Jimmy, man, you don't hang out no more. Markie's using Jack's growly voice, has his jaw stuck out the way Jack's gets. All's you do anymore, man, Markie says, still being Jack, you sit in front of the firehouse with that old fart McCardle, like the two of you, you're in charge of looking at stuff.

Jimmy flips his empty beer can into the air, swats it over so Markie has to duck.

Oh, man, says Markie, you're lucky the girls took the potato salad inside.

What, you're telling me you'd start a food fight? In your own backyard?

You started it already! Anyway, it's not my backyard, it's old man O'Neill's.

Marian comes out onto the porch right then, asks if Jimmy's ready to go. Markie says, Marian, you just did a really good thing, you just saved Jimmy's ass.

From what? Marian says, looking around to the back of Jimmy, like she needs to see what's wrong with his ass.

Potato salad, says Markie, nodding darkly, like that's his most serious weapon.

Oh my God, says Marian, her eyes getting wide.

Yeah, says Jimmy, I'm getting scared, we better go.

Markie walks with Jimmy and Marian up the driveway to the front of the house. When they get to the sidewalk, Markie says, Jimmy, man, that stuff we were talking about? Maybe I could do it.

Jimmy looks at him. Maybe, he says.

Yeah, why not?

Jimmy nods. Just, you have to not say you got it from me. Because he'd blow it off then.

Got you.

What are you guys talking about? Marian wants to know.

Boy talk. I ask you what you and Sally were cracking up about in the kitchen? Jimmy kisses Marian on the nose.

No, but if you had, I'd have told you.

That's because you're nicer than me.

Marian smacks him on the arm, lightly.

Markie says, Jimmy, you're in trouble now.

Yeah, says Jimmy, but I know a way out. He wraps his arms around Marian, presses her close, kisses her in a way he doesn't usually do out on the street. Finally he moves his face an inch away from hers, asks, Am I still in trouble?

You sure are, says Marian, but now it's a completely different kind.

―――

Abraham Lincoln and the Pig

October 31, 2001

Four tables bodyguarded by two chairs each lounged on the sidewalk outside the Bird. Phil thought, Nice day to sit outside. Too bad Kevin probably wouldn't see it that way. He pushed through the door and sure enough spotted Kevin in the far corner booth, the one most shadowed.

The Bird, Phil saw, was his kind of saloon. Atmosphere-free. No concession at all to Halloween, not a ghost or goblin. Scratched tables, mismatched chairs, neon beer signs. Though the five-foot flag above the bar, he'd give odds that was new. A scattering of solitary drinkers drifted foggily through the afternoon, staring at nothing, lost in private reasons. On the walls, photos of Little League teams down the years. Phil wondered, as he made his way to the back, which of those smiling uniformed boys was Jimmy McCaffery, which was Eddie Spano, which was Jack Molloy. Which was Markie. Boys with their teammates, shoulder to shoulder, squinting and smiling into the bright future. Two dead at twenty-three, one dead last month. The one still living, a career criminal. Ah, youth.

"Your team photos here?" he asked as he slid into the booth opposite Kevin.

"What?" Kevin sat off-kilter, favoring his right leg. His crutches leaned in the corner.

"Didn't the Bird sponsor your Little League team?"

Kevin said, "What are you asking that for?" but he pointed across the room. "Those."

Phil turned to look, saw Kevin as he'd been at nine, at ten, at twelve. The boy he'd never disappointed.

"Uncle Phil—"

The waitress materialized, hovered beside them. Her bleached-blond presence felt like a reprieve. Phil wanted her to stay. But after she'd run down the list of beer on tap and in bottles, what was there to keep her there? He supposed he could ask about scotches, gins, five-star brandies, but he'd always despised opponents whose delaying tactics were that obvious, that desperate. You're not prepared, don't show up. He asked for a Guinness and watched her leave to get it. Kevin was already working on a bottle of Bud.

"Uncle Phil—" Kevin said again, but Phil raised his hand.

"Kev, listen."

Kevin stopped, did as Phil said. All right, now you have to tell him something. In a minute. When the beer comes. No, now, before he starts again. "I don't know what's going on, okay?" The look Kevin gave him, it wasn't okay. "I don't know what happened to that reporter, if he killed himself or someone killed him. But—no, wait—but there are a couple things I never told you, or your mother. I'll tell you now if you want."

Kevin nodded.

Jump, Phil told himself. The net will appear. Or it won't. Looking into Kevin's eyes, so like Sally's, he said, "I met with Jimmy McCaffery every couple of months for eighteen years. Sometimes in a bar like this, sometimes in my office. Once at one of your games. The Tornados, a play-off game. You tripled. Do you remember?"

Kevin looked blank, then he shrugged. "They were always good. The Tornados. We played them lots of times."

Phil nodded. The waitress brought his Guinness, but she didn't stick around. Story of his life.

Kevin said, "Why'd you meet with Uncle Jimmy?"

A sip of beer. "He gave me money. Cash. I'd put it in a bank account, an escrow account in your mother's name, and write her a check every month."

"From the State."

"Well, obviously not. But yes, those checks."

"Why?"

"Your father was dead. You were a baby. Your mother needed the money."

"Goddamn it, Uncle Phil!" At Kevin's shout the waitress's head whipped around like a searchlight. The bartender's, too, in case something was blowing up he'd need to take care of. Phil raised an apologetic hand, shook his head. The bartender nodded: Okay, but watch your-selves. Screw you, Phil thought, that was more action than you've seen in here all week.

Kevin leaned forward. If this were a negotiating session, Phil would have pulled back and also leaned a little to one side. That way he'd control the distance between them and make it clear, too, that he was the one controlling it. But he didn't do any of that. There was too much distance already.

"I mean, why you and Uncle Jimmy?" Kevin lowered his voice, but now it wore a sharp and ragged edge. "I thought you didn't even like each other. Why the bullshit?"

Of course that's what he meant. "Jimmy said your mother wouldn't have taken the money from him. From anyone."

"Bullshit," Kevin repeated.

Kevin drank. Phil waited. Never offer information, never answer the question that wasn't asked. "Why did the paper say the money might have come from Eddie Spano?" Kevin demanded.

"It had to come from somewhere. They don't think it could have been Jimmy's. It's too much money."

"Where did it come from?"

Answer half the question: "What Jimmy gave me, I don't know where it came from."

"What the fuck do you mean, you don't know?"

"I never asked him."

"He just hands you thousands in cash every couple months for eigh-teen fucking years, and you never ask where it comes from?"

"Kev, I work with criminals. There are a lot of things I'm better off not knowing."

"Criminals?"

"I don't mean Jimmy!" Like hell you don't. "Generally, always, all I want to know is that I'm not involved in anything illegal. Beyond that, sometimes the less information I have, the better."

"If you were thinking like that, you were thinking there was some-thing bad to know."

Phil said nothing, spiraling down.

"If you never asked him"—this sarcastically, a tone he'd never heard from Kevin before—"how could you know you weren't *involved in any-thing illegal?*"

"My job . . ." Phil drank, a stall while he tried to find a way to regain altitude. "Your father asked me to look after you and your mother while he was gone."

"I still—"

"Your father was my responsibility, Kev."

Kevin's answer was what he'd been taught, but with a new, unsure note. "You did everything you could. Mom always said."

Okay, Kevin. It's been nice knowing you. "I let him—I encouraged him—to plead to something I was sure he didn't do."

Phil watched that hit Kevin like arctic air. Then he said: "I don't think he shot Jack Molloy. I never did."

"If my dad—then who do you think did?"

It wasn't really a question, just an automatic reaction. Like a blink to clear your eyes when you're not sure what you're seeing. Phil let it go, waited for the next one.

"No one else was there," Kevin said. "Just them. Jack Molloy and my dad."

"I think someone else was."

Kevin stared, and drank, and stared, and said, "Uncle Jimmy? You think Uncle Jimmy was there? You think Jimmy did it?"

No answer from Phil.

"Oh, fuck you, Uncle Phil! Fuck you, that's nuts!"

"It was his money."

"Or someone else's. You just said."

"Or someone else's. But it came through Jimmy. Why? If he didn't know something?"

"Something like what?"

"If he didn't do it, he knew who did."

"My dad did it. By accident. Uncle Jimmy was my dad's best friend!"

"Everyone says that."

"You don't believe it?"

"That's not what I mean." No? Then why did you say it like that, that icy edge?

Phil waved to the waitress, who nodded and went behind the bar to the tap, didn't even approach. Thanks a lot, honey. "I didn't meet any of those people—your father, Jimmy, any of them—until after Markie was arrested. I was new in private practice, but everything I'd done since the day I left law school was criminal defense. I didn't know whose friend was whose around here, but I knew Markie was lying. I could smell it."

"And you didn't do anything?"

"He wouldn't let me. He told me exactly what he'd told the police, and his story never changed. 'Jack shot at me, I shot back, I was scared, I never thought I'd hit him.' In the end I was goddamn grateful to be offered the plea on the gun charge, because Markie was ready to go to trial."

"Because he thought you'd get him off. Because he trusted you."

That was a punch in the gut. "Kevin—" Thank God, the waitress and the new beers. She gave them one each, grabbed up the empties, and left. Come on, honey, don't you want to sit and chat?

"Kev, for God's sake. He kept insisting he'd done it. What the hell defense did I have? Insanity? I'm not a magician." Oh, but that's wrong. Ask anyone on the other side. They'll tell you: Constantine's a sorcerer, a conjuror, a spell-caster. Rabbits from hats, pickpockets from jail, gangsters from prison and flash! into the Witness Protection Program because, presto change-o, Phil Constantine can turn drug dealers into cooperators and accused murderers into innocent men.

But only since Markie. Only since he'd started to see Markie Keegan's eyes looking out of every new client's face.

The waitress made a circuit of the room, bringing fresh drinks to men who hadn't called for them. It was likely that outside the sun was moving across the sky but in here the light didn't change and the silence didn't change and nothing changed except the way Kevin looked at Phil.

Phil turned from that look, focused on the names and dates and loves dug into the table.

"The front booth," Kevin said quietly. Phil looked up. "My dad carved his initials and my mom's in a heart in the front booth. Did you ever tell my mom my dad was lying?"

"She didn't believe it, he wouldn't admit it. I stopped saying it."

"Did you tell Uncle Jimmy?"

Guinness, thought Phil, used to taste better than this. "In the beginning. When I still thought if I could find the truth I could get Markie off. I tried, Kev. I tried to find the truth." Why had he said that? What would Kevin care, what he'd tried, what he'd failed at?

"What did you say to him? Uncle Jimmy, in the beginning?"

"I told him I was sure Markie was lying. I asked him if he knew what really happened. Because everyone told me he was Markie's friend. I asked if Markie had said anything to him. I asked . . ."

"What?"

"I asked if he knew who Markie was trying to protect. He said no. He asked me how light a sentence I thought I could get Markie. I said I didn't think Markie was guilty and I wanted the truth. Jimmy said, What if what Markie's saying is the truth? Or it's not but he keeps saying it? What will happen to him?

"I said if we could sell the self-defense story, maybe we could get a plea deal, no charges in the death, only the gun. There was no way out of the gun. I said with no priors, upstanding citizen, wife and child, probably I could play the violin a little and get the minimum, sixteen months. A possibility of probation, no jail time, if he gave up the gun dealer."

"But he didn't."

"Because he didn't know who it was. Because he hadn't bought the gun."

"He told you that?"

"No, dammit, Kevin, he didn't tell me that! He swore to me he'd bought it from some guy in some bar in Tottenville. He didn't remember the name of the guy, or the bar, or the street the bar was on, or how to get to the street the bar was on. I took the train out to Tottenville one Saturday and spent the whole goddamn day wandering around. You been to Tottenville?" Tottenville, twenty years ago a mini-Appalachia holding down the southern end of Staten Island, where rusting cars were lawn ornaments and chickens shared the yards with scruffy dogs.

"We don't go down there much."

"From Pleasant Hills. You think in 'seventy-nine anyone did? After everyone Markie knew threw their cash together so he could make bail, I made him drive me back there. To look for the bar. A complete bust. I asked him why he'd been down there. He said, No real reason. He said he had no real reason for buying the gun or for carrying it that night. He said he didn't know why Jack was so pissed, he'd just been trying to help, to set Jack straight. He swore to me he and Jack were alone. He told me he wasn't protecting anybody. He told me bullshit, Kev. And it was all he'd tell me."

Kevin said nothing, sat so still it was almost possible for Phil to believe he hadn't heard him.

"I could see what was going to happen," Phil said quietly. "He was going to prison. He was going to do someone else's time—a lot of time, Kev—and there wasn't a goddamn thing I could do." Phil remembered it, that airless feeling in his chest. No countermove. No fake, no palmed ace, no magic flowers bursting from an empty hand. "And then out of the blue I got a call from an ADA, offering a plea on the gun. Pretty much the deal I'd outlined to Jimmy, almost exactly that. We had nothing, and they were offering a plea. Do you understand what that means?"

Kevin shook his head.

Shit, thought Phil, of course he understands, no one could miss it.

But maybe not. Phil remembered a Panthers game, ten-year-old Kevin leaning on his coach, limping off from second, his ankle bloody (Phil gripping Sally's hand, shaking his head to keep her from the dugout). Kevin's face was white with pain, but he was dry-eyed. No tears, until he saw his coach and the other team's coach screaming at each other nose to nose, until he saw the fury in his teammates' eyes, until he understood he'd been spiked on purpose by the sliding runner. When he cried, it wasn't because of the hurt and the blood. It was bewilderment and surprise that someone would be so deliberately cruel.

So maybe he really didn't get it.

Or maybe he just wanted to make Phil say it.

"It meant a fix, Kev."

Phil drained his Guinness. "Kev, look where I was. What I had. I didn't know this town, I didn't know where the fix was coming from. My client was a guy I liked, young, with a family. The plea deal was good. Especially if you believed he'd pulled the trigger. And I seemed to be the only one who didn't.

"Maybe I could've found the truth, if I'd kept digging. But I couldn't be sure that was the best thing for Markie. Whatever the truth was, Markie was my client, and he didn't want it out. Maybe he was right, in terms of whatever the hell was going on in Pleasant Hills, things I didn't understand."

That was it. What else was he going to say? And where was the mistake? What should he have done differently? What had brought him to this dead room with Kevin silent across a scarred table? What had he done wrong?

Kevin looked at him and answered Phil's unasked question: "And you were in love with my mom."

MARIAN'S STORY
Chapter 11

———

The Water Dreams

October 31, 2001

Such strange things, words, Marian thought. They create poetry, and death sentences, and lies. They describe how it feels to make love, or to freeze to death. Without words people would remain as unconnected as rooted trees, unable to approach each other, yearning, but forever alone, on a vast plain.

"Tom?"

Marian stared at Tom in the unfamiliar room, noisier, she was sure, than when they'd arrived. Words were being chattered, shouted, whispered, and flung everywhere all around them, masking and disguising one another, and Marian understood none of them, least of all the ones Tom had just spoken.

Tom slumped in his chair, as though trying to move away from Marian, away from his own past and the memories his words were summoning the way a magician's spell summons evil spirits. She was suddenly terrified he'd get up and leave, leave her, leave her alone here where nothing looked right and all the words had different meanings. In the comics Jimmy used to read—Bizarro World, that was where these things happened. Bizarro World, from *Superman*.

"We were all there that night," Tom said. "All four of us. It wasn't Markie and Jack having a few beers on the building site. It was Markie, Jimmy, Jack, and me."

"I don't understand."

"I know. Just listen." A breath. "Jack was drunk. I—I guess we all were. Jack pulled out a gun and started waving it around. He was pissed as hell."

This needed to be clearer, it really did. "Why?"

"Something Markie said. Jack and Markie'd been talking, a day or two back. That's what it seemed like, anyway. I don't really know, my brother wasn't making a lot of sense. He was pissed, and he kept saying Markie was full of shit and he was going to kill him."

"That's what Markie said happened." Marian's voice sounded very faint to her.

"We tried to talk Jack down," Tom said. "Jimmy and me both. He was— he should have calmed down. You know. He usually did, or he went away steaming and came back when it was okay. But he was so drunk, Marian. And the gun. He fired off a shot, blew a hole in that fucking two-by-four."

Suddenly every word was sharp, each meaning unmistakable. Was it better this way?

"I thought he'd stop then," Tom said. "See how stupid it was, and stop. But he aimed at Markie and shot again."

Tom raised his beer and gazed at her, and this time Marian knew he was not seeing her, he was seeing a skeleton house, his brother, his friends.

"Markie froze. He froze like he always did. What the hell did he think he was doing, Marian?"

Marian didn't know whether Tom meant Jack, or Markie, and in any case she had no idea, none.

"After the second shot Jimmy tackled Markie. Knocked him out of the way." Tom gulped more beer. "Everything Jack was—everything we all were, Marian, everything, it was all there, you could see it all. Like this bright light was shining. Like we were naked. No, no, not naked. Like you could, like you could see right through us."

Tired to the bone from waiting, waiting so many years, Marian said it for him. "It was Jimmy, wasn't it?"

Tom raised his eyes to her. "It . . ." He looked down again, shook his head. "I can't, Marian. And it doesn't matter."

"It was—"

"Don't you see? What each of us was. What we always were. It was right there."

"Tom—"

"Marian?" He was pleading for something. How could that be? Tom always had the answers, the smart ideas. Tom never needed anything. Tom was the one other people asked for things from. It was she who'd asked the question, the only question that had ever mattered, ever, the one question, because of that, she'd never asked.

And now she had to hear Tom's answer.

But Tom said, "Marian, I can't. And it doesn't matter."

PHIL'S STORY
Chapter 12

Turtles in the Pond

Kevin and Phil sat in the lifeless air of the Bird while Phil told Kevin the story of how he'd failed Markie. Kevin listened to all of Phil's reasons, then made his accusation: "And you were in love with my mom."

To be accused of love, Phil thought. If there ever was a circumstance where guilty was the same as innocent, this has got to be it.

"Your mother and I, Kev—that came much later."

Phil found his body tensing, his muscles set, like in a game. Like this morning's game. Over and over he'd blocked Brian's shot, blocked it though Brian was bigger than he, stronger, but Phil had studied Brian as he studied them all. He had counters for every move. If one thing didn't work, he tried another. He'd learned to do that. His whole life, he'd worked at that.

"I did everything I could for your dad, Kev. Your mother and I—"

Kevin waved this off, whatever Phil had been going to say. "I've heard this since I was a kid. You guys didn't get together until a long time later. That doesn't mean it wasn't on your mind."

Phil looked around. God, for a breeze to blow through this bar! Just something to breathe. Or, hell, to blow the top off, sweep us all up, fling us someplace else, some other time. Ancient Egypt, Camelot, Timbuktu. September 10.

It didn't happen, not a gust, not a zephyr. Phil didn't know what else to do, so he went on. "Markie wanted the plea, Kev. I got . . . I got the feeling he knew it was coming. But he said no, he didn't know, he just hoped. He just said, Great, I'll take it. It's fine.

"Fine? Kev, it was better than fine. Sixteen months, he'd be out in five and change. Manslaughter, he'd been looking at years. Years away from you and Sally. I could see how that was killing him. I tried to use it to get him to tell me the truth, but he never changed his story."

"Couldn't that mean it was true?"

"It could. Sure it could." This wasn't the point he wanted to argue with Kevin right now. He didn't want to argue anything with Kevin. Right now or any other time. "Anyway, that should've been it for me. Case over, win or lose, I'm gone. But he asked me to look after you guys. So I told Sally she could call me if she needed anything. There's always paperwork, things to do. She wanted to take you up there on visiting day. I showed her how. Things like that." Nothing from Kevin. Phil said the rest: "Then Markie died. Kev . . . ?"

"What?"

"Nothing." Phil had been about to say, Could we get out of here? Walk around, move, breathe some air, talk where there aren't any walls? But he'd forgotten about the crutches. "Nothing."

As though it was important for Kevin to hear the rest, he went on. "After that—after he died—I told your mom I'd hook her up with another lawyer. Everyone in Pleasant Hills was blaming me. I shouldn't have let him take the plea. I should've gotten him sent somewhere safer. I should've done something.

"I understood. I was the outsider, they had to blame someone. I didn't want Sally caught up in that. But she told me it wasn't my fault, and she wanted me to stay helping her, if I didn't mind. Kev, that's all it was. For a long time."

That, and Sally's eyes, changing from emerald glass to storm-swept, distant sea.

"So when Jimmy wanted to start giving you money—whoever's money it was—I was the logical guy to come to."

Finally, something from Kevin. A growl: "And you just took it? You thought Uncle Jimmy shot that guy and let my dad go to jail, and you just took his money?"

"Shit, Kev! Should I have told him to go fuck himself? What did I have? A gut feeling something's rotten and it's Jimmy McCaffery? You see who he is today—that's who he always was! The stained-glass saint. Me? I was the loser Jew lawyer from the other side of the harbor." Phil saw, or thought or hoped he saw, a cloud of uncertainty in Kevin's eyes. Move in on that, leverage it. "And I'll say this: I never saw him do anything that contradicted that. Everyone looked up to him. Including you."

"What the fuck—?"

"He raised you, Kev! As much as I did. And he"—how to put it?—
"he meant more to you. No, hear me out. I was fun, Kev, I was there,
you could count on me, but Jimmy was the guy you wanted to be. Who
the hell wouldn't? It would have broken your heart, and your mother's,
if I could have proved what I knew."

"What you *thought*!"

"Okay, thought." Making my point, said Phil to himself, to Kevin,
silently. "Even more reason to keep my mouth shut. Kev, I followed his
career all these years. He saved a lot of lives. He *was* a hero. Except, if
I was right, this one time. One time. And the money? Wherever it came
from, he was using it to help people I loved."

Kevin flinched at the word. Phil wondered, Can this really be the
first time I've said it to him?

"So who the hell was I to screw that up?" He leaned toward Kevin.
"For what? To prove how smart I was? What good would it have done?"

"What about justice? You didn't care?"

Phil opened his hands. Empty. "I think about that every day. About
Markie and every client since. I don't know what it means."

"You don't know? For Christ's sake, Uncle Phil! You're a lawyer!"

The universe of innocence in that outburst would have made Phil
laugh with delight, if things were different. Instead, he leaned toward
Kevin again and tried to explain.

"The other side—the prosecution—they talk about justice all the
time. Paying your debts. Justice for the victims. But I see guys like
Markie. Guys with family, friends, guys who had something going. Then
one fuckup, their lives are over. Who's the justice for, Kevin? What
does it look like?"

Kevin gave no answer. How could he? There was no answer.

But he had another question.

"Eddie Spano?"

Phil nodded. "You mean, if the money was his?"

"Because you can't be telling me Uncle Jimmy was . . . I don't know
what the fuck, Spano's hit man or something? And we—and that was
the payoff? You can't—"

"No, no. But there was a turf thing, the Molloys and the Spanos. I
think either Jimmy or your dad was a go-between."

"Spano was there, too? That night?"

"No. I thought about that, but no. I don't think Jimmy or Markie
would have protected him. I think something was going on, some
arrangement Eddie Spano and Jack Molloy were working out, through

somebody, Jimmy or Markie. And Molloy got drunk, started shooting, got shot, just like Markie said. But I don't think Markie shot him. I think it was Jimmy."

"Then why would Spano—"

"Maybe that's where the gun came from, from Spano, and Jimmy had that on him. So Jimmy squeezed a little out of him every month. Not a lot, not so much Spano would rather do something else about it. Just enough to keep Jimmy quiet and help you guys out."

Through narrowed eyes Kevin watched him. Shit, Phil thought. He suddenly knew what his clients must feel when they saw the end coming, when they realized Phil's magic wasn't going to work.

Slowly, Kevin said, "When I was thirteen, the money doubled. You said it was a cost-of-living thing, the state was adjusting it. What was that? Uncle Jimmy squeezing Spano harder? After ten years?"

Phil shook his head. One more. One more and it's over. "That was me."

Kevin stared.

"Your mother wanted to send you to St. Ann's."

"You paid for that?"

"I make money. What the hell was I going to do with it?"

"Jesus Christ. Jesus Christ." Kevin shook his head, looking as though he were standing on Mars staring at the scenery. "That was always a big deal to her. Your money. That she wasn't taking your fucking money."

"I know."

"It was important. She always said. You and her, she said, that was a special thing. But what kept us going was her working, and Dad's money from the State. Her and Dad. It was important."

"I know."

"How much of this did you tell that reporter?" Kevin's voice was tight. If he wasn't hurt, he'd have started it already, Phil thought. Lurched across the table, grabbed my shirt, thrown me. I'm bigger, he's younger. How would it come out?

"None of it. It was none of his goddamn business. Everything he put in the paper was on the public record, just that no one ever looked for it before. As soon as he found it, I knew it was big trouble."

"Why did someone kill him?"

"Maybe they didn't. Maybe he jumped. Kevin?"

"What?"

"If someone did kill him, it wasn't me."

The silence began again, and stretched on and on, until Phil started to wonder if anyone, anything, in this room would ever move anymore.

Then Kevin slid to the end of the booth. He pushed to his feet and leaned for his crutches. He set them where he needed them and gripped them, Phil thought, tighter than he had to: his knuckles were white. Without another word or a look at Phil he swung away, through the room. As he shouldered the door, a flare of bright light filled the opening, as though something had exploded the very moment Kevin left.

Well, sure, thought Phil.

It had.

———

Turtles in the Pond

October 31, 2001

Marian walked with Tom along the streets of Pleasant Hills. He wasn't telling her something, and she didn't know what it was. That was almost funny, not funny but almost, considering what he had told her, and how much she had not wanted to hear it.

When they'd first left the bar (it was all a little runny to Marian, like a watercolor, but she did not think Tom had paid for their meal and drinks, just signaled to the bartender and pointed to the table as he rose from his chair), she had been glad of the cool and the quiet and the dark. Tom had his hand on her arm, and he'd steered her off the avenue at the first corner they came to, so even the thin traffic and unambitious neon of a Pleasant Hills evening was behind them. Quiet streets, cars in the driveways, yellow glows from the windows. On porches, carved pumpkins sneered. The flickering candlelight inside them made them seem to move their mouths, whispering terrible things. Ghosts swung from tree limbs, but these were just cloth, not the real ghosts of Pleasant Hills.

This was the oldest section of town, not far from where they'd grown up. Marian knew whose houses these were, and if she didn't, she knew whose they had been: the Leslies, old man Callahan, the crazy Curren sisters. Marian knew which of these trees were good for climbing and what birds sang in them, though no birds sang now, this dark, this late. What she did not know was what the secret was that Tom was keeping.

Tom had always had secrets, well, of course he had, he was Tom Molloy, so many things his family knew and did that the rest of them did not know. And he had secrets now that Marian would not think of trying to unearth. How hard it had been to have his children grow up around the corner with Vicky instead of under his own roof. How Mike the Bear had felt when Tom sold or gave away or let fall into ruin or burned down the disparate parts of the empire Big Mike had built. Whether Tom thought he had ever brought a smile, a real smile, to his mother's sad eyes.

About some things, Marian would never ask.

Tom had secrets; she had a secret, too, one she'd been hiding forever. That hideous knife-scaled thing had crawled out between them in Flanagan's, fouled the air, driven them outdoors, and was now following them, hissing, through the streets. (Marian shivered, was barely able to keep from looking behind; Tom put his arm across her shoulders.) And so she wondered, What other secret could there be? What else was worth hiding, once this truth was out?

"Tell me," she said.

"Tell you what?" Tom pulled her closer to him. She was grateful. She wanted to answer him, but she did not know how to demand his secret, how to shrilly insist, when it was his arm that was keeping her warm. So she asked something else.

"Why did—did Jimmy"—she stumbled, and it made her stammer, or maybe it was the other way—"why did he let Markie say it was him? Markie went to jail—" To her horror, she started to cry.

Tom gave her a handkerchief, Tom gave her time. "It wasn't supposed to happen the way it did." Marian scrubbed at her eyes. Tom said, "He was supposed to serve maybe five months, get paroled, everything would be fine."

"What do you mean, 'supposed to'?"

"It's what we thought," Tom said, looking as they passed the McCrae house with its big new addition.

"When did you think that? Who said to think that?"

She knew her voice was rising. Tom's was patient. "Markie had no priors, he had no sheet. He was going to keep his head down inside. It shouldn't have been a problem."

"That lawyer bastard, it was all his idea, right?"

Tom turned his face to her. Even in the dark she could see the blue of his eyes. No, she couldn't. It was just that she knew about his eyes, with Tom she believed things without having to see them. "Constantine?" he said. "He didn't even get the case until way after we'd worked it out. He came in after Markie was arrested. He believed the story the way Markie told it."

She wasn't sure what Tom was saying: on these quiet streets there was too much noise, though maybe it was in her head, what sounded like sobbing. Tom was likely to be right. Yes, of course. But it could not be that Phil was innocent in all this.

" 'Worked it out,' " she said. "What does that mean?"

"Markie and Jimmy and me. Our story. We worked it out together."

"Why did he let him?"

"Who let who?"

"Why did Jimmy let Markie!"

Tom said, "Because Markie wanted to." Tom stopped and faced her, in front of the house that used to be the O'Briens', five kids, they were fun to play with but they moved away. "Jimmy was always saving Markie's ass. You remember how it was. Markie wanted to be the hero, just for once."

A breeze rustled the leaves above them. Someone's cat trotted across a lawn, stopped and froze when it saw them, then hissed and scooted back.

Marian felt strange. If she and Tom were telling secrets on the streets of Pleasant Hills, they shouldn't be adults. When they were all children and they did this, whispered to each other, everything they said was important, of course it was, but there was another thing they knew. They never said it, but they knew it and that was that no matter how serious something was, it could all be made right again. Somebody could make it right.

Even when Marian's mother died.

Marian had felt very bad. All the kids tried hard to be nice to her. Everyone invited her to their houses to play and the moms gave them extra cookies. Marian knew everyone was trying to make her feel better, but she didn't want to play. She wasn't sure she wanted to feel better. She just wanted to sit scrunched up in the corner of the fence in her own backyard and think about her mom.

Sometimes she did that. Other times she went to the other kids' houses, because her dad was very sad, too, and she could tell he liked it for her to go to play. And sometimes she stayed home and helped Aunt Fiona look after her sisters and her baby brother. Aunt Fiona, who came from someplace far away, was very nice, but she didn't know things like where the Band-Aids were, or that Betty cried if you let her applesauce touch her peas.

One day when Marian was sitting against the fence with her knees pulled up tight she heard scratchy footsteps on the gravel driveway. Tom slipped through the secret passage between the house and the garage.

"Hi," Tom said.

"Hi."

She waited for him to say something else but he just sat down next to her. Marian first thought she wanted Tom to go away, but then when he was just quiet and she went back to thinking about her mom she thought maybe she liked it that he was there.

After a while Tom turned his head to look at her. "You know what my mom says? She says your mom went to Heaven."

Marian nodded. She didn't want to talk because her throat felt sore.

"She says, the way you and your dad and everyone, the way you feel all sad and lonely? She says that's how God felt. Your mom was on earth and God got lonely. He missed her so much he asked her to come to Heaven."

God was lonely? He missed her mommy? That made Marian very sad, and she started to cry.

"But," said Tom fast, "but Heaven's beautiful. It's got clouds and flowers and oceans and stuff, pretty music, too, my mom says, and she says your mom likes it. She's just waiting for you to come."

Marian sniffled. Her mom liked pretty music. "Waiting for me?"

"Uh-huh," said Tom. "If you're good you go to Heaven when you die. Don't you know that?"

Marian thought maybe she did, but she wasn't positive. "I can go to Heaven?" she asked, just to make sure. "Where Mommy is?"

"Uh-huh."

Marian wiped her eyes and thought about this, about the clouds and flowers and oceans. "Can Daddy go there, too?"

"Everybody who's good."

"Betty? And Eileen and Patty? And Davey?"

"Everybody."

"And Aunt Fiona?"

Tom grinned and poked her in the ribs. "*Every*body."

Marian squirmed; it tickled where Tom poked her. "You?" she asked. "And Jimmy? And Jack? And Sally, and Markie, and Vicky?"

Every time Marian said a name, Tom poked her. She kept saying more names—"Your mom? Your dad? Sister Hilda?"—and then she poked him, too, and then they were saying everyone's name they could think of and poking each other and squirming and giggling.

When they ran out of names they both plopped back against the fence, tired from giggling. Tom was still smiling but something Marian thought of made her sad again.

"How do you know?" she asked.

"Know what?"

"About going to Heaven?" What if Tom was wrong, that was the thing she'd thought of.

"My mom says God promised."

God promised. God already thought about this and had it all planned, and Tom's mom knew about it; probably the other grown-ups did, too, her dad and everyone.

She thought of something else about Heaven. "Do everyone's dogs and cats go there, too? And the elephant from Spivey's Circus? Are there animals in Heaven?"

"If they're good. You just have to be good, then you can go."

Marian thought about the elephant sitting on a cloud, and she smiled, but Tom wasn't smiling, he had a serious face, even kind of sad. "What's the matter?" she asked.

He shook his head. "Nothing."

She leaned against him, and then he smiled.

The sun lit up the lilies her mom had planted along the fence. There was grass growing in with them. Her mom always said grass belonged on the lawn. When it grew where the flowers were, it needed to be pulled out so the flowers could get big. Marian knew how to do that. Maybe later she would, maybe after lunch. She wasn't less sad when she thought about her mom now, or less lonely. But she hadn't known she was scared until now. Now that Tom had told her about Heaven, she thought she might not be scared anymore.

"Are you sure?" she asked Tom, one more time.

Tom nodded and told her he was sure.

That was how it used to be. God had thought about everything, and even the things the grown-ups couldn't make better, God had planned out. Everything was under control even if you didn't understand it. Even if you didn't like it, there was a reason.

Marian still believed in God. She still believed, she tried her hardest to believe, that the world was unfolding according to His plan. She had always done her best to try to understand her part in that plan. The work she had made her life—MANY, her volunteer work, the boards on which she served, and now, God help her, the McCaffery Fund—was the way she tried to follow the path God had chosen for her.

She'd done this although, from the night Jack died, that path—always so bright before, so straight and wide—had twisted and darkened, plunging into thickets, thorns, and shadows. She'd kept on following, growing more determined as the way became more difficult: as Markie died, and Jimmy left her, and she moved away from Pleasant Hills.

On September 11, the path had vanished altogether. Still she'd gone on blindly, hoping to break into a clearing and find it again, shining ahead. And now with no path to guide her, she stood on the sidewalk in Pleasant Hills with Tom, stalked by a terrifying truth.

"Markie," she said to Tom. It had gotten cooler while they stood, facing each other, and she shivered. "He wanted to save somebody?"

Tom nodded.

"How?" And also she meant, From what?

Tom said, "It was Markie's fault that Jack was so pissed off. It was his fault, everything that happened, Markie said. He said if anyone even knew Jimmy was there, just if he was even there, he'd get kicked off the Job."

Off the Job. Out of the department. If Jimmy got in trouble, they wouldn't let him be a fireman. That would have been like not letting him breathe.

"And me," Tom said, "who I was, if they found me there, they'd have thrown a party."

Tom looked down. Marian suddenly wanted to take him in her arms, to hold him and say, Who you were, Tom, not who you are. But she couldn't move.

"Markie said he wanted to be the one. No way Markie was taking this fall, Jimmy said, he could forget that. Markie had a wife and kid. A manslaughter sentence, it was years.

"Markie said, No, not manslaughter, he'd tell them Jack was shooting, they'd see it was self-defense, he'd get off.

"But not from the gun, I told them. The gun wasn't licensed, there was no way out of the gun.

"But that could be a good thing. It could give the cops something to convict Markie on, so they'd look good. And it would be a short sentence. Maybe even no jail time, a guy like Markie."

A vision flashed in front of Marian, so complete and real it stopped her breath: how it would be if Markie hadn't gone to jail. He and Sally would have a house, maybe right on this street; close, anyway, to where she and Jimmy lived. She'd have watched from the kitchen window as her kids, hers and Jimmy's, grew up playing with Kevin and his red-haired brothers and sisters in each other's backyards. With Tom and Vicky's kids, too, Tom and Vicky probably never breaking up because if Markie hadn't gone to jail, hadn't died, the world would not have changed. Everyone would miss Jack, but Jack would have gone away anyway, to Atlanta, someplace, Jack wouldn't have been one of them now, no matter what.

"You couldn't—you couldn't have just run away?" Why was she asking Tom that? What did it matter what they could have done? And that would have been wrong, so wrong. But the beautiful world of her vision was fading, and she grasped for it. "Couldn't you all just pretend you weren't there? Why did anyone have to know?"

"Because it was Jack. The cops would've thought some Molloy-Spano thing was going on. They'd have leaned on everyone. They'd have found witnesses who saw the four of us together, they'd have dug up evidence. It would have all come out, that we were there. No, someone had to step up, to stop any of that."

"And you decided it would be Markie."

"It was what Markie wanted. The way we talked about it, in the end that's how it went down, except Constantine couldn't get him out of doing jail time, but the sentence was short."

"Did he know?" Marian whispered. "Did Phil know it wasn't Markie?"

"I don't think he bought the whole thing, but Markie never changed his story." Tom looked across the street, to a white house, its windows dark. Marian couldn't remember who lived there. "It was a stupid prison fight," Tom said softly. "It all worked so well, and then that."

Marian looked at Tom in the streetlit night but didn't see him. She saw instead Jimmy's face turning white as he listened on the phone, heard him asking, What? What? as though the person on the other end were babbling. She saw Jimmy's eyes when he slipped the receiver down and stood there empty-handed. His eyes terrified her. They looked as though they had seen something he wanted very very much, watched it vanish away.

Tom put his arm around Marian's shoulders. "You're so cold," he said. "Come on." Marian didn't think she could move. But she was surprised and grateful to find that her immobility could not withstand Tom's decision that they should walk.

They stepped over tree roots that had years ago tilted the sidewalks up. They turned left at this corner and right at that, and now Marian saw that the house at the end of the block was Tom's. Tom's new house. No, that was silly. Tom had lived here for thirteen years.

With his arm still around Marian, Tom took out his keys. They jingled as he unlocked the door, and they clinked when he dropped them on the shelf. He stepped aside for her to go before him, pressing his hand lightly on her back to guide her to the kitchen. "I'll make coffee," he said. "Then I'll take you home."

"I can take the ferry." It was a long drive to her loft from here. Especially now, with so many streets and the Brooklyn Battery Tunnel still closed. The bridge, the expressway, another bridge, north on the East Side, across Manhattan, south on the West Side. Why should Tom have to do that? The ferry, which she could take alone, was much more direct.

Tom's mouth turned up at the corner. "Not in your condition."

I'm in a condition? Marian was surprised. Had she had too much to drink? Could that explain the feeling she had that the ground was shifting, that dark, unexplained things were happening just beyond where she could see?

She watched Tom as he reached into the cabinet for the can of coffee, watched him spoon grounds into the basket. She loved the smell of ground coffee. She inhaled deeply; he looked up and caught her at it, and they both smiled. Why had Tom never remarried? Marian wondered while he ran water into the pot, while he poured it right out again into the machine. Or why hadn't Vicky? Or Marian's dad? Or, for that matter, after Jimmy left her, why hadn't she ever married at all? Why the crowded days, the busy evenings, the travel and concerts and meals and all the young men, no house, no garden, no pets, no children, nothing of the life she'd been sure she'd have when she was lying awake in the basement apartment in the Cooleys' house and listening to the beat of Jimmy's heart?

The coffeemaker began to gurgle.

Tom took two mugs from the drainboard, from the refrigerator a quart of milk. The milk was for her: Tom always remembered things about you. Steam rose from the coffee as he poured it from the pot. He glanced at her and smiled again, that smile that said every smart thing Tom Molloy did was partly yours and that seeing you was the best thing that had happened to him all day.

Marian smiled back.

How blue his eyes were.

Laura's Story
Chapter 12

———

The Water Dreams

Angelo Zannoni, leaning on his balcony rail, turned to Laura. "You want some tea?"

Mentally she shook herself. She'd been, she realized, mesmerized by the lights sparkling on the water, by the clear air. Boats came and went, stars stood still. From this balcony everything seemed so ordered, so predictable. The universe unfolding. As long as you couldn't see over the treetops to the tip of Manhattan.

Or hear the echoing silence of Harry's apartment.

"No. No, thank you. I don't want to take up any more of your time." She bent for her tape recorder, dropped her notebook into her bag.

"You see a lot of things waiting for me to do?" Zannoni didn't pause for her to answer but pulled open the sliding glass and waited for her to pass into the nearly bare living room. Laura glanced into the kitchen as he walked her to the door. Vacant countertops, no pots or pans or canisters. A kettle on the stove. A single white dish towel folded over the oven door handle. She found herself wishing for a quick peek into the bedroom. She had a mental picture of scarlet draperies, bowls of rose petals, lush nudes reclining in massive gold-framed oil paintings.

And she could hear Harry's delighted laugh at the absurdity of her vision.

And was thrilled at the sound.

Luckily, Reporter-Laura was still paying attention to work. At the door, about to shake Zannoni's hand and say thanks and goodbye, something occurred to her. "Can I ask you one more thing? You said you talked to the detective who knew the Molloys and the Spanos best. Who was that?"

Zannoni shook his head, as though refusing an answer; but he stopped, said, "Oh, what the hell," and said, "Charlie Rosoff. Jewish, see?"

Laura didn't see.

"Not Irish, not Italian. It wasn't like the goombahs or the micks trusted Rosoff. But at least they all knew Charlie didn't belong to the other guys."

"Can I find him?"

A brief look, then, "He's brass now. At Police Plaza."

Laura whipped out her cell phone as soon as she left Fitzgerald Drive behind. The newsroom number was on her speed dial, but she had to punch in the letters of Jesselson's name because she didn't know his extension. Oh, Hugh, she pleaded, be working late. Half a ring, then, "Jesselson."

Thank God. "Hugh, it's Laura."

"Hey." It seemed to her that was a pleased "Hey," but immediately on its heels was "What's up?"

"A cop named Charlie Rosoff?"

"Assistant Commissioner. Operations."

"Hard to see?"

"Normally, doesn't have to be. Relies on his personality. Real people repellent."

"What do you mean 'normally'?"

"Not normal down there, now."

"Will I have trouble getting to him?"

"Maybe."

"Can you help?" She was doing it, too, Laura realized: talking as though each word came with a price tag.

"Right now?"

"Yes."

"Maybe. How come?"

"Your man Zannoni gave me his name. Rosoff was in the Staten Island precinct in 'seventy-nine when the Molloy shooting happened."

"I'll call. Your number?"

She gave Jesselson her cell phone number. The phone rang again before she'd reached Main Street.

"He's pissed, but he'll see you."

"Why's he pissed?"

"About to go home. And no love between cops and firefighters, but nobody likes what we're saying about McCaffery."

"Why's he seeing me?"

"Told him you're wacko. Said you'd print lies if he didn't."

One Police Plaza was a glass-and-red-brick slab near City Hall, a building that tried to impress by height inside and out, by complicated interior brickwork that she supposed was art, by echoing hard surfaces and a totally unintelligible circulation system that she supposed was security. She showed her ID and had her bag inspected at three different desks, went through two metal detectors, and was led from the ninth-floor elevator to a door with "Assistant Commissioner Charles Rosoff" gold-leafed on it, by a stony-faced policewoman who looked as if she'd just as soon shoot Laura as take her a step farther.

Rosoff was a scowling, balding man with huge hands. He didn't stand when she came in, just looked at his watch and growled, "Fifteen minutes." The policewoman shut the door behind them.

"I appreciate—"

"Don't bother. The only reason I stayed, Jesselson says you're a fly-off-the-handle broad with a bug up your—a bee in your bonnet about the Jack Molloy shooting, from back in the goddamn Dark Ages." Gee, thanks, Hugh, Laura thought. "He said you didn't get the straight shit, you'd make it up. You do that, the department might sue your rag, and your own personal ass, except we're a little busy right now. In case you haven't noticed, Miss"—he glanced at a pad in front of him—"Stone—Miss Stone, there's a war on at the moment, and we're in the front lines. No one gives a fart about what happened on Staten Island a thousand years ago. Now you have fourteen minutes."

He sat back with another glance at his watch.

Laura sat without invitation. Around here a man with a wooden leg might not be invited to sit. She didn't take out a recorder; there'd be no point in even asking. She switched both of them on in her bag while she reached for her pad and pen, began speaking before she'd pulled those out, so Rosoff couldn't start again and chew up the rest of her time. "Just a few questions." She caught the sharp icy edge in her voice. Laura Stone, a fly-off-the-handle broad. So crazy she'll print lies. Don't mess with me. "I understand when you were at the 124, you were the detective with the most knowledge about the Molloys and the Spanos."

"Understand from where?"

"A retired sergeant named Angelo Zannoni."

"Zannoni." Rosoff snorted. "I remember that asshole. He and his partner—Miller—they thought they were Starsky and Hutch. Okay, so the locals were my hobby. So?"

"Two things. One: the manslaughter charges filed against Mark Keegan were dropped, and the plea deal was only on the gun charge. Why?"

"Not our choice. The DAs do that. We just haul 'em in. DAs charge 'em."

"Based on evidence you supply."

Rosoff shrugged, his combative eyes fixed on Laura's.

"All right," said Laura, in a voice that really said: uh-huh, well, we'll come back to that. "Two: the thing that seems to have sparked the fight that night between Molloy and Keegan was a phony rumor that the cops were cracking down on Molloy's gang. Where did it come from?"

Rosoff stared at her. "Where did you get that?"

"Why?"

"It's crap."

"It was about something else?"

"No idea."

"I'm sorry, that's not true. The lawyer told me. Phillip Constantine."

"That fuck?" Rosoff laughed, an unpleasant bark. "That may be the one good thing comes out of all this, if that piece-of-shit lawyer goes down."

"Constantine told me," said Laura, careful not to react to Rosoff's language, certain he expected her to, "because he said it would all come out anyway. So: it's true, right?"

Rosoff picked up a thin gold pen from his desk and tossed it down immediately. "Shit. Yeah, okay, it's true."

"Where did the rumor come from?"

"No idea."

"Come on. The cop who knew the most about these people? Didn't you wonder?"

"Sure I wondered. But I don't know."

"Did Eddie Spano plant it?"

"Not likely. Keegan wouldn't've trusted anything he got from any butthole buddy of Spano's."

"So where did he get it?"

"Why don't you ask that lawyer fuck?"

"He says he doesn't know."

"You asked him?"

"How the hell else would I know what he said?" Laura snapped.

"You believe him?"

Laura thought she heard a note of uncertainty in Rosoff's growl. This was probably not a man who got snapped at very much.

"A defense attorney? As if." She could hear Reporter-Laura cheering her on. "But whatever he does know, he's too slippery to tell me." Laura let contempt for the slippery leak into her voice. She looked Rosoff straight in the eye, to say: As opposed to my admiration for the blunt and straightforward, for any man brave enough to let the chips fall where they may.

Rosoff met Laura's stare, then cocked his head, as though he'd learn something if he saw her from a new angle. She didn't move. The window behind him was filled with black water and black sky, the lights of boats and stars and the Verrazano Narrows Bridge. One of the cargo ships Laura had been watching from Angelo Zannoni's terrace was slipping into the distance, going to a new job in a new place. Laura wondered if it had finished the work it had come here to do, or if that job had been disrupted, ruined by the attacks, the collapse, the new world.

"Fuck," Rosoff said. "You're gonna skewer this guy McCaffery no matter what, right?"

"I'm looking for the truth," Laura declared. She rolled on before he could snarl out his thoughts on truth. "I think McCaffery had something to do with Jack Molloy's death and he's been paying off Mark Keegan's family ever since. I think the money's not his, and that means someone else was also involved, probably Spano. I think the investigation into all this is what led to the death of a reporter on my paper."

"That guy who jumped off the bridge? That was suicide."

"It was murder."

Rosoff peered at her again and didn't speak. Hey, come on, Laura thought, you can't run out the clock like that, it's not fair.

Fair? Laura felt an icy wash slip over her skin as she heard Harry's voice, mocking and amused. After everything that's happened, Stone, you're still complaining when things aren't *fair*?

Rosoff snapped his head around to look in the direction Laura was looking, toward the window. Water lay flat and moonlight sparkled, boats drifted, the bridge stood. He spun back. "What's the matter with you? You look like you saw a ghost."

A plane, Laura realized he meant. A jet banking low. Or an explosion in the harbor, a new billowing black cloud.

"Just thinking," she managed. "Just remembering something."

Under his breath Rosoff muttered, "Shit."

"About McCaffery?" Laura prompted, trying to behave like the hard-edged reporter she'd been a few seconds ago, though her face was hot and her heart was pounding. Harry, she thought, for pity's sake, I'm working! Leave me alone! No! No, wait, no, don't!

"Harry Randall," Rosoff said. "What makes you think the guy didn't jump?"

However much of Rosoff's time Laura had left, it wasn't enough to explain that. She settled on "I knew him."

Rosoff's right hand scratched at something on the thumbnail of the left one. "Any other time," he said, and he seemed to be talking as much to himself as to Laura, "I'd be happy to help. To see one of those showboat Fire Department pretty boys get what's coming to him, it wouldn't bother me in the least. Now . . ." He kept his eyes on his huge hands.

"Now," he went on, "maybe this is bigger than him. What happened back then doesn't matter. What happened to that reporter doesn't matter. People look at these guys, they went running into that hellhole, didn't come out, people need them to be better than the rest of us. Even if this one beat his wife, that one cheated on his taxes. They're dead now. Anything bad McCaffery did, he's not gonna do it again. He's not a guy now, he's a legend. What's wrong with that?"

"Because someone killed Harry," Laura said. "Because the truth matters. Even now."

"What you're telling me," Rosoff said, "you're not gonna stop."

"No, I'm not."

"Shit." He stood. Laura thought he was going to march to the door, yank it open, and toss her out, but all he did was turn to face the window. "Well," he said, his back to her, "what the fuck do I know? Maybe you're right. Maybe the truth does matter. Right now, only thing that matters to me is we catch the motherfuckers who did this. Pound them into ashes. But maybe someday I'll feel different. Maybe something else will start mattering again."

He stood silent, his broad back unmoving. When he spoke, he did not face Laura.

"That story, that we were about to come down on Jack Molloy? Like you said, it was lies. That point in time, we had nothing different than we ever had, nothing that would've stuck. The story was planted, and I was never sure why. I don't know how it got to Keegan. But I've always been pretty sure it came from us."

"From you?"

"In those days, it wasn't like now. Guys were in Al Spano's pocket. And the Molloys'. Tom, Jack, Big Mike—they all had their own guys, bought and paid for. Nothing I could do about those guys, the bent ones, but I kept an eye on them. There was one guy. Ted O'Hagan. Bad temper, sticky fingers. A real piece of work. He's dead now, four, five years. DUI, into a tree in Jersey."

Laura waited, watching Rosoff watch the water.

"O'Hagan," said Rosoff. "Good cop name, right? From a cop family. A couple of things he said later made me figure it was him gave the story out. Funny thing was, I had him pegged as working for Tom Molloy. Must've changed sides when I wasn't looking. A mick working for Spano. Bet they paid him double." Rosoff turned slowly; his eyes met hers. "I thought I knew. I thought I knew what was going on, and come to find out I don't know shit. How can you fight these bastards when you don't know shit?"

Laura didn't answer. Rosoff's gaze hardened again. "Yeah," he said bitterly, sitting down. "Molloy. McCaffery. What the hell else do you want to know?"

Rosoff had softened briefly, but he was ice again. Laura had seen this before: it happened all over New York now. Strangers turned to each other for comfort, then caught themselves and turned away. A new etiquette had arisen to cover the situation, and Laura followed it, framing her next question, returning to the topic, not acknowledging what both she and Rosoff knew: that for a moment he hadn't been talking about O'Hagan or Spano or Molloy. That bent cops and gangsters were not the only bastards he didn't know how to fight.

MARIAN'S STORY
Chapter 13

———

Abraham Lincoln and the Pig

November 1, 2001

An unfamiliar light woke Marian, a brightness sneaking under the bottom of a window shade to poke her in the eye. That wasn't very nice. Especially since she had a headache. Sunshine was lovely, she thought groggily, but why couldn't it stay outside until she was ready? Squinting, she tried to make out what it was she was looking at as she moved her gaze around the room. Without her glasses she couldn't be positive, but it seemed to her she didn't recognize any of it.

And slowly she realized something else: she wasn't alone. Her back was warm, someone else's up against it.

And her mouth was sticky and dry. And the headache.

Oh no, she thought wearily. What did I do?

What bar did I sweep into this time, what young man did I select, allow to buy me drinks? Flirt with and make promises to? What will I have to extricate myself from now? What tangles will there be to delicately slip out of, never detaching as gracefully as you'd want?

When will I learn?

She turned gently, not wanting him to awaken until she saw who it was, until she remembered, until she'd had a chance to think. She prided herself on one thing: she had never not remembered. In the morning, she always knew their names and whatever it was about them she had learned while their eyes were holding hers over cocktails or wine, while the comings and goings of a public place surrounded the two of them and their hands touched quite by accident as they toasted their luck in having met.

But she had to admit that the remembering sometimes took longer now than it had once.

So she gently lifted herself on her elbows to peer over the bare shoulder of the sleeping man beside her, to see who he was.

It was Tom.

Oh my God, it was Tom. How could this be, how could this have happened? The room spun, Marian's heart pounded wildly. What would she say to Jimmy, to Vicky? How could she have done this? What kind of a person was she?

Tom stirred, and Marian jerked away, almost horrified, not wanting to touch him. Then, as he continued to sleep, she peered at him, looked more closely. It was Tom, no question about it. But why did he look so strange? Why did he look so *old*?

Then memory, like a landslide. She had never not remembered.

There was nothing she needed to tell Jimmy. Jimmy was dead. And what had she ever told Jimmy, what had he told her, since that windy spring morning so long ago (spring, when things were supposed to grow and flourish and begin) when he had told her goodbye?

And Vicky? Tom and Vicky had split years ago. From childhood, Vicky had been the promised consort of the crown prince, and it was he whom she adored, he whom she married. When Tom abdicated, Vicky left him. What Tom did did not matter to Vicky anymore.

In her mind, Marian saw last night. She and Tom had had coffee. Good coffee, hers sweet and light, chasing the chill from her bones. And then Tom was going to take her home. But Marian, who had lived alone so long—Marian, who was always the first to feel confined, to see the wide endless highway of a new romance narrowing into a rutted road, who had always believed freedom meant more to her than love, because freedom was sure and love could not be counted on—Marian had not wanted to be alone last night.

Not after what she had heard from Tom. Not after the hissing formless fear that had followed them down the quiet streets.

And Tom, who could read minds, knew that.

Or maybe Tom had not wanted to be alone, either. Often that was true of the young men, the men who took Marian home, or came back home with her. They wanted no more than anyone wanted: a night or a week or a lifetime of shutting out the dark, pretending that love was truth. That love would last. That aloneness was not stretched around you like your own skin, and the cost of piercing it was not always, only, pain.

The sheets rustled as Tom lifted his arm, rubbed his hand over his face. He dropped his arm again, and she thought he was still asleep, but though his eyes were closed, his hand searched for and found hers. And then his eyes opened.

"Hey," Tom said, smiling, his voice low and scratchy.

"Hey," said Marian.

Tom pushed himself up on his elbows, kissed her, and fell back again. "It's okay," he said.

"What is?"

"Whatever you were thinking wasn't okay."

Marian stared at him for a moment, then settled down close. He opened his arm to her, curled it around her, his movements seamless with hers. If she could stay like this forever, wrapped in the warmth of Tom's arm, then maybe things really would be okay.

But she couldn't.

And they already weren't.

Tom brought Marian a glass of water and some aspirin, and then he went to take a shower. She drank all the water because a hangover was partly dehydration—oh, she had this down—and she stayed in bed, doing breathing exercises and meditating, trying not to think of last night, and the last weeks, and what had happened and what any of it meant. Tom emerged from the bathroom with a towel wrapped around his waist so she could have his bathrobe. She took a very hot shower, and by the time she came out, she felt better.

She could hear Tom downstairs moving around the kitchen as she dressed. She disliked getting back into yesterday's clothes; she always disliked that, which was one of the reasons she generally brought the young men home with her. Fresh clothes, and her own shampoo.

Her purse was downstairs, so she borrowed Tom's comb. He had no hair dryer, so after she got her hair essentially organized, it was on its own. The young men, she reflected, taking one last look in the mirror and heading for the stairs, the Manhattan young men, they all had hair dryers.

She smelled Tom's good coffee from the top of the stairs; by the time she reached the kitchen, he had poured her a cup, in the same black mug she had used last night. Or maybe this morning he was using that one, and she was using his.

"Scrambled eggs?" he asked. In a pan on the stove, butter made little spitting sounds as it started to melt.

"Let me make them."

"No way. I'm trying to impress you."

"You already have."

He grinned. "I mean, in the kitchen."

Marian felt herself flush from her breasts to her scalp. Tom politely turned away, still grinning.

Breakfast was orange juice, eggs, toast, and more coffee. She sipped her coffee and watched him bring the plates to the table, and as he sat, she finally faced the thought she had been turning from all morning.

Jimmy's papers, what he had left behind.

His legacy. Oh, if any of this were funny, that would be a laugh.

If the papers Jimmy had left told the true story of Jack's death—and what else, what subject was there?—then the legendary James McCaffery, the hero people needed so desperately to believe in in these terrible times, the legend that should have been Jimmy's legacy, would be destroyed. All the brave and selfless acts over the years, the risks, the rescues, would mean nothing. The man responsible for them would be revealed to be not who people thought he was, and it would change things, and one more thing people believed was solid and beautiful and good would turn into choking, crumbling rubble.

And drinking Tom's coffee, watching Tom, Marian thought: Not only Jimmy.

Tom Molloy had gone from bad to good, from dangerous taker to generous giver. He had left the path he was born to follow and gone another way. He had put his heart into it. Now, perhaps, Marian understood why. But the perilous truths Jimmy left behind could destroy Tom, too.

And the Fund. All the good the Fund could do, *she* could do, could be gone also.

It couldn't happen. It mustn't happen. Jimmy was already gone, and Markie, and Jack. And now, the good that was left, to be scorched into lifelessness and scattered like ash in a city choking on ashes?

No.

"Tom?"

"Hmm?"

"Jimmy—I think he told the story, Tom. He left some record of it. That reporter said so."

Tom didn't seem surprised or upset. That heartened her; that was the old Tom. It was comforting, in the same way as her small fantasies—the cabin in the woods—comforted her.

"She said that to me, too," Tom said. "Papers. Do you believe it?"

"What if he did? If he wrote it all down? If he wrote down the truth?"

Tom's blue eyes regarded her. "I'll deny it."

Marian was confused. "You'll—?"

"I'm the only one left, Marian. I'll say he was writing a novel, these papers are just notes for it. Lots of firefighters write novels. I could even say I knew he was, that he told me about it."

Doubtfully, Marian said, "Do you think that would work?"

Tom pushed back his chair, came and stood behind her, kneading her shoulders with powerful, sure hands.

"It was an accident," he said softly. "That night, what happened to my brother, my God, Marian, it was a lifetime ago, and it was an *accident.*"

His fingers found the fear in her shoulders, the foreboding at the base of her skull, found them and broke them down and commanded them away.

"Jimmy was a hero," he said. "Why can't people keep their heroes, when they need them?"

Heroes, Marian thought, surrendering to Tom's hands. Everyone had to have heroes.

From the *New York Tribune*, November 1, 2001

1979 SLAYING REEXAMINED
NEW EVIDENCE CASTS DOUBT
ON ORIGINAL STORY

Old Crime May Be Tied to Reporter's Death
Nature of Hero Firefighter's Involvement Still Uncertain

by Laura Stone

Captain James McCaffery of Ladder Co. 62 died a hero on September 11, like hundreds of other New York City firefighters. Unlike many of his fallen brothers, however, it appears that McCaffery may have gone to his death hiding decades-old secrets that are only now coming to light.

A recent article in the *New York Tribune* by Harry Randall, a three-time Pulitzer Prize–winning reporter, began to probe some of these secrets. Randall died on October 29 under circumstances now considered suspicious and possibly related to his investigation of incidents in McCaffery's past.

The questions surrounding McCaffery stem from the death of Jack Molloy, stepson of alleged crime figure Michael "Mike the Bear" Molloy. Jack Molloy died from a single gunshot in September 1979. Mark Keegan, a close friend of Capt. McCaffery's, was convicted of weapons possession but never charged with homicide. Keegan claimed he and Molloy were alone at the time of the shooting. He said Molloy was drunk and attacked him, and that he fired in self-defense. At the time no one who knew Keegan could explain why he was carrying a gun or where he had obtained it, nor did Keegan offer an explanation. The precise nature of the dispute between Molloy and Keegan that led Molloy to fire two shots was never clear to police or prosecutors. Keegan was himself slain in prison five months later.

New evidence uncovered by the *Tribune,* however, suggests that a third man may have been present. "It had to be him," said a retired police officer with close ties to the case, referring to McCaffery and speaking on condition of anonymity. In addition to evidence the NYPD is unwilling to reveal, the anonymous source pointed to the money trail uncovered by the late Mr. Randall. Payments purportedly from the State of New York were made through Keegan's defense attorney, Phillip Constantine, to the Keegan family for eighteen years. The money did not, however, come from the State. Constantine refused to discuss the origin of the funds, but admits to meeting with McCaffery many times over the years. The NYPD source suggests that though the money may have come through McCaffery, it is unlikely to have been his.

The *Tribune* has also discovered the subject of the argument between Molloy and Keegan on the fatal night. According to Constantine, Keegan had previously informed Molloy that the police were on the verge of shutting down Molloy's criminal activities. Molloy, however, had his own informants in the NYPD and discovered that this story was untrue.

This was confirmed by NYPD Assistant Commissioner Charles Rosoff, a sergeant at the 124th Precinct at that time. Both Commissioner Rosoff and the anonymous police source speculate that the rumor of a crackdown may have originated with Edward Spano, an alleged organized crime figure on Staten Island with reputed ties to the Bonnano crime family.

Commissioner Rosoff, in an interview at One Police Plaza, said Keegan had been well liked and had a reputation for picking up information. "If you wanted to plant a story, he's the guy you'd plant it on," the Commissioner said. Asked whether the story was planted by the NYPD, he denied it. He alleged that both the Molloy and Spano organizations had police officers on their payrolls. When asked to speculate on the source of the false story, both Commissioner Rosoff and the anonymous police source pointed to the dismantling of the Molloy organization soon after Jack Molloy's death and the subsequent growth of the alleged Spano criminal network.

"Maybe Spano invented the story to scare Molloy out of town, got it to Keegan through a cop so Keegan would think it was the real deal," Commissioner Rosoff said. Then Spano might have offered Jack Molloy a deal to take over Molloy's operations. This offer might have been made through an intermediary, possibly McCaffery.

Commissioner Rosoff went on to suggest this further scenario: after Keegan's death, McCaffery may have pressed Spano into making payments to Keegan's young family—the mysterious payments "from the State"—as the price of his own silence regarding Spano's involvement. When asked whether the information McCaffery could have revealed was enough to prompt Spano to agree to blackmail, the Commissioner said, "Think about this: what if Keegan wasn't the shooter? What if it was McCaffery? If he was there that night to negotiate for Spano, that could get Spano sent up. Keegan takes the fall because he's promised a fix and a payoff. When Keegan dies, McCaffery tells Spano the money better keep coming. If I was Spano, I'd pay."

The *Tribune* has also discovered that McCaffery left behind a set of papers, which the late Mr. Randall is believed to have seen shortly before his death, and that are believed to concern the Molloy shooting. Marian Gallagher, McCaffery's ex-fiancée and currently the director of the More Art, New York! Foundation and the newly established McCaffery Memorial Fund, claims to be skeptical about the papers' existence. Constantine, Mark Keegan's attorney and a close friend of Keegan's widow, admits they may exist but claims he has not seen them. There is reason to believe Randall would have exposed the contents of McCaffery's papers, had he lived.

The investigation is continuing.

Marian's Story
Chapter 14

———

Leaving the Cat

November 1, 2001

Marian took the long way past the park because she liked to look at it. The sunlight glowed and the breeze was fresh, whisking tan and yellow leaves along the sidewalk. Someone—whoever lived now in the Faherty house—had planted a Japanese maple, and it blazed red as a fire.

She'd called the office and told Elena she'd be in by lunchtime. When she'd left his house, Tom had offered to drive her. But the day was so beautiful, why not walk? And there was more to it, and Tom knew that and did not insist. Marian was on her way to see Sally and Kevin, and the more was this: she did not want to have to explain to Sally why she was with Tom so early in the morning. Not, she reminded herself firmly, that there was anything wrong with what she and Tom had done. They were adults, neither of them promised to anyone else, neither of them being unfaithful by accepting the comforts of the other's arms.

But it did seem . . . upside down, somehow. No more so than the rest of the world now, and no one was hurt, and no one would mind. And Sally would never ask. With a quiet smile she would wait for Marian to tell her what the sight of Marian getting out of Tom's car already had. She would wait, but she would expect to be told, and she would deserve that, because that was who Sally and Marian were to each other.

Marian had only ever had one secret she had not told Sally; she doubted if Sally had any she had not shared. And Marian's secret had always been less a secret than a trembling fear, less a monster than a grasping shadow. Until last night. Until Tom's words had released the hissing serpent truth. Marian dreaded being alone with that serpent, that secret, that truth; she always had. Her horror of its hot breath on her neck had driven her into Tom's arms, as into the arms of all the young men over all the years. This was what Marian knew. This was the one thing she had always kept from Sally.

And on this bright morning, on her way to Sally's, Marian walked.

It was Kevin who answered the door, leaning on his crutches. His unshaven face was sprinkled with the beginnings of a beard that would grow in as red as his hair, if he let it. His T-shirt and boxer shorts were sleep-rumpled. From knee to ankle his right leg was bandaged, and still that was an improvement: the bandage in the beginning had enclosed his thigh also, but skin had not been grafted there, and that burn had soon healed. The shiny scar there matched the one on his right wrist, also unbandaged now.

Kevin's surprised smile appeared half a beat late, but it was the same sunshine beam he'd been giving her since, she swore, the day he was born.

Kevin was eight hours old when Marian first saw him, his hair already red and his arms and legs already in motion. She'd planned just to go to the hospital nursery and take a look, not to bother Sally (though when Markie called Jimmy and Marian to tell them about it, to tell them it was a boy, he and Sally had a son, he said Sally felt great, he said it was an easy delivery, maybe an hour, the baby just popped out; he told them Sally's mom said that meant the boy would never give them any trouble). But when Marian got off the elevator, Markie was in the corridor, looking through the glass, grinning at the babies. His grin was so big it included them all, but when a nurse came and picked one up, Marian thought the way he smiled then would split his face in half.

"I guess that's him?" she said.

"It sure is. Isn't he great?"

"Yes. He's great."

"It's time for Sally to feed him. Come on, say hello."

So Marian visited with Sally and Markie while Sally nursed Kevin. "It usually takes a while," Markie told her. "Like a day, the nurse said, before they really figure out how to do it. But this kid, he figured it out already."

Sally looked tired but radiant. Because, Marian thought, being this happy makes you radiant. When Kevin was finished nursing, Markie took him from Sally, wrapped his blankets a little better—his blankets, as far as Marian could see, were just fine—and asked Marian if she wanted to hold him.

"Really?"

Markie grinned and handed Kevin to her. Marian had held babies before, many babies, many times. She took him with practiced hands, cradled him in experienced arms, and found he was the smallest, softest, warmest thing she'd ever known. Holding him, wondering at his tiny eyelashes and his miniature fingers, Marian found herself suddenly overwhelmed with two sensations she had always thought of as separate, even contradictory: an enormous energy and a deep, boundless peace.

Kevin stirred in her arms. He opened his eyes, and then he smiled right at her, a wide smile like his father's, of recognition and joy. They can't even *see* yet, Marian tried to tell herself as her heart leaped, they can't make expressions, he doesn't have any idea who you are or who anybody is or *anything*. None of that, true though it all was, had any effect on her whatsoever. Marian had never been happier than she was at that moment, holding her best friend's baby, and she knew she never would be until she was out of school and Jimmy was out of the Academy and on the Job and they had babies of their own.

Now, a lifetime later, Kevin stood at the door, smiling that same smile. "Aunt Marian, I didn't know you were coming over today."

Something was caught in Marian's throat; she had to clear it to answer. "Me either. Is it too early?"

"I just got up." He looked abashed, the way he used to when he was a little boy and she caught him in mischief. "But Mom's been up for hours. Come on in."

He moved aside so she could pass in front of him. She turned back to say something, something innocuous about the beauty of the day, and found herself unable to speak, overtaken by the same fullness of heart she had felt on his first day on earth. Caught by this, she watched Kevin push the door shut with the tip of one crutch. It was an unconscious act; he appeared to be preoccupied, thinking about something else, and he did not notice her eyes on him as he swung himself down the short hall. He moved smoothly and quickly, and in his casual, newly learned grace, Marian saw, and was dazzled by, hope.

Kevin's world had changed. Friends had died. He was disabled, though only, thank God, temporarily; he was in daily pain—yet he'd adapted. And when he was finally rid of the crutches, back on the Job, and once more the man he had been—different, but the same—he would adapt to that, too.

Since September 11 Marian had been grateful to be middle-aged, glad at least that she'd had her youth, under some clouds and some looming shadows to be sure, but not like this. Her heart had ached for the young people who would have to live the rest of their lives with the knowledge of what had happened and what therefore, at any moment, could happen again. But watching Kevin now, Marian became less sure that she was fortunate in this. Perhaps the sheer forward momentum of youth, the impulsiveness and lack of subtlety (the subtlety that could be in people her age a cause of, and cover for, an unwillingness to choose and commit), would carry the young through into a world whose changes they would accept, adjust to, and even thrive within.

"You should see him when he's clean." Sally's voice startled Marian. She spun to find Sally in the kitchen doorway behind her.

"What?"

"Kevin. He's much more worth staring at after his shower. He's almost handsome if you can get him to shave."

Kevin dropped himself onto a chair and rolled his eyes.

Marian said, "Was I staring?"

Sally hugged her and murmured, "A little, but who could blame you?" She crossed to the kitchen table, kissed Kevin's cheek, took the crutches, and propped them in a corner. "What are you doing out here so early?" she asked Marian. "Did you stay with your dad last night? Want some coffee?" She brought out three yellow cups and saucers from the cabinet and put the coffeepot on the table.

"Thanks, Mom," Kevin said, pouring coffee, reaching for the sugar.

"Could I have tea?" Marian asked.

"Real tea? Or smelly flowers?"

"Flowers, thanks. Kevin, darling, you can just unwrinkle your nose."

When he was four, Kevin had asked Marian why she always drank smelly flowers. He hadn't understood what was funny, but that she'd laughed was good enough for him. From then on, for years, he'd clapped his hand to his head in mock horror and announced, "Smelly flowers!" every time the chamomile tea box came off the shelf.

"How do you feel?" Marian asked Kevin.

He shrugged. "Pretty good, I guess."

She peered more closely. "You look like you're worried about something. Is your therapy going all right?"

"The PT?" Kevin glanced down at his leg. "It's going fine."

"His physical therapist says he's improving faster than she expected. She says he's impressive. Fantastic, extraordinary, unbelievable—"

"No, Mom, that was you. Mrs. Cummings said I sweat a lot."

"Same thing. Marian, did you have breakfast?"

"Yes, thanks. Can I help you do something?" Marian made the offer quickly, before Sally could ask where she'd eaten. Marian's father liked to take her out to breakfast whenever she stayed over in Pleasant Hills.

"No, I have it under control." Into melted butter Sally broke three eggs. She popped bread into the toaster and sliced a grapefruit in half. The scents of domesticity, of the life Marian had not had, crowded the sunny air like phantoms.

Sally asked, "Are you sure you don't want anything?"

"No, the tea will be perfect, thanks."

Marian felt herself distracted. She tried to force herself to focus on her task, but before she could begin, Sally asked quietly, "Did you see the paper this morning?"

Marian nodded.

"What?" said Kevin. "What's in it?"

Sally reached for the *New York Tribune* from the counter and handed it to her son. It was already folded to the story on the bottom of the front page, the story Tom had read aloud to Marian an hour earlier, Tom glancing up from time to time, Marian's hand lifting to cover her mouth as though to smother despair.

Marian watched Sally cook, watched Kevin read. His face could hide anger no better than it could joy. When it came time to turn to the inside pages, he snapped the paper to a new fold. His skin flushed, his scowl deepened.

Marian waited until she judged he was finished, though his eyes remained on the newspaper. She took a breath and said, "Listen, you guys. I came over to talk to you about something serious."

Now Kevin looked up. Sally, back at the stove, turned to regard Marian over her shoulder. The two concerned pairs of eyes so exactly alike, so dear to her. Marian thought, Can I take it back? Can I leave them out of this? Hasn't it been terrible enough for them? Why don't I just say, No, never mind, I'll handle it, you guys just go on doing what you're doing, it's enough.

But of course she couldn't. It wasn't her choice. Earlier, watching

Tom drink coffee, she had seemed to choose, but it wasn't her decision. The real choice was Jimmy's, made long ago. All Marian had done, all she'd been able to do, was to determine to take whatever action she must to limit the damage now.

"What is it, honey?" Sally set Kevin's eggs in front of him. "Is everything all right?"

Such an odd question, in these times. Is *anything* all right? would have been better, and even that Marian was not certain she could answer.

"These newspaper stories," she began. She would have said more, but Sally raised a hand to stop her.

"There's no need to discuss them," Sally said. Standing next to Kevin, she laid her hand on his shoulder. "I don't believe any of it."

"Sal—"

"No, honey, really. It's okay. I don't believe Jimmy was there, and I certainly don't believe he shot Jack. That's so completely *ridiculous*. Someone could only say that who never knew him. That he let Markie go to prison? Jimmy? And," she went on, as Marian's stomach twisted, "Jimmy would never have had anything to do with a man like Eddie. Any of the Spanos, anytime. It just isn't true."

"Sal," Marian said gently. "Sal, the money—"

Sally shook her head. "I know."

"You know what?"

"I know about the money." Sally spoke quietly, like someone admitting a wrongdoing.

Confused, Marian asked, "You know?"

Sally said slowly, "It was Phil's." Kevin twisted in his chair to look at her. She met his gaze. "That's right, isn't it, Marian?"

Kevin flushed and turned away. He looked at neither of them as with a fork he broke the yolks of the eggs.

"Phil's?" Marian spoke uncertainly.

Sally came around the table to slip into the chair next to Marian. She picked up a teaspoon and turned it over between finger and thumb. "He always wanted to give me money. I never let him. I never wanted him to think it was that." She stopped the spoon in midtwirl as if catching herself in a bad habit she'd meant to break. She put it gently down. "Phil always wanted to take care of us. He wanted me to marry him."

Kevin lifted his eyes to her. "He asked you? When?" His voice was uneven.

"Over and over. Honey, I'm sorry. I know you'd have liked that, to have a dad. But he wouldn't move here."

"Move here?"

When Kevin asked that, Sally frowned, as if she'd heard something untrue, as if someone had said something she could not let pass. "No," she said. "No, that's not fair. It wasn't . . . Phil said he'd buy us a house anywhere, in Manhattan, or Brooklyn Heights, or maybe up in Westchester. Just not here. I said, only here."

Marian had a feeling there was something she should do, say, right now, some step she should take, but how could you take steps on such treacherous, shifting soil? Kevin was watching his mother with his lips pressed tight.

"When I said I'd only marry him if he moved here, he said it wouldn't be good for you, for me, if he did that. Because he'd been Markie's lawyer. Because he's Jewish. And it's true, those things would have made it hard. But it wasn't that."

"Then what was it?" Kevin asked.

"It was—that we had to live here—I said it because I knew he'd say no."

Kevin's forehead creased. "I don't get it."

"No, I don't suppose you do," Sally said softly. She reached across the table to touch Kevin's cheek, as though her hands could tell him something words never could. "The way we lived, Kev, I don't know if you can understand this, but it's the only way we could have lived. I love Phil. I do. I gave him everything I could. But not everything I had. There was always Markie. Still. Always.

"So I . . . it was like in a fairy tale. Do something impossible, and you win the princess's hand. But you know what happens in fairy tales. Only the right prince can do it. The monster kills the other ones when they try.

"Phil knew that. He knew I made it impossible on purpose, and he knew he wasn't that prince. So he . . . you could say he agreed. To call it impossible. He agreed not to try. So that we could go on. So that we could have as much as we had."

The teakettle began to whistle. Marian started to rise, but Sally was there before her. She turned off the burner, poured steaming water into Marian's cup, and returned the kettle to the stove. When she sat again, she picked up her coffee and said, "I thought, all these years . . . it was somehow like Markie was still taking care of us. I was grateful for the money, of course I was. It meant I could stay home when you were little. But even more, it was something Markie was still giving us, every month, and that made it so precious. . . .

"But it wasn't. Now it turns out it wasn't. Do you see?"

Sally asked that of Kevin. He didn't answer. She turned to Marian. The question hung in the air.

"Of course," Marian whispered. This wasn't true. Marian did not know what she saw. She had stepped through a familiar gate into a landscape so alien, it might have been on a different world or from another time. She did not understand what she was seeing, but she knew what Sally had to hear. "Of course."

"I wish Phil hadn't done this," Sally said. "I wish he'd been straight with me. All those years . . . But what the paper's saying about Jimmy? That just can't be true."

Marian wanted to leap up, to take Sally in her arms and protect her forever from evil, from disappointment and truth. But it was too late for that, far too late.

She kept her seat. She looked from Sally to Kevin, wondering what the right thing was. To hold her tongue? Or to say what she had come to say?

How could she, now?

But how could she not?

LAURA'S STORY
Chapter 13

———

Breathing Smoke

November 1, 2001

In the office, Laura typed up notes, checked her e-mail, made a list. She waited for the morning meeting to start so it could end so she could get to work. She was close, very close, she could feel it. And the story in this morning's edition, already tucked into briefcases and open on breakfast tables all over New York, should, if things went right, bring her much closer, work like a depth charge, blasting to the surface all the ugly bottom-feeders that scuttled through the dark.

The newsroom was a deadline-driven place; clocks studded its walls, columns, desks. Laura glanced at them, at her own wristwatch, at the numbers in the corner of her computer screen. All were identical, and none had progressed more than a minute since the last time her eyes had made this sweep. That made it nine minutes until the meeting started, twenty-nine until it was over—no, now twenty-eight, hooray. When four more endless minutes had dissolved, she began to gather her things. That way she could take off as soon as Leo waved them all away. She had just picked up her cell phone from her desk when it started to ring.

Well, if that don't beat all, she heard Harry drawl.

Harry! Laura's heart drummed wildly. Oh, Harry, don't! I can't work, she explained earnestly, I can't stay focused if you keep doing this. Don't you want me to work? Don't you want me to find out the truth?

I already know it, my little flounder, Harry said.

But I don't. The world doesn't.

Are you sure you want to? You and the world?

Of course! Why wouldn't I?

A lot of reasons.

Reasons not to know the truth? You know I don't believe that.

Well, then, said Harry (and Laura could have sworn she saw him shrug, though she couldn't see him at all), *well, then,* he said, *answer that damn phone.*

Laura snapped her eyes to the phone in her hand. It was still ringing. Flip, press. "Laura Stone."

"You that reporter? The *Tribune?*" A familiar, impatient voice.

"Yes, I am. Who—?"

"Eddie Spano. What the hell is this crap in your paper?"

Laura's heart, pounding from her encounter with the unruly ghost of Harry, stilled in expectation. "Mr. Spano. I'm glad you called."

"Sure you are. I read one more word of this crap, Miss Stone, you'll find out I have some damn nasty lawyers."

"Would you like a chance to tell your story?"

"I don't have a story. None of this McCaffery shit has anything to do with me."

"I'd like to tell my readers that."

"What's stopping you?"

"I need to talk to you."

"What about?"

"I'd like your explanation—"

"I have nothing to explain!"

"Your theory, then. I'd like to talk about what's going on, from your perspective."

"From my—"

"May I come talk to you?"

"Shit," Spano breathed. "Yeah. Yeah, you better come out here. Come out, and I'll set you straight."

He spat out an address. Then a thud, and silence: he'd slammed down his phone.

Laura thumbed hers off.

Harry? See? I'm getting close.

She waited. Nothing. In the vast, empty silence, Leo plowed out of his office, leading the morning swarm toward the conference room.

Midmorning, Laura standing at the ferry's front rail, watching the hills on Staten Island become larger and clearer. A beautiful day. Another beautiful day.

Laura was headed out to one of Eddie Spano's construction sites, the address he'd given her. According to Jesselson, Spano was connected to more than a dozen Staten Island businesses, all of them dirty or, if clean, fronts for dirty ones. "Spano? Hands-on. A headquarters-in-the-saddle type," Jesselson had told her.

"This place," Laura asked, "where he told me to come. Harry went there. What's it like?"

"His project du jour. Luxury development. Chapel Pointe."

What chapel? Laura wondered. And when her cab left her at the gate in a chain-link fence around acres of mud in the center of Staten Island, as far from the water in every direction as you could get, she also wondered, What pointe?

Laura had not met Eddie Spano. Her one conversation with him had been by phone. Harry, though, had been to Chapel Pointe and—just a week ago? in her last lifetime?—had described the place to her.

"Very biblical," Harry had said, raising his gin bottle high above his glass to make a dramatic waterfall. " 'Every valley shall be exalted and every hill made low.' Also every tree chopped down and every blade of grass bulldozed into eternity. Thus shall the dwellings of men be created. They may be luxurious, but I promise you, when our Mr. Spano's Townhomes at Chapel Pointe are finished, they will be *ugly*." He took a drink. "And his coffee's bad."

"So's the *Tribune*'s."

"The *Tribune*"—Harry had wagged his finger at her severely—"is not Italian. It has no cultural responsibility to serve drinkable coffee."

"You're in a good mood." Laura had sidled over to him, kissed him, gin and all.

He had kissed her back but then said, "To the contrary. I have work to do."

"Can't it wait?"

"The man who loves you would be only too happy to let it wait. However, the man you love had better get back to work."

"They're the same man."

"No," Harry said softly. "I think not."

And Harry, glass in one hand, bottle in the other, had taken himself to his desk to work on his story, the work Laura had been so sure was the right thing for him to do.

* *

The construction trailers belligerently displayed World Trade Center posters, American flags, patriotic bumper stickers. God Bless America. United We Stand. These Colors Don't Run.

Laura clomped across plywood sheets laid over the mud, followed by the appraising territorial stares of dirt-streaked men in hard hats.

In Lower Manhattan men just like these were heroes now. They were given thumbs-up signs and bottles of water, flowers and applause as they rode in pickup trucks or wearily walked away from Ground Zero, after a day or a night—the work on the site was around the clock—spent burning through twisted steel columns and clawing with backhoes at chunks of concrete, moving the gigantic bulk of the rubble aside so the inch by inch search for the lost could go on.

The *Tribune* had run stories, and would run more, about these men. The nobility of manual labor. The courage and dedication of the workers who climbed the tangled, smoking wreckage. The drained and driven men who slept on church pews and ate at the tent they called the Taj Mahal, who asked for extra shifts and objected, refused, when ordered to take a day off, ordered to go home. Rescue workers, they were still called, though there was no one to rescue anymore, there was no one to save.

Laura stopped in the sunlight to study Chapel Pointe. She watched the rumbling earth movers, gazed at the wooden homes-to-be rising against the hard blue sky. She smelled sawdust and mud, heard the percussion of hammers, the whine of drills; and was caught off guard by an emotion she hardly dared look at straight-on. In front of her were things being built. *Built.* Not dismantled, bucket of dust by chunk of concrete, not untangled, uncompounded, lifted and removed, not disassembled but *created.* Yes, they were ugly. That didn't matter. What mattered was that the way they were was the way they were intended to be.

Hope. Laura, whose religion had always been truth, whose prayers were always words, named what she was feeling and then caught her breath. She waited for horror and fear, despair and loneliness and anger, to flood her heart and drown this once-familiar, lately unknown sensation. It didn't happen. Hope shrank and retreated, but remained: glowing, she thought, in an eerie, hypnotic way, like a light underwater. Laura, amazed, walked tentatively forward, seeing something she'd thought she'd never see again: possibility.

She squinted in the sun, eager to move. Eager to finish this work. She scanned the trailers for the one that belonged to the Chapel Pointe Development Corp. She climbed its stairs and knocked on its door. Her headache had started, but that was good. Now she'd speak to Eddie Spano.

Now she'd find the truth.

MARIAN'S STORY
Chapter 15

A Hundred Circling Camps

November 1, 2001

In the sun-drenched silence of Sally's kitchen Marian tried to find a way to say what she had come for, some way better than she had planned. But there was no good way.

Marian had never permitted herself the luxury of shrinking from difficult duties. She sipped her tea and she said, "Jimmy." Her voice shocked her; it boomed in the silence, was harsh in the sunlight. She'd meant to speak softly; she'd thought she had. She went on before one of the many reasons not to go on could find her. "Jimmy left papers. Something he'd written."

Sally nodded. "That's what the *Tribune* says. Do you think he did?"

"Yes."

"What do you think is in them?"

Marian said, "The truth."

Kevin's head snapped her way, and his eyes locked on Marian's.

Marian met them and saw there a storm that she had never seen before. Oh my God, she thought, wanting to look away and finding she could not. Oh my God. *He knows.*

"The truth?" Sally said. "About the money?"

The cozy sunlight pouring into Sally's kitchen, the smell of tea and toast and the presence of two people she had always loved: these things should have made Marian feel embraced. At home, and safe. Before, they always had. But now, locked onto Kevin's eyes, she had a sense she was stumbling, directionless, through smoking, twisted ruins.

With difficulty, she said, "And more." She answered Sally without looking away from Kevin, because she could not.

Kevin could have held Marian there, staring into her eyes, as long as he wanted, all day, all night, there would have been nothing she could do. But instead he broke his grip. He flung the newspaper onto the counter and went back to his eggs, jabbing the yolks with toast, spearing the whites with a fork as though this was something they deserved.

"What more?" Sally asked. "What more?"

"Whatever was going on—" Marian had to pause, to force her ragged heart to slow. To cover this need she sipped her tea. Chamomile, a common weed that flourished in cold dry air. Its fragrant white flowers blanketed alpine meadows in Switzerland, whose mountains were famously its source; but Marian, attending a conference in Anchorage a few years earlier, had come upon a miniature forest of it growing through the cracked, oil-spattered asphalt of a parking lot.

"I think," Marian said, "I think something happened back then that we still don't know. Maybe you're right about the money, Sally. But whatever was going on, it's clear that"—*tread carefully, Marian*—"that Phil wasn't the only person hiding something. Jimmy was, too. No, Kevin, let me go on."

Kevin had begun, "Aunt Marian—" but Marian was suddenly using her conference-table voice, and like most people who heard it, he stopped midsentence.

"I don't care what happens to Phil—I'm sorry, but you guys know how I feel—but Jimmy's reputation is something else." She shot Kevin a look; a lifetime of meetings had honed her instinct for impending interruptions and how to quash them. "Whatever happened back then, maybe it was what we always thought, and maybe it was something different. If it was something Jimmy . . . something he felt bad about, then it seems to me he spent a lot of money and a lot of his life making up for it."

"Wait," said Sally. Marian heard a world of uncertainty in that one word. "You can't believe the money came from Jimmy. . . ?"

"Sally?" *Oh God,* Marian thought, *why do I have to do this?* "Sally, it did."

Sally stared. "What are you—"

"Phil told me."

A pause. "Phil?" Sally spoke Phil's name as though it were a word whose meaning had changed without warning. "Phil told you?"

"I'm sorry, honey. God, I'm sorry. That's what he said." Marian put her hand over Sally's. "From Jimmy. All these years."

"But he—I don't believe it."

"I don't know," Marian said helplessly, "whether it's true. But it's what he said."

"To the reporter? Phil told him that?"

"He says not. He says he never told anyone but me."

"Why . . ."

"Why did he tell me? I got the feeling he wanted me to help make it all right with you."

Sally was shaking her head, back and forth, back and forth. "It's just not true."

"Maybe not," said Marian. "Maybe it isn't. But, Sal? Phil and Jimmy, they didn't like each other, but they got together, lots of times, over the years. Why?"

"Aunt Marian?" Kevin's voice was insistent, angry. "You can't be saying you believe that?" With *that* he stabbed a finger at the *Tribune,* at the serpent-filled world of distortions and half-truths and real truths crowded into a two-inch-wide column of type.

Marian shook her head. Not *that.* She was not taken in by *that. That* was manufactured, a Frankenstein monster cobbled out of whatever fragments of truth a reporter had dug out of the smoking rubble. Salamanders, she thought. Weren't those the lizards that rose mythically from fire, indestructible, crawling out of the ashes when all else had been consumed? Yes, salamanders. The old firehouses sometimes had them carved on the beams above the doors. Engine 168 had them; Jimmy had shown her.

Marian could hear that salamander truth hissing now. She forced herself to speak above it. "What they're implying, most of it's probably lies. About Jimmy, and about Phil, too." She added that without believing it, but it was possible, and it would help win Sally over. Although the hope that flooded Sally's eyes when she said it was almost unbearable to see.

"Jimmy's a hero," she said softly. "He was always a hero, except, if anything in the *Tribune*'s right, except maybe once. Somehow. I don't know how." *Oh God,* she thought, *how can I be lying like this?* She continued bitterly, punishing herself. "Something. It changed him, whatever it was."

Suddenly her words began to come fast. She felt like a machine caught and racing, unregulated, unstoppable. "But now, now he's a symbol. Of courage, sacrifice, things people need to believe in. Whatever the truth is, what people need now to help them through what happened is more important. I think Jimmy would think so, too. I think he always thought that, or he'd have told the truth—all the truth—back then. You can't change the . . . mistakes of the past. You can only build the future."

She was dismayed, yes, even frightened, to see the storm still raging in Kevin's eyes. *What do you believe? What do you know?*

But Marian did not ask, and Kevin did not speak.

"Marian?" Sally said. "You really think, you think whatever happened then . . . Markie and Jack . . . you think it wasn't what they told us?"

All Marian could do was nod her head and wish she were somewhere infinitely far away.

"And that's what you think Jimmy . . . what he wrote down?" Sally's question was so hushed Marian could barely hear it.

"Whatever it is," Marian said, "whatever it is, if someone finds it, people will read it who didn't know him, didn't know any of them, any of us. They'll make judgments. Nothing good will come of it, Sally." *Breathe in, breathe out, in, out. Find a calm place.* "And," she said, "it's the only thing they have."

"The only thing people have?"

"No." Marian shook her head. "The *Tribune.* Whoever's investigating. In Phil's case, the Ethics Commission." She waited for the earth to open up and swallow her. She hoped it would. How could she be doing this, using Sally's love for Phil as just another tool of her own, another implement to shape the structure she had concluded must be built?

"Without what Jimmy wrote," she said, "it's just speculation. It will go away. It's a hot story now, but it will cool, with so much else going on."

"Aunt Marian." Kevin pronounced the words carefully, as though he was afraid they were going to give him trouble. " 'The only thing they have.' But the paper"—he jerked his thumb at the *Tribune,* lying in bread crumbs—"they say they haven't seen them, Uncle Jimmy's papers. Only that reporter who died, they say he saw them. Where are they? Who has them?"

And at last Marian had reached the center of the labyrinth, the reason she had torn apart their sunny morning. "I don't know. I hoped you knew."

"*Me?*" Kevin's eyes widened. "I never even knew about them, until the *Tribune.* Mom?"

"No, I didn't know."

Both pairs of green eyes resting on her, waiting.

"Are you . . . sure?" asked Marian. To Kevin: "He left you his things."

It was Sally who answered. "I cleaned out his apartment," she told Marian. "Kevin was at Burke, and I thought . . . anyway, it was me." She took a breath. "There wasn't anything like that there. He didn't have much. Shirts, pants. His dress uniform. Some books." Softly, she smiled. "I wouldn't have thought . . . *The Confessions of Saint Augustine.* Some books about Buddhism. But nothing from those days. Not even old photographs. A picture of Kevin, from when he graduated the Academy. But not any old ones."

None? Not any?

Oh, please, this is not important, Marian begged herself wildly, feeling her spirit plunge as though a cliffside path had crumbled suddenly beneath her feet. *That Jimmy had not kept a photograph of her, not a single one, as she had of him, just the one, all these years in her bedside table*—what had she expected? What had she any right to hope for?

She forced herself to speak. "Even if they were there," she said, "the papers, even if you found them, wouldn't be the ones the reporter saw. There must be copies. Who has those?"

Kevin's face was dark and hard. With a shock Marian recalled a day long ago: Kevin at thirteen, Marian arriving to pick him up after school. She had entered the gate at St. Ann's at the start of a schoolyard brawl. Kevin had looked exactly this way in the seconds before he threw himself at a bigger boy. She'd run over and pulled the boys apart, had told them they should be ashamed of themselves, civilized people did not settle arguments with violence. She had made them shake hands. Marching Kevin out of the yard, she'd asked him what the fight was about. Kevin, still crimson, said without looking at her, "He said I had no dad because my dad was a killer and he died in jail. He said my mom was screwing a Jew."

Now, empty of the certainties she'd had that afternoon, Marian said to Kevin, "Couldn't there be something, something Jimmy told you about, just so someone would know? That you never knew what it was, but you knew it was important to him? Because"—she raced to say this; she couldn't help herself, but that was good, because maybe the truth of it was powerful enough to force things to turn out the way they must, the way she needed them to—"because, Kevin, besides fighting fires, you're the thing he loved most in the world."

Kevin's eyes fastened on hers again, but not to hold her, she thought, not to bind her. More, this time, to be held.

"Kevin?" Sally asked softly. "Was there anything like that, that Jimmy ever talked about?"

"He wouldn't have. It's not like that. I'm a probie. He's—he was Jimmy McCaffery. He was lowering guys on ropes when I was a kid. He had anything important to say to someone, maybe when I had a few years on the Job it might be me. I was thinking that. I was thinking, maybe someday it could be just, you know, Jimmy. Not Uncle Jimmy. Maybe someday. But not yet.

"The only thing I have, besides the books Mom said—his shirts don't fit me—" He swallowed and had to start again. "The only thing, from the memorial service, is his helmet. The guys gave it to me."

He swiped at his eyes and looked away. Sally reached across the table, withdrew her hand without touching him. Silence as thick as the sunlight filled the room. Sally asked Marian, "Where do you think they are? Whatever's in them, these papers?"

"I don't know," Marian answered. "But we need to find them—we need to find them—before that reporter does."

Kevin's chair scraped across the floor as he pushed back from the table, reaching for his crutches.

"Kev?" Sally stood as he levered himself up. "Honey?"

Kevin shook his head and kept going. Sally took a step as though to follow but stopped herself. Marian didn't watch him go but she heard, she felt, the hard slam of his door.

Phil's Story
Chapter 13

———

The Water Dreams

November 1, 2001

Early morning at the Y, but no game today, so Phil was running. Long rhythmic strides, faster than comfortable so it wouldn't get easy. Though this track, tenth of a mile, God he hated it. The same thing, past the same point, forty times, you have to be kidding. Before, even in bad weather, he ran outdoors. Down from his place, through the streets to a park. Either side of the island, up along the river. But now you couldn't run downtown. The ash, the rubble, the trucks. The nervous National Guardsmen. The smell. He couldn't breathe that air. Not like you breathed when you ran. Couldn't take it in, deep in his lungs. Couldn't make it part of him. He'd tried, early on. It had made him sick.

Sixteen. The track, braced on angles, circled the gym. Volleyball practice today, some league team. These guys were good. Long volleys, sharp smashes. Worthy distraction. But not a game Phil took to. You stayed in one place, any given play. Doomed it for him.

Twenty-four. Heart pounding. Runner's high starting. He lived for that. Since September 11, the only time, the only place, he ever felt there was a point: a run, a game. In court? For the clients, so he kept at it. For himself? No. Now, just here. What this point was? No idea. All brain chemicals. Sure, he knew. Supplied by evolution, thank you, ma'am. So you'd run across savannahs. Away from predators. Toward your prey.

Thirty. Could he talk to Sally? Kevin? And say what? Last night, with Kevin: to do that again? But suppose he knew? If he could know, prove it was true? McCaffery, what he did? Phil was the messenger. First urge, kill the messenger.

Thirty-two. Talk to Spano. This might work. With Kev. Take him, show him. Might work. High getting higher. Phil's favorite chemical, always came last, flooding his brain: kicking in hope.

Thirty-seven. Faster, the last three faster. Breath burning, heart hammering. Outrunning thought. Sally, cold voice on the phone. Kevin, back turned. Spano. Huge vast generous fresh breeze of hope. Outrun it all.

Thirty-eight. Pain everywhere, lungs desperate. Legs still pumping. Why? He couldn't remember. Maybe that's the reason.

Forty. Hallelujah.

Slow the pace.

Spano.

Heart pounding.

Find the truth.

Jog one.

For Sally. For Kevin.

Sweat dripping.

Walk one.

Enough.

Laura's Story
Chapter 14

———

Sutter's Mill

November 1, 2001

Afterward, whenever Laura reviewed her tapes—and she'd had both recorders going, of course she had, and both recorders played back exactly the same sounds, told exactly the same story, of course they did (it was like watching the film of the second plane hitting, the footage looped endlessly on TV and you watched it over and over, helplessly hoping this time it would be different)—none of the early part, the interview when she'd been sitting alone with Eddie Spano, sounded familiar to her. It was as though she were listening to the sound track of a film she hadn't seen. It wasn't until the knock, the creaking open of the trailer door, the new voice, that the images started to come; and even then, they were spotty. Until the shouting started. This she remembered. This sprang into full view. The rest of the morning from that point on was clear and sharp to her, full of detail, unrolling in perfect sync with her tapes, and no matter what she did, she was sure—she was afraid—she would never be able to stop seeing it.

Here, at the beginning, on the tape, was Eddie Spano, just as she entered his office. (He'd been sitting behind his desk, a bald, pudgy man. Had he looked up? He must have. Had he stood? No, he hadn't.) Impatient growl: "What?"

Her own voice, words she'd said a million times but didn't now remember saying to Eddie Spano. "Laura Stone, *New York Tribune.*"

"Great." A snort, caught for all time. "Go ahead, sit down. Or stand, I don't care. This isn't an interview. This is an order. Lay the fuck off."

(A rustle on the tape. Laura sitting down?)

"Mr. Spano, my paper has information—"

"Your paper hasn't got shit." (A small sound, a slap? Spano, irritated, closing the file in front of him; it might be that.) "I hardly knew Jimmy McCaffery, I don't know that goddamn lawyer, I never gave Keegan's widow any fucking money. I don't know anything about any of this shit, and I'm tired of seeing my name every fucking day in your fucking paper. Is that clear enough?"

Her voice again, persistent. "What was your involvement in the death of Jack Molloy?"

"You don't listen, do you?"

"If I'm wrong, show me where. What was your—"

"Zip. Zero. Nada. None. I make my point, or I have to draw you a picture?"

"I'm interested in the truth, Mr. Spano."

"Bullshit. You and your paper are interested in smearing shit all over me. I don't know what I ever did to you, but, sweetie, people who play with fire get burned. Ask Jimmy McCaffery."

"What can you tell me about the negotiations going on before Jack Molloy's death?"

"Negotiations? Jesus Christ, lady, what's wrong with you? What the fuck are you talking about?"

"You and Molloy were making some kind of deal. What was it?"

"Deal?" (A change in Spano's voice. This must be when he adjusted his game to Laura's, to her tough-broad-reporter, to her cold eyes that told him she'd faced down nastier specimens than Eddie Spano. At least, that's what her eyes were supposed to be saying. That was how, heading over in the cab, she'd decided to approach him. Had she? It sounded like that, on the tape. But she didn't know. She didn't know.) "What was this 'deal' supposed to be about?"

"After Jack Molloy died, you ended up with a lot of the Molloy empire."

"*Empire?* Shit, you're killing me. Molloy was a punk, his old man was a small-time ass-wipe."

"But you don't deny you wound up running the Molloy rackets?"

"Rackets? You learn to talk like that from the movies?"

"You don't deny it?"

"Of course I deny it. I don't know anything about any 'rackets.' I'm a businessman."

"What kind of business?"

"Real estate. Insurance. I have investments all over this island."

"So did Big Mike Molloy. Drugs, gambling—"

"Lady, are you too stupid to live?"

"Was Harry Randall?"

"What?"

"Too stupid to live. Someone murdered Harry Randall. He was breaking this story, and—"

"Fuck this shit! Lady, that's enough. One more word of this shit in the paper, and—"

Now—there, on the tape—now the knock, now the hinges whining. Now the pictures started.

Eddie Spano, swinging his flushed face from Laura to the door. "Oh fuck, what now? Who the hell—?"

And the new voice. "Phil Constantine, Mr. Spano." A pause, and then, "I work for you."

Laura could see them standing just inside: the lawyer tall—taller than he'd seemed in his own office, and she remembered thinking that was odd—suit and tie, mud spots on his polished shoes. The young man— this must be Kevin Keegan, she realized, the center of this storm—red hair, muscled, and leaning on crutches. This picture was a snapshot, though, not a movie yet.

But the sound track went on.

"You work for—wait, you're that lawyer fuck? Jesus! What is this? Are you as psycho as she is? You do not work for me. I don't know what the hell you people want—"

"I just want to hear you say it, Eddie." Constantine was smiling. Laura saw that. Smiling. A glittering, hungry grin. "I've been your bag-man for twenty years, and I just want to hear you say it. I want you to tell Kevin what it's all been about."

"Look. Shit. I don't know what you people are up to, but I've had enough." A scraping sound as Spano pushed back his chair. Laura had an idea he'd been about to say something else, but Constantine's eyes had caught hers, and Spano saw that. "Fuck," Spano said instead. "What? You two in this together? This some kind of shakedown? Get the fuck out of here. All of you. Out."

"Ms. Stone, that means you," Constantine said. "We'll leave soon, too, Eddie. But I passed your money to Sally Keegan for eighteen years. I was a good boy. I didn't ask questions. Jimmy McCaffery said it was his, I closed my eyes and covered my ears and passed it on.

"I'm likely to be disbarred, Eddie. I may even go to jail. I just want to know what it was all about. I want Kevin to know. Ms. Stone." Now Constantine turned to Laura, and the details filled in, spreading from the center to the farthest edges as Constantine said to her, "Ms. Stone, get lost. Mr. Spano wants this off the record. So do I."

Laura was not about to get lost. What reporter could leave a scene like this? But she was thinking furiously. It was obviously her presence that was making Spano deny he'd used Constantine to pass the money; what reason would he have to lie to Constantine, even if McCaffery had been their go-between, even if the two had never met? If she left, so they could have this out alone, could she hide somewhere, lurk under the windows, eavesdrop? Outside a trailer on concrete blocks in the mud of a building site? The men with the American flag decals on their hard hats would spot her, circle toward her, surround her like a pack of wolves.

No, she'd stay until Spano had her physically thrown out (and maybe he wouldn't; after all, think how that would look in the paper) and play them off against each other. She'd done that before. It wasn't so hard. Everyone wanted to come out looking good, everyone wanted his story to be the one that was believed.

That was Laura's plan. "If you—" She never got any further than that.

"Fuck that!" Keegan exploded. "Let her stay! Let her hear it, let everyone hear it!"

"Kev—"

"No, Uncle Phil." Keegan's voice took on a different tone, a tone Laura knew. She'd heard it in the voices of people she'd interviewed in those first days after the towers fell, people coming to accept what they had been desperately fighting: that the "missing" posters, the hospital searches, the frantic digging at Ground Zero, could not help them. It was the voice of someone admitting the shattering truth that a loved one was gone, and in that voice Kevin Keegan said, "No, Uncle Phil."

———

The Way Home

November 1, 2001

"Kevin." Constantine spoke quietly to the young man, as though the two were alone. As though they stood on some wind-blasted height where nothing grew and nothing lived and everything had been torn away but the truth.

Keegan shook his head. "Don't. Don't tell me more lies, Uncle Phil. No more. You lied all my life."

"Not about what was important." Like voices on the tapes Laura had heard of calls made from the upper floors of the towers, people who understood they were certainly doomed but were determined to maintain contact until the end, Constantine's voice was calm. "Not about what mattered."

"To *you*!" Keegan shouted. "What mattered to *you*! Me and my mom—oh, fuck. Fuck you!"

The young man looked wildly around, as much, Laura thought, to break the spell of Constantine's eyes as anything else. He spotted her but moved on, too furious to care who she was or what she'd heard. Constantine's eyes watched the young man the way you'd stare after a priceless possession torn away in a hurricane.

Keegan fixed on Eddie Spano. "You," he said hoarsely. "I want to know. My dad, Uncle Jimmy, what was it about?"

"I don't know what the hell—"

"Don't do that! Don't lie like him, no more bullshit! Who shot Jack Molloy? Was it Uncle Jimmy?"

"Kid, I—"

Constantine said, "Kevin—"

"Why did my dad go to jail? What was the money for?"

From Spano: "I got no fucking idea!"

From Constantine: "Kev—"

"Uncle Jimmy's papers," Keegan hissed at Spano. "What he wrote. Is that what's in them?"

"Papers? What fucking papers?"

"You lying bastard! *Tell me!*"

"Get the fuck out of here! You're fucking crazy, all of you! Get out!"

Keegan, green eyes blazing, swung forward on his crutches with a speed that took Laura by surprise. He shoved Spano against the wall before anyone could move. The whole trailer rocked. "Tell me the truth!" The crutches clattered to the floor. Keegan squeezed Spano's throat. Spano clawed Keegan's face as Keegan shouted, "What did my father do? Why did he go to jail? Tell me the truth! Tell me! Tell me!"

Spano pushed and twisted; Constantine grabbed Keegan, tried to pull him away. "Kevin! Come on, Kev, come on!"

Keegan swung at Constantine. The blow was unbalanced and badly timed but had the unstoppable force of betrayal behind it. Constantine's head snapped back. Keegan, weight shifting to his bad leg, fell forward, seizing Spano again.

Spano struggled half out of Keegan's grip. Keegan pounded and punched. Laura wasn't sure if he knew who he was hitting, what he was screaming. Spano was shouting, too. And Constantine, not shouting, talking, talking to Keegan, blood on his face as he wrapped his arms around the young man, trying to make him stop, trying at the same time, Laura realized, not to hurt him.

Laura had jumped up but had not neared the struggling men. She was a reporter, she stood apart. Her chair had fallen over, but she was in the spot she'd been in since she arrived and so was in the perfect place to see when Spano, still caught in Keegan's grip, pounded, screamed at, bloodied, yanked open the desk drawer. He shouted, "Fuck you, you fucking lunatic!" and there was a gun in his hand.

From the *New York Tribune,* November 2, 2001

FIREFIGHTER SLAIN IN
SHOOTING INCIDENT

Survived Fall of North Tower

by Hugh Jesselson

Probationary Firefighter Kevin Keegan, who was pulled to safety by fellow firefighters from under burning debris when the World Trade Center's north tower collapsed on September 11, was killed yesterday in a shooting incident on Staten Island. Keegan was hit in the chest by a single bullet. He was taken to Staten Island Hospital, where he died three hours later.

Police have arrested Edward Spano, of Pleasant Hills, a reputed organized crime figure with alleged ties to the Bonnano crime family. Spano has been charged with manslaughter and reckless endangerment.

The shooting happened yesterday morning in Spano's office at Chapel Pointe, a luxury Staten Island residential development. The circumstances surrounding the shooting are still under investigation.

Spano, as first reported by the *Tribune* on October 29, is believed to have been the source of payments made over nearly two decades to the dead man's family. These payments were made through attorney Phillip Constantine, a longtime Keegan family friend. Constantine, present at the scene of yesterday's shooting, was injured but refused medical attention. He was taken into custody and released this morning with no charges filed against him.

Also present was *Tribune* reporter Laura Stone, who was interviewing Spano at his office when Constantine entered with Keegan.

When Spano ordered the three to leave, a fight began. Spano

pulled a gun from his desk and pointed it at Keegan. Laura Stone said, "It just made him madder. He jumped on Spano and choked him. Constantine tried to pull him back and the gun went off."

Police have subpoenaed the bank records for the escrow account Constantine maintained for the Keegan family. It is alleged by some sources that the cash for the payments was passed from Spano to Constantine by FDNY Captain James McCaffery, who died on September 11.

Edward Spano will be arraigned today on Staten Island. He is expected to enter a plea of self-defense.

The investigation is continuing.

LAURA'S STORY
Chapter 16

———

*The Invisible Man
Steps Between You and the Mirror*

November 2, 2001

Morning in the newsroom. Laura, as always, early; other reporters drifting in one by one, stopping by her desk to ask, How are you doing? Are you okay? All of them sympathetic, all of them kind. But some—the honest ones, Laura thought—not suppressing their ironic and envious smiles when they said, Hell of a way to get a story.

Five clocks in plain view, none of them moving. Just get through the meeting, Laura told herself. Just that.

Laura's desk phone ringing. No, she thought, no, whoever you are and whatever you want, I can't. Even as she thought that, she grabbed the receiver up.

"Laura Stone."

"Owen McCardle."

An unfamiliar voice, a familiar name. Laura cast about. "I'm sorry—"

"Friend of Jimmy McCaffery's."

Yes. "Yes, I remember. You were at Engine 168. Harry interviewed you."

"I want to talk to you."

"Mr. McCardle, after what just happened—"

"I want you to come here."

"I—"

"It's goddamn important, Miss Stone."

Anger slammed Laura as though McCardle's fist had pounded her through the electronic distance between them.

Laura closed her eyes. But that brought, not longed-for emptiness, but—again, once again—the sight of Kevin Keegan, swaying, clutching his bloodied chest. Staring not at Edward Spano, the man who'd shot him, but at Phil Constantine, motionless, frozen. Only his eyes reached for Keegan. Then Keegan fell.

I want to go home, Laura thought. Not to Harry's empty apartment, or her own, not to anyplace in this ruined city. *Home.*

"It's goddamn important." McCardle's voice, each word separate, a boiling fury.

Too tired to argue, Laura said, "All right." What choice was there? With the sinking feeling that she knew the answer, she asked, "Where is 'here'?"

The ferry ride, one more time. Manhattan shrank as Laura stood on the back of the boat in the bright sun and watched. She didn't want to look forward, couldn't bear to see anything more coming toward her.

From the terminal she took a cab, leaning back against the seat. After yesterday, she was not ready to be seen in Pleasant Hills.

The cab drove past a school, a red-brick building she hadn't noticed before. The thought struck her: *I could teach.* English lit. Shakespeare, Yeats, Auden. The echoing halls of her midwestern high school came to her, the blaze of golden trees in autumn, the blue of the lake. *Let Jesselson have the rest of this. Let him do the digging to prove Spano killed Harry. I'll leave. I'll get out now. There's still time.*

The idea was comforting and also exciting. Yes. After this interview. Whatever McCardle had, she'd take it down, hand it to Jesselson, pack up, and fly home.

Would you mind, Harry? she asked. *Now that I'm this close, now that it's this obvious? Do I have to stay, and watch, the way we all watched the towers burn and fall and keep burning? This time, can't I turn away?*

The house where the cab left her was compact, well kept. A white fence edged the front yard. Against it, yellow and orange chrysanthemums burned. The doorbell sounded a three-note chime, and the door was opened instantly by a man who had surely been waiting, waiting. He said, "Laura Stone?" and moved aside to let her in as though the answer were not in doubt.

She replied, "Mr. McCardle?" though there was no question about that, either. He had a drooping gray mustache, the rough, uneven skin of a man who spends his time outdoors, and angry gray eyes.

Unnerved by those eyes, Laura stopped just inside the door and asked as he closed it, "What's this about?"

McCardle shut the door, strode into the living room, pointed to the sofa. He sat in an easy chair but didn't speak. How shall I handle this, what should I do? Laura wondered. She waited for instructions from Reporter-Laura, but none came. And at that—Reporter-Laura's silence, her absence—a slow tide of fear began to rise.

"Jimmy McCaffery gave me that ten years ago." McCardle's hands remained on the arms of his chair, but his eyes moved to a thick, yellowed envelope on the table beside Laura. "He said, Owen, hold this for me. Don't have to do anything with it, just keep it. I said, What the hell's in it, kid? Your will, something like that? He said, It's the truth. I just think it should be someplace. What do you mean, the truth? I said. About what? I'm not sure, he said. But I know it's the truth.

"So I kept it. Pretty much forgot about it. Even when Jimmy died. A lot of guys gone that day, a lot to think about." McCardle's rough hand brushed at something on his pants leg. "I've been down at the pit, every day. You find this guy's belt buckle, that guy's wedding ring. Guys you knew. You know what that's like?"

Inside the fence at Ground Zero, Laura had seen the firefighters stop and lift something, some small, crumpled thing, from the dust and rubble. She'd tried to imagine what that was like.

She shook her head.

McCardle fixed his fierce gray eyes on her again.

"Wasn't until your paper ran that story. Not the first ones, about Jimmy, or Kevin. That other one, about the money, where it came from. I read it and thought, This is crap, I knew Jimmy, when he was here, when he was Superman. And then, like he was in the room, I saw him handing me that, saying, Owen, keep this for me, it's the truth.

"So I dug it out. I read it. I called that reporter, Randall, I made him read it.

"Next thing I know, Randall takes a dive off the bridge. Shit. I put that thing back in the desk. No one needs anyone else dying, not now. But at least, I think, at least the lies about Jimmy'll stop.

"But they don't. You just don't let it go. More and more crap, worse and worse—"

McCardle's hands were gripping the arms of his chair so tightly they threatened to rip the fabric. The muscle along his jaw bulged, ropy and thick.

"And now Kevin. Goddammit. Goddammit! You did that, Miss Stone. You got Kevin killed."

Mutely, Laura shook her head.

McCardle boiled up out of his chair. He loomed over Laura. She thought he was going to seize her, hit her, tear her in half. She did nothing to stop him.

"Read it," he snarled, and slammed out of the room, out of the house, leaving her alone.

Boys' Own Book
Chapter 15

How to Find the Floor

September 11, 1979

It's Jimmy and Markie, Tom and Jack, on a hot autumn night. Sitting in sawdust, lounging against skeletal walls made from spaced lengths of two-by-four, they sip beer from six-packs scattered at their feet and watch the moon.

No one'll ever see this again, says Tom, gazing through the strips of rafter, the naked wooden lines overhead.

Markie pops a top, wants to know, What are you talking about?

Tomorrow, the next day, says Tom, they'll be putting the roof on. That spot you're sitting on, Markie, man, no one'll ever see the moon from right there again.

Unless the house burns down, laughs Markie. Like if Jimmy's asleep on the truck or something. Then you can see the moon from here.

House burns down, that spot's gone, too, says Tom. Nope, no more moons from here. He lifts his beer can to the moon, to say goodbye.

Jack snorts. This's gonna be the bedroom. Some just-married guy moves in here, you can bet he'll be seeing plenty of moons.

No one answers.

It was Jack's idea to come out here tonight. Everyone else agreed, shrugging, saying, Sure. It's not so often they hang together anymore, the four of them. Tom and Vicky have a kid now, Michael, and Vicky's pregnant again, due in March. Markie's got the job and his family. Jimmy's working a fireman's tours, and anyway there's this strange thing between him and Jack. And a strange thing, too, between Jack and Tom, different from when they were kids, when Tom knew what to say to his brother, when he knew what would work to calm Jack down.

So when Jack says, Let's get some beer, go out to Coleman Road, they all say, Yeah, sounds good. Since they were kids, this was a thing they did, hang out on the construction sites in the neighborhood. It makes them theirs. Jimmy sees it this way: you can't stop people from changing your world. There are too many people, and you never know what they're planning until it's too late. But what you can do, you can make the changes part of you. You can take changes inside you as though you're big and they're small. Instead of letting the changes be something that makes you choke, you can breathe them in.

Sometimes it works, sometimes it doesn't.

He doesn't say this to the others, and he's not sure they have the same reasons why they want to come out to the half-built houses and drink beer (instead of chasing each other around and throwing dirt bombs, that's what hanging out meant when they were kids). Sometimes—always, back then, but now just sometimes—the girls come with them; but mostly, like tonight, as though they'd talked to each other about it (they never have), they don't tell the girls where they're headed. Just, Me and the guys, we're going to have a couple beers.

Even Marian. Jimmy thinks she'd get it; at least, she'd get why he does it. But Marian doesn't hang out with Jack or Tom anymore. She never tells Jimmy not to, she never tells him what to do about anything unless he asks her what she thinks, and the funny thing is, he knows she still likes Tom, everyone does. And Jack, he always made Marian laugh, and Jimmy knows she misses Jack, misses laughing like that. But she doesn't hang out with them anymore.

Tonight it was Jack's idea, but he's been in a lousy mood the whole night. Markie seems a little weird, too, Jimmy can't put his finger on it. Jumpy maybe, and pretending like he's not.

That thing Markie was going to tell Jack about, the thing Mike the Bear asked Jimmy to help him out with that afternoon in Flanagan's, Markie says he told him.

What did he say? Jimmy asked Markie this last weekend, the two of them hammering asphalt shingles back onto the roof of the O'Neills' porch. Old man O'Neill, he can't do this stuff for himself anymore, and Jimmy and Markie don't have much else to do on a Saturday afternoon.

Bullshit, says Markie.

He said Bullshit?

Yeah.

What does he mean, bullshit? He doesn't think it's true?

Uh-uh. Markie leans way over for the bucket of nails that's by Jimmy. He slips, grabs, but gets nothing. He's about to slide, he's headed right for the edge of the roof, but Jimmy's got his foot braced against the tree that leans on the porch, and he grabs Markie, pulls him, and then Markie sticks his foot out against the tree, too.

Jesus Christ, man. Jimmy breathes, waits for his heart to stop kicking his chest. Jesus Christ. You come over here, let me do that part, says Jimmy. Markie grins as he and Jimmy crawl over each other on the roof, so Markie's near the tree.

Jimmy grabs a handful of nails on the way, drops them in his shirt pocket so he doesn't have to lean over for the bucket. He sticks four in his mouth for the first shingle on that side, takes them out one by one, and hammers them in. He waits till he's done before he says, You're telling me Jack doesn't buy it? He doesn't believe it, that the cops are closing in?

I didn't know what the hell else to say, says Markie. I told him. I said man, they're coming to roll you up, Jack, man, you gotta cool it, you gotta be Mr. Clean. He wanted to know where I got it. I said I heard it around. He said, Bullshit. He said, Stuff like that, if it's true, you don't hear it around.

Hmmm. Jimmy's got nails in his mouth again, so he just grunts, pushes hard on a shingle that's supposed to slip under the next one but it doesn't want to go where it belongs. When he finally gets it in and hammered down, he says, Could be he's right about that.

Well, what the hell, where did *you* hear it? That's what you told me, you heard it around.

Yeah, well, says Jimmy. He isn't sure he wants to say to Markie, Mike the Bear told me, me and him had a drink at Flanagan's and he asked me for help. That seems wrong, Jimmy telling Big Mike's secret: that he'd come up against something he couldn't take care of on his own. Jimmy's thinking what to say when Sally calls from down in the yard, do they want a Coke or something?

We're almost done, shouts Jimmy.

Markie says, Yeah, Jimmy, man, can you give me a hand with this one? Jimmy pulls himself over to where Markie is, and they wrestle the last couple of shingles together.

Now they're sitting, all four of them, on rough plywood sheets in a spill of moonlight under the outline of a roof that'll be getting its own shingles soon. Jack's drinking more than everyone else, and he's talking louder when he talks, but mostly he's quiet.

Just to be saying something, because usually he likes quiet, but this is a kind he doesn't, Jimmy says, I heard they're putting up a subdivision over on Fitzgerald, too, soon. Condos, that's what I heard.

Tom nods, like he knows Jimmy's right, but Jack says, Bullshit. He says, I'm tired of people hearing shit, it's all bullshit. Markie looks real quick at Jack, and then away, but Jack is watching Markie. People hear shit, says Jack. People tell other people. Fucks everyone up, it's all a pile of crap.

Tom says, Fuck, Jack, why don't you yell a little more, I don't think you woke up those people across the street yet.

Jimmy peers into the dark. A faraway streetlight shows where across the street is, where the finished houses are, with people in them. Not so easy to wake those people up from here, he thinks, we might as well be off in the woods. But he doesn't say it, because it would be okay with him if Jack stopped yelling.

Listen, you guys, says Tom. It's too hot out here, let's go get a nightcap at the Bird before last call.

He stands and brushes off his jeans. Jimmy puts his beer can down, but Markie and Jack aren't moving.

People hear shit, Jack says, it's because someone else told them.

Tom says, What the hell's your problem tonight?

Tom's glaring down at Jack.

My problem? And now Jack jumps up, too, faster than Jimmy thought he could, as much as he had to drink. My *problem* is this asshole is telling me bullshit. He's trying to scare me, how about that shit? Puny Markie Keegan's trying to scare the crap out of Jack Molloy.

Jack laughs, but not like something's funny, says, What the fuck, Markie? You think you can scare me because of some made-up crap? You think that?

It's what I heard, Markie says, spreading his hands, and at the same time Tom says, What are you talking about?

You cocksucker, says Jack, I swear to God, Markie, you piss me off, who told you to feed me that bullshit?

Markie starts, No one told me.

But he can't finish because Jack's yelling: Fuck, Markie, fuck! Who're you working for?

Working for? Markie repeats the words like he's amazed Jack said them, like when they were kids and Jack said something so dirty the rest of them wouldn't dare even try it; except Markie, Markie always used to try. He says, Hey, Jack.

What bullshit? Tom says in a low voice, each word crammed with dynamite. Jack swings around to stare at Tom. Jimmy thinks for a second about standing up like they are; instead he inches a little closer across the plywood to where Markie's sitting.

Jack says, You want to know what bullshit?

Jack's glaring at Tom, swaying a little to keep his balance. Like he's on a ship, thinks Jimmy. Or like the wind's blowing only where he is.

You want to know what bullshit? Okay, says Jack, I'll tell you. This asshole—he points at Markie—he's been telling me the cops have all this bullshit. Operation Jack or some damn shit, files on me and evidence up their buttholes and if I don't lay off they'll throw me in the fucking can. That's what bullshit.

Tom looks at Markie.

Markie says, It's what I heard.

Where? says Tom, like he doesn't quite get something.

Just, says Markie, just around.

Balls, spits Jack.

Just around? Tom asks Markie. You just heard this?

Markie nods.

Guys? Jimmy says. I heard it, too.

Jack goes wild.

Oh, fuck! Oh, shut the fuck up, Superman! Who the hell's gonna tell shit like this to you? To either of you? Squeaky clean motherfuckers like you? This shit was true, you'd be the last guys in hell to hear it.

But here's the punch line, Jack says, with his hands opening and closing. He takes a step closer to Markie. Markie's looking up. Jack's between him and the moon. The joke about this bullshit, says Jack, it's crap. It's lies. It's not fucking true.

Tom steps up, too, so he won't be behind Jack. He says, How do you know?

Fuck you, little brother. You think you're the only Molloy with cops in his pocket?

Jack's growling now, like a dog warning you to back off. Like King, when they were all kids. When the dog was trapped and couldn't get away.

Tom tries: Jack—

I pay good money to find out shit like this! Jack yells. Markie tells me this shit, I ask my guys, What about it? They say it's news to them.

They check around, come back, and say it's bullshit from ass to tits. So what I want to know, Markie, what I fucking want to know is *what fucking motherfucker told you to tell me this shit?*

I—

Because it fucked me up, Markie.

Jack's voice is suddenly quiet, and as hot as the night is, Jimmy goes ice cold.

It was my time, Markie, Jack says in that soft voice. Dad was ready. Did you know that? he asks Tom.

Tom shakes his head.

Atlanta, next month, Jack says. I was on my way, I was out of here. And now, Jack says, in a whisper, and Jimmy hears it like a crackling flame, like a fire in the walls, you can't see it, but it's devouring everything where it hides. And now he says I'm too hot. He says, if I made so much noise the NYPD is coming after me, even with all the guys I bought, then I'm too hot for Atlanta.

Tom speaks now, but the words he says, he says them like he doesn't trust them. Did you tell Dad? That your guys say it's crap?

Of course I fucking told him! He says where he heard it, it's not crap.

Tom tries again. So you'll cool off, he tells Jack. A couple of months—

NO! shouts Jack. No, that's not what he said! What he said, he doesn't know, he doesn't know if there's going to be any kind of place there for me. For a guy like me. He said he wasn't sure anyway, but I wanted it so much, he figured what the hell, he'd send me. But this shit changed his mind. He said I better plan on staying here. A guy like me.

Jack's looking at the three of them. His shoulders drop. Not yelling now, almost sad, like he's asking them for something, Jack says: You guys. You have what you wanted. Why can't I?

He asks them again, harder: *Why can't I?*

Jimmy wants to answer Jack's question. He wants to say something to Jack, to help. Marian would know how to talk to Jack, like always when they were kids. Jimmy wishes he'd said to Marian, Come on with us, he wishes Marian were here. He wishes they all were: Marian, and Vicky and Sally. Like it was back then, if you got mad at somebody, you could turn away and hang with somebody else. If the girls were here, Marian would make a joke with Jack, or Vicky would roll her eyes to say to Jack, Oh, please, or Sally would smile at Jack and Jack would do anything, like any of them always would, for Sally.

But the girls aren't here, so Jimmy thinks, what can he do for Jack, what can he say? But like when you're at a call and you can't see or smell anything, everything's dark and quiet and you're not sure what you're supposed to do and then with no warning the fire from the walls explodes in a deadly roar, like that, Jack explodes.

So don't hand me that heard-it-around shit! he howls at Markie. *Tell me who it was!*

Even in just the light from the moon and the faraway streetlight, Jack's face is red and burning, Jimmy can see it.

It was Spano, wasn't it? Jack yells. You're fucking working for that wop asshole, and he wants to cut me down! Eddie, right? He doesn't give a rat's ass about Tom or Dad, but what *I* got Eddie wants! That's right, right, Markie? You're lying for that fucking wop?

No, says Markie, Jack, that's stupid.

Stupid? Who's fucking stupid? You're fucking stupid, Markie! You and that fucking wop Eddie!

Jack, says Tom, what are you talking about? Why would it be Eddie?

Who the fuck else? Who's gonna do shit like this to me? Shit! This didn't happen, I'm outta here, Eddie could have it all, good fucking riddance! But he couldn't wait! And what the fuck, Markie, you had to help him? Why'd you do this to me, Markie? *Why?*

Jimmy says, Jack. Jack, listen.

Oh fuck! Oh fuck, Superman! SHUT THE FUCK UP! screams Jack, and there's a gun in his hand.

Tom says, right away: Jack. Put it down.

This is Tom, the old Tom, he knows everything about you, he's only telling you to do what you want to do anyway, and everyone always does it.

Jack, Tom says again, but Jack doesn't even look at him. Jack, this is fucked up, man, put that thing down.

Jimmy hears something in Tom's voice he never heard before. Jimmy flashes back: a warehouse fire last month, four alarms. A roof collapse takes a guy from a ladder company with it. His brothers on radios, searching frantically; the guy at first responding, but sounding so exhausted; then apologizing; I'm sorry, guys. I can't. Going silent. Jimmy's there when they bring the body up.

Jack, don't, says Tom again, in that guy's voice.

Tom, Jack says, hard and so cold, Little brother, I should've stopped listening to you years ago.

Jack takes a swaying step toward Markie, looks at him. *Say it,* he screams at Markie. *Say it was Eddie!* You're sucking that wop mother-fucker's dick, and I want to hear you say it!

Markie opens his mouth, maybe he's going to say it, maybe he'd say whatever Jack wants him to, but nothing comes out.

Jack, says Tom.

Jimmy, too, he says, Jack, and he starts to stand.

Fucker! screams Jack, and the gun screams, too, the loudest bang Jimmy's ever heard, the brightest flash he's ever seen. Splinters fly out of the wood above Markie's head. Jimmy dives for Markie, pushes him down flat. Tom grabs Jack's arm, but Jack flings him off. They both stumble. Jack's the one who's stinking drunk, but it's Tom who can't stay on his feet. He thuds onto the plywood, a sawdust cloud flying up around him.

Jack points the gun again. Jimmy's covering Markie, so Jack shoots at Jimmy. The bullet slams into the wood an inch from Jimmy's face. The third shot, Jimmy hears it and thinks he's dead, dead for sure, but he doesn't feel anything. He twists around, looks up at Jack. Jack is standing over him, and Jimmy waits for him to shoot again, but Jack just says, Fuck. He says, Oh, you fucker.

Then he falls.

Jimmy turns, looks for Tom. Tom's on his belly, covered in sawdust, right arm straight out, and there's a gun in his hand.

It's like some freezing wind came and blasted them all, changed them to ice or to frozen stones and it's been centuries now, forever, and still no one can move.

That's how it feels, but Jimmy knows it can't be true. The echoes of Tom's shot are still fading as he scrambles across the plywood to where Jack's sprawled. He checks for a pulse in Jack's neck, they taught him that in paramedic class, but he doesn't have to do it. He already knows. The dark spot on the front of Jack's shirt is small, but the blood under him is spreading so fast, the sawdust can't soak it up.

Jack, says Tom, whispering. Jack.

Tom, still flat on his belly, stares at his hand, his own hand with his own gun in it, his eyes wild like he's seeing a monster he never knew was there on the end of his arm. Very gently, he puts the gun down on a bed of sawdust, like now that it's quiet he doesn't want to make it mad again. He lurches to his knees and crawls over to where Jack is, leans close to Jack. I'm sorry, he says. Oh, Jesus, Jack, I'm sorry, man, come on.

Jimmy takes hold of Tom's arm, pulls him back. Don't, Jimmy says. Tom, man, there's nothing you can do.

Tom looks at Jimmy like Jimmy's speaking Chinese.

I have to, Tom whispers. I'm supposed to do something.

You can't.

When he gets like that. I'm supposed to do something. Get him to stop. I'm supposed to. Jack? Hey, Jack, hey, man—

Tom, says Jimmy. Tom, he's gone.

Tom looks at Jimmy like he still doesn't understand a word. Markie gets up, moving like he's asleep. He crouches down with them, all three of them next to Jack. Jack's gun is lying in the sawdust, too, like Tom's, two coiled serpents, resting now like they just fought a battle.

Something happens Jimmy's never seen before: Tom starts to cry.

After a while, it's not very long, Tom pulls away from Jimmy, from where Jimmy's been holding him tight. Jesus, Tom says. Shit.

He would've killed us, says Jimmy. Me and Markie. You, too, maybe. Jimmy's shirt is damp on his shoulder, from Tom's crying, and he can't stop shivering.

Tom looks down at Jack, like maybe something's going to happen, like maybe he's wrong about what happened already. Softly he says again, Jesus.

Nobody else says anything.

Then Tom says, Mom.

This'll kill my mom, says Tom.

Jimmy sees her, Mrs. Molloy, he sees her eyes watching Jack, and he knows this is what she's been afraid of, been waiting for all his life. Something like this, Jack getting in the kind of trouble no one gets out of.

I'm supposed to look out for him, says Tom. My job, make sure something like this doesn't happen to him. He laughs, a quick growling bark. Shit, he whispers, oh shit. This will kill her. Jack . . . Tom doesn't finish that. He can't say the word.

He whispers, And me going down for it! Jesus.

You saved our lives, says Markie. He was shooting at us. You won't go down.

Don't you know who I am? says Tom, raw and wild. The cops'll fucking love it, one Molloy wasting the other! Oh, you bet your ass I'm going down for the rest of my fucking life.

Jimmy knows that's right. The cops won't let this go.

And like the cops were wolves, like they smelled blood in the night air, Jimmy hears sirens, far away, coming closer.

Shit, oh shit, says Tom.

Come on, says Markie. He grabs the bag, starts shoving the beer cans back in it.

Wait, says Tom.

What the fuck for? Markie scoops up Tom's gun like it's just another beer can, drops it in the bag. He says, They find you here, you're fucked. Jimmy, they find *you* here, maybe you don't go to jail, but they'll kick your ass off the Job, you know they will.

This hits Jimmy hard. Markie might be right.

Or they'll tell you, says Markie, they'll say to stay on the Job, you gotta rat Tom out.

When Markie says this, Jimmy feels like he's buried under tons of concrete, like he can't breathe.

The sirens howl louder.

Tom rubs his hand over his head, and Jimmy can see now he's thinking, he's working this out. No, Tom says. They find Jack like this, they'll think it's the Spanos. Dad'll send guys over there. They'll send guys back. A fucking war. Oh, Christ.

Tom? says Markie. You can think what to do later. You guys have to get the fuck out of here now.

Us guys? says Jimmy.

Yeah, says Markie. You gotta go.

The sirens wail louder.

Markie pushes them, both of them, to the edge of the plywood floor. Jimmy thinks, *Markie*. Markie's figuring what to do. Everybody's listening to Markie. But Markie never thinks past now, this minute. Markie never thinks ahead.

Wait, Jimmy says. Stop. He looks at Tom, at Markie; at Jack, sprawled on the unfinished floor. He wants to take it all in, until he knows what to do. He doesn't know what to do.

Markie says, Jimmy, the Job. You want to stay on the Job? You think that's gonna happen, they find you here?

There's a sweep of lights in the trees.

Jim, says Tom. Jimmy, man?

They look at each other, Tom and Jimmy. Jimmy's looking for that light Tom gets in his eyes, the thing that says he had a smart idea, he knows the answer. Looking for it, but doesn't see it.

Markie jumps down, says, Come on, you guys, come on. Tom jumps, too. They both stand looking up at Jimmy.

Just before he jumps, just before he runs, Jimmy looks up through the roof beams, up at the sky, like maybe something there can help him know what to do.

The moon's gone.

Boys' Own Book
Chapter 16

———

Breathing Smoke

September 12, 1979

Markie, man, you're fucking crazy!

Jimmy's said these words a million times before, on the playground, in the classroom, in someone's backyard. He's saying them now, again, from the shotgun seat of Markie's car. The ragtop's down, Tom's in the back, the sun's hot even though it's early in the morning and it glitters on the water just beyond the dead end where they're parked.

Jimmy's thinking about last night. Tom and Markie are, too, Jimmy knows that, how can they think about anything else? Last night's like a huge tall building when you're standing right in front of it, it fills up the world and there's nothing else there.

Last night: Jimmy and Markie and Tom run through the woods as cop car headlights stab into the half-built houses on Coleman Road. They leave Jack on the plywood floor, to be found and photographed and taken away by men who don't like him, men whose job it is to find who killed him but who will give each other little cold smiles when they hear he's dead.

This is fucked, Jimmy says last night, when they circle around to Markie's car, the ragtop parked in the turn-off, the vinyl filled with tree shadows. I can't— He stops. He doesn't know what he can't do. Or what he can.

Yeah, says Tom. I know. Just till morning, man. Give me till morning, I have to think.

Jimmy knows what Tom's thinking about: his mom. Jack, it's too late, there's no thinking that'll help Jack now. Tom's doing what he always does, pushing right past the problem he can't solve, looking for the one he can do something about.

And Jimmy's thinking about the Job. About what Markie said would happen if anyone knew Jimmy was there when Jack got killed.

Jesus, man, Jimmy says.

But he doesn't say, No.

When Jimmy gets home, Marian's asleep. He takes a shower, pounding and cold, like sometimes at the firehouse after a run, most of the guys soaping off in hot steamy water but Jimmy thinking hot water's a lot like fire, how can it wash away what fire leaves behind? The shower he takes tonight is hard and icy, but it doesn't feel like it washes anything away.

He gets into bed very quietly. Marian turns, smiles in her sleep. He kisses her, puts his arm over her, pretends to fall asleep right away.

An hour later the phone rings.

Marian jumps, and Jimmy does, too, though as soon as he hears it, he knows he's been expecting it. Marian's eyes are worried, she watches him while he answers, because nothing good ever comes from a phone call in the middle of the night.

It's Tom. He's talking quietly, like he doesn't want anyone else to hear. The cops were here, he says.

Jimmy doesn't say anything, waits for Tom.

They came to tell me about Jack, Tom says. And Jimmy, man? Shit, Jimmy. Markie, says Tom. Markie confessed.

Jimmy is confused. He asks Tom, What are you talking about?

After he dropped you and me off, Tom says, he went back there. He told them Jack was shooting at him, and he shot at Jack just to scare him, he didn't mean to hit him, but he's a lousy shot. He said he got scared and ran but now he came back.

Wait, says Jimmy, wait.

What's Jimmy asking Tom to wait for? He doesn't know.

Tom says, They have him at the station, he's making a statement. That's what the cops said. They said he gave them the gun.

The gun? Jimmy feels stupid, he doesn't understand anything.

When he said he'd get rid of it, with the cans? He didn't. He gave it to them. He told them it's his.

Why?

Jesus, Jim. Why do you fucking think?

Shit, says Jimmy. He knows why. He wants to say, So he can be a fucking hero, so he can save your ass. And mine. This is Markie, climbing a tree without thinking how he's going to get down, like always, like always.

But Jimmy can't say this to Tom, because Marian's watching him, her eyes wide now because she knows for sure something bad's going on. Her hand is in his, like she wants to help him, like whatever the bad thing is, it'll be better if the two of them know about it together.

Jim? says Tom.

What?

Marian's there with you?

Yes, Jimmy says.

Say I called to tell you about . . . about Jack. Don't say anything else. I got to find out what's going on. I got to think, what to do.

Jimmy nods as though Tom could see him. He puts the phone down, turns to Marian, but he can't say anything, he just looks at her and then suddenly wraps his arms around her, holds her close.

She's warm, and he's so cold.

Now it's morning, the sun's pouring down on Jimmy and Markie and Tom in the car, but Jimmy's still cold.

They didn't arrest Markie last night, they let him go home because the way he told the story about shooting Jack, it was self-defense and there's nothing to say it wasn't. The cops all know Markie, the cops all know everyone in Pleasant Hills, they know Markie has a kid, they don't see him going anywhere. Markie's grinning.

See, he says, it's what I figured. I'm an upstanding citizen. They believed me. Everybody'll believe me. It was an accident, it was because he was shooting at me. This way you guys are cool, and even, no one thinks it was Eddie, so there's no war. Your guys, Tom, yours and Big Mike's, they don't go after Eddie's guys, and Eddie's guys don't come back over here. Nobody gets popped, man. Everybody's cool.

You're fucking crazy, Jimmy says again, and he knows this thing Markie's doing, it's wrong; but he's thinking about how they didn't arrest Markie, thinking maybe, just maybe, this is wrong but it could be a good answer.

Then Tom, who's been quiet since he got in the car, Tom says, The gun.

No, says Markie, grinning wider, like he thought of this, too. No, it's okay. I wiped it. I wrapped my hand on it like I shot it. Even if they find your prints on it, Tom, I'll say I showed it to you a couple days ago. Everything's cool.

The gun's not registered, says Tom.

So? Markie says.

Markie, man, even if they buy the whole rest of it, Tom says, they'll still send you up for the gun.

But, says Markie, and his grin wobbles. What do you mean? Just the gun?

Yeah, says Tom. He closes his eyes, leans on the backseat like he's too tired to say anything else.

But, says Markie again. But I'm clean. I'm an upstanding citizen.

Tom's eyes open. He jerks forward. Christ, where have you been? he shouts. It's their big thing. *Get the guns off the street!* You were just carrying it and they caught you, maybe you might get off, suspended sentence, whatever, you're so fucking upstanding. You shoot someone with an unlicensed gun, self-defense, it doesn't matter, you're fucked. They'll send you up for it, sure as shit.

Everything's silent, the trees aren't even rustling, the birds aren't singing.

Then Markie says, How long?

What?

For the gun. How long?

Markie, fuck, you're not serious, says Jimmy.

Tom starts to say something. Then he stops. He keeps staring at Markie, but his face changes. He seems to Jimmy like maybe he's seeing something different from what he thought he was.

Tom says, First offense, no priors? Good lawyer, sixteen months. Behave inside, you're out in five.

Okay, says Markie.

What the fuck? says Jimmy.

Five months, Markie says. He swallows, looks down quickly. Because listen. Because now I said I did it. If I say I didn't, they'll want to know why I said it in the first place. They'll want to know who I'm—what I know. What the hell can I say?

Jimmy wants to say, Dammit, Markie, you should've thought of that before. But what's the point? Markie never thought ahead in his life, why would he do it now?

Markie says, Tom goes down for this, he's fucked for good. I mean, years, he'll spend years inside.

Markie looks at Tom, and Tom nods.

That fucks Vicky, too, says Markie, and the kids, Mikey and the baby you got coming. And your mom, look what happens to her. And Jimmy? Jimmy, anyone finds out you were there, you're fucked, too.

Everything Markie just said is right. Still. Jimmy shakes his head, says to Markie, No.

Jimmy? says Markie. It's not your choice.

Markie looks at Tom, and Tom looks at Markie. Jimmy can see they're saying something between themselves, without any words.

Then Tom says, Maybe I can fix it. He nods. I can talk to some guys.

It sounds like Tom's trying to make them feel better by telling them that, but Jimmy thinks it's not him and Markie he's really talking to.

Just, says Tom, to make sure they don't charge Markie with anything except the gun. I can do that. My guys can. And, Markie, man, I swear, if it doesn't work like that, if they throw anything else at you, or the sentence is long, any shit like that, I swear to God I'll come clean, man. I swear it.

Wait, says Jimmy. But like last night, he doesn't know what he's asking Tom to wait for. You guys are nuts, says Jimmy. You can't. You're crazy.

I want to. Markie's voice is quiet. I want to save people, one time. *I* want to be Superman, just once. Jimmy, you do it all the time. You always did it. Just one time, I want to do it.

But Sally and Kevin, says Jimmy.

It'll be better, says Markie, it'll be better for me with them, if I always know, from now on if I always know I did this. I saved people, one time.

Jimmy's sticky with sweat. He doesn't know what to say. He keeps thinking of words to use, then seeing how they'll mess things up, trip him up, make it worse. The sun crawls higher in the sky. The other side of the backseat, the place next to Tom where Jack should be, the sun's glaring off the vinyl there because there's nothing to stop it.

And Jimmy's thinking, *Jack*.

If Jack knew what Markie was doing, Jack would slap Markie on the back, say, Markie, man, I knew you had balls!

If Jack knew about this, thinks Jimmy, Jack would love it.

BOYS' OWN BOOK

Chapter 17

———

The Bodies of the Birds

February 16, 1980

Markie's dead.

Jimmy doesn't know what to do. It's like he knows what the words mean, but he still doesn't understand them.

Jimmy remembers hearing the words, the first time was two days ago. He remembers answering the phone, it's Sally, she's crying and telling him. He tells Marian, and the two of them run, pulling their coats on they run on the sidewalk. There's a cop at Sally's, a guy named Rosoff, Jimmy knows him a little, the way a fireman knows a cop. He came to tell Sally, and he stayed until someone could come, but he sure looks glad he can leave now.

What happened? Jimmy asks, and Sally sits there crying with Marian's arms around her and tells them. Markie got into a fight with some guy, the guy told Markie to do something and maybe Markie didn't do it fast enough or maybe he did it and that made the guy even madder, but anyway he stabbed Markie, and now Markie's dead.

Jimmy remembers that, Sally telling that story, Sally crying. He remembers everything that happened, everything everyone said, every minute all day as people came and went. Sally's family, friends, the neighbors.

Sally's mom, still some red in her gray hair, Jimmy remembers her picking up Kevin, who's all smiley and bouncy because all these people are over, Kevin likes people around. Sally's mom starts to cry, holding Kevin, and Kevin looks confused and then scared and then he cries, too.

Jimmy's answering the door, he made that his job. He opens it one time to find Tom and Vicky, Vicky brought cookies and Tom brought whiskey. Vicky comes right in the house, but Tom and Jimmy stand, one inside and one outside. Jimmy looks into Tom's eyes, eyes as blue as the sea or the sky. Sally comes up behind Jimmy, holds out her hand to Tom, he takes it and hugs her, and Jimmy stands aside, watches Tom go in.

Jimmy's in the living room, listening to everyone saying things that don't make sense. He's not drinking because he's on duty later, at least until Marian whispers to him maybe he wants to get someone to take his shift?

He doesn't, he really doesn't; what Jimmy wants more than anything is to go to the firehouse, like this was a regular day, the guys'll all be there, ragging on each other, and what Jimmy wants then is for a call to come in and all at once it's the bell and the sirens, racing onto the truck and flying through the streets to get to oily black smoke and heat like a wall. He wants water exploding out of the hose to meet the starving flames reaching out to eat you and you have to beat them back and you do, you do, and you win and it's over. And then he wants another call, and another one, because while you're battling the dragon, you have to *do* it, you have no time to think, and that's what he wants, because if he thinks, all he can think is: *Markie's dead.*

That was yesterday. Now, today, Jimmy leaves Marian at Sally's, early in the morning before the people start to come. He gives the girls time to be alone, and he goes out to the rocks under the bridge.

It's a cold day, windy, no sun, the sky's gray and the water's gray, too, just darker. Jimmy watches the ships crawl by as though he's looking for a special one, but the ships he sees, they're all black freighters, they're all the same. The gulls circle, screeching and diving. The gulls, the cold steel of the bridge, the rocks Jimmy's sitting on, everything's gray, like the water and the sky. Jimmy thinks, Goddamn you all.

Jim?

Jimmy snaps his head around.

It's Tom.

Tom stands there on the edge of the rock behind Jimmy, like he's not going to come any closer unless Jimmy says it's okay.

Jimmy doesn't say that. He doesn't say anything. He just turns back to watching the water.

For a long time there's nothing but the ships and the crying gulls. It's so long that Jimmy thinks Tom left, or maybe he was never there at all.

Then a pebble clicks along the rock, tumbles off the edge and into the water. Jimmy hears footsteps crunch, and Tom's standing beside him.

Tom unslings the canvas backpack he's carrying and he sits. Brought some coffee, he says. He takes out a Thermos, a couple of Styrofoam cups. The coffee steams as he pours. He hands a cup to Jimmy. Jimmy wraps both hands around it; he's never been this cold before.

Jim, says Tom.

At first that's all Tom says. He drinks his coffee. It's black, the way Jimmy and Tom both like it.

Jim, if you want to come clean, I won't try to stop you.

A yacht plows out under the bridge, throwing up a white trail. Who the hell's that asshole? Jimmy wonders. It's February, what's he thinking, he can just go out and have a good time on a day like this?

I'll go with you, Tom says. I'll tell the truth, everything.

Jimmy drinks his coffee.

That what you want? says Tom. I'll do it.

What I want, Jimmy says, I want Markie not to be dead.

Tom nods. Yeah, he says. Yeah, no shit, man. So do I.

A fireboat steams by, the *John J. Harvey* maybe, Jimmy was on the *Harvey* once, doing some training. Jimmy thinks, Good for them, good for those guys, on their way to a job. He thinks about the fire under his skin that he feels at a job, not feeling it now, now he's too cold, now he can't feel anything.

I have an idea, says Tom.

Jimmy turns to stare. You have an idea? You have a fucking idea?

Tom says, Jim, listen. Please, just listen.

Fuck, says Jimmy. But he doesn't get up, he doesn't stand and go climbing over the rocks and leave Tom there alone.

It's all my fault, says Tom, I know that, but I can't change what happened. No way I can bring Markie back. Jack, either.

Jimmy doesn't know, he really doesn't know, how much is Tom's fault, but he knows "all" is wrong. It was Tom who shot Jack. But Jack wasn't shooting at Tom, he was shooting at Markie and at him. It was Tom who went along with Markie's unbelievably stupid idea, to say he shot Jack. But Jimmy didn't stop them. Could he have? That's another thing he doesn't know. But this is a thing he does know: it wasn't Tom's idea for Markie to go to Jack, to tell him about the cops, the story that turned out to be bullshit, the story that made Big Mike decide not to send Jack to Atlanta, the story that made Jack so mad.

That wasn't Tom's idea. It was Jimmy's.

Tom says, My fault, Jim. But all I can do, man, all I can do now, I can think about what's going to happen. How I can make it up.

Jimmy doesn't see any way, how to do that, but he sips his coffee and listens.

You know Markie didn't have any kind of insurance, Tom says, any of that shit. Since Kevin came along, Sally's been staying home, that was what her and Markie wanted. If she'd worked, they could've lived someplace nicer, but they wanted her home. Now she's gonna get a job, not be home with Kevin, he has no dad and no mom at home either?

Yeah? says Jimmy. So?

What was Markie making, Tom asks, down at the garage? Ten thousand? I can do that. A little more, even. Thousand a month, so she can stay home.

Tom's not looking at Jimmy, he's staring out over the water, maybe looking for the same ship Jimmy can't find.

No, says Jimmy.

Tom says, Why? not like he's arguing, just like he wants to know.

Where that money comes from, says Jimmy. That's why this happened. That's why Markie's dead.

Tom nods slowly, drinks his coffee, is quiet for a long time. Then he says, I'll get out. My dad, says Tom. You see how old he got, the last couple months? My mom, since Jack, the way she is, he can't do anything anymore except take care of her. He's sure as hell not taking care of business. I'm supposed to be. But screw it, man. I can fold it up. Not overnight, I can't do that. I got people I have to take care of. But I'll get out. If the money's clean, you think I can give it to Sally? You think then?

Jimmy finishes his coffee. Tom passes over the Thermos. Jimmy unscrews the cap, pours some more. He lifts the Thermos to Tom, but Tom's not done yet with what he has.

She won't take it, says Jimmy. You know Sally. She doesn't like help.

Not from me, Tom says. But if she doesn't know. If she thinks it's Markie.

Markie? How the hell is it Markie?

New York State, says Tom. They should have been protecting him. He was in their prison. What if we sue them?

Are you crazy? We won't get shit, says Jimmy.

No, says Tom. But if we say we sued them. And this is their money. Jimmy shakes his head.

That lawyer, says Tom. Constantine. He'd go along. He could say he's the one who sued. She'd believe it if he said it.

Why would he? Why would he do it?

You seen the way he looks at her?

Jimmy says, What?

I'm just saying. Maybe he doesn't even know. Sally, I know she doesn't, all she can think about is Markie. But still. For her, he'd do it. It's not illegal. It's a lie, but it's not illegal.

Tom stops. He sips some coffee and then says, like he doesn't want to say this part but he has to: It would have to be you who talks to him, Jimmy. He won't say yes if it's me. But if you say it's you, your money, you're borrowing against your Department insurance or something, you want Sally to have it but you know she won't take it.

Jimmy turns to the gray water again, and the black ships. He can't think of anything to say. Anything.

It was my story, says Tom.

What?

The bullshit story that got Jack so pissed? Had nothing to do with Eddie Spano. Came from me.

What the fuck? What are you saying?

This cop. O'Hagan. My guy. I told him, tell my dad this and that. I thought Dad would send Jack out of town. Atlanta, maybe. To cool him off.

You told him?

Jack was too hot, Jimmy. They weren't ready to roll him up, but they would've, sooner or later.

Tom waits a minute, then says, But not just that. You remember, you and me, we talked about Markie? About him and Jack, we were worried about him getting in trouble because of Jack?

Yeah, well, says Jimmy, and he's surprised how savage his own voice sounds.

Tom drinks his coffee. Jimmy gets the strange idea that Tom's collecting himself, getting ready like a fireman does, before he charges into the flame wall.

And not just you and me, talking about it, Tom says. Marian said to me how she was afraid, she thought Jack was going to get too deep into something, get into some kind of thing he couldn't get out of.

Marian? I thought, says Jimmy, I thought Marian and you . . .

Yeah, says Tom. I was surprised. I liked it that she talked to me like that, it'd been a long time.

A long time, thinks Jimmy, looking at the bridge arching away. It's all been such a long time.

Tom says, I looked at it, Jim. Markie, you're worried about him, Marian's worried about him and Jack, too. I'm thinking, if Jack fucks Markie up, it'll be Sally, too, and little Kev. And Vicky's been after me, I spend too much time cleaning up after my brother, worrying about my mom because of Jack, like that. Everyone's worried and everyone wants the same thing. I looked at it.

Jimmy watches the ships, coming and going, back and forth. He wonders who's in charge, someone must be or they'd all crash, wreck each other. He thinks back to so many times when they were kids, Tom having a good idea because of something everybody wanted.

Tom rubs his eyes like it's too bright out here, on this gray day. He says, So I went to O'Hagan. I said, Tell my dad it's like this, that you have this operation going. Jimmy, I swear, I thought Dad would send Jack, send him someplace. I thought Jack would get to go to Atlanta, that he'd get what he wanted out of this, too! Shit, Jim.

Tom looks into his coffee cup; it's empty. He says, I don't know how the story got to Markie. It was supposed to be my dad. I don't know how.

After that Tom doesn't say anything else. They sit on the rocks, Jimmy not saying anything either, just looking, just taking it all in. A gull screeches, soars and knifes into the water, comes up silent, flaps away. It must have caught what it wanted, Jimmy thinks.

Jim, Tom says, you let me know. Whatever you want, I'll do it.

Jimmy doesn't turn to watch as Tom walks away, but he hears him go.

PHIL'S STORY
Chapter 14

———

The Old Masters
(Sailing Calmly On)

November 2, 2001

On the ferry. On the way back. No, not back. That would mean a journey done. A place not home, from which he was returning. But there was no home now, and no returning.

People stared, moved away. Because of the blood. On his face, his own. Scrubbed and stanched, but still slowly bleeding. He was still bleeding. On his shirt, on his jacket, Kevin's. So much death, death everywhere, and still people backed away, because of blood.

Phil stood in the wind outside, the Brooklyn side, and stared at the bridge. Brigadoon, Camelot, Shangri-la, all vanished. Never real, but where he'd lived. Gone now. Gone.

His last night on Staten Island—oh yes, what else was it?—and spent in jail.

"I love you," he'd told Sally, calling on the prisoner's pay phone. The air was rank, the walls too close.

She'd said—sadly, softly—"It doesn't matter."

When they'd let him out, he'd gone right over, but she wouldn't let him in.

Now, on the boat, he took out his phone, tried again to call her. Again, as all morning, all day yesterday, only ringing. No connection to be made.

He slipped the phone away, back in his pocket, his shirt stiff with blood.

If she had answered?

What was he thinking to say?

Marian's Story
Chapter 16

———

First In, Last Out

November 2, 2001

Marian walked out onto the deck of the ferry, on the east side. The boat seemed to lurch; she thought she might fall, but did not. She stood in shadow, aware of people moving uneasily away: something in her face, her eyes, making them uncomfortable, making them uncertain. Marian was uncertain, also: uncertain how she'd come to be on the boat, uncertain where she was going. Uncertain of everything, and yet it was all so clear, every minute, every second.

The phone ringing, Kevin in his room picking up before Sally could. A few minutes later, Kevin, dressed but not shaved, reaching into the kitchen for his keys.

"That was Uncle Phil." Sally flushed; Kevin went on, "He wants me to meet him."

"Why?"

"He wants to show me something. Be back later, Mom. Goodbye, Aunt Marian." His smile, not the sunburst, but a sweet, sweet one. It seemed slightly sad to Marian, this smile, but of course she didn't say that to Sally. Sally had enough on her mind.

Goodbye, Aunt Marian.

More tea in Sally's kitchen, Marian and Sally talking, at first about Jimmy's papers, where they could be, what could be in them. Then their mood lightening, trading gossip, then just talking, as best friends, as they always had.

The phone ringing, high-pitched, Sally laughing at a joke Marian had made as she reached for it.

Racing to the hospital, Marian driving Sally's car, Marian no more fit to drive than Sally, her skin cold and her stomach churning, but she knew it was right. (Strangely, frighteningly, she took the keys, she took the wheel, because she heard Jimmy tell her to, heard Jimmy saying it was right.)

The hours there, and then the doctor, and then Sally in Marian's arms, wailing, sobbing, and Marian, too, and nothing she could do.

And the hours since. At the hospital, police officers with questions. Back at Sally's house, family, friends. Firefighters. The telephone ringing, nonstop, unbearable, finally silenced, turned off, still ringing and ringing, thought Marian, but no one could hear. Sally, white, silent, motionless.

Sally's mother, finally, asking everyone to leave, thanking them all, asking them to go home. But not me, surely, Marian thought, not me, to leave, to be alone now. Not me, too. Marian the last friend remaining, as she'd been the first, Marian expecting to stay.

Sally, green eyes finding Marian from across a vast, lifeless desert. Sally saying nothing, shaking her head.

Marian spending the night at her father's house, sitting in the yard for a long time before going to bed. Her mother's flower beds were overgrown with grass.

Now, on the ferry, Marian watched the clouds, the ships, the hills. The place where she'd grown up, where her heart had remained, grew unimaginably distant as the boat plowed without remorse toward the opposite shore.

If only, she thought: if only she could have spoken to Sally, across the desert of Sally's eyes, if only she could have found words. If only she'd found words for Kevin: Where are you going, Kevin, what are you planning, I'm sorry if I upset you, Kevin, don't go.

Why hadn't she found the words?

And so she stood now by the rail of the ferry, watching the gulls circle, watching the bridge, watching, on this perfect, beautiful day, watching everything slip away.

LAURA'S STORY
Chapter 17

————

Abraham Lincoln and the Pig

November 2, 2001

In the gathering twilight, Laura sat on the deck of the ferry. Not the front, to see the glittering towers of Manhattan reach for her; not the back, to see Staten Island's angry hills grimly cheering her departure. Not the west side, where the Statue of Liberty still welcomed the wretched. Laura sat outside on a wooden bench on the ferry's east side and stared at the Verrazano Narrows Bridge, the last place where Harry had stood.

She saw the bridge waver, she felt the tears hot on her cheeks, and she knew her fellow passengers were aware that she was crying. But in New York now, people burst into tears in public places. No one knew why, but everyone knew why. Strangers would comfort you if you let them, and they would leave you alone if that was what you wanted, and that was what Laura wanted, and people must have seen that because they left her alone.

"Harry?" Laura whispered.

The sun was setting, the sky had gone cold.

"Harry?"

The wind blew over her and was sharp as a blade.

"Harry?"

Yes, I'm here, came the gentle answer.

"Harry!"

He asked, *Do you see now?*

Laura swallowed. Her throat was parched. "We were wrong."

No, Harry said softly, I *was wrong. That is to say: years ago, when the fact finally dawned on my thick brain that the truth was—contrary to the sermon I'd been preaching all my life—neither obtainable nor by any means the highest good, at* that *time I was right. And when I met you, my little starfish, I should have told you that. But you were so beautiful.*

"Me? I've never—"

Beautiful. So alive. It wasn't even that you'd never lost hope. You didn't need hope. You had religion. You wanted nothing but the truth. And my good fortune, when you consented to spend your time with me, astounded me. But I was sly. I knew. I knew which man you loved. Not the old and tired one who'd dedicated himself to not making waves. *He wasn't the man you loved, Laura. You were in love with the crusading truth-seeker. Harry Randall, star reporter. For you—for you—I became that man again.*

"Harry? Harry . . ."

Harry waited politely, but Laura could find no words. He resumed: *And then Owen McCardle gave me Jimmy McCaffery's papers. I read them, as you have. And I could see. Yes, the scales fell from my eyes, the clouds lifted, the floodwaters of illusion receded. Write it however you want. I saw the harm I'd done and the harm that was coming. I saw my selfishness and my guilt. So much destroyed, so that a washed-up drunk could keep a love that was never really his.*

"It was yours!"

No. The man you loved died long ago. He should never have returned. Look at the mess he made.

"But couldn't . . . Couldn't you have . . . Once you knew . . . A retraction . . . ?"

You said it yourself, Harry's voice came sadly. *"First in, last out."* A retraction *wouldn't have mattered. Or even been read. I'd destroyed a hero. I'd deliberately broken hearts. Given people who never even knew Captain McCaffery one more reason for hopelessness in a season of despair.* Harry, invisible in the clear autumn air, spread his arms wide.

"You can't have known. You can't have seen this coming."

The shrug. Harry's shrug. *Not this exactly. Something like it. It doesn't matter.*

"Harry?" Laura's throat hurt so much, ached so badly, she hoped, after this, to never have to speak again. But she had to ask: "What they said. It was true?"

What I said—what I said and you, my love, echoed and elaborated after I was gone—was not true. What they said was.

Laura, speaking what felt like her last words: "You jumped."

Harry, replying, confirming, pronouncing sentence: *I jumped.*

Boys' Own Book
Chapter 18

—

The Invisible Man
Steps Between You and the Mirror

September 11, 2001

Jimmy folds his T-shirt and shorts into his gym bag, slings it over his shoulder as he leaves the basement apartment that's been his for twenty years. Since spring he's been going to yoga classes at a place around the corner from the firehouse, will be heading there today at the end of his shift. Needs to stay flexible, Jimmy does: he's forty-six, and though he's got his eye on a Battalion Chief's spot in the next year or two (and been told over the back fence he has a good shot at it), at Ladder 62 he's Captain. He's got to be ready, when the bell rings, for the ax, the flames, the smothering smoke and heat like a wall. He's got men depending on him, men who follow him.

Some of the guys, they rag on him about it—Hey, when you do the stork one, they give you a baby to deliver?—but the guys rag on the officers anyway, it's part of what makes the firehouse what it is, your brothers yanking your chain. And Jimmy has to admit, you need a good laugh, you could do worse than watch him try to stand on his head. But, he tells the guys, there's a dozen twenty-five-year-old girls there standing on *their* heads, so maybe it's not so bad.

And delivering babies, he's done that seven times already since he came on the Job.

Jimmy's up early today so he can take the long way, down around the tip of the island. This is something he does sometimes, just walk and look and think. He's got a lot on his mind, nothing he can't handle, but he needs to think what to do, make a plan for each thing. Two of his guys are out for a couple of days—Doherty's sick, and Logan's wife just had twins—so he's got to work their replacements into the rotation. He's got a probie, Adams, three months out of the Academy, green like Kevin; Jimmy'll have to come up with some drills for the kid, doesn't want him just sitting around. And Gino Aiello: Jimmy needs to call him, to see how the Deputy Chief's coming on that favor he promised, getting Kevin assigned to 62 for a few months. Kev asked for 168 in Pleasant Hills, same as Jimmy did out of the Academy, and Jimmy thinks that's great, a good place for him. He can serve out his whole time in that house the way Jimmy'd been planning to before; but first he needs experience, he needs knowledge. Kev's up for the transfer, and Jimmy wants to get him here, show him, teach him, before it's too late. Because when Jimmy moves to the Battalion, he won't be running a house day-to-day anymore.

Jimmy's picked up coffee from the Pakistani guy at the newsstand. He peels back the lid, sips it as he walks. It's good; it always is, from that place, a lot better than the guys make at 62. Either he's got to get some Italian guy transferred to 62, Jimmy decides, or he's got to detail one of those micks to learn to make decent coffee.

This early, New York's still shaking off sleep, getting started on the day. A neighbor, walking a funny yellow mutt, greets him: Perfect weather, she says, and strolls away smiling. As Jimmy passes the Y, he hears the thud of a basketball on the hardwood; God, those guys must love that game, to come out at this hour. He crosses the highway to the path by the Hudson, watches the sun glinting off the silver water. A bird and an airplane cross high overhead, going in opposite directions, and Jimmy has to smile: they look the same size.

At the tip of Manhattan, Jimmy stands at the rail near the ferry terminal. On a morning as clear as this, he can see the Verrazano Narrows Bridge arching away, see Staten Island across the harbor, see the boat docking there as one approaches here. Watching the ferry come in, Jimmy spots some young guy on the deck, dark-haired, broad-shouldered, not too tall, but standing straight, like Jimmy himself when he was young. Staring straight ahead, like Jimmy himself.

Twenty-five years old: Jimmy's on the ferry. Two hours, back and forth five times already, how stupid is that, but he can't decide.

It's a February day, the sky that hard blue it only gets in winter, everything sharp and fresh. Not like that gray day last week, sitting under the bridge with Tom.

When Jimmy first gets on the boat, he goes to the front. The sunlight glints on the water as Manhattan grows and grows. When he can't decide, he stays there while the boat heads the other way. The towers of the skyline throw bursts of light at him, but they keep getting smaller. After that he goes inside and buys coffee and stares through the window. The glass is so clouded and scratched that he can't make anything out.

Jimmy's thinking this: More than anything, he wants to stop keeping this secret. For months it's been inside him, filling up places that should have been for other things. This secret is changing him, and Jimmy doesn't want it anymore. He wants to stand up and say, This is what happened that night on Coleman Road. This is why Jack is dead, and why Markie.

But if he does that, what happens?

One thing, Sally would find out Markie chose to be where he was. He didn't have to leave her and Kevin and put himself where this could happen to him, but he did. As bad as things are for Sally now, Jimmy thinks knowing that would be much worse.

And Tom goes to prison. Peggy Molloy's lost both sons then.

And if Tom's in prison, he's not giving money to Sally, that idea he had about giving her money. Jimmy could give her some himself, but he doesn't make that much, and he's just a fireman, he never will.

And Vicky. She just had a baby, hers and Tom's second. Vicky and Sally, both raising their kids without fathers, Jimmy thinks about that.

And this, too: Tom says if that's what it takes, he'll go straight. That would be a good thing, God, yes, Jimmy knows. For Tom, for Vicky, for a lot of people.

Through the beat-up glass Jimmy sees sunlight flash off something, it looks like a flame. And again he thinks, what he wants is to not have this secret anymore. He wants to walk into a fire and have it burned away. That's what it would feel like, he thinks, if he told it. It would hurt, like getting burned, but he'd be clean after that.

But if he does that, who's saved?

Only Jimmy.

The other way, it's better for everybody else. Jimmy can't see anyone, besides him, that the other way—Tom's way—isn't better for.

The boat groans into the slip back at home, back on Staten Island. Jimmy goes outside on the side where the Verrazano Narrows Bridge is, and when the boat pulls out from the slip he stands in the wind and the sunlight, so strong in winter it's not yellow, it's pure white but it doesn't warm you. He watches the bridge slide by, watches Staten Island get small.

When they get close to the Manhattan side, Jimmy checks his pocket for Phil Constantine's address. He moves to the front and he watches the towers come close. As the boat slides into the slip, sunlight bounces off the windows at the top of the World Trade Center, the ones highest in the air. It sparkles off the water at the end of the island. It's so bright it even glitters on the pathway stones, worn smooth by so many people over so much time.

The sun's a huge fireball burning in the sky, and Jimmy wants to be the sun. That strong. That clean. That distant.

But Jimmy's a twenty-five-year-old guy standing on the steel deck of a ferry. When it docks, when they lower the ramp, he takes one more minute, like he's still not sure. He's not. But he heads down the slope with the people around him. Jimmy stands for a moment at the rail, looking back. Then he turns, leaves Superman on the boat, and walks out onto the streets of Lower Manhattan.

And at the rail now, Jimmy stands there, in that same place, different, after so many years, but the same. The ferry that docked is pulling out again, carrying people across the water. Jimmy finishes his coffee. He checks his pocket for his St. Florian medal that his mother gave him his first week in the Academy; and for Marian's photograph, the single one he's kept all these years. They're both there, they always are; he's taken them into each house as he's transferred, slips them into the pocket of his dress uniform for ceremonies and funerals. But he's always checked for them as he's heading for the firehouse, and he checks now.

Jimmy glances at the river and the ferry one more time. Then he turns and walks out onto the streets of Lower Manhattan.

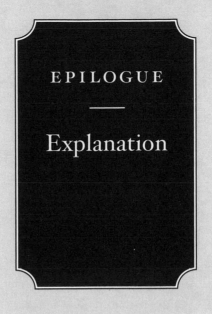

EPILOGUE

———

Explanation

Secrets No One Knew

> We lost voices
> Lives
> Loved ones
> Secrets no one knew

> —Sarah Williams, 17, "Voices" (excerpt),
> from *Wordsmiths: A Teen Poetry Journal*

Tree, Falling

A tree falls in the forest; no one is there to hear it. To whom does it make a difference, then, whether it makes a sound?

Complicated Work

> What is a good man but a bad man's teacher?
> What is a bad man but a good man's job?

> —Lao-Tse

The Man Who Sat by the Door

A New York City police officer tells this story: I took my wife upstate to visit my uncle Rob. To get away for a few days, you know? This was maybe a month after 9/11. Rob used to be a warden, one of the prisons up the Hudson. They call them medium security, but, trust me, they're tough places. He retired long ago, kids are all grown and gone, wife died years back. Talks about moving to Florida, but still lives in the same house he used to, across the street from the main gate. So the first night up there, Rob makes lasagna, we talk for a while, then my wife and I are ready to turn in. Rob takes us to this bedroom upstairs, says good night, heads downstairs again. You staying up for a while? I ask him. No, I'm going to sleep, he says. I sleep here. He points to a chair in the living room, facing the door. Got used to it years ago, he says. And damn if he doesn't sit down in that chair, fully dressed—even shoes—and sleep like that until morning. And all I could think was, I thought *I* was putting in a lot of overtime. You know?

The Old Masters
(Sailing Calmly On)

About suffering they were never wrong,
The Old Masters: how well they understood
Its human position; how it takes place
While someone else is eating or opening a window or just
    walking dully along . . .
In Brueghel's *Icarus,* for instance: how everything turns
    away
Quite leisurely from the disaster; the ploughman may
Have heard the splash, the forsaken cry,
But for him it was not an important failure . . .
. . . and the expensive delicate ship that must have seen
Something amazing, a boy falling out of the sky,
Had somewhere to get to and sailed calmly on.

—W. H. Auden, "Musée des Beaux Arts"

THE WOMEN IN THE TENT

As unidentified bodies and parts of bodies were brought in re-frigerated trucks to the morgue tents after September 11, a group of Stern College students—religious Jews in their teens and early twenties—took it upon themselves to ask for rabbinical dispensation to allow them to relieve their male counterparts in sitting with the bodies and reciting the prayers for the dead, who, according to Jewish custom, must not be left alone between death and burial. By Jewish law women may recite prayers over the bodies of women but not those of men. Of many of the remains brought to the morgue, it was unknown whether they were male or female. Nevertheless, permission was granted.

FIRST IN, LAST OUT

Captain Patrick Brown, one of the most decorated firefighters in the history of the FDNY, lost his life in the north tower on September 11. At his memorial service, held at St. Patrick's Cathedral on what would have been Captain Brown's forty-ninth birthday, pallbearers carried an American flag made of flowers, on which rested his helmet. Captain Brown, in the tradition of FDNY officers, was first in and last out at any fire, entering ahead of his men and not leaving until they were all out safely. Ladder 3, the company he commanded, lost twelve men on September 11. Captain Brown's memorial service was the last.

THE WAY HOME

A resident of downtown Manhattan, interviewed on the street, September 12: "My son asked, 'Mommy, you always told me if I got lost I should just look for the towers and I could find my way home. How will I find my way home now?' That's how we all feel. We'll just have to come up with another way to find our way home."

A Hundred Circling Camps

I have seen Him in the watch fires
Of a hundred circling camps
They have builded Him an altar
In the evening dews and damps
You can read the righteous sentence
By the dim and flaring lamps
His truth is marching on.

—"The Battle Hymn of the Republic"

Sutter's Mill

In California in 1848 John Augustus Sutter tried to keep from the world the knowledge that gold had been found on his land. His motive was not a desire to be the only one to mine this gold, rather a hope of avoiding the mining entirely. The gold might have made him rich. But Sutter had come to the valleys of central California to plant oranges and lemons, to watch the sun ripen the fruits on his trees, and to listen to the birds singing in them in the morning. Mining the gold, which in the end he could not prevent, destroyed all that, as Sutter knew it would.

Leaving the Cat

Two women, New Yorkers, old friends, met for coffee sometime during the week after September 11, still talking in the slow, subdued tones of shock. The first said she had packed a knapsack with hiking boots, a sweater, a bottle of water, placed it in the front closet, in the event of evacuation. The second said she'd located the cat carrier, moved it near her apartment door for the same reason. The first woman, eyebrows raised, said, "You're taking your cat?" She paused, looking away; for a time both were silent. "It didn't occur to me," the first woman finally said, "to take the cat."

The Water Dreams

A woman who lives near Ground Zero was in the Caribbean on September 11. As a child she had nearly drowned in the ocean, was dragged through the waves to shore by a friend. (They were both surprised at the friend's unexpected strength.) For years she was troubled by nightmares: wild, luminous green water inexorably rising behind glass walls. The nightmares had long since passed, until the night of September 11, when, after an endless day spent alternately staring at the TV in the hotel bar and walking along the seawall, an exhausted sleep finally overtook her. A Caribbean hurricane howled around her hotel room, and dreams of green water and glass walls woke her twice. Since then the dreams have not stopped.

Turtles in the Pond

A lifelong New Yorker, walking through Chinatown in August, came upon an old woman selling two live turtles in a cardboard box. The turtles, an illicit dinner delicacy, were over eight inches long. Tightly wrapped in plastic net bags, they could hardly move; but they struggled, tiny, pushing gestures, little twists of their heads. He asked the woman the price; she sold them to him for ten dollars apiece. Sweating in the afternoon heat, he carried them in their cardboard box a mile and a half across town to a pond in Battery Park City, where he released them among the lily pads and the koi. Three weeks later the pond was clogged with debris and dust from the falling towers of the World Trade Center. Everything in it died.

Breathing Smoke

. . . I walk uptown chain-smoking, while downtown people
are dying from breathing smoke.

—Alison Shapiro, in the October 2, 2001, issue of *The Spectator,*
the student newspaper of Stuyvesant High School

How to Find the Floor

In the days after September 11, two friends spoke on the
phone. Not wanting to break the connection, they searched for
topics to talk about, though only one thing was on their minds,
the same as on everyone's. One of the two was a man with a dis-
ability. "Did you know I'm using a cane now?" he said. "It's not
that I can't walk; I can. It's just that sometimes I feel like I can't
find the floor." My God, that's how I feel, the other thought,
though she said nothing. I know where it is, I must be standing
right on it, where else could I stand? But I can't find it. I can't
find the floor.

Abraham Lincoln and the Pig

An old story about Abe Lincoln: riding through the country-
side in a carriage with a friend, Lincoln spotted a pig stuck in a
fence. The pig was squealing and writhing, but it couldn't get
loose. Lincoln stopped the carriage, took off his jacket, and wrestled the pig out from the rails. The pig trotted off. Lincoln, covered with sweat, mud, and bruises, returned to the carriage.

"Was that your pig?" his friend asked.

"No," Lincoln answered, picking up the reins.

"Your neighbor's?"

"I don't know the man who owns this land."

"Well, that was awfully good of you, then," said the friend. "To put yourself to so much trouble for a stranger's pig."

Lincoln said, "I didn't do it for the pig."

"For the owner, then? Whoever he is?"

"No. For myself."

"For yourself?"

"Yes," said Lincoln. "I don't want to have to lie awake all night listening to that damn pig squealing in my head."

THE BODIES OF THE BIRDS

The fireballs that erupted when the planes hit the towers of the World Trade Center scorched the feathers from the wings of sparrows, finches, grackles, pigeons, and seagulls hundreds of yards away. Small charred corpses were found as far north as Houston Street.

THE INVISIBLE MAN STEPS BETWEEN YOU AND THE MIRROR

The undead, so legends say, though visible to the eye and capable of great destruction, don't appear in mirrors. The Invisible Man, though, who cannot be seen at all: does his presence, as it is said, distort reflections?